THE COLLECTED

FABLES OF

AMBROSE

BIERCE

THE COLLECTED

FABLES OF

AMBROSE

BIERCE

Edited, with Introduction
and Commentary, by

S . T . JOSHI

Ohio State University Press

Columbus

Frontispiece: Photograph of Ambrose Bierce (PS1097.Z5 A3 1922a copy 2), Clifton Waller Barrett Library of American Literature, Special Collections Department, University of Virginia Library.

The fables "The Vigilant Guardian," "The Lady and the Tiger," "A Faulty Rigging," "King and Parrot," "A Hope of Return," and "Bullet & Bone" are taken from the Ambrose Bierce Scrapbooks, vol. 19, Bierce-Danzinger Collection (MSS 5992-a), Clifton Waller Barrett Library of American Literature, Special Collections Department, University of Virginia Library.

Library of Congress Cataloging-in-Publication Data
Bierce, Ambrose, 1842–1914?
[Fables]
The collected fables of Ambrose Bierce / edited, with introduction and commentary, by S.T. Joshi.
p. cm.
Includes bibliographical references and index.
ISBN 0-8142-0842-8 (alk. paper)
1. Fables, American. I. Joshi, S. T., 1958- II. Title.
PS1097 .A6 2000b
818'.402 — dc21   99-052375

Text and jacket design by Diane Gleba Hall.
Type set in 11/14 Bulmer by Tseng Information Systems, Inc.
Paper (ISBN: 978-0-8142-5045-7)

9 8 7 6 5 4 3 2

CONTENTS

INTRODUCTION

Ambrose Bierce (1842-1914?) wrote nearly 850 fables in a literary and journalistic career that spanned more than forty years. Less than half of these fables have been reprinted from their original appearances in newspapers and magazines of a century or more ago, and Bierce himself reprinted scarcely more than a third of them in the two editions of his *Fantastic Fables* (1899, 1911). Bierce's fables are unique of their kind, and yet they reveal a thorough familiarity with the long history of the fable as a literary form; indeed, much of their brilliance resides in their adaptation and expansion of that form.

What sets Bierce's fables apart from others of their kind—aside from their sheer quantity and their consistent brilliance—is their pungently satirical "morals," their skewering of a wide array of political, social, and even literary foibles, and their exemplification of Bierce's sharp skepticism in regard to human character and endeavor. The man who urged a budding writer to remember that "this is a world of fools and rogues, blind with superstition, tormented with envy, consumed with vanity, selfish, false, cruel, cursed with illusions—frothing mad!"[1] spent a lifetime enunciating that view in his fables.

THE FABLE

The tradition of the fable in English — especially in America — cannot be said to be notably distinguished. Certainly, if we look at the rich history of the poem, the drama, the novel, and the short story, we find the fable presenting only intermittent instances of brilliance and long periods of mediocrity or neglect.

Matters are not helped by the fact that the precise nature and characteristics of the fable are difficult to specify. The canonical definition by the Greek rhetorician Theon — "a fictitious story picturing a truth"[2] — could be applied to virtually all literary forms that make some claim to presenting "truth" within the context of fiction. Nor, as we shall see presently, is compactness a requisite of the fable, although most of those in the Aesopic tradition are preeminent instances of literary concision. Similarly, the utterance of an explicit "moral," whether at the beginning (*promythium*) or at the end (*epimythium*), was considered optional even in antiquity. The use of animals as interlocutors is predominant but not exclusive in the ancient fable, whose characters can consist of ordinary human beings, gods, and even on rare occasions inanimate objects.

What is not in doubt, of course, is that the fable as a literary form is as old as literature itself. The two dominant traditions are the Aesopic fable and the "Eastern" fable arising out of India or the Middle East. The former is far more familiar to English-speaking readers, although the latter may predate it by more than a millennium.

Whether there ever was a writer named Aesop is open to doubt. If he did exist (and his most diligent scholar, Ben Edwin Perry, believes he did), then he "came originally from Thrace, not from Phrygia; . . . he was at one time a slave on the island of Samos in the service of a man named Iadmon; who later freed him; . . . [and] he was a contemporary of the poetess Sappho in the early sixth century B.C."[3] It was, however, not until the fourth century B.C.E. that the Aesopic fables (in prose) were collected by Demetrius of Phalerum. At that time the fable was not conceived by the Greeks as a literary form, but rather as a means for rhetorical ornament in oratory. It only became a literary form when the Latin poet Phaedrus (first half of the first century C.E.) and the Greek poet Babrius (second half of the first century C.E.) adapted many of the Aesopic fables into verse. It is from the work of these two poets that the bulk of the fables that we call "Aesop's" are known.

The Eastern fable derives from an entirely different tradition, although at a later period it may have been influenced by the Aesopic tradition. Fables or fablelike material can be found as early as 1800 B.C.E. in wisdom books, but the two chief volumes of Eastern fables are the *Fables of Bidpai* (or *The Book of Kalilah and Dimnah,* also known as the *Panchatantra*) and *The Tales of Marzuban* by Sa'd al-Warawini. The former originated in India as part of Buddhist literature; it was brought to Persia no later than 570 C.E. The latter was originally composed in Old Persian in the early thirteenth century C.E. The Eastern fable is significantly different from the Aesopic form in being considerably longer (some fables are tantamount to short stories or even novellas) and more discursive, so that the "moral" is not as easily discernible as in the compressed Aesopic version. Bidpai (or Pilpay) was translated into English as early as 1570 by Thomas North, with other translations appearing in 1747 (anonymous), 1818 (by John Milford), and 1819 (by Wyndham Knatchbull). But the Eastern fable has had minimal influence upon English and American literature.

William Caxton translated Aesop's fables from the French in 1484, but it was Roger L'Estrange's translation (1692–99) that made Aesop a familiar name to English readers. It was followed by Samuel Croxall's translation of 1722, which continued to be reprinted far into the nineteenth century. Translations by Thomas James (1848) and George Fyler Townsend (1867) were also widely read, as was Christopher Smart's 1765 verse translation of Phaedrus.

It was, indeed, in poetic form that the fable became popular; but in the process it withdrew further and further from the Aesopic original. The fables of Jean de La Fontaine (1621–95), published in twelve books between 1668 and 1693, are largely versified renditions of Aesop, but some of La Fontaine's later fables are original. Dryden's *Fables Ancient and Modern* (1700) are merely retellings of stories out of Homer, Ovid, Boccaccio, and Chaucer; his long introduction — certainly a masterwork of criticism in its own right — never mentions Aesop. John Gay's *Fables* (fifty of them published in 1727, sixteen more in 1738) are a perfect delight, for once matching the compactness of the Aesopic original and adding a refined elegance that only Georgian poetry can achieve. But whether we should even regard such book-length "fables" as Bernard Mandeville's *Fable of the Bees* (1714) or such modern works as George Orwell's *Animal Farm* (1945) as fables at all is an open question; certainly they have departed from the Aesopic original in form, and perhaps even in substance. The mere use of animals as characters in place of human beings to point a moral may not be sufficient to classify a work as a fable, for modern fantasy literature is full of such instances.

BIERCE AND THE FABLE

We do not know what edition of Aesop was read by Ambrose Bierce; but that he had read Aesop at a relatively early stage of his literary career is evident, as adaptations of the Greek fabulist appear in his earliest fables. He had read La Fontaine at some point as well: he quotes the adage "An empty stomach has no ears" in one of his early fables (48) and also in a late article, although in the latter he attributes it to Rabelais.[4] Another fable (419) adapts a fable found only in La Fontaine. That Bierce, however, must have been at least casually familiar with the Eastern fable is clear from his earliest fables, "The Fables of Zambri, the Parsee." These appeared in two series in the British humor magazine *Fun* in 1872-73, and were reprinted with some revisions and reorganizations in Bierce's *Cobwebs from an Empty Skull* (1874). And yet, the Zambri fables have little connection with the Eastern fable aside from random elements of setting and nomenclature; they are direct and compact rather than lengthy and discursive, and several of them manifestly adapt well-known fables of the Aesopic tradition.

What led Bierce to write these fables, which precede nearly the whole of his output of short fiction? A better question might be why Bierce did not write more of them; for in the fable Bierce seemed to find an ideal means to convey his pungent opinions on life, literature, and society, and his mastery of the fable is only symptomatic of his mastery of many of the shortest and most condensed literary forms in English. This is hardly the place for a detailed study of Bierce's life,[5] let alone his thought,[6] or even his views on satire; but some notes on these subjects may help to place his fables in their proper context.

After growing up as a poor farm boy in Ohio and Indiana and participating in some of the most horrific battles of the Civil War, Bierce eventually settled down in San Francisco. His earliest literary work was journalism for the *San Francisco News Letter and California Advertiser* (1868-72); but in the three and a half years of his tenure on this weekly paper he was no cub reporter, but rather the imposing "Town Crier" who wrote a column of random opinion on any subject that entered his mind. The columns may each have been up to 2,500 words in length, but they comprised dozens of discrete paragraphs, some no more than a sentence or two in length. This was a practice Bierce maintained for nearly the whole of his literary and journalistic career.

His first "fable" may perhaps date to this period, if the following item — from the "Town Crier" column of 16 September 1871 and reprinted under the

title "The Pridies" in an early collection, *Nuggets and Dust* (1873) — counts as
a fable:

> Mr. Pridy and his female returned home, drawn by a pair
> of horses. (Mr. P. and his f. had been driving for their health.)
> Straightway appeared upon the scene ten white-headed Pridies, of
> assorted sizes, screaming like infuriated fiends, leaping like mani-
> acs, and gesticulating like a tempest of windmills. A nice way to
> welcome these staid and respectable parties! The horses turned
> aside in disgust, sprang deliberately off a bank, sank breathless
> through the yielding air, stopped when they got to the bottom, and
> Madame Pridy was a melancholy remain.
> MORAL: If people *will* have children — Bah! of course they
> will.[7]

Mildly amusing as this is, it does not greatly resemble the fables even of his
early period, let alone the great fables of *Fantastic Fables*.

Bierce's transplantation to England in 1872 was in all likelihood meant
to be permanent, but in the event it lasted only three years. Almost immediately upon his arrival he began writing the Zambri fables for the weekly comic
journal *Fun*, edited by Thomas Hood the Younger, with whom Bierce rapidly
became close friends. Sometimes as many as eight fables would appear in one
issue, at other times as few as two. They were published under the pseudonym he used for the bulk of his English period, Dod Grile; and the first series
of fifty-seven fables proved popular enough that a second series of seventy-
eight began publication after a two-month hiatus. In light of Bierce's later
work in the fable form, the Zambri fables appear loose and a little verbose;
they perhaps strain a little too hard to be funny. Like much of Bierce's writing
at this time, they are apprentice work by a young man who knows perhaps too
well that he is clever and gifted; but, like the best apprentice work, they are a
harbinger of better things to come.

When Bierce's wife, Mollie, already burdened with two small children
and with a third on the way, tired of London literary life and returned to San
Francisco in the spring of 1875, Bierce felt he had no recourse but to follow
her a few months later. After two years of literary quiescence he joined the
staff of the newly formed weekly paper the *Argonaut*. Bierce reprinted a good
many of the Zambri fables in the paper but wrote no new fables; the bulk of his
creative work went into his controversial column "Prattle," which consisted
as before of discrete paragraphs of commentary. It was at this time that he
began writing a series of "Fables and Anecdotes" in the voice of an imaginary

backwoods boy, Little Johnny, a character that had evidently proved popular with British readers of *Fun*, where Johnny had made his debut; but these "fables"—written in an almost impenetrable patois of deliberate solecisms and misspellings—are so radically different from Bierce's other work in the fable form that they have not been included here. They are, in any event, so voluminous that they would require a volume—perhaps several volumes—all to themselves.

After a bootless effort in 1880–81 to mine gold in the Black Hills of the Dakota Territory, Bierce returned to San Francisco. Denied his old job at the *Argonaut*, he quickly gained employment as associate editor of another weekly paper, the *Wasp*, where his tart wit found a ready haven. For five and a half years he ground out weekly "Prattle" columns (only 1,500 words each, however) for the *Wasp*, along with a wide range of poetry, fiction, humorous sketches, memoirs, and essays.

But what of fables? In December 1883 a column of fables entitled "Anecdotes of Animals" appeared; and in September and October of 1884 five columns of fables, headed either "Fables without Political Morals" or "Fables without Political Meaning," were published. All are unsigned. Are they by Bierce? There is clearly a great deal of unsigned material by Bierce in the *Wasp;* and he had used or would use two of the three titles of these fables in other work ("Anecdotes of Animals" had appeared in the *Argonaut* for some Little Johnny material; "Fables without Morals" was a long-running if sporadic column in the *San Francisco Examiner*). Given this, and given the thoroughly Biercian style and content of these fables, I believe their attribution to Bierce is sound.

It was in the *Wasp*, of course, that Bierce began his *Devil's Dictionary:* it first appeared in serial form beginning in 1881. This work is Bierce's greatest triumph of concision: he can pack more venom in a single sentence, sometimes in a single word, than any writer in literature. On occasion he would elaborate his definitions with little stories that are manifestly fables. I have included seven of them in this volume.

By the fall of 1886 Bierce was out of a job again, and it was only in the spring of the next year that—as he relates with his typically understated wit[8] —the twenty-three-year-old William Randolph Hearst came to Bierce's house in Oakland and asked him to be the star editorial writer for the *San Francisco Examiner.* For the next twenty years Bierce was allowed unprecedented space and editorial freedom to expound on whatever topics he wished. Although the bulk of his creative work went into the writing of "Prattle," which attained epic proportions in bulk, sizzling satire, and notoriety, Bierce also produced the majority of his short fiction—both the Civil War stories that went into *Tales of Soldiers and Civilians* (1891) and the supernatural tales that fill *Can Such Things Be?* (1893)—along with poems, essays, and, of course, fables. More than six hundred fables were written in the twenty years Bierce worked for the *Examiner* and, later, for Hearst's *Cosmopolitan,* and it was here that he came into his own as a fabulist.

The opportunity to collect Bierce's fables into a book did not, however, emerge until 1899.[9] The previous year Putnam's had reissued Bierce's first story collection—now titled (after the 1892 London edition) *In the Midst of Life*—and shortly thereafter agreed to publish a volume of fables. *Fantastic Fables* appeared in early 1899 and contained only 245 fables. I say "only" because Bierce had by this time written twice as many fables for the *Examiner* alone, let alone his earlier fables for *Fun* (which, as with nearly all his English writing, he seemed intent on forgetting) and (assuming they are his) the *Wasp. Fantastic Fables* itself consists almost entirely of fables published in the *Examiner* between 1887 and 1893—which, indeed, represents the bulk of Bierce's output in this form. In this volume appear forty-seven fables in the section "Æsopus Emendatus," originally published in the *Oakland Tribune* for 1890, at a time when Bierce—probably at the urging of his friend Edward F. Cahill, editor of the *Tribune*—was contributing to this small rival of the *Examiner* across the bay.[10] It is in these fables that Bierce reveals most thoroughly his knowledge of Aesop, for here we find piquant revisions of the moral thrust of many familiar Aesopic fables—revisions that signal Bierce's impatience with the conventional morality found in Aesop, and which exhibit facets of Bierce's hardheaded perception of human folly and duplicity.

From this point on, Bierce's production of fables becomes sporadic. It had, perhaps, always been so: even during the heyday of his work for the *Examiner* (1887-99), months or even a year or two would pass between the publication of fables. There are no fables for the whole of 1888, and none between an unprecedentedly long period between September 1893 and November 1896, although some of this latter period (February to May 1896) was occupied with Bierce's lobbying against a funding bill advocated by railroad baron Collis P. Huntington; the bill's defeat in Congress was Bierce's greatest journalistic triumph.[11] In late 1899 Bierce was forced to move to Washington, D.C., for health reasons (the fogs in San Francisco were playing havoc with his steadily worsening asthma), and for the next decade he would have repeated disputes with Hearst and his editors over their tampering with the work he submitted. His columns and other matter were now first appearing in the *New York Journal* (later *American*), to be reprinted a week or two later in the *Examiner;* some material appeared only in the *Journal.* Perhaps Bierce's creative energies were also flagging; his columns grew shorter and less pungent, and both his stories and his fables appeared more intermittently.

Nevertheless, Bierce had a large supply of fables ready for any contemplated reprint of *Fantastic Fables;* but when that dream turned into a reality — as part of the sixth volume of his *Collected Works* (1909–12) — Bierce chose to include only fifty-nine new fables, while at the same time dropping ten fables from the first edition of *Fantastic Fables.*[12] Eight of these new fables are "Fables in Rhyme," originally published between 1897 and 1902. Curiously, Bierce inserted, before the "Æsopus Emendatus" section, a series of fifteen "Fables from *Fun,*" which are extensively revised versions of some Zambri fables. These are so altered from their original appearances that I have included them as an appendix to the Zambri fables.

Bierce manifestly gave considerable thought to the arrangement and content of the fables he chose to collect in book form, and I have accordingly followed his wishes by preserving the sequence and text of both the Zambri fables (as published in *Cobwebs from an Empty Skull*) and the revised *Fantastic Fables* (as published in the *Collected Works*). Bierce's revisions were almost always for the better, although in some cases he truncated fables so that they would be even more pointed than before; I have included the omitted portions, along with other significant variants, in my commentary.

ANALYSIS AND ASSESSMENT

The reasons for Bierce's failure to include more than half of his fabular output in book form are intimately connected with the nature and purpose of the fable as he apparently conceived it. (We have no writing by Bierce on the fable as a literary form, not even any prefaces to his books of fables, so that his views on the fable must be inferred by random comments in letters or newspaper columns and by the character of the fables themselves.) His fables undergo a striking development in both form and content, so that his greatest fables — those of the 1890s — underscore many facets of his personal philosophy more powerfully, pungently, and piquantly than anything he wrote, with the exception of *The Devil's Dictionary.*

But what is that philosophy? Bierce of course was not a philosopher, and one should not expect any systematic exposition of his views. A series of comments made as early as 1872, in the persona of the departing "Town Crier," may be as succinct an expression of his worldview as we will find:

> The only talents that he has are a knack at hating hypocrisy, cant, and all sham, and a trick of expressing his hatred. . . . Be as decent as you can. Don't believe without evidence. Treat things divine with marked respect—don't have anything to do with them. Do not trust humanity without collateral security; it will play you some scurvy trick. Remember that it hurts no one to be treated as an enemy entitled to respect until he shall prove himself a friend worthy of affection. Cultivate a taste for distasteful truths. And, finally, most important of all, endeavor to see things as they are, not as they ought to be.[13]

What we find here are a series of assertions stressing the following points: skepticism, specifically of politics and religion; distrust of the sincerity of many human motives; and, overarchingly, an unflinching quest to see through the layers of "hypocrisy, cant, and . . . sham" that mask so much human behavior. It is, indeed, no accident that that final remark anticipates his later definition of "Cynic" in *The Devil's Dictionary:* "A blackguard whose faulty vision sees things as they are, not as they ought to be." Bierce strove, both in his personal comportment and in his public utterances, to adhere to the bulk of these assertions throughout his life.

"The Fables of Zambri, the Parsee" only broach some of these issues, and do so in a way that rarely departs radically from the Aesopic fabular form that Bierce is imitating. The cynicism encapsulated in the remark that human beings are "every way inferior to snakes—except in malice" (59) is found only rarely in these fables, and many of the moral failings they chastise are commonplace: making a virtue of necessity (7, 34), using trickery to gain an advantage or to escape punishment (2, 16, 108), self-preservation overcoming family feeling (31). Perhaps somewhat more specifically Biercian are those fables that satirically display pure and unadulterated viciousness within the family circle (33, 90): Bierce, in his "Town Crier" period, claimed to take delight in reporting accounts of the suicide of a beleaguered husband or wife, a parent's murder of his or her children, and the like. To be sure, much of this malevolent glee was designed merely for shock value and cannot be said to echo any personal sentiment on Bierce's part; but its underlying purpose—to show to his Victorian readers that the sanctity and placidity of family life is a "sham" worth exposing—is clear.

Several fables touch upon religious credulity (15, 32, 95) and again echo many comments found in the "Town Crier" columns. But nineteenth-century religion's great foe, science, is not exempt from ridicule (102)—although perhaps here the satire is directed more specifically at the folly of individual scientists. Bierce also found the pomposity, impracticality, and credulity of philosophers a target too good to pass up (62, 69).

Bierce's most radical departure from the fabular tradition was the use of fables for purposes of political satire, but we find only the slightest hints of this in the Zambri fables. Fable 38 may be Bierce's first political fable, although its theme (a king wishes to avoid the usurpation of his throne during his absence) is very general. On the other hand, fable 44, in its attack on Fabian socialism, is too specific to have any broader political message.

As it is, the greatest significance of the Zambri fables may be in their gradual departure from the standard Aesopic form. While almost all the fables utilize animals as interlocutors, one delightful fable (50) plays upon this very usage: a man is terrified when he comes upon a succession of animals who speak to him. Many of the fables lack explicit morals altogether; others present "morals" that are really no morals at all (see 86), or morals that are deliberately self-deflating by reason of their literalness or triviality; still others end up being merely the excuses for puns (13, 113) or other self-parodic jokes.

It is evident that, in the ten-year interval between the Zambri fables and the series of fifty fables found in the *Wasp* (1883-84), Bierce's conception of the fable underwent a considerable change. These fables, although perhaps not of the high quality we find in *Fantastic Fables* and others written during his *Examiner* period, nevertheless approach those fables in form and substance far more than do the Zambri fables. That five out of the six groups of *Wasp* fables have the word "political" in the title is sufficient to indicate the shift of focus. Several of these fables (481, 495) directly address the presidential election of 1884, when those Republicans who deserted their party's chosen candidate, James G. Blaine, gained the sobriquet "Mugwumps." (Bierce later confessed that he was one of them.) [14] Here we have not only few animals as characters but such eccentric interlocutors as a "Record Without a Blot," a "Grasping Monopoly," a "Brilliant Peroration," and so on.

It is difficult to characterize the nearly six hundred fables Bierce wrote for the *Examiner*, but we can start by noting that he has by now almost entirely given up the traditional fabular practice of using animals as interlocutors. In one of the few instances in which he does so, the intent is to make a joke on the physical resemblance of animals to certain human beings who are the targets of his satire: in 198, a zebra is likened to a man in a penitentiary, while a kangaroo with a full pouch brings to mind a thieving legislator. (The fable is perhaps an adaptation of one of the Zambri fables [65], where a somewhat similar idea is found.)

It is also instructive to examine which fables Bierce chose to reprint in *Fantastic Fables* and which he did not. It is certainly the case that the overwhelming bulk of the fables collected in the volume deal with political, legal, or social topics; and Bierce appears intent on presenting only those fables that might be capable of conveying some broader moral or political point. Indeed, the rapidity with which Bierce digested some incident in local, national, or international politics and extracted its quintessence in a fable is remarkable. Accordingly, Bierce either rewrote some fables (usually by replacing a specific name with a generalized description) when reprinting his fables in book form, or chose not to reprint some of his best fables at all, in the apparent belief that some topical fables (especially on local events) would be too recondite to a general readership or had lost their punch after the incidents themselves had passed from public consciousness.

If this is indeed Bierce's motivation, then it seems at least partly contradictory to his normal practice. The overwhelming bulk of his literary and journalistic work — even his fiction — is satirical; and from the beginning of his career Bierce had allied himself with the tart, mordant satire of Juvenal as opposed to the mild, genial satire of Horace. Moreover, throughout the course of his life Bierce justified his attacks on specific individuals — many of whom would now have achieved merited oblivion had they not been embalmed in Bierce's own work — as being typical of all satiric practice:

> In satirizing real persons I follow the example of *all* satirists who succeed. It does not at all matter how obscure, or how anything-else, the persons satirised may be; the merit is *in the satire*. Do you suppose that the merit of Heine's, of Pope's, or Byron's attacks on *persons* — has any relation to the personality . . . of the objects of it. The merit is *intrinsic*. Nobody cares who was hit — nobody reads, for example, the explanatory notes to "The Dunciad" or the "English Bards and Scotch Reviewers", which fool publishers think it necessary to insert. These things of mine would have the same literary value (and I'm bound to assume that they have *some*) if they bore any other names than the ones they do bear. Would it add anything to the interest of a personal satire to entitle it "Atticus" instead of "Arthur McEwen"? I'm not running a guessing game: I prefer human names as Byron did.[15]

But perhaps, in his fables, he considered not only the persons but some of the issues (such as a controversy over the location of the Post Office site in San

Francisco, or the building of the City Hall tower) so remote from his readers' present interests that even the satire had lost much of its sting.

In *Fantastic Fables,* then, are any number of general attacks on "hypocrisy, cant, and . . . sham." The repeated satires on the venality of lawyers (160, 226), politicians (172, 205, 248, 258, 265), and courts (195, 220, 235, 270) are what one might expect from a "cynic" determined to "see things as they are," and parallels to many of these views can readily be found in his journalism.

More to the point, perhaps, are Bierce's censures on the stupidity of the electorate (271), which provides frequent opportunity for demagoguery (255, 263, 354); for it is here that we approach the essence of Bierce's own political philosophy. Bierce refused to ally himself with either political party of the day, feeling that there was an abundance of rascality on both sides; if in his journalism he finds more to attack in Republicans than in Democrats, that may only be because the former were in power for a large portion of the later nineteenth century. But Bierce's attacks go far beyond mere abuses of the democratic system; he condemns the very foundations of that system (see 294, 842). His magisterial satirical novella, "Ashes of the Beacon" (1909), delivers an obvious but still unanswerable refutation of democracy: "An inherent weakness in republican government was that it assumed the honesty and intelligence of the majority, 'the masses,' who were neither honest nor intelligent" (*CW* 1.61). What solution Bierce had to offer is not on record; perhaps he felt there was no solution.

Given Bierce's long tenure in California, it is not surprising that, even in *Fantastic Fables,* a book intended for a broader audience, he presented fables attacking the leniency of California courts (182, 201): Bierce constantly lamented the ease with which defendants whom he believed clearly guilty were acquitted, and the reluctance of jurors and judges to impose the death penalty. Related to this complaint is Bierce's scorn and contempt for anarchists (see 310, 345). It is difficult in our age to realize the widespread alarm that the anarchist movement caused throughout Europe and America, and Bierce is not alone in thinking that even philosophical anarchists secretly sought the violent overthrow of all government. Such concerns were bolstered by the suspicion (erroneous in many cases) that anarchists were behind the assassination of several world leaders, including President William McKinley in 1901.[16]

Some of Bierce's later fables in *Fantastic Fables* do attack specific individuals in the McKinley and Roosevelt administrations; indeed, in one case (339) the subject of attack is not mentioned by name, as Bierce presumably felt that he was sufficiently notorious that his audience would readily grasp the allusion. The writer and political theorist Edward Bellamy is also a target

(403). Such personal satires, however, are rare. In most cases where Bierce's fables are not general, he jeers at institutions or phenomena that had long earned his wrath. The attack on state militias (158) may seem puzzling to those who have not read Bierce's relentless criticisms of such bodies as being mere play soldiers who are useless in cases of actual conflict. In his later fables the army itself does not escape scrutiny (324, 330, 331), and his fable (346) on the military's careless waste of money would seem very timely today. A number of fables poking fun at women poets (174), reporters (218), and writers in general (262, 274) echo long-standing complaints on Bierce's part. Bierce had an exceptionally narrow view of woman's proper place in society, so that it is by no means surprising that he opposed woman suffrage and ridiculed women politicians (344).

In *Fantastic Fables* Bierce is not shy in ridiculing religion (or, perhaps more specifically, religious people) on a variety of grounds: venality (159), intolerance (197, 207, 301), illiteracy (299), cynicism (317), and the like. Bierce himself was manifestly an agnostic, perhaps an atheist; and he well knew that hypocrisy, cant, and sham had as wide a field of play in religion as in politics.

It would of course be too limiting to state that Bierce's later fables are solely on political, religious, or social topics. One piquant phase of his fabular output is a series of fables on literary subjects, especially literary criticism. As a writer whose patience had been tried on numerous occasions by careless or inept critics, Bierce was not slow to poke fun at them (150, 318). Bad poets (350) were also a sore trial to Bierce, if the frequency of their skewering in his journalism is any indication.

As noted, Bierce's uncollected fables were probably consigned by their author to apparent oblivion because he felt that they did not allow for generalization. It is in these uncollected pieces that we find fables on political and other events of the 1890s that had already faded out of public consciousness by the turn of the century: the threat of a war with Chile in 1891 (677), the World's Fair of 1893 (707), the Cuban crisis of 1896 (766). It is perhaps a little surprising that, in 1911, Bierce decided to reprint none of his several fables about the Spanish-American War or the war in the Philippines; but perhaps some of the issues he dealt with—for instance, the controversy over naval maneuvers at the Battle of Santiago (see 802)—seemed to him too recondite or insignificant to evoke a responsive chord in his audience. At any rate, it is in these uncollected fables that we see most clearly Bierce's absorption of the political events of the day and his deftness in molding their elements of absurdity, hypocrisy, or grotesqueness for purposes of pungent satire.

Can Bierce be considered America's greatest prose fabulist? Very few names can be put forth as his equals, let alone his superiors. The Uncle Remus stories of Joel Chandler Harris (1848–1908) are remarkable specimens of their kind, an affecting distillation of African American folklore; but they are more of the nature of short stories or vignettes than fables, at least in terms of length (the shortest of them is at least 750 words, the longest up to 2,500 words). They first appeared in the Atlanta *Constitution* in 1879—after Bierce had written his Zambri fables but well before he began his later work in the fable form— and were collected in *Uncle Remus, His Songs and His Sayings* (1880) and many other volumes. Bierce, however, showered abuse on Harris for his use of dialect, a literary practice he abominated.

Then there is George Ade (1866–1944), who achieved spectacular if transient fame with *Fables in Slang* (1900), first published in the Chicago *Record* for 1897. Ade's fables—collected in more than a dozen volumes—are considerably longer than Bierce's, and to my taste reveal an arch sophistication and preciousness that seriously disfigure them as literary works; and their colloquialism dates them far more than Bierce's austere classicism. Some advocates may find Ade's "amiable cynicism"[17] appealing, but my feeling is that the majority of literate readers will prefer Bierce's deliberately unamiable cynicism. The mere fact that Bierce used the title "Fables without Slang" for several columns in 1901 and 1902 suggests that he did not look upon Ade's work with favor; and a passage in his "Small Contributions" column in *Cosmopolitan* for July 1907, subtitled "Some Sober Words on Slang," clinches the matter: "Among large classes of our countrymen, [slang] is held in so high esteem that whole books of it are put upon the market with profit to author and publisher. One of the most successful of these, reprinted from many of our leading newspapers, is called, I think, 'Fables in Slang'—containing, by the way, nothing that resembles a fable. This unspeakable stuff made its author rich, and naturally he 'syndicated' a second series of the same."[18] In spite of the advocacy of H. L. Mencken,[19] Ade's work seems to have lapsed into obscurity.

As for the *Fables for Our Time* (1940) and *Further Fables for Our Time* (1956) by James Thurber (1894–1961), they are as inimitable as any of Thurber's other works. His fables too tend to be somewhat milder than Bierce's, although tarter than Ade's. One should not allow mere quantity to determine aesthetic worth, but certainly the sheer number of fables by Bierce contained in this volume dwarf the few dozen by Thurber, and not many would deny that the best of Bierce's can easily hold their own with the best of Thurber's. Both Ade and Thurber affix explicit, if wry, morals at the end of their fables, creating a certain mechanical effect that Bierce avoids by allowing readers to deduce the morals for themselves.

Comparisons are inevitably odious, so it is perhaps fruitless to dwell on the issue of America's greatest fabulist. Suffice it to say that both the quantity and consistently high quality of Ambrose Bierce's fables should guarantee them a place in the canon of American literature, especially now that they are at last all available for consultation. Whether we regard them as the ultimate American homage to Aesop, or as the outpourings of a writer never inclined to suffer fools gladly, or even as a contribution to the literature of fantasy, Bierce's fables engage our admiration by their wit, their concision, and preeminently by their exposure of the follies, hypocrisies, and absurdities of our human species.

—S. T. Joshi

NOTES

1. "To Train a Writer" (1899), rpt. in *A Sole Survivor: Bits of Autobiography*, ed. S. T. Joshi and David E. Schultz (Knoxville: University of Tennessee Press, 1998), p. 248.

2. Ben Edwin Perry, "Introduction," *Babrius and Phaedrus* (Cambridge, MA: Harvard University Press; London: William Heinemann, 1965), p. xx.

3. Perry, p. xxxv.

4. "Concerning Wit and Humor," *SFE* (23 March 1903): 12.

5. The best biography remains Carey McWilliams's *Ambrose Bierce: A Biography* (1929); all subsequent biographical work derives largely from it. For some glimpses of Bierce's life as expressed in his own words, see *A Sole Survivor*.

6. For which see Lawrence I. Berkove, "Ambrose Bierce's Concern with Mind and Man," Ph.D. diss., University of Pennsylvania, 1962.

7. "The Pridies," in *Nuggets and Dust Panned Out in California* (London: Chatto & Windus, 1873), p. 33.

8. See "A Thumb-Nail Sketch" (1912), in *A Sole Survivor*, pp. 201–5.

9. In an undated letter to Carroll Carrington (envelope postmarked 28 February 1898), Bierce takes note of the fact that Carrington has seen an advertisement for *Fantastic Fables* from a publisher named Way & Williams, but Bierce writes: "They have as yet not even sent me a contract to sign, nor has there been any correspondence about terms; so I think it odd that they should announce something that they have not really bought" (ms., University of Virginia). Shortly thereafter Bierce came to terms with Putnam's for the book.

10. The "Æsopus Emendatus" columns derive from four of the five columns published in the *Tribune* between 12 July and 9 August 1890. Oddly, no fables from the column of 19 July were reprinted; perhaps Bierce somehow did not have access to this column when compiling *Fantastic Fables*.

11. Two unsigned columns of fables appeared in the *Examiner* at this time, "Aesop's Fables Up to Date" (20 March 1896) and "Aesop Up to Date" (23 April 1896); but they are manifestly not by Bierce.

12. One of these fifty-nine fables is derived from a section of a column for *Cosmopolitan* entitled "Negligible Epigrams." Although a few other items in this and other collections of Bierce's epigrams might pass for fables, I have resisted the temptation to include them.

13. "The Town Crier," *San Francisco News Letter* (9 March 1892): 9.

14. "Prattle," *SFE* (8 July 1888): 4; rpt. *A Sole Survivor,* p. 219.

15. Bierce to Herman Scheffauer [c. September 1902]; ms., Bancroft Library, University of California.

16. There is a further irony here, as far as Bierce was concerned. Some years later the political enemies of William Randolph Hearst claimed that McKinley's assassin had been led to his crime by reading the Hearst papers, and specifically a poetic squib by Bierce himself in which he appeared to predict or even to encourage the assassination. See "A Thumb-Nail Sketch," *A Sole Survivor,* pp. 202-3.

17. Lee Coyle, *George Ade* (New York: Twayne, 1964), p. 43.

18. "Small Contributions," *Cosmopolitan Magazine* 43, No. 3 (July 1907): 335.

19. See "George Ade," in *Prejudices: First Series* (1919).

❧

A NOTE ON THIS EDITION

As mentioned in the introduction, I have respected Bierce's own order and selection of fables in both "The Fables of Zambri, the Parsee" (as published in *Cobwebs from an Empty Skull*) and *Fantastic Fables* (as published in volume 6 of his *Collected Works*). I have accordingly placed the uncollected fables in various sections following these two groups of fables. Readers interested in studying Bierce's fables in absolute chronological order can do so by consulting "A Chronology of Bierce's Fables."

Although this is not a variorum edition, I have included significant textual variants in my commentary. The book versions of the fables contain only a few typographical errors; what is more remarkable, even the newspaper appearances of the uncollected fables seem to have been printed with exceptional accuracy. I have, however, silently corrected a few errors in the texts. I have numbered the fables consecutively throughout the volume for ease of indexing and of cross-referencing in the commentary, and because the bulk of Bierce's uncollected fables were published without titles. Save where indicated, the fables are referred to in the commentary and bibliography by number.

In the commentary I have supplied dates of first publication of each fable as well as selected reprints. This bibliographical information should not be considered exhaustive, as some of the fables (especially those in *Fantastic Fables*) have been reprinted many times. Complete bibliographical citations can be found in "A Chronology of Bierce's Fables." I have in addition supplied elucidations of political, literary, and other allusions in the fables, and have referred the reader to the Aesopic originals that Bierce has adapted in some of his fables; the numbers refer to the numbers used by Ben Edwin Perry to designate Aesopic fables in his appendix ("An Analytical Survey of Greek and Latin Fables in the Aesopic Tradition") to *Babrius and Phaedrus* (see my introduction above, note 2), which correspond with the Greek and Latin texts of the fables printed in Perry's *Aesopica* (University of Illinois Press, 1952). I have resisted the tendency to explain Bierce's jokes, but in a few cases have done so when I have felt that the joke was sufficiently obscure to general readers as to require elucidation.

My index of titles is self-explanatory. I have included titles of all fables that bear titles, as well as the more significant variant titles (as noted in the commentary). The index of characters lists significant characters in the fables; I have capitalized all the characters in the index whether they appear in the actual fables with initial capital letters or not. For characters that appear in the form of a noun with an accompanying adjective, it is best to search in the index under the noun.

As with all my Bierce work, I am grateful to David E. Schultz both for his assistance in locating some of the works included in this book and for his general knowledge of Bierce and his work. Lawrence I. Berkove, Alan Gullette, and Mindi Rayner have also provided assistance and encouragement. I have done most of my research at the New York Public Library, New York University Library, Columbia University Library, University of Minnesota Library, St. Cloud State University Library (St. Cloud, MN), the Huntington Library and Art Gallery, and the Bancroft Library of the University of California. I am grateful to the Alderman Library of the University of Virginia for permission to publish the text of six of Bierce's fables contained in a manuscript in its possession.

❧

THE FABLES OF ZAMBRI,

THE PARSEE

1.

A certain Persian nobleman obtained from a cow gipsy a small oyster. Holding him up by the beard, he addressed him thus:

"You must try to forgive me for what I am about to do; and you might as well set about it at once, for you haven't much time. I should never think of swallowing you if it were not so easy; but opportunity is the strongest of all temptations. Besides, I am an orphan, and very hungry."

"Very well," replied the oyster; "it affords me genuine pleasure to comfort the parentless and the starving. I have already done my best for our friend here, of whom you purchased me; but although she has an amiable and accommodating stomach, *we couldn't agree*. For this trifling incompatibility — would you believe it? — she was about to stew me! Saviour, benefactor, proceed."

"I think," said the nobleman, rising and laying down the oyster, "I ought to know something more definite about your antecedents before succouring you. If you couldn't agree with your mistress, you are probably no better than you should be."

People who begin doing something from a selfish motive frequently drop it when they learn that it is a real benevolence.

2.

A rat seeing a cat approaching, and finding no avenue of escape, went boldly up to her, and said:

"Madam, I have just swallowed a dose of powerful bane, and in accordance with instructions upon the label, have come out of my hole to die. Will you kindly direct me to a spot where my corpse will prove peculiarly offensive?"

"Since you are so ill," replied the cat, "I will myself transport you to a spot which I think will suit."

So saying, she struck her teeth through the nape of his neck and trotted away with him. This was more than he had bargained for, and he squeaked shrilly with the pain.

"Ah!" said the cat, "a rat who knows he has but a few minutes to live, never makes a fuss about a little agony. I don't think, my fine fellow, you have taken poison enough to hurt either you or me."

So she made a meal of him.

If this fable does not teach that a rat gets no profit by lying, I should be pleased to know what it does teach.

3.

A frog who had been sitting up all night in neighbourly converse with an echo of elegant leisure, went out in the grey of the morning to obtain a cheap breakfast. Seeing a tadpole approach,

"Halt!" he croaked, "and show cause why I should not eat you."

The tadpole stopped and displayed a fine tail.

"Enough," said the frog: "I mistook you for one of us; and if there is anything I like, it is frog. But no frog has a tail, as a matter of course."

While he was speaking, however, the tail ripened and dropped off, and its owner stood revealed in his edible character.

"Aha!" ejaculated the frog, "so that is your little game! If, instead of adopting a disguise, you had trusted to my mercy, I should have spared you. But I am down upon all manner of deceit."

And he had him down in a moment.

Learn from this that he would have eaten him anyhow.

4.

An old man carrying, for no obvious reason, a sheaf of sticks, met another donkey whose cargo consisted merely of a bundle of stones.

"Suppose we swop," said the donkey.

"Very good, sir," assented the old man; "lay your load upon my shoulders, and take off my parcel, putting it upon your own back."

The donkey complied, so far as concerned his own encumbrance, but neglected to remove that of the other.

"How clever!" said the merry old gentleman, "I knew you would do that. If you had done any differently there would have been no point to the fable."

And laying down both burdens by the roadside, he trudged away as merry as anything.

5.

An elephant meeting a mouse, reproached him for not taking a proper interest in growth.

"It is all very well," retorted the mouse, "for people who haven't the capacity for anything better. Let them grow if they like; but *I* prefer toasted cheese."

The stupid elephant, not being able to make much sense of this remark, essayed, after the manner of persons worsted at repartee, to set his foot upon his clever conqueror. In point of fact, he did set his foot upon him, and there wasn't any more mouse.

The lesson imparted by this fable is open, palpable: mice and elephants look at things each after the manner of his kind; and when an elephant decides to occupy the standpoint of a mouse, it is unhealthy for the latter.

6.

A wolf was slaking his thirst at a stream, when a lamb left the side of his shepherd, came down the creek to the wolf, passed round him with considerable ostentation, and began drinking below.

"I beg you to observe," said the lamb, "that water does not commonly run uphill; and my sipping here cannot possibly defile the current up where you are, even supposing my nose were no cleaner than yours, which it is. So you have not the flimsiest pretext for slaying me."

"I am not aware, sir," replied the wolf, "that I require a pretext for loving chops; it never occurred to me that one was necessary."

And he dined upon that lambkin with much apparent satisfaction.

This fable ought to convince any one that of two stories very similar one needs not necessarily be a plagiarism.

7.

An old gentleman sat down, one day, upon an acorn, and finding it a very comfortable seat, went soundly to sleep. The warmth of his body caused the acorn to germinate, and it grew so rapidly, that when the sleeper awoke he found himself setting in the fork of an oak, sixty feet from the ground.

"Ah!" said he, "I am fond of having an extended view of any landscape which happens to please my fancy; but this one does not seem to possess that merit. I think I will go home."

It is easier to say go home than to go.

"Well, well!" he resumed, "if I cannot compel circumstances to my will, I can at least adapt my will to circumstances. I decide to remain. 'Life' — as a certain eminent philosopher in England will say, whenever there shall be an England to say it in — 'is the definite combination of heterogeneous changes, both simultaneous and successive, in correspondence with external co-existences and sequences.' I have, fortunately, a few years of this before me yet; and I suppose I can permit my surroundings to alter me into anything I choose."

And he did; but what a choice!

I should say that the lesson hereby imparted is one of contentment combined with science.

8.

A caterpillar had crawled painfully to the top of a hop-pole, and not finding anything there to interest him, began to think of descending.

"Now," soliloquized he, "if I only had a pair of wings, I should be able to manage it very nicely."

So saying, he turned himself about to go down, but the heat of his previous exertion, and that of the sun, had by this time matured him into a butterfly.

"Just my luck!" he growled, "I never wish for anything without getting it. I did not expect this when I came out this morning, and have nothing prepared. But I suppose I shall have to stand it."

So he spread his pinions and made for the first open flower he saw. But a spider happened to be spending the summer in that vegetable, and it was not long before Mr. Butterfly was wishing himself back atop of that pole, a simple caterpillar.

Hæc fabula docet that it is not a good plan to call at houses without first ascertaining who is at home there.

9.

It is related of a certain Tartar priest that, being about to sacrifice a pig, he observed tears in the victim's eyes.

"Now I'd like to know what is the matter with *you?*" he asked.

"Sir," replied the pig, "if your penetration were equal to that of the knife you hold, you would know without inquiring; but I don't mind telling you. I weep because I know I shall be badly roasted."

"Ah," returned the priest, meditatively, having first killed the pig, "we are all pretty much alike: it is the bad roasting that frightens us. Mere death has no terrors."

From this narrative learn that even priests sometimes get hold of only half a truth.

10.

A dog being very much annoyed by bees, ran, quite accidentally, into an empty barrel lying on the ground, and looking out at the bung-hole, addressed his tormentors thus:

"Had you been temperate, stinging me only one at a time, you might have got a good deal of fun out of me. As it is, you have driven me into a secure retreat; for I can snap you up as fast as you come in through the bung-hole. Learn from this the folly of intemperate zeal."

When he had concluded, he awaited a reply. There wasn't any reply; for the bees had never gone near the bung-hole; they went in the same way as he did, and made it very warm for him.

The lesson of this fable is that one cannot stick to his pure reason while quarrelling with bees.

11.

A fox and a duck having quarrelled about the ownership of a frog, agreed to refer the dispute to a lion. After hearing a great deal of argument, the lion opened his mouth to speak.

"I am very well aware," interrupted the duck, "what your decision is. It is that by our own showing the frog belongs to neither of us, and you will eat him yourself. But please remember that lions do not like frogs."

"To me," exclaimed the fox, "it is perfectly clear that you will give the frog to the duck, the duck to me, and take me yourself. Allow me to state certain objections to—"

"I was about to remark," said the lion, "that while you were disputing, the cause of contention had hopped away. Perhaps you can procure another frog."

To point out the moral of this fable would be to offer a gratuitous insult to the acuteness of the reader.

12.

An ass meeting a pair of horses, late one evening, said to them:

"It is time all honest horses were in bed. Why are you driving out this time of day?"

"Ah!" returned they, "if it is so very late, why are you out riding?"

"I never in my life," retorted the ass angrily, "knew a horse to return a direct answer to a civil question."

This tale shows that this ass did not know everything.

[The implication that horses do not answer questions seems to have irritated the worthy fabulist. —TRANSLATOR.]

13.

A stone being cast by the plough against a lump of earth, hastened to open the conversation as follows:

"Virtue, which is the opposite of vice, is best fostered by the absence of temptation!"

The lump of earth, being taken somewhat by surprise, was not prepared with an apophthegm, and said nothing.

Since that time it has been customary to call a stupid person a "clod."

14.

A river seeing a zephyr carrying off an anchor, asked him, "What are you going to do with it?"

"I give it up," replied the zephyr, after mature reflection.

"Blow me if *I* would!" continued the river; "you might just as well not have taken it at all."

"Between you and me," returned the zephyr, "I only picked it up because it is customary for zephyrs to do such things. But if you don't mind I will carry it up to your head and drop it in your mouth."

This fable teaches such a multitude of good things that it would be invidious to mention any.

15.

A peasant sitting on a pile of stones saw an ostrich approaching, and when it had got within range he began pelting it. It is hardly probable that the bird liked this; but it never moved until a large number of boulders had been discharged; then it fell to and ate them.

"It was very good of you, sir," then said the fowl; "pray tell me to what virtue I am indebted for this excellent meal."

"To piety," replied the peasant, who, believing that anything able to devour stones must be a god, was stricken with fear. "I beg you won't think these were merely cold victuals from my table; I had just gathered them fresh, and was intending to have them dressed for my dinner; but I am always hospitable to the deities, and now I suppose I shall have to go without."

"On the contrary, my pious youth," returned the ostrich, "you shall go within."

And the man followed the stones.

The falsehoods of the wicked never amount to much.

16.

Two thieves went into a farmer's granary and stole a sack of kitchen vegetables; and, one of them slinging it across his shoulders, they began to run away. In a moment all the domestic animals and barn-yard fowls about the place were at their heels, in high clamour, which threatened to bring the farmer down upon them with his dogs.

"You have no idea how the weight of this sack assists me in escaping, by increasing my momentum," said the one who carried the plunder; "suppose *you* take it."

"Ah!" returned the other, who had been zealously pointing out the way to safety, and keeping foremost therein, "it is interesting to observe how a common danger makes people confiding. You have a thousand times said that I could not be trusted with valuable booty. It is an humiliating confession, but I am myself convinced that if I should assume that sack, and the impetus it confers, you could not depend upon your dividend."

"A common danger," was the reply, "seems to stimulate conviction, as well as confidence."

"Very likely," assented the other, drily; "I am quite too busy to enter into these subtleties. You will find the subject very ably treated in the Zend-Avesta."

But the bastinado taught them more in a minute than they would have gleaned from that excellent work in a fortnight.

If they could only have had the privilege of reading this fable, it would have taught them more than either.

17.

While a man was trying with all his might to cross a fence, a bull ran to his assistance, and taking him upon his horns, tossed him over. Seeing the man walking away without making any remark, the bull said:

"You are quite welcome, I am sure. I did no more than my duty."

"I take a different view of it, very naturally," replied the man, "and you may keep your polite acknowledgments of my gratitude until you receive it. I did not require your services."

"You don't mean to say," answered the bull, "that you did not wish to cross that fence!"

"I mean to say," was the rejoinder, "that I wished to cross it by my method, solely to avoid crossing it by yours."

Fabula docet that while the end is everything, the means is something.

18.

An hippopotamus meeting an open alligator, said to him:

"My forked friend, you may as well collapse. You are not sufficiently comprehensive to embrace me. I am myself no tyro at smiling, when in the humour."

"I really had no expectation of taking you in," replied the other. "I have a habit of extending my hospitality impartially to all, and about seven feet wide."

"You remind me," said the hippopotamus, "of a certain zebra who was not vicious at all; he merely kicked the breath out of everything that passed behind him, but did not induce things to pass behind him."

"It is quite immaterial what I remind you of," was the reply.

The lesson conveyed by this fable is a very beautiful one.

19.

A man was plucking a living goose, when his victim addressed him thus:

"Suppose *you* were a goose; do you think you would relish this sort of thing?"

"Well, suppose I were," answered the man; "do you think *you* would like to pluck me?"

"Indeed I would!" was the emphatic, natural, but injudicious reply.

"Just so," concluded her tormentor; "that's the way *I* feel about the matter."

20.

A traveller perishing of thirst in a desert, debated with his camel whether they should continue their journey, or turn back to an oasis they had passed some days before. The traveller favoured the latter plan.

"I am decidedly opposed to any such waste of time," said the animal; "I don't care for oases myself."

"I should not care for them either," retorted the man, with some temper, "if, like you, I carried a number of assorted water-tanks inside. But as you will not submit to go back, and I shall not consent to go forward, we can only remain where we are."

"But," objected the camel, "that will be certain death to you!"

"Not quite," was the quiet answer, "it involves only the loss of my camel."

So saying, he assassinated the beast, and appropriated his liquid store.

A compromise is not always a settlement satisfactory to both parties.

21.

A sheep, making a long journey, found the heat of his fleece very uncomfortable, and seeing a flock of other sheep in a fold, evidently awaiting for some one, leaped over and joined them, in the hope of being shorn. Perceiving the shepherd approaching, and the other sheep huddling into a remote corner of the fold, he shouldered his way forward, and going up to the shepherd, said:

"Did you ever see such a lot of fools? It's lucky I came along to set them an example of docility. Seeing me operated upon, they'll be glad to offer themselves."

"Perhaps so," replied the shepherd, laying hold of the animal's horns; "but I never kill more than one sheep at a time. Mutton won't keep in hot weather."

The chops tasted excellently well with tomato sauce.

The moral of this fable isn't what you think it is. It is this: The chops of another man's mutton are *always* nice eating.

22.

Two travellers between Teheran and Bagdad met half-way up the vertical face of a rock, on a path only a cubit in width. As both were in a hurry, and etiquette would allow neither to set his foot upon the other even if dignity had permitted prostration, they maintained for some time a stationary condition. After some reflection each decided to jump round the other; but as etiquette did not warrant conversation with a stranger, neither made known his intention. The consequence was they met, with considerable emphasis, about four feet from the edge of the path, and went through a flight of soaring eagles, a mile out of their way!*

* This is infamous! The learned Parsee appears wholly to ignore the distinction between a fable and a simple lie.

—TRANSLATOR.

23.

A stone which had lain for centuries in a hidden place complained to Allah that remaining so long in one position was productive of cramps.

"If thou wouldst be pleased," it said, "to let me take a little exercise now and then, my health would be the better for it."

So it was granted permission to make a short excursion, and at once began rolling out into the open desert. It had not proceeded far before an ostrich, who was pensively eating a keg of nails, left his repast, dashed at the stone, and gobbled it up.

This narration teaches the folly of contentment: if the ostrich had been content with his nails he would never have eaten the stone.

24.

A man carrying a sack of corn up a high ladder propped against a wall, had nearly reached the top, when a powerful hog passing that way leant against the bottom to scratch its hide.

"I wish," said the man, speaking down the ladder, "you would make that operation as brief as possible; and when I come down I will reward you by rearing a fresh ladder especially for you."

"This one is quite good enough for a hog," was the reply; "but I am curious to know if you will keep your promise, so I'll just amuse myself until you come down."

And taking the bottom rung in his mouth, he moved off, away from the wall. A moment later he had all the loose corn he could garner, but he never got that other ladder.

MORAL. — An ace and four kings is as good a hand as one can hold in draw-poker.

25.

A young cock and a hen were speaking of the size of eggs. Said the cock:

"I once laid an egg—"

"Oh, you did!" interrupted the hen, with a derisive cackle. "Pray how did you manage it?"

The cock felt injured in his self-esteem, and, turning his back upon the hen, addressed himself to a brood of young chickens.

"I once laid an egg—"

The chickens chirped incredulously, and passed on. The insulted bird reddened in the wattles with indignation, and strutting up to the patriarch of the entire barn-yard, repeated his assertion. The patriarch nodded gravely, as if the feat were an every-day affair, and the other continued:

"I once laid an egg alongside a water-melon, and compared the two. The vegetable was considerably the larger."

This fable is intended to show the absurdity of hearing all a man has to say.

26.

Seeing himself getting beyond his depth, a bathing naturalist called lustily for succour.

"Anything *I* can do for you?" inquired the engaging octopus.

"Happy to serve you, I am sure," said the accommodating leech.

"Command *me*," added the earnest crab.

"Gentleman of the briny deep," exclaimed the gasping *savant*, "I am compelled to decline your friendly offices, but I tender you my scientific gratitude; and, as a return favour, I beg, with this my last breath, that you will accept the freedom of my aquarium, and make it your home."

This tale proves that scientific gratitude is quite as bad as the natural sort.

27.

Two whales seizing a pike, attempted in turn to swallow him, but without success. They finally determined to try him jointly, each taking hold of an end, and both shutting their eyes for a grand effort, when a shark darted silently between them, biting away the whole body of their prey. Opening their eyes, they gazed upon one another with much satisfaction.

"I had no idea he would go down so easily," said the one.

"Nor I," returned the other; "but how very tasteless a pike is."

The insipidity we observe in most of our acquaintances is largely due to our imperfect knowledge of them.

28.

A wolf went into the cottage of a peasant while the family was absent in the fields, and falling foul of some beef, was quietly enjoying it, when he was observed by a domestic rat, who went directly to her master, informing him of what she had seen.

"I would myself have dispatched the robber," she added, "but feared you might wish to take him alive."

So the man secured a powerful club and went to the door of the house, while the rat looked in at the window. After taking a survey of the situation, the man said:

"I don't think I care to take this fellow alive. Judging from his present performance, I should say his keeping would entail no mean expense. You may go in and slay him if you like; I have quite changed my mind."

"If you really intended taking him prisoner," replied the rat, "the object of that bludgeon is to me a matter of mere conjecture. However, it is easy enough to see you have changed your mind; and it may be barely worth mentioning that I have changed mine."

"The interest you both take in me," said the wolf, without looking up, "touches me deeply. As you have considerately abstained from bothering me with the question of how I am to be disposed of, I will not embarrass your counsels by obtruding a preference. Whatever may be your decision, you may count on my acquiescence; my countenance alone ought to convince you of the meek docility of my character. I never lose my temper, and I never swear; but, by the stomach of the Prophet! if either one of you domestic animals is in sight when I have finished the conquest of these ribs, the question of *my* fate may be postponed for future debate, without detriment to any important interest."

This fable teaches that while you are considering the abatement of a nuisance, it is important to know which nuisance is the more likely to be abated.

29.

A snake tried to shed its skin by pulling it off over his head, but, being unable to do so, was advised by a woodman to slip out of it in the usual way.

"But," said the serpent, "this is the way *you* do it!"

"True," exclaimed the woodman, holding out the hem of his tunic; "but you will observe that my skin is brief and open. If you desire one like that, I think I can assist you."

So saying, he chopped off about a cubit of the snake's tail.

30.

An oyster who had got a large pebble between the valves of his shell, and was unable to get it out, was lamenting his sad fate, when — the tide being out — a monkey ran to him, and began making an examination.

"You appear," said the monkey, "to have got something else in here, too. I think I'd better remove that first."

With this he inserted his paw, and scooped out the animal's essential part.

"Now," said he, eating the portion he had removed, "I think you will be able to manage the pebble yourself."

To apprehend the lesson of this fable one must have some experience of the law.

31.

An old fox and her two cubs were pursued by dogs, when one of the cubs got a thorn in his foot, and could go no farther. Setting the other to watch for the pursuers, the mother proceeded, with much tender solicitude, to extract the thorn. Just as she had done so, the sentinel gave the alarm.

"How near are they?" asked the mother.

"Close by, in the next field," was the answer.

"The deuce they are!" was the hasty rejoinder. "However, I presume they will be content with a single fox."

And shoving the thorn earnestly back into the wounded foot, this excellent parent took to her heels.

This fable proves that humanity does not happen to enjoy a monopoly of paternal affection.

32.

A man crossing the great river of Egypt, heard a voice, which seemed to come from beneath his boat, requesting him to stop. Thinking it must proceed from some river-deity, he laid down his paddle and said:

"Whoever you are that ask me to stop, I beg you will let me go on. I have been asked by a friend to dine with him, and I am late."

"Should your friend pass this way," said the voice, "I will show him the cause of your detention. Meantime you must come to dinner with *me*."

"Willingly," replied the man, devoutly, very well pleased with so extraordinary an honour; "pray show me the way."

"In here," said the crocodile, elevating his distending jaws above the water and beckoning with his tongue — "this way, please."

This fable shows that being asked to dinner is not always the same thing as being asked to dine.

33.

An old monkey, designing to teach his sons the advantage of unity, brought them a number of sticks, and desired them to see how easily they might be broken, one at a time. So each young monkey took a stick and broke it.

"Now," said the father, "I will teach you a lesson."

And he began to gather the sticks in a bundle. But the young monkeys, thinking he was about to beat them, set upon him, all together, and disabled him.

"There!" said the aged sufferer, "behold the advantage of unity! If you had assailed me one at a time, I would have killed every mother's son of you!"

Moral lessons are like the merchant's goods: they are conveyed in various ways.

34.

A wild horse meeting a domestic one, taunted him with his condition of servitude. The tame animal claimed that he was as free as the wind.

"If that is so," said the other, "pray tell me the office of that bit in your mouth."

"That," was the answer, "is iron, one of the best tonics in the *materia medica.*"

"But what," said the other, "is the meaning of the rein attached to it?"

"Keeps it from falling out of my mouth when I am too indolent to hold it," was the reply.

"How about that saddle?"

"Fool!" was the angry retort; "its purpose is to spare me fatigue; when I am tired, I get on and ride."

35.

Some doves went to a hawk, and asked him to protect them from a kite.

"That I will," was the cheerful reply; "and when I am admitted into the dovecote, I shall kill more of you in a day than the kite did in a century. But of course you know this; you expect to be treated in the regular way."

So he entered the dovecote, and began preparations for a general slaughter. But the doves all set upon him and made exceedingly short work of him. With his last breath he asked them why, being so formidable, they had not killed the kite. They replied that they had never seen any kite.

36.

A defeated warrior snatched up his aged father, and, slinging him across his shoulders, plunged into the wilderness, followed by the weary remnant of his beaten army. The old gentleman liked it.

"See!" said he, triumphantly, to the flying legion; "did you ever hear of so dutiful and accommodating a son? And he's as easy under the saddle as an old family horse!"

"I rather think," replied the broken and disordered battalion, with a grin, "that Mr. Æneas once did something of this kind. But *his* father had thoughtfully taken an armful of lares and penates; and the accommodating nature of *his* son was, therefore, more conspicuous. If I might venture to suggest that you take up my shield and scimitar —"

"Thank you," said the aged party, "I could not think of disarming the military; but if you would just hand me up one of the heaviest of those dead branches, I think the merits of my son would be rendered sufficiently apparent."

The routed column passed him up the one shown in the immediate foreground of our sketch, and it was quite enough for both steed and rider.

Fabula ostendit that History repeats itself, with variations.

37.

A pig who had engaged a cray-fish to pilot him along the beach in search of mussels, was surprised to see his guide start off backwards.

"Your excessive politeness quite overcomes me," said the porker, "but don't you think it rather ill bestowed upon a pig? Pray don't hesitate to turn your back upon me."

"Sir," replied the cray-fish, "permit me to continue as I am. We now stand to each other in the proper relation of *employé* to employer. The former is excessively obsequious, and the latter is, in the eyes of the former, a hog."

38.

The king of tortoises desiring to pay a visit of ceremony to a neighbouring monarch, feared that in his absence his idle subjects might get up a revolution, and that whoever might be left at the head of the State would usurp the throne. So calling his subjects about him, he addressed them thus:

"I am about to leave our beloved country for a long period, and desire to leave the sceptre in the hands of him who is most truly a tortoise. I decree that you shall set out from yonder distant tree, and pass round it. Whoever shall get back last shall be appointed Regent."

So the population set out for the goal, and the king for his destination. Before the race was decided, his Majesty had made the journey and returned. He found the throne occupied by a subject, who at once secured by violence what he had won by guile.

Certain usurpers are too conscientious to retain kingly power unless the rightful monarch be dead; and these are the most dangerous sort.

39.

A spaniel at the point of death requested a mastiff friend to eat him.

"It would soothe my last moments," said he, "to know that when I am no longer of any importance to myself I may still be useful to you."

"Much obliged, I am sure," replied his friend; "I think you mean well, but you should know that my appetite is not so depraved as to relish dog."

Perhaps it is for a similar reason we abstain from cannibalism.

40.

A cloud was passing across the face of the sun, when the latter expostulated with him.

"Why," said the sun, "when you have so much space to float in, should you be casting your cold shadow upon me?"

After a moment's reflection, the cloud made answer thus:

"I certainly had no intention of giving offence by my presence, and as for my shadow, don't you think you have made a trifling mistake? — not a gigantic or absurd mistake, but merely one that would disgrace an idiot."

At this the great luminary was furious, and fell so hotly upon him that in a few minutes there was nothing of him left.

It is very foolish to bandy words with a cloud if you happen to be the sun.

41.

A rabbit travelling leisurely along the highway was seen, at some distance, by a duck, who had just come out of the water.

"Well, I declare!" said she, "if I could not walk without limping in that ridiculous way, I'd stay at home. Why, he's a spectacle!"

"Did you ever see such an ungainly beast as that duck!" said the rabbit to himself. "If I waddled like that I should go out only at night."

MORAL, BY A KANGAROO. — People who are ungraceful of gait are always intolerant of mind.

42.

A fox who dwelt in the upper chamber of an abandoned watch-tower, where he practised all manner of magic, had by means of his art subjected all other animals to his will. One day he assembled a great multitude of them below his window, and commanded that each should appear in his presence, and all who could not teach him some important truth should be thrown off the walls and dashed to pieces. Upon hearing this they were all stricken with grief, and began to lament their hard fate most piteously.

"How," said they, "shall we, who are unskilled in magic, unread in philosophy, and untaught in the secrets of the stars — who have neither wit, eloquence, nor song — how shall we essay to teach wisdom to the wise?"

Nevertheless, they were compelled to make the attempt. After many had failed and been dispatched, another fox arrived on the ground, and learning the condition of affairs, scampered slyly up the steps, and whispered something in the ear of the cat, who was about entering the tower. So the latter stuck her head in at the door, and shrieked:

"Pullets with a southern exposure ripen earliest, and have yellow legs."

At this the magician was so delighted that he dissolved the spell and let them all go free.

43.

One evening a jackass, passing between a village and a hill, looked over the latter and saw the faint light of the rising moon.

"Ho-ho, Master Redface!" said he, "so you are climbing up the other side to point out my long ears to the villagers, are you? I'll just meet you at the top, and set my heels into your insolent old lantern."

So he scrambled painfully up to the crest, and stood outlined against the broad disc of the unconscious luminary, more conspicuously a jackass than ever before.

44.

A bear wishing to rob a beehive, laid himself down in front of it, and over-turned it with his paw.

"Now," said he, "I will lie perfectly still and let the bees sting me until they are exhausted and powerless; their honey may then be obtained without opposition."

And it was so obtained, but by a fresh bear, the other being dead.

This narrative exhibits one aspect of the "Fabian policy."

45.

A cat seeing a mouse with a piece of cheese, said:

"I would not eat that, if I were you, for I think it is poisoned. However, if you will allow me to examine it, I will tell you certainly whether it is or not."

While the mouse was thinking what it was best to do, the cat had fully made up her mind, and was kind enough to examine both the cheese and the mouse in a manner highly satisfactory to herself, but the mouse has never returned to give *his* opinion.

46.

An improvident man, who had quarrelled with his wife concerning household expenses, took her and the children out on the lawn, intending to make an example of her. Putting himself in an attitude of aggression, and turning to his offspring, he said:

"You will observe, my darlings, that domestic offences are always pun-ished with a loss of blood. Make a note of this and be wise."

He had no sooner spoken than a starving mosquito settled upon his nose, and began to assist in enforcing the lesson.

"My officious friend," said the man, "when I require illustrations from the fowls of the air, you may command my patronage. The deep interest you take in my affairs is, at present, a trifle annoying."

"I do not find it so," the mosquito would have replied had he been at leisure, "and am convinced that our respective points of view are so widely dissimilar as not to afford the faintest hope of reconciling our opinions upon collateral points. Let us be thankful that upon the main question of bloodlet-ting we perfectly agree."

When the bird had concluded, the man's convictions were quite un-
altered, but he was too weak to resume the discussion; and, although blood is
thicker than water, the children were constrained to confess that the stranger
had the best of it.

This fable teaches.

47.

"I hate snakes who bestow their caresses with interested partiality or fastidious discrimination," boasted a boa constrictor. "*My* affection is unbounded; it
embraces all animated nature. I am the universal shepherd; I gather all manner
of living things into my folds. Entertainment here for man and beast!"

"I should be glad of one of your caresses," said a porcupine, meekly; "it
has been some time since I got a loving embrace."

So saying, he nestled snugly and confidingly against the large-hearted
serpent—who fled.

A comprehensive philanthropy may be devoid of prejudices, but it has its
preferences all the same.

48.

During a distressing famine in China a starving man met a fat pig, who, seeing
no chance of escape, walked confidently up to the superior animal, and said:

"Awful famine! isn't it?"

"Quite dreadful!" replied the man, eyeing him with an evident purpose:
"almost impossible to obtain meat."

"Plenty of meat, such as it is, but no corn. Do you know, I have been compelled to eat so many of your people, I don't believe there is an ounce of pork
in my composition."

"And I so many that I have lost all taste for pork."

"Terrible thing this cannibalism!"

"Depends upon which character you try it in; it is terrible to be eaten."

"You are very brutal!"

"You are very fat."

"You look as if you would take my life."

"You look as if you would sustain mine."

"Let us 'pull sticks,' " said the now desperate animal, "to see which of us
shall die."

"Good!" assented the man, "I'll pull this one."

So saying, he drew a hedge-stake from the ground, and stained it with the brain of that unhappy porker.

MORAL. — An empty stomach has no ears.

49.

A snake, a mile long, having drawn himself over a roc's egg, complained that in its present form he could get no benefit from it, and modestly desired the roc to aid him in some way.

"Certainly," assented the bird, "I think we can arrange it."

Saying which, she snatched up one of the smaller Persian provinces, and poising herself a few leagues above the suffering reptile, let it drop upon him to smash the egg.

This fable exhibits the folly of asking for aid without specifying the kind and amount of aid you require.

50.

An ox meeting a man on the highway, asked him for a pinch of snuff, where-upon the man fled back along the road in extreme terror.

"*Don't* be alarmed," said a horse whom he met; "the ox won't bite you."

The man gave one stare and broke across the meadows.

"Well," said a sheep, "I wouldn't be afraid of a horse; *he* won't kick."

The man shot like a comet into the forest.

"Look where you're going there, or I'll thrash the life out of you!" screamed a bird into whose nest he had blundered.

Frantic with fear, the man leapt into the sea.

"By Jove! how you frightened me," said a small shark.

The man was dejected, and felt a sense of injury. He seated himself mood-ily on the bottom, braced up his chin with his knees, and thought for an hour. Then he beckoned to the fish who had made the last remark.

"See here, I say," said he, "I wish you would just tell me what in thunder this all means."

"Ever read any fables?" asked the shark.

"No — yes — well, the catechism, the marriage service, and — "

"Oh, bother!" said the fish, playfully, smiling clean back to the pectoral fins; "get out of this and bolt your Æsop!"

The man did get out and bolted.

[This fable teaches that its worthy author was drunk as a loon. — TRANS-LATOR.]

51.

A lion pursued by some villagers was asked by a fox why he did not escape on horseback.

"There is a fine strong steed just beyond this rock," said the fox. "All you have to do is to get on his back and stay there."

So the lion went up to the charger and asked him to give him a lift.

"Certainly," said the horse, "with great pleasure."

And setting one of his heels into the animal's stomach, he lifted him about seven feet from the ground.

"Confound you!" roared the beast as he fell back.

"So did you," quietly remarked the steed.

52.

A mahout who had dismounted from his elephant, and was quietly standing on his head in the middle of the highway, was asked by the animal why he did not revert and move on.

"You are making a spectacle of yourself," said the beast.

"If I choose to stand upside down," replied the man, "I am very well aware that I incur the displeasure of those who adhere with slavish tenacity to the prejudices and traditions of society; but it seems to me that rebuke would come with a more consistent grace from one who does not wear a tail upon his nose."

This fable teaches that four straight lines may enclose a circle, but there will be corners to let.

53.

A dog meeting a strange cat, took her by the top of the back, and shook her for a considerable period with some earnestness. Then depositing her in a ditch, he remarked with gravity:

"There, my feline friend! I think that will teach you a wholesome lesson; and as punishment is intended to be reformatory, you ought to be grateful to me for deigning to administer it."

"I don't think of questioning your right to worry me," said the cat, getting her breath, "but I should like to know where you got your licence to preach at me. Also, if not inconsistent with the dignity of the court, I should wish to be informed of the nature of my offence; in order that I may the more clearly apprehend the character of the lesson imparted by its punishment."

"Since you are so curious," replied the dog, "I worry you because you are too feeble to worry me."

"In other words," rejoined the cat, getting herself together as well as she could, "you bite me for that to which you owe your peaceful existence."

The reply of the dog was lost in the illimitable field of ether, whither he was just then projected by the kick of a passing horse. The moral of this fable cannot be given until he shall get down, and close the conversation with the regular apophthegm.

54.

People who wear tight hats will do well to lay this fable well to heart, and ponder upon the deep significance of its moral:

In passing over a river, upon a high bridge, a cow discovered a broad loose plank in the flooring, sustained in place by a beam beneath the centre.

"Now," said she, "I will stand at this end of the trap, and when yonder sheep steps upon the opposite extreme there will be an upward tendency in wool."

So when the meditative mutton advanced unwarily upon the treacherous device, the cow sprang bodily upon the other end, and there was a fall in beef.

55.

Two snakes were debating about the proper method of attacking prey.

"The best way," said one, "is to slide cautiously up, endwise, and seize it thus" — illustrating his method by laying hold of the other's tail.

"Not at all," was the reply; "a better plan is to approach by a circular side-sweep, thus" — turning upon his opponent and taking in *his* tail.

Although there was no disagreement as to the manner of disposing of what was once seized, each began to practise his system upon the other, and continued until both were swallowed.

The work begun by contention is frequently completed by habit.

56.

A man staggering wearily through the streets of Persepolis, under a heavy burden, said to himself:

"I wish I knew what this thing is I have on my back; then I could make some sort of conjecture as to what I design doing with it."

"Suppose," said the burden, "I were a man in a sack; what disposition would you make of me?"

"The regular thing," replied the man, "would be to take you over to Constantinople, and pitch you into the Bosphorus; but I should probably content myself with laying you down and jumping on you, as being more agreeable to my feelings, and quite as efficacious."

"But suppose," continued the burden, "I were a shoulder of beef—which I quite as much resemble—belonging to some poor family."

"In that case," replied the man, promptly, "I should carry you to my larder, my good fellow."

"But if I were a sack of gold, do you think you would find me very onerous?" said the burden.

"A great deal would depend," was the answer, "upon whom you happened to belong to; but I may say, generally, that gold upon the shoulders is wonderfully light, considering the weight of it."

"Behold," said the burden, "the folly of mankind: they cannot perceive that the *quality* of the burdens of life is a matter of no importance. The question of pounds and ounces is the only consideration of any real weight."

57.

A ghost meeting a genie, one wintry night, said to him:

"Extremely harassing weather, friend. Wish I had some teeth to chatter!"

"You do not need them," said the other; "you can always chatter those of other people, by merely showing yourself. For my part, I should be content with some light employment: would erect a cheap palace, transport a light-weight princess, threaten a small cripple—of jobs of that kind. What are the prospects of the fool crop?"

"For the next few thousand years, very good. There is a sort of thing called Literature coming in, shortly, and it will make our fortune. But it will be very bad for History. Curse this phantom apparel! The more I gather it about me the colder I get."

"When Literature has made our fortune," sneered the genie, "I presume you will purchase material clothing."

"And you," retorted the ghost, "will be able to advertise for permanent employment at a fixed salary."

This fable shows the difference between the super natural and the natural "super": the one appears in the narrative, the other does not.

58.

"Permit me to help you on in the world, sir," said a boy to a travelling tortoise, placing a glowing coal upon the animal's back.

"Thank you," replied the unconscious beast; "I alone am responsible for the time of my arrival, and I alone will determine the degree of celerity required. The gait I am going will enable me to keep all my present appointments."

A genial warmth began about this time to pervade his upper crust, and a moment after he was dashing away at a pace comparatively tremendous.

"How about those engagements?" sneered the grinning urchin.

"I've recollected another one," was the hasty reply.

59.

Having fastened his gaze upon a sparrow, a rattlesnake sprang open his spanning jaws, and invited her to enter.

"I should be most happy," said the bird, not daring to betray her helpless condition, but anxious by any subterfuge to get the serpent to remove his fascinating regard, "but I am just lost in contemplation of yonder green sunset, from which I am unable to look away for more than a minute. I shall turn to it presently."

"Do, by all means," said the serpent, with a touch of irony in his voice. "There is nothing so improving as a good, square, green sunset."

"Did you happen to observe that man standing behind you with a club?" continued the sparrow. "Handsome fellow! Fifteen cubits high, with seven heads, and very singularly attired; quite a spectacle in his way."

"I don't seem to care much for men," said the snake. "Every way inferior to serpents — except in malice."

"But he is accompanied by a *really interesting* child," persisted the bird, desperately.

The rattlesnake reflected deeply. He soliloquized as follows:

"There is a mere chance—say about one chance in ten thousand million—that this songster is speaking the truth. One chance in ten thousand million of seeing a really interesting child is worth the sacrifice demanded; I'll make it."

So saying, he removed his glittering eyes from the bird (who immediately took wing) and looked behind him. It is needless to say there was no really interesting child there—nor anywhere else.

MORAL.—Mendacity (so called from the inventors) is a very poor sort of dacity; but it will serve your purpose if you draw it sufficiently strong.

60.

A man who was very much annoyed by the incursions of a lean ass belonging to his neighbour, resolved to compass the destruction of the invader.

"Now," said he, "if this animal shall choose to starve himself to death in the midst of plenty, the law will not hold *me* guilty of his blood. I have read of a trick which I think will 'fix' him."

So he took two bales of his best hay, and placed them in a distant field, about forty cubits apart. By means of a little salt he then enticed the ass in, and coaxed him between the bundles.

"There, fiend!" said he, with a diabolic grin, as he walked away delighted with the success of his strategem, "now hesitate which bundle of hay to attack first, until you starve—monster!"

Some weeks afterwards he returned with a wagon to convey back the bundles of hay. There wasn't any hay, but the wagon was useful for returning to his owner that unfortunate ass—who was too fat to walk.

This ought to show any one the folly of relying upon the teaching of obscure and inferior authors.*

---

* It is to be wished our author had not laid himself open to the imputation of having perverted, if not actually invented, some of his facts, for the unworthy purpose of bringing a deserving rival into disfavour.

—TRANSLATOR.

61.

One day the king of the wrens held his court for the trial of a bear, who was at large upon his own recognizance. Being summoned to appear, the animal came with great humility into the royal presence.

"What have you to say, sir," demanded the King, "in defence of your inexcusable conduct in pillaging the nests of our loyal subjects wherever you can find them?"

"May it please your Majesty," replied the prisoner, with a reverential gesture, repeated at intervals, and each time at a less distance from the royal person, "I will not wound your Majesty's sensibilities by pleading a love of eggs; I will humbly confess my course of crime, warn your Majesty of its probable continuance, and beg your Majesty's gracious permission to enquire — What is your Majesty going to do about it?"

The king and his ministers were very much struck with this respectful speech, with the ingenuity of the final inquiry, and with the bear's paw. It was the paw, however, which made the most lasting impression.

Always give ear to the flattery of your powerful inferiors: it will cheer you in your decline.

62.

A philosopher looking up from the pages of the Zend-Avesta, upon which he had been centring his soul, beheld a pig violently assailing a cauldron of cold slops.

"Heaven bless us!" said the sage; "for unalloyed delight give me a good honest article of Sensuality. So soon as my 'Essay upon the Correlation of Mind-forces' shall have brought me fame and fortune, I hope to abjure the higher faculties, devoting the remainder of my life to the cultivation of the propensities."

"Allah be praised!" soliloquized the pig, "there is nothing so godlike as Intellect, and nothing so ecstatic as intellectual pursuits. I must hasten to perform this gross material function, that I may retire to my wallow and resign my soul to philosophical meditation."

This tale has one moral if you are a philosopher, and another if you are a pig.

63.

"Awful dark—isn't it?" said an owl, one night, looking in upon the roosting hens in a poultry-house; "don't see how I am to find my way back to my hollow tree."

"There is no necessity," replied the cock; "you can roost there, alongside the door, and go home in the morning."

"Thanks!" said the owl, chuckling at the fool's simplicity; and, having plenty of time to indulge his facetious humour, he gravely installed himself upon the perch indicated, and shutting his eyes, counterfeited a profound slumber. He was aroused soon after by a sharp constriction of the throat.

"I omitted to tell you," said the cock, "that the seat you happen by the merest chance to occupy is a contested one, and has been fruitful of hens to this vexatious weasel. I don't know *how* often I have been partially widowed by the sneaking villain."

For obvious reasons there was no audible reply.

This narrative is intended to teach the folly—the worse than sin!—of trumping your partner's ace.

64.

A fat cow who saw herself detected by an approaching horse while perpetrating stiff and ungainly gambols in the spring sunshine, suddenly assumed a severe gravity of gait, and a sedate solemnity of expression that would have been creditable to a Brahmin.

"Fine morning!" said the horse, who, fired by her example, was curvetting lithely and tossing his head.

"That rather uninteresting fact," replied the cow, attending strictly to her business as a ruminant, "does not impress me as justifying your execution of all manner of unseemly contortions, as a preliminary to accosting an entire stranger."

"Well, n—no," stammered the horse; "I—I suppose not. Fact is I—I— no offence, I hope."

And that unhappy charger walked soberly away, dazed by the preternatural effrontery of that placid cow.

When overcome by the dignity of any one you chance to meet, try to have this fable about you.

65.

"What have you there on your back?" said a zebra, jeeringly, to a "ship of the desert" in ballast.

"Only a bale of gridirons," was the meek reply.

"And what, pray, may you design doing with them?" was the incredulous rejoinder.

"What am I to do with gridirons?" repeated the camel, contemptuously. "Nice question for *you*, who have evidently come off one!"

People who wish to throw stones should not live in glass houses; but there ought to be a few in their vicinity.

66.

A cat, waking out of a sound sleep, saw a mouse sitting just out of reach, observing her. Perceiving that at the slightest movement of hers the mouse would recollect an engagement, she put on a look of extreme amiability, and said:

"Oh! it's you, is it? Do you know, I thought at first you were a frightful great rat; and I am *so* afraid of rats! I feel so much relieved — you don't know! Of course you have heard that I am a great friend to the dear little mice?"

"Yes," was the answer, "I have heard that you love us indifferently well, and my mission here was to bless you while you slept. But as you will wish to go and get your breakfast, I won't bore you. Fine morning — isn't it? *Au revoir!*"

The fable teaches that it is usually safe to avoid one who pretends to be a friend without having any reason to be. It wasn't safe in this instance, however; for the cat went after the departing rodent, and got away with him.

67.

A man pursued by a lion, was about stepping into a place of safety, when he bethought him of the power of the human eye; and, turning about, he fixed upon his pursuer a steady look of stern reproof. The raging beast immediately moderated his rate per hour, and finally came to a dead halt, within a yard of the man's nose. After making a leisurely survey of him, he extended his neck and bit off a small section of his victim's thigh.

"Beard of Arimanes!" roared the man; "have you no respect for the Human Eye?"

"I hold the human eye in profound esteem," replied the lion, "and confess its power. It assists digestion if taken just before a meal. But I don't understand why you should have two and I none."

With that he raised his foot, unsheathed his claws, and transferred one of the gentleman's visual organs to his own mouth.

"Now," continued he, "during the brief remainder of a squandered existence, your lion-quelling power, being more highly concentrated, will be the more easily managed."

He then devoured the remnant of his victim, including the other eye.

68.

An ant laden with a grain of corn, which he had acquired with infinite toil, was breasting a current of his fellows, each of whom, as is their etiquette, insisted upon stopping him, feeling him all over, and shaking hands. It occurred to him that an excess of ceremony is an abuse of courtesy. So he laid down his burden, sat upon it, folded all his legs tight to his body, and smiled a smile of great grimness.

"Hullo! What's the matter with *you?*" exclaimed the first insect whose overtures were declined.

"Sick of the hollow conventionalities of a rotten civilization," was the rasping reply. "Relapsed into the honest simplicity of primitive observances. Go to grass!"

"Ah! then we must trouble you for that corn. In a condition of primitive simplicity there are no rights of property, you know. These are 'hollow conventionalities.' "

A light dawned upon the intellect of that pismire. He shook the reefs out of his legs; he scratched the reverse of his ear; he grappled that cereal, and trotted away like a giant refreshed. It was observed that he submitted with a wealth of patience to manipulation by his friends and neighbours, and went some distance out of his way to shake hands with strangers on competing lines of traffic.

69.

A snake who had lain torpid all winter in his hole took advantage of the first warm day to limber up for the spring campaign. Having tied himself into an intricate knot, he was so overcome by the warmth of his own body that he fell asleep, and did not wake until nightfall. In the darkness he was unable to find his head or his tail, and so could not disentangle and slide into his hole. Per consequence, he froze to death.

Many a subtle philosopher has failed to solve himself, owing to his inability to discern his beginning and his end.

70.

A dog finding a joint of mutton, apparently guarded by a negligent raven, stretched himself before it with an air of intense satisfaction.

"Ah!" said he, alternately smiling and stopping up the smiles with meat, "this is an instrument of salvation to my stomach — an instrument upon which I love to perform!"

"I beg your pardon!" said the bird; "it was placed there specially for me, by one whose right to so convey it is beyond question, he having legally acquired it by chopping it off the original owner."

"I detect no flaw in your abstract of title," replied the dog; "all seems quite regular; but I must not provoke a breach of the peace by lightly relinquishing what I might feel it my duty to resume by violence. I must have time to consider; and in the meantime I will dine."

Thereupon he leisurely consumed the property in dispute, shut his eyes, yawned, turned upon his back, thrust out his legs divergently, and died.

For the meat had been carefully poisoned — a fact of which the raven was guiltily conscious.

There are several things mightier than brute force, and arsenic* is one of them.

---

*In the original, *"pizen;"* which might, perhaps, with equal propriety have been rendered by "caper sauce."

— TRANSLATOR.

71.

The King of Persia had a favourite hawk. One day his Majesty was hunting, and had become separated from his attendants. Feeling thirsty, he sought a stream of water trickling from a rock, took a cup, and pouring some liquor into it from his pocket-flask, filled it up with water, and raised it to his lips. The hawk, who had been all this time hovering about, swooped down, screaming "No you don't!" and upset the cup with his wing.

"I know what is the matter," said the King; "there is a dead serpent in the fountain above, and this faithful bird has saved my life by not permitting me to drink the juice. I must reward him in the regular way."

So he called a page, who had thoughtfully presented himself, and gave directions to have the Remorse Apartments of the palace put in order, and for the court tailor to prepare an evening suit of sackcloth-and-ashes. Then summoning the hawk, he seized and dashed him upon the ground, killing him very dead. Rejoining his retinue, he dispatched an officer to remove the body of the serpent from the fountain, lest somebody else should get poisoned. There wasn't any serpent—the water was remarkable for its wholesome purity!

Then the King, cheated of his remorse, was sorry he had slain the bird; he said it was a needless waste of power to kill a bird who merely deserved killing. It never occurred to the King that the hawk's touching solicitude was with reference to the contents of the royal flask.

Fabula ostendit that a "twice-told tale" needs not necessarily be "tedious"; a reasonable degree of interest may be obtained by intelligently varying the details.

72.

A herd of cows, blown off the summit of the Himalayas, were sailing some miles above the valleys, when one said to another:

"Got anything to say about this?"

"Not much," was the answer. "It's airy."

"I wasn't thinking of that," continued the first; "I am troubled about our course. If we could leave the Pleiades a little more to the right, striking a middle course between Boötes and the ecliptic, we should find it all plain sailing as far as the solstitial colure. But once we get into the Zodiac upon our present bearing, we are certain to meet with shipwreck before reaching our aphelion."

They escaped this melancholy fate, however, for some Chaldean shepherds, seeing a nebulous cloud drifting athwart the heavens, and obscuring a favourite planet they had just invented, brought out their most powerful telescopes and resolved it into independent cows—whom they proceeded to slaughter in detail with the instruments of smaller calibre. There have been occasional "meat showers" ever since. These are probably nothing more than—

[Our author can be depended upon in matters of fact; his scientific theories are not worth printing.—TRANSLATOR.]

73.

A bear, who had worn himself out walking from one end of his cage to the other, addressed his keeper thus:

"I say, friend, if you don't procure me a shorter cage I shall have to give up zoology; it is about the most wearing pursuit I ever engaged in. I favour the advancement of science, but the mechanical part of it is a trifle severe, and ought to be done by contract."

"You are quite right, my hearty," said the keeper, "it *is* severe; and there have been several excellent plans proposed to lighten the drudgery. Pending the adoption of some of them, you would find a partial relief in lying down and keeping quiet."

"It won't do—it won't do!" replied the bear, with a mournful shake of his head, "it's not the orthodox thing. Inaction may do for professors, collectors, and others connected with the ornamental part of the noble science; but for *us*, we must keep moving, or zoology would soon revert to the crude guesses and mistaken theories of the azoic period. And yet," continued the beast, after the keeper had gone, "there is something novel and ingenious in what the underling suggests. I must remember that; and when I have leisure, give it a trial."

It was noted next day that the noble science had lost an active apostle, and gained a passive disciple.

74.

A hen who had hatched out a quantity of ducklings, was somewhat surprised one day to see them take to the water, and sail away out of her jurisdiction. The more she thought of this the more unreasonable such conduct appeared, and the more indignant she became. She resolved that it must cease forthwith. So she soon afterward convened her brood, and conducted them to the margin of a hot pool, having a business connection with the boiling spring of Doo-sno-swair. They straightway launched themselves for a cruise—returning immediately to the land, as if they had forgotten their ship's papers.

When Callow Youth exhibits an eccentric tendency, give it him hot.

75.

"Did it ever occur to you that this manner of thing is extremely unpleasant?" asked a writhing worm of the angler who had impaled him upon a hook. "Such treatment by those who boast themselves our brothers is, possibly, fraternal — but it hurts."

"I confess," replied the idler, "that our usages with regard to vermin and reptiles might be so amended as to be more temperately diabolical; but please to remember that the gentle agonies with which we afflict *you* are wholesome and exhilarating compared with the ills we ladle out to one another. During the reign of His Pellucid Reflugence, Khatchoo Khan," he continued, absently dropping his wriggling auditor into the brook, "no less than three hundred thousand Persian subjects were put to death, in a pleasing variety of ingenious ways, for their religious beliefs."

"What that has to do with your treatment of *us*," interrupted a fish, who, having bitten at the worm just then, was drawn into the conversation, "I am quite unable to see."

"That," said the angler, disengaging him, "is because you have the hook through your eyeball, my edible friend."

Many a truth is spoken in jest; but at least ten times as many falsehoods are uttered in dead earnest.

76.

A wild cat was listening with rapt approval to the melody of distant hounds tracking a remote fox.

"Excellent! *bravo!*" she exclaimed at intervals. "I could sit and listen all day to the like of that. I am passionately fond of music. *Ong-core!*"

Presently the tuneful sounds drew near, whereupon she began to fidget; ending by shinning up a tree, just as the dogs burst into view below her, and stifled their songs upon the body of their victim before her eyes — which protruded.

"There is an indefinable charm," said she — "a subtle and tender spell — a mystery — a conundrum, as it were — in the sounds of an unseen orchestra. This is quite lost when the performers are visible to the audience. Distant music (if any) for your obedient servant!"

77.

Having been taught to turn his scraps of bad Persian into choice Latin, a parrot was puffed up with conceit.

"Observe," said he, "the superiority I may boast by virtue of my classical education: I can chatter flat nonsense in the language of Cicero."

"I would advise you," said his master, quietly, "to let it be of a different character to that chattered by some of Mr. Cicero's most admired compatriots, if you value the privilege of hanging at that public window. 'Commit no mythology,' please."

The exquisite fancies of a remote age may not be imitated in this; not, perhaps, from a lack of talent, so much as from a fear of arrest.

78.

A rat, finding a file, smelt it all over, bit it gently, and observed that, as it did not seem to be rich enough to produce dyspepsia, he would venture to make a meal of it. So he gnawed it into *smithareens** without the slightest injury to his teeth. With his morals the case was somewhat different. For the file was a file of newspapers, and his system became so saturated with the "spirit of the Press" that he went off and called his aged father a "lingering contemporary"; advised the correction of brief tails by amputation; lauded the skill of a quack rodentist for money; and, upon what would otherwise have been his deathbed, essayed a lie of such phenomenal magnitude that it stuck in his throat, and prevented him breathing his last. All this crime, and misery, and other nonsense, because he was too lazy to worry about and find a file of nutritious fables.

This tale shows the folly of eating everything you happen to fancy. Consider, moreover, the danger of such a course to your neighbour's wife.

*I confess my inability to translate this word: it may mean "flinders."

— TRANSLATOR.

79.

"I should like to climb up you, if you don't mind," cried an ivy to a young oak.

"Oh, certainly; come along," was the cheerful assent.

So she started up, and finding she could grow faster than he, she wound round and round him until she had passed up all the line she had. The oak, however, continued to grow, and as she could not disengage her coils, she was just lifted out by the root. So that ends the oak-and-ivy business, and removes a powerful temptation from the path of the young writer.

80.

A merchant of Cairo gave a grand feast. In the midst of the revelry, the great doors of the dining-hall were pushed open from the outside, and the guests were surprised and grieved by the advent of a crocodile of a tun's girth, and as long as the moral law.

"Thought I'd look in," he said, simply, but not without a certain grave dignity.

"But," cried the host, from the top of the table, "I did not invite any saurians."

"No — I know yer didn't; it's the old thing, it is: never no wacancies for saurians — saurians should orter keep theirselves *to* theirselves — no saurians need apply. I got it all by 'eart, I tell yer. But don't give yerself no distress; I didn't come to beg; thank 'eaven I ain't drove to that yet — leastwise I ain't done it. But I thought as 'ow yer'd need a dish to throw slops and broken wittles in it; so I fetched along this 'ere."

And the willing creature lifted off the cover by erecting the upper half of his head till the snout of him smote the ceiling.

Open servitude is better than covert begging.

81.

A gander being annoyed by the assiduous attendance of his ugly reflection in the water, determined that he would prosecute future voyages in a less susceptible element. So he essayed a sail upon the placid bosom of a clay-bank. This kind of navigation did not meet his expectations, however, and he returned with dogged despair to his pond, resolved to make a final cruise and go out of commission. He was delighted to find that the clay adhering to his hull so defiled the water that it gave back no image of him. After that, whenever he left port, he was careful to be well clayed along the water-line.

The lesson of this is that if all geese are alike, we can banish unpleasant reflections by befouling ourselves. This is worth knowing.

82.

The belly and the members of the human body were in a riot. (This is not the riot recorded by an inferior writer, but a more notable and authentic one.) After exhausting the well-known arguments, they had recourse to the appropriate threat, when the man to whom they belonged thought it time for *him* to be heard, in his capacity as a unit.

"Deuce take you!" he roared. "Things have come to a pretty pass if a fellow cannot walk out of a fine morning without alarming the town by a disgraceful squabble between his component parts! I am reasonably impartial, I hope, but man's devotion is due to his deity: I espouse the cause of my belly."

Hearing this, the members were thrown into so extraordinary confusion that the man was arrested for a windmill.

As a rule, don't "take sides." Sides of bacon, however, may be temperately acquired.

83.

A man dropping from a balloon struck against a soaring eagle.

"I beg your pardon," said he, continuing his descent; "I never *could* keep off eagles when in my descending node."

"It is splendid to meet so pleasing a gentleman, even without previous appointment," said the bird, looking admiringly down upon the lessening aeronaut; "he is the very pink of politeness. How extremely nice his liver must be. I will follow him down and arrange his simple obsequies."

This fable is narrated for its intrinsic worth.

84.

To escape from a peasant who had come suddenly upon him, an opossum adopted his favourite expedient of counterfeiting death.

"I suppose," said the peasant, "that ninety-nine men in a hundred would go away and leave this poor creature's body to the beasts of prey." [It is notorious that man is the only living thing that will eat the animal.] "But *I* will give him good burial."

So he dug a hole, and was about tumbling him into it, when a solemn voice appeared to emanate from the corpse: "Let the dead bury their dead!"

"Whatever spirit hath wrought this miracle," cried the peasant, dropping upon his knees, "let him but add the trifling explanation of *how* the dead can perform this or any similar rite, and I am obedience itself. Otherwise, in goes Mr. 'Possum by these hands."

"Ah!" meditated the unhappy beast, "I have performed one miracle, but I can't keep it up all day, you know. The explanation demanded is a trifle too heavy for even the ponderous ingenuity of a marsupial."

And he permitted himself to be sodded over.

If the reader knows what lesson is conveyed by this narrative, he knows — just what the writer knows.

85.

Three animals on board a sinking ship prepared to take to the water. It was agreed among them that the bear should be lowered alongside; the mouse (who was to act as pilot) should embark upon him at once, to beat off the drowning sailors; and the monkey should follow, with provisions for the expedition — which arrangement was successfully carried out. The fourth day out from the wreck, the bear began to propound a series of leading questions concerning dinner; when it appeared that the monkey had provided but a single nut.

"I thought this would keep me awhile," he explained, "and you could eat the pilot."

Hearing this, the mouse vanished like a flash into the bear's ear, and fearing the hungry beast would then demand the nut, the monkey hastily devoured it. Not being in a position to insist upon his rights, the bear merely gobbled up the monkey.

86.

A lamb suffering from thirst went to a brook to drink. Putting his nose to the water, he was interested to feel it bitten by a fish. Not liking fish, he drew back and sought another place; but his persecutor getting there before him administered the same rebuff. The lamb being rather persevering, and the fish having no appointments for that day, this was repeated a few thousand times, when the former felt justified in swearing:

"I'm eternally boiled!" said he, "if ever I experienced so many fish in my life. It is discouraging. It inspires me with mint sauce and green peas."

He probably meant amazement and fear; under the influence of powerful emotions even lambs will talk "shop."

"Well, good bye," said his tormentor, taking a final nip at the animal's muzzle; "I should like to amuse you some more; but I have other fish to fry."

This fable teaches a good quantity of lessons; but it does *not* teach why this fish should have persecuted this lamb.

87.

A mole, in pursuing certain geological researches, came upon the buried carcase of a mule, and was about to tunnel him.

"Slow down, my good friend," said the deceased. "Push your mining operations in a less sacrilegious direction. Respect the dead, as you hope for death!"

"You have that about you," said the gnome, "that must make your grave respected in a certain sense, for at least such a period as your immortal part may require for perfect exhalation. The immunity I accord is not conceded to your sanctity, but extorted by your scent. The sepulchres of moles only are sacred."

> To moles, the body of a lifeless mule
> A dead mule's carcase is, and nothing more.

88.

"I think I'll set my sting into you, my obstructive friend," said a bee to an iron pump against which she had flown; "you are always more or less in the way."

"If you do," retorted the other, "I'll pump on you, if I can get any one to work my handle."

Exasperated by this impotent conservative threat, she pushed her little dart against him with all her vigour. When she tried to sheathe it again she couldn't, but she still made herself useful about the hive by hooking on to small articles and dragging them about. But no other bee would sleep with her after this; and so, by her ill-judged resentment, she was self-condemned to a solitary cell.

The young reader may profitably beware.

89.

A Chinese dog, who had been much abroad with his master, was asked, upon his return, to state the most ludicrous fact he had observed.

"There is a country," said he, "the people of which are eternally speaking about 'Persian honesty,' 'Persian courage,' 'Persian loyalty,' 'Persian love of fair play,' &c., as if the Persians enjoyed a clear monopoly of these universal virtues. What is more, they speak thus in blind good faith — with a dense gravity of expression that is simply amazing."

"But," urged his auditors, "we requested something ludicrous, not amazing."

"Exactly; the ludicrous part is the name of their country, which is — "

"What?"

"Persia."

90.

There was a calf, who, suspecting the purity of the milk supplied him by his dam, resolved to transfer his patronage to the barn-yard pump.

"Better," said he, "a pure article of water, than a diet that is neither fish, flesh, nor fowl."

But, although extremely regular in his new diet — taking it all the time — he did not seem to thrive as might have been expected. The larger orders he drew, the thinner and more transparent he became; and at last, when the shadow of his person had become to him a vague and unreal memory, he repented, and applied to be reinstated in his comfortable sinecure at the maternal udder.

"Ah! my prodigal son," said the old lady, lowering her horns as if to permit him to weep upon her neck, "I regret that it is out of my power to celebrate your return by killing the fatted calf; but what I can I will do."

And she killed the him instead.

*Mot herl yaff ecti onk nocksal loth ervir tu esperfec tlyc old.**

---

* The learned reader will appreciate the motive which has prompted me to give this moral only in the original Persian.

—Translator.

91.

"There, now," said a kitten, triumphantly, laying a passive mouse at the feet of her mother. "I flatter myself I am coming on with a reasonable degree of rapidity. What will become of the minor quadrupeds when I shall have attained my full strength and ferocity, it is mournful to conjecture!"

"Did he give you much trouble?" inquired the aged ornament of the hearth-side, with a look of tender solicitude.

"Trouble!" echoed the kitten, "I never had such a fight in all my life! He was a downright savage — in his day."

"My Falstaffian issue," rejoined the Tabby, dropping her eyelids and composing her head for a quiet sleep, "the above is a *toy* mouse."

92.

A crab who had travelled from the mouth of the Indus all the way to Ispahan, knocked, with much chuckling, at the door of the King's physician.

"Who's there?" shouted the doctor, from his divan within.

"A bad case of *cancer*," was the complacent reply.

"Good!" returned the doctor; "I'll *cure* you, my friend."

So saying, he conducted his facetious patient into the kitchen, and potted him in pickle. It cured him — of practical jocularity.

May the fable heal *you*, if you are afflicted with that form of evil.

93.

A certain magician owned a learned pig, who had lived a cleanly gentlemanly life, achieving great fame, and winning the hearts of all the people. But perceiving he was not happy, the magician, by a process easily explained did space permit, transformed him into a man. Straightway the creature abandoned his cards, his timepiece, his musical instruments, and all other devices of his profession, and betook him to a pool of mud, wherein he inhumed himself to the tip of his nose.

"Ten minutes ago," said the magician, reprovingly, "you would have scorned to do an act like that."

"True," replied the biped, with a contented grunt; "I was then a learned pig; I am now a learned man."

94.

"Nature has been very kind to her creatures," said a giraffe to an elephant. "For example, your neck being so very short, she has given you a proboscis wherewith to reach your food; and I having no proboscis, she has bestowed upon me a long neck."

"I think, my good friend, you have been among the theologians," said the elephant. "I doubt if I am clever enough to argue with you. I can only say it does not strike me that way."

"But, really," persisted the giraffe, "you must confess your trunk is a great convenience, in that it enables you to reach the high branches of which you are so fond, even as my long neck enables me."

"Perhaps," mused the ungrateful pachyderm, "if we could not reach the higher branches, we should develop a taste for the lower ones."

"In any case," was the rejoinder, "we can never be sufficiently thankful that we are unlike the lowly hippopotamus, who can reach neither the one nor the other."

"Ah! yes," the elephant assented, "there does not seem to have been enough of Nature's kindness to go round."

"But the hippopotamus has his roots and his rushes."

"It is not easy to see how, with his present appliances, he could obtain anything else."

This fable teaches nothing; for those who perceive the meaning of it either knew it before, or will not be taught.

95.

A pious heathen who was currying favour with his wooden deity by sitting for some years motionless in a treeless plain, observed a young ivy putting forth her tender shoots at his feet. He thought he could endure the additional martyrdom of a little shade, and begged her to make herself quite at home.

"Exactly," said the plant; "it is my mission to adorn venerable ruins."

She lapped her clinging tendrils about his wasted shanks, and in six months had mantled him in green.

"It is now time," said the devotee, a year later, "for me to fulfil the remainder of my religious vow. I must put in a few seasons of howling and leaping. You have been very good, but I no longer require your gentle ministrations."

"But I require yours," replied the vine; "you have become a second nature to me. Let others indulge in the delights of gymnastic worship; you and I will 'suffer and be strong'—respectively."

The devotee muttered something about the division of labour, and his bones are still pointed out to the pilgrim.

96.

A fox seeing a swan afloat, called out:

"What ship is that? I wish to take passage by your line."

"Got a ticket?" inquired the fowl.

"No; I'll make it all right with the company, though."

So the swan moored alongside, and he embarked,—deck passage. When they were well off shore the fox intimated that dinner would be agreeable.

"I would advise you not to try the ship's provisions," said the bird; "we have only salt meat on board. Beware the scurvy!"

"You are quite right," replied the passenger; "I'll see if I can stay my stomach with the foremast."

So saying he bit off her neck, and she immediately capsizing, he was drowned.

MORAL—highly so, but not instructive.

97.

A monkey finding a heap of cocoa-nuts, gnawed into one, then dropped it, gagging hideously.

"Now this is what *I* call perfectly disgusting!" said he; "I can never leave anything lying about but some one comes along and puts a quantity of nasty milk in it!"

A cat just then happening to pass that way began rolling the cocoa-nuts about with her paw.

"Yeow!" she exclaimed; "it is enough to vex the soul of a cast-iron dog! Whenever I set out any milk to cool, somebody comes and seals it up tight as a drum!"

Then perceiving one another, and each thinking the other the offender, these enraged animals contended, and wrought a mutual extermination. Whereby two worthy consumers were lost to society, and a quantity of excellent food had to be given to the poor.

98.

A mouse who had overturned an earthen jug was discovered by a cat, who entered from an adjoining room and began to upbraid him in the harshest and most threatening manner.

"You little wretch!" said she, "how dare you knock over that valuable urn? If it had been filled with hot water, and I had been lying before it asleep, I should have been scalded to death."

"If it had been full of water," pleaded the mouse, "it would not have up-set."

"But I might have lain down in it, monster!" persisted the cat.

"No, you couldn't," was the answer; "it is not wide enough."

"Fiend!" shrieked the cat, smashing him with her paw, "I can curl up real small when I try."

The *ultima ratio* of very angry people is frequently addressed to the ear of the dead.

99.

In crossing a frozen pool, a monkey slipped and fell, striking upon the back of his head with considerable force, so that the ice was very much shattered. A peacock, who was strutting about on shore thinking what a pretty peacock he was, laughed immoderately at the mishap. N.B. — All laughter is immoderate when a fellow is hurt — if the fellow is oneself.

"Bah!" exclaimed the sufferer; "if you could see the beautiful prismatic tints I have knocked into this ice, you would laugh out of the other side of your bill. The splendour of your tail is quite eclipsed."

Thus craftily did he inveigle the vain bird, who finally came and spread his tail alongside the fracture for comparison. The gorgeous feathers at once froze fast to the ice, and — in short, that artless fowl passed a very uncomfortable winter.

100.

A volcano, having discharged a few million tons of stones upon a small vil-lage, asked the mayor if he thought that a tolerably good supply for building purposes.

"I think," replied that functionary, "if you give us another dash of granite, and just a pinch of old red sandstone, we could manage with what you have already done for us. We would, however, be grateful for the loan of your crater to bake bricks."

"Oh, certainly; parties served at their residences." Then, after the man had gone, the mountain added, with mingled lava and contempt: "The most insatiable people I ever contracted to supply. They shall not have another pebble!"

He banked his fires, and in six weeks was as cold as a neglected pudding. Then might you have seen the heaving of the surface boulders, as the people began stirring forty fathoms beneath.

When you have got quite enough of anything, make it manifest by asking for some more. You won't get it.

101.

"I entertain for you a sentiment of profound amity," said the tiger to the leopard. "And why should I not? for are we not members of the same great feline family?"

"True," replied the leopard, who was engaged in the hopeless endeavour to change his spots; "since we have mutually plundered one another's hunting grounds of everything edible, there remains no grievance to quarrel about. You are a good fellow; let us embrace!"

They did so with the utmost heartiness; which being observed by a contiguous monkey, that animal got up a tree, where he delivered himself of the wisdom following:

"There is nothing so touching as these expressions of mutual regard between animals who are vulgarly believed to hate one another. They render the brief intervals of peace almost endurable to both parties. But the difficulty is, there are so many excellent reasons why these relatives should live in peace, that they won't have time to state them all before the next fight."

102.

A woodpecker, who had bored a multitude of holes in the body of a dead tree, was asked by a robin to explain their purpose.

"As yet, in the infancy of science," replied the woodpecker, "I am quite unable to do so. Some naturalists affirm that I hide acorns in these pits; others maintain that I get worms out of them. I endeavoured for some time to reconcile the two theories; but the worms ate my acorns, and then would not come out. Since then, I have left science to work out its own problems, while I work out the holes. I hope the final decision may be in some way advantageous to me; for at my nest I have a number of prepared holes which I can hammer into some suitable tree at a moment's notice. Perhaps I could insert a few into the scientific head."

"No-o-o," said the robin, reflectively, "I should think not. A prepared hole is an idea; I don't think it could get in."

MORAL. — It might be driven in with a steam-hammer.

103.

"Are you going to this great hop?" inquired a spruce cricket of a labouring beetle.

"No," replied he, sadly, "I've got to attend this great ball."

"Blest if I know the difference," drawled a more offensive insect, with his head in an empty silk hat; "and I've been in society all my life. But why was I not invited to either hop or ball?"

He is now invited to the latter.

104.

"Too bad, too bad," said a young Abyssinian to a yawning hippopotamus.

"What is 'too bad'?" inquired the quadruped. "What is the matter with you?"

"O, I never complain," was the reply; "I was only thinking of the niggard economy of Nature in building a great big beast like you and not giving him any mouth."

"H'm, h'm! it was still worse," mused the beast, "to construct a great wit like you and give him no seasonable occasion for the display of his cleverness."

A moment later there were a cracking of bitten bones, a great gush of animal fluids, the vanishing of two black feet — in short, the fatal poisoning of an indiscreet hippopotamus.

The rubbing of a bit of lemon about the beaker's brim is the finishing-touch to a whiskey punch. Much misery may be thus averted.

105.

A salmon vainly attempted to leap up a cascade. After trying a few thousand times, he grew so fatigued that he began to leap less and think more. Suddenly an obvious method of surmounting the difficulty presented itself to the salmonic intelligence.

"Strange," he soliloquized, as well as he could in the water, — "very strange I did not think of it before! I'll go above the fall and leap downwards."

So he went out on the bank, walked round to the upper side of the fall, and found he could leap over quite easily. Ever afterwards when he went upstream in the spring to be caught, he adopted this plan. He has been heard to remark that the price of salmon might be brought down to a merely nominal figure, if so many would not wear themselves out before getting up to where there is good fishing.

106.

"The son of a jackass," shrieked a haughty mare to a mule who had offended her by expressing an opinion, "should cultivate the simple grace of intellectual humility."

"It is true," was the meek reply, "I cannot boast an illustrious ancestry; but at least I shall never be called upon to blush for my posterity. Yonder mule colt is as proper a son —"

"Yonder mule colt?" interrupted the mare, with a look of ineffable contempt for her auditor; "that is *my* colt!"

"The consort of a jackass and the mother of mules," retorted he, quietly, "should cultivate the simple thingamy of intellectual whatsitsname."

The mare muttered something about having some shopping to do, threw on her harness, and went out to call a cab.

107.

"Hi! hi!" squeaked a pig, running after a hen who had just left her nest; "I say, mum, you dropped this 'ere. It looks wal'able; which I fetched it along!" And splitting his long face, he laid a warm egg at her feet.

"You meddlesome bacon!" cackled the ungrateful bird; "if you don't take that orb directly back, I'll sit on you till I hatch you out of your saddle-cover!"

MORAL. — Virtue is its only reward.

108.

A rustic, preparing to devour an apple, was addressed by a brace of crafty and covetous birds:

"Nice apple that," said one, critically examining it. "I don't wish to disparage it—wouldn't say a word against that vegetable for all the world. But I never can look upon an apple of that variety without thinking of my poisoned nestling! Ah! so plump, and rosy, and—rotten!"

"Just so," said the other. "And you remember my good father, who perished in that orchard. Strange that so fair a skin should cover so vile a heart!"

Just then another fowl came flying up.

"I came in all haste," said he, "to warn you about that fruit. My late lamented wife ate some off the same tree. Alas! how comely to the eye, and how essentially noxious!"

"I am very grateful," the young man said; "but I am unable to comprehend how the sight of this pretty piece of painted confectionery should incite you all to slander your dead relations."

Whereat there was confusion in the demeanour of that feathered trio.

109.

"The Millennium is come," said a lion to a lamb. "Suppose you come out of that fold, and let us lie down together, as it has been foretold we should."

"Been to dinner to-day?" inquired the lamb.

"Not a bite of anything since breakfast," was the reply, "except a few lean swine, a saddle or two, and some old harness."

"I distrust a Millennium," continued the lamb, thoughtfully, "which consists *solely* in our lying down together. My notion of that happy time is that it is a period in which pork and leather are not articles of diet, but in which every respectable lion shall have as much mutton as he can consume. However, you may go over to yonder sunny hill and lie down until I come."

It is singular how a feeling of security tends to develop cunning. If that lamb had been out upon the open plain he would have readily fallen into the snare—and it was studded very thickly with teeth.

110.

"I say, you!" bawled a fat ox in a stall to a lusty young ass who was braying outside; "the like of that is not in good taste!"

"In whose good taste, my adipose censor?" inquired the ass, not too respectfully.

"Why — h'm — ah! I mean it does not suit *me*. You ought to bellow."

"May I inquire how it happens to be any of your business whether I bellow or bray, or do both — or neither?"

"I cannot tell you," answered the critic, shaking his head despondingly; "I do not at all understand it. I can only say that I have been accustomed to censure all discourse that differs from my own."

"Exactly," said the ass; "you have sought to make an art of impertinence by mistaking preferences for principles. In 'taste' you have invented a word incapable of definition, to denote an idea impossible of expression; and by employing in connection therewith the words 'good' and 'bad,' you indicate a merely subjective process in terms of an objective quality. Such presumption transcends the limit of the merely impudent, and passes into the boundless empyrean of pure cheek!"

At the close of this remarkable harangue, the bovine critic was at a loss for language to express his disapproval. So he said the speech was in bad taste.

111.

A bloated toad, studded with dermal excrescences, was boasting that she was the wartiest creature alive.

"Perhaps you are," said her auditor, emerging from the soil; "but it is a barren and superficial honour. Look at me: I am one solid mole!"

112.

"It is very difficult getting on in the world," sighed a weary snail; "very difficult indeed, with such high rents!"

"You don't mean to say you pay anything for that old rookery!" said a slug, who was characteristically insinuating himself between the stems of the celery intended for dinner. "A miserable old shanty like that, without stables, grounds, or any modern conveniences!"

"Pay!" said the snail, contemptuously; "I'd like to see you get a semi-detached villa like this at a nominal rate!"

"Why don't you let your upper apartments to a respectable single party?" urged the slug.

The answer is not recorded.

113.

A hare, pursued by a dog, sought sanctuary in the den of a wolf. It being after business hours, the latter was at home to him.

"Ah!" panted the hare; "how very fortunate! I feel quite safe here, for you dislike dogs quite as much as I do."

"Your security, my small friend," replied the wolf, "depends not upon those points in which you and I agree, but upon those in which I and the dog differ."

"Then you mean to eat me?" inquired the timorous puss.

"No-o-o," drawled the wolf, reflectively, "I should not like to promise *that;* I mean to eat a part of you. There may be a tuft of fur, and a toe-nail or two, left for you to go on with. I am hungry, but I am not hoggish."

"The distinction is too fine for me," said the hare, scratching her head.

"That, my friend, is because you have not made a practice of hare-splitting. I have."

114.

"Oyster at home?" inquired a monkey, rapping at the closed shell.

There was no reply. Dropping the knocker, he laid hold of the bell-handle, ringing a loud peal, but without effect.

"Hum, hum!" he mused, with a look of disappointment, "gone to the sea-side, I suppose."

So he turned away, thinking he would call again later in the season; but he had not proceeded far before he conceived a brilliant idea. Perhaps there had been a suicide! —or a murder! He would go back and force the door. By way of doing so he obtained a large stone, and smashed in the roof. There had been no murder to justify such audacity, so he committed one.

The funeral was gorgeous. There were mute oysters with wands, drunken oysters with scarves and hat-bands, a sable hearse with hearth-dusters on it, a swindling undertaker's bill, and all the accessories of a first-rate churchyard circus—everything necessary but the corpse. That had been disposed of by the monkey, and the undertaker meanly withheld the use of his own.

MORAL.—A lamb foaled in March makes the best pork when his horns have attained the length of an inch.

115.

"Pray walk into my parlour," said the spider to the fly.
"That is not quite original," the latter made reply.
"If that's the way you plagiarize, your fame will be a fib—
But I'll walk into your parlour, while I pitch into your crib.
But before I cross your threshold, sir, if I may make so free,
Pray let me introduce to you my friend, 'the wicked flea.' "
"How do you?" says the spider, as his welcome he extends;
" 'How doth the busy little bee,' and all our other friends?"
"Quite well, I think, and quite unchanged," the flea said; "though I learn,
In certain quarters well-informed, 'tis feared 'the worm will turn.' "
"Humph!" said the fly; "I do not understand this talk—not I!"
"It is 'classical allusion,' " said the spider to the fly.

116.

A polar bear navigating the mid-sea upon the mortal part of a late lamented walrus, soliloquized, in substance, as follows:

"Such liberty of action as I am afflicted with is enough to embarrass any bear that ever bore. I can remain passive, and starve; or I can devour my ship, and drown. I am really unable to decide."

So he sat down to think it over. He considered the question in all its aspects, until he grew quite thin; turned it over and over in his mind until he was too weak to sit up; meditated upon it with a constantly decreasing pulse, a rapidly failing respiration. But he could not make up his mind, and finally expired without having come to a decision.

It appears to me he might almost as well have chosen starvation, at a venture.

117.

A sword-fish having penetrated seven or eight feet into the bottom of a ship, under the impression that he was quarrelling with a whale, was unable to draw out of the fight. The sailors annoyed him a good deal, by pounding with hand-spikes upon that portion of his horn inside; but he bore it as bravely as he could, putting the best possible face upon the matter, until he saw a shark swimming by, of whom he inquired the probable destination of the ship.

"Italy, I think," said the other, grinning. "I have private reasons for believing her cargo consists mainly of consumptives."

"Ah!" exclaimed the captive; "Italy, delightful clime of the cerulean orange — the rosy olive! Land of the night-blooming Jesuit, and the fragrant *lazza-rone!* It would be heavenly to run down gondolas in the streets of Venice! I *must* go to Italy."

"Indeed you must," said the shark, darting suddenly aft, where he had caught the gleam of shotted canvas through the blue waters.

But it was fated to be otherwise: some days afterwards the ship and fish passed over a sunken rock which almost grazed the keel. Then the two parted company, with mutual expressions of tender regard, and a report which could be traced by those on board to no trustworthy source.

The foregoing fable shows that a man of good behaviour need not care for money, and *vice versâ*.

118.

A facetious old cat seeing her kitten sleeping in a bath tub, went down into the cellar and turned on the hot water. (For the convenience of the bathers the bath was arranged in that way; you had to undress, and then go down to the cellar to let on the wet.) No sooner did the kitten remark the unfamiliar sensation, than he departed thence with a willingness quite creditable in one who was not a professional acrobat, and met his mother on the kitchen stairs.

"Aha! my steaming hearty!" cried the elder grimalkin; "I coveted you when I saw the cook put you in the dinner-pot. If I have a weakness, it is hare — hare nicely dressed, and partially boiled."

Whereupon she made a banquet of her suffering offspring.*

Adversity works a stupendous change in tender youth; many a young man is never recognized by his parents after having been in hot water.

*Here should have followed the appropriate and obvious classical allusion. It is known our fabulist was classically educated. Why, then, this disgraceful omission?

— TRANSLATOR.

119.

"It is a waste of valour for us to do battle," said a lame ostrich to a negro who had suddenly come upon her in the desert; "let us cast lots to see who shall be considered the victor, and then go about our business."

To this proposition the negro readily assented. They cast lots: the negro cast lots of stones, and the ostrich cast lots of feathers. Then the former went about his business, which consisted in skinning the bird.

MORAL. — There is nothing like the arbitrament of chance. That form of it known as *trile-bi-joorie* is perhaps as good as any.

120.

An author who had wrought a book of fables (the merit whereof transcended expression) was peacefully sleeping atop of the modest eminence to which he had attained, when he was rudely awakened by a throng of critics, emitting adverse judgment upon the tales he had builded.

"Apparently," said he, "I have been guilty of some small grains of unconsidered wisdom, and the same have proven a bitterness to these excellent folk, the which they will not abide. Ah, well! those who produce the Strasburg *pâté* and the feather-pillow are prone to regard *us* as rival creators. I presume it is in course of nature for him who grows the pen to censure the manner of its use."

So speaking, he executed a smile a hand's-breadth in extent, and resumed his airy dream of dropping ducats.

121.

For many years an opossum had anointed his tail with bear's oil, but it remained stubbornly bald-headed. At last his patience was exhausted, and he appealed to Bruin himself, accusing him of breaking faith, and calling him a quack.

"Why, you insolent marsupial!" retorted the bear in a rage; "you expect my oil to give you hair upon your tail, when it will not give me even a tail. Why don't you try under-draining, or top-dressing with light compost?"

They said and did a good deal more before the opossum withdrew his cold and barren member from consideration; but the judicious fabulist does not encumber his tale with extraneous matter, lest it be pointless.

122.

"So disreputable a lot as you are I never saw!" said a sleepy rat to the casks in a wine-cellar. "Always making night hideous with your hoops and hollows, and disfiguring the day with your bunged-up appearance. There is no sleeping when once the wine has got into your heads. I'll report you to the butler!"

"The sneaking tale-bearer," said the casks. "Let us beat him with our staves."

"Requiescat in pace," muttered a learned cobweb, sententiously.

"Requires a cat in the place, does it?" shrieked the rat. "Then I'm off!"

To explain all the wisdom imparted by this fable would require the pen of a pig, and volumes of smoke.

123.

A giraffe having trodden upon the tail of a poodle, that animal flew into a blind rage, and wrestled valorously with the invading foot.

"Hullo, sonny!" said the giraffe, looking down, "what are you doing there?"

"I am fighting!" was the proud reply; "but I don't know that it is any of your business."

"Oh, I have no desire to mix in," said the good-natured giraffe. "I never take sides in terrestrial strife. Still, as that is my foot, I think—"

"Eh!" cried the poodle, backing some distance away and gazing upward, shading his eyes with his paw. "You don't mean to say—by Jove it's a fact. Well, that beats *me!* A beast of such enormous length—such preposterous duration, as it were—I wouldn't have believed it! Of course I can't quarrel with a non-resident; but why don't you have a local agent on the ground?"

The reply was probably the wisest ever made; but it has not descended to this generation. It had so very far to descend.

124.

A dog having got upon the scent of a deer which a hunter had been dragging home, set off with extraordinary zeal. After measuring off a few leagues, he paused.

"My running gear is all right," said he; "but I seem to have lost my voice."

Suddenly his ear was assailed by a succession of eager barks, as of another dog in pursuit of him. It then began to dawn upon him that he was a particularly rapid dog: instead of having lost his voice, his voice had lost him, and was just now arriving. Full of his discovery, he sought his master, and struck for better food and more comfortable housing.

"Why, you miserable example of perverted powers!" said his master; "I never intended you for the chase, but for the road. You are to be a draught-dog—to pull baby about in a cart. You will perceive that speed is an objection. Sir, you must be toned down; you will be at once assigned to a house with modern conveniences, and will dine at a French restaurant. If that system do not reduce your own, I'm an 'Ebrew Jew!'"

The journals next morning had racy and appetizing accounts of a canine suicide.

125.

A gosling, who had not yet begun to blanch, was accosted by a chicken just out of the shell:

"Whither away so fast, fair maid?" inquired the chick.

"Wither away yourself," was the contemptuous reply; "you are already in the sere and yellow leaf; while I seem to have a green old age before me."

126.

A famishing traveller who had run down a salamander, made a fire, and laid him alive upon the hot coals to cook. Wearied with the pursuit which had preceded his capture, the animal at once composed himself, and fell into a refreshing sleep. At the end of a half-hour, the man stirred him with a stick, remarking:

"I say!—wake up and begin toasting, will you? How long do you mean to keep dinner waiting, eh?"

"Oh, I beg you will not wait for me," was the yawning reply. "If you are going to stand upon ceremony, everything will get cold. Besides, I have dined. I wish, by-the-way, you would put on some more fuel; I think we shall have snow."

"Yes," said the man, "the weather is like yourself—raw, and exasperatingly cool. Perhaps this will warm you." And he rolled a ponderous pine log atop of that provoking reptile, who flattened out, and "handed in his checks."

> The moral thus doth glibly run —
>   A cause its opposite may brew;
> The sun-shade is unlike the sun,
>   The plum unlike the plumber, too.
> A salamander underdone
>   His impudence may overdo.

127.

A humming-bird invited a vulture to dine with her. He accepted, but took the precaution to have an emetic along with him; and immediately after dinner, which consisted mainly of dew, spices, honey, and similar slops, he swallowed his corrective, and tumbled the distasteful viands out. He then went away, and made a good wholesome meal with his friend the ghoul. He has been heard to remark, that the taste for humming-bird fare is "too artificial for *him*." He says, a simple and natural diet, with agreeable companions, cheerful surroundings, and a struggling moon, is best for the health, and most agreeable to the normal palate.

People with vitiated tastes may derive much profit from this opinion. *Crede experto.*

128.

A certain terrier, of a dogmatic turn, asked a kitten her opinion of rats, demanding a categorical answer. The opinion, as given, did not possess the merit of coinciding with his own; whereupon he fell upon the heretic and bit her — bit her until his teeth were much worn and her body much elongated — bit her good! Having thus vindicated the correctness of his own view, he felt so amiable a satisfaction that he announced his willingness to adopt the opinion of which he had demonstrated the harmlessness. So he begged his enfeebled antagonist to re-state it, which she incautiously did. No sooner, however, had the superior debater heard it for the second time than he resumed his intolerance, and made an end of that unhappy cat.

"Heresy," said he, wiping his mouth, "may be endured in the vigorous and lusty; but in a person lying at the very point of death such hardihood is intolerable."

It is always intolerable.

129.

A tortoise and an armadillo quarrelled, and agreed to fight it out. Repairing to a secluded valley, they put themselves into hostile array.

"Now come on!" shouted the tortoise, shrinking into the inmost recesses of his shell.

"All right," shrieked the armadillo, coiling up tightly in his coat of mail; "I am ready for you!"

And thus these heroes waged the awful fray from morn till dewy eve, at less than a yard's distance. There has never been anything like it; their endurance was something marvellous! During the night each combatant sneaked silently away; and the historian of the period obscurely alludes to the battle as "the naval engagement of the future."

130.

Two hedgehogs having conceived a dislike to a hare, conspired for his extinction. It was agreed between them that the lighter and more agile of the two should beat him up, surround him, run him into a ditch, and drive him upon the thorns of the more gouty and unwieldy conspirator. It was not a very hopeful scheme, but it was the best they could devise. There was a chance of success if the hare should prove willing, and, gambler-like, they decided to take that chance, instead of trusting to the remote certainty of their victim's death from natural cause. The doomed animal performed his part as well as could be reasonably expected of him: every time the enemy's flying detachment pressed him hard, he fled playfully toward the main body, and lightly vaulted over, about eight feet above the spines. And this prickly blockhead had not the practical sagacity to get upon a wall seven feet and six inches high!

This fable is designed to show that the most desperate chances are comparatively safe.

131.

A young eel inhabiting the mouth of a river in India, determined to travel. Being a fresh-water eel, he was somewhat restricted in his choice of a route, but he set out with a cheerful heart and very little luggage. Before he had proceeded very far up-stream he found the current too strong to be overcome without a ruinous consumption of coals. He decided to anchor his tail where it then was, and *grow* up. For the first hundred miles it was tolerably tedious work, but when he had learned to tame his impatience, he found this method of progress rather pleasant than otherwise. But when he began to be caught at widely separate points by the fishermen of eight or ten different nations, he did not think it so fine.

This fable teaches that when you extend your residence you multiply your experiences. A local eel can know but little of angling.

132.

Some of the lower animals held a convention to settle for ever the unspeakably important question, What is Life?

"Life," squeaked the poet, blinking and folding his flimsy wings, "is — ." His kind having been already very numerously heard from upon the subject, he was choked off.

"Life," said the scientist, in a voice smothered by the earth he was throwing up into small hills, "is the harmonious action of heterogeneous but related faculties, operating in accordance with certain natural laws."

"Ah!" chattered the lover, "but that thawt of thing is vewy gweat blith in the thothiety of one'th thweetheaht." And curling his tail about a branch, he swung himself heavenward and had a spasm.

"It is *vita!*" grunted the sententious scholar, pausing in his mastication of a Chaldaic root.

"It is a thistle," brayed the warrior: "very nice thing to take!"

"Life, my friends," croaked the philosopher from his hollow tree, dropping his lids over his cattish eyes, "is a disease. We are all symptoms."

"Pooh!" ejaculated the physician, uncoiling and springing his rattle. "How then does it happen that when *we* remove the symptoms, the disease is gone?"

"I would give something to know that," replied the philosopher, musingly; "but I suspect that in most cases the inflammation remains, and is intensified."

Draw your own moral inference, "in your own jugs."

133.

A heedless boy having flung a pebble in the direction of a basking lizard, that reptile's tail disengaged itself, and flew some distance away. One of the properties of a lizard's camp-follower is to leave the main body at the slightest intimation of danger.

"There goes that vexatious narrative again," exclaimed the lizard, pettishly; "I never had such a tail in my life! Its restless tendency to divorce upon insufficient grounds is enough to harrow the reptilian soul! Now," he continued, backing up to the fugitive part, "perhaps you will be good enough to resume your connection with the parent establishment."

No sooner was the splice effected, than an astronomer passing that way casually remarked to a friend that he had just sighted a comet. Supposing itself menaced, the timorous member again sprang away, coming down plump before the horny nose of a sparrow. Here its career terminated.

We sometimes escape from an imaginary danger, only to find some real persecutor has a little bill against us.

134.

A jackal who had pursued a deer all day with unflagging industry, was about to seize him, when an earthquake, which was doing a little civil engineering in that part of the country, opened a broad chasm between him and his prey.

"Now here," said he, "is a distinct interference with the laws of nature. But if we are to tolerate miracles, there is an end of all progress."

So speaking, he endeavoured to cross the abyss at two jumps. His fate would serve the purpose of an impressive warning if it might be clearly entertained; but the earth having immediately pinched together again, the research of the moral investigator is baffled.

135.

"Ah!" sighed a three-legged stool, "if I had only been a quadruped, I should have been happy as the day is long—which, on the twenty-first of June, would be considerable felicity for a stool."

"Ha! look at me," said a toadstool; "consider my superior privation, and be content with your comparatively happy lot."

"I don't discern," replied the first, "how the contemplation of unipedal misery tends to alleviate tripedal wretchedness."

"You don't, eh!" sneered the toadstool. "You mean, do you, to fly in the face of all the moral and social philosophers?"

"No; not unless some benefactor of his race shall impel me."

"H'm! I think Zambri the Parsee is the man for that kindly office, my dear."

This final fable teaches that he is.

APPENDIX: FABLES FROM *FUN*

11A. [Litigation]

A Fox and a Duck having quarreled about the ownership of a frog, referred the matter to a Lion. After hearing a deal of argument the Lion opened his mouth to deliver judgment.

"I know what your decision is," said the Duck, interrupting. "It is that by our own showing the frog belongs to neither of us, and you will eat him yourself. Permit me to say that this is unjust, as I shall prove."

"To me," said the Fox, "it is clear that you will give the frog to the Duck and the Duck to me and take me yourself. I am not without experience of the law."

"I was about to explain," said the Lion, yawning, "that during the arguments in this case the property in dispute has hopped away. Perhaps you can procure another frog."

15A. [A Family Resemblance]

A Negro seeing an Ostrich began pelting him with stones. When a considerable number had been flung the Ostrich turned to and ate them.

"Pray tell me," he said, "to what virtue I am indebted for this excellent meal."

"To generosity," the Negro answered, now eager to conciliate one whom he thought miraculously gifted; "if it had not been for a charitable impulse I should have eaten those stones myself."

"My good fellow," said the Ostrich, "it seems that some of the lesser human virtues are not readily distinguishable from an imperfect digestion."

19A. [Candor as an Inexpediency]

A Man was plucking a live Goose, when the bird addressed him thus:

"Suppose that you were a goose; do you think that you would relish this sort of thing?"

"Suppose that I were," said the Man; "do you think that you would like to pluck me?"

"Indeed I should!" was the natural, emphatic, but injudicious reply.

"Just so," concluded her tormentor, pulling out another handful of feathers; "that is the way that *I* feel about it."

21A. [Docility's Reward]

A Sheep making a long journey found the heat of her fleece insupportable, and seeing a flock of others in a fold, evidently in expectation, leaped over and joined them in the hope of being shorn. Perceiving the Shepherd approaching, and the other sheep huddling into a remote corner of the fold, she shouldered her way forward and said:

"Your flock is insubordinate; it is fortunate that I came along to set them an example of docility. Seeing me operated on, they will be glad to offer themselves."

"Thank you," said the Shepherd, "but I never kill more than one at a time. Mutton does not keep well in warm weather."

30A. [Diagnosis]

An Oyster who had got a large pebble between the valves of his shell and was unable to get it out was lamenting his untoward fate, when a Monkey ran to him — the tide being out — and began an examination.

"You appear," said the Monkey, "to have got something else in here, too. I will remove that first."

He inserted his paw and scooped out the body of the patient.

"Now," said he, devouring it, "I think you will be able to endure the pebble without inconvenience."

34A. [Apologia Servilitatis]

A Wild Horse meeting a Domestic One, taunted him with his condition of servitude. The tamed animal claimed that he was as free as the wind.

"If that is so," said the other, "pray what is the office of that bit in your mouth?"

"That," was the answer, "is iron, one of the best tonics known."

"But what is the meaning of the rein attached to it?"

"That keeps it from falling from my mouth when I am too indolent to hold it."

"How about the saddle?"

"It spares me fatigue: when I am tired I mount and ride."

43A.

An Ass wandering near a village in the evening saw the light of the rising moon beyond a hill.

"Ho-ho, Master Redface," said he, "you are going to point out my long ears to the villagers, are you? I'll meet you at the crest and set my heels into you!"

So he scrambled painfully up to the crest and stood outlined against the broad disc of the unconscious luminary, a more conspicuous ass than ever before.

68A.

Laden with a grain of wheat which he had acquired with infinite toil, an Ant was breasting a current of his fellows, each of whom, as is their etiquette, insisted on stopping him, feeling him all over and shaking hands. It occurred to him that an excess of ceremony is an abuse of courtesy; so he laid down his burden, sat upon it, folded all his legs and smiled a smile of great grimness.

"Hello!" said his Fellow Ants, "what is the matter with you?"

"Sick of the hollow conventionalities of an effete civilization," was the rasping reply — "returned to the simplicity of primitive life."

"Ah! then we must trouble you for that grain. In the primitive life there are no rights of property."

A great white light fell upon the understanding of that rebellious insect. He rose and grappling the grain of wheat trotted away with alacrity. It was observed that he submitted with a wealth of patience to manipulation by his friends and neighbors and went long distances out of his way to shake hands with strangers on competing lines of traffic.

77A. [An Injunction]

Having been taught Greek, a Parrot was puffed up with conceit.

"Observe," said he, "the advantages of a classical education! I can chatter nonsense in the tongue of Plato."

"I should advise you," said his Master, quietly, "to let it be nonsense of a character somewhat different from that of some of Plato's most admired compatriots if you value the privilege of hanging at that open window. Commit no mythology, please."

93A. [Reversion]

A certain Magician had a Learned Pig who had lived a cleanly, gentlemanly life, achieving a wide renown and winning the hearts of the people, attending his elevating performances. But perceiving that the creature was unhappy, the Magician transformed him to a man. Straightway the man abandoned his cards, his timepiece, his musical instruments and the other devices of his profession, and betook himself to a pool of mud, wherein he inhumed himself to the tips of his nose, grunting with sodden satisfaction.

109A. [The Premature Millennium]

"The Millennium is come," said a Lion to a Lamb inside the fold. "Come out and let us lie down together, as it has been foretold that we shall."

"Have you brought along the little child that is to lead us?" the Lamb asked.

"No; I thought that perhaps a child of the shepherd would serve."

"I distrust a Millennium that requires the shepherd to supply both the feast and the leader of the revel. My notion of that happy time is that it is to be a period in which mutton is unfit to eat and a lion the product of the sculptor's art."

Finding no profit in dissimulation, the Lion walked thoughtfully away and candidly dined on the village priest.

110A. [The Critic]

"I say, you," bawled a fat Ox in a stall to a lusty young Ass who was braying outside; "the like of that is not in good taste."

"In whose good taste, my adipose censor?" inquired the Ass, not too respectfully.

"Why—ah—h'm. I mean it does not suit me. You should bellow."

"May I ask how it concerns you whether I bellow or bray, or do both, or neither?"

"I cannot tell you," said the Ox, shaking his head despondingly—"I do not at all understand the matter. I can only say that I have been used to censure all discourse that differs from my own."

"Exactly," said the Ass; "you have tried to make an art of impudence by calling preferences principles. In 'taste' you have invented a word incapable of definition to denote an idea impossible of expression, and by employing the word 'good' or 'bad' in connection with it you indicate a merely subjective process, in terms of an objective quality. Such presumption transcends the limits of mere effrontery and passes into the boundless empyrean of pure gall!"

The bovine critic having no words to express his disapproval of this remarkable harangue, said it was in bad taste.

120A. [The Contented Fabulist]

An Author who had wrought a book of fables (the merit whereof transcended expression) was peacefully sleeping atop of his modest eminence, when he was rudely roused by a throng of Critics uttering adverse judgment on the incomparable tales.

"Apparently," said he, "I have been guilty of some small grains of unconsidered wisdom, and it is a bitterness to these good folk, the which they will not abide. Ah, well, those who produce the Strasburg *pâté* and the feather pillow regard *us* as rival creators. Doubtless it is in course of nature for those who grow the pen to censure the manner of its use."

So speaking, he executed a smile a hand's-breadth in extent and resumed his airy dream of dropping ducats.

129A.

A Tortoise and an Armadillo, having quarreled, repaired to a secluded spot to vindicate their honor by an appeal to arms.

"Now, then," shouted the Tortoise, shrinking into the innermost recesses of his shell, "come on!"

"Very well," assented the Armadillo, coiling up tightly in his coat of mail, "I am ready for you!"

An historian of the period obscurely alludes to the incident as foreshadowing the naval engagement of the future.

134A. [An Infraction]

A Jackal in pursuit of a Deer was about to seize it, when an earthquake opened a broad and deep chasm between him and his prey.

"This," said he, "is a pernicious interference with the laws of Nature. I refuse to recognize such irregularity."

So he resumed the chase, endeavoring to cross the abyss by two leaps.

FANTASTIC FABLES

136. Moral Principle and Material Interest

A Moral Principle met a Material Interest on a bridge wide enough for but one.

"Down, you base thing!" thundered the Moral Principle, "and let me pass over you!"

The Material Interest merely looked in the other's eyes without saying anything.

"Ah," said the Moral Principle, hesitatingly, "let us draw lots to see which of us shall retire till the other has crossed."

The Material Interest maintained an unbroken silence and an unwavering stare.

"In order to avoid a conflict," the Moral Principle resumed, somewhat uneasily, "I shall myself lie down and let you walk over me."

Then the Material Interest found his tongue. "I don't think you are very good walking," it said. "I am a little particular about what I have underfoot. Suppose you get off into the water."

It occurred that way.

137. The Crimson Candle

A Man lying at the point of death called his wife to his bedside and said:

"I am about to leave you forever; give me, therefore, one last proof of your affection and fidelity. In my desk you will find a crimson candle, which has been blessed by the High Priest and has a peculiar mystical significance. Swear to me that while it is in existence you will not remarry."

The Woman swore and the Man died. At the funeral the Woman stood at the head of the bier, holding a lighted crimson candle till it was wasted entirely away.

138. Escutcheon and Ermine

A Blotted Escutcheon, rising to a question of privilege, said:

"Mr. Speaker, I wish to hurl back an allegation and explain that the spots upon me are the natural markings of one who is a direct descendant of the sun and a spotted fawn. They come of no accident of character, but inhere in the divine order and constitution of things."

When the Blotted Escutcheon had resumed his seat a Soiled Ermine rose and said:

"Mr. Speaker, I have heard with profound attention and entire approval the explanation of the honorable member, and wish to offer a few remarks on my own behalf. I, too, have been foully calumniated by our ancient enemy, the Infamous Falsehood, and I wish to point out that I am made of the fur of the *Mustela maculata,* which is dirty from birth."

139. The Ingenious Patriot

Having obtained an audience of the King an Ingenious Patriot pulled a paper from his pocket, saying:

"May it please your Majesty, I have here a formula for constructing armor plating which no gun can pierce. If these plates are adopted in the Royal Navy our warships will be invulnerable and therefore invincible. Here, also, are reports of your Majesty's Ministers, attesting the value of the invention. I will part with my right in it for a million tumtums."

After examining the papers, the King put them away and promised him an order on the Lord High Treasurer of the Extortion Department for a million tumtums.

"And here," said the Ingenious Patriot, pulling another paper from another pocket, "are the working plans of a gun that I have invented, which will pierce that armor. Your Majesty's royal brother, the Emperor of Bang, is eager to purchase it, but loyalty to your Majesty's throne and person constrains me to offer it first to your Majesty. The price is one million tumtums."

Having received the promise of another check, he thrust his hand into still another pocket, remarking:

"The price of the irresistible gun would have been much greater, your Majesty, but for the fact that its missiles can be so effectively averted by my peculiar method of treating the armor plates with a new —"

The King signed to the Great Head Factotum to approach.

"Search this man," he said, "and report how many pockets he has."

"Forty-three, Sire," said the Great Head Factotum, completing the scrutiny.

"May it please your Majesty," cried the Ingenious Patriot, in terror, "one of them contains tobacco."

"Hold him up by the ankles and shake him," said the King; "then give him a check for forty-two million tumtums and put him to death. Let a decree issue declaring ingenuity a capital offence."

140. Officer and Thug

A Chief of Police who had seen an Officer beating a Thug was very indignant, and said he must not do so any more on pain of dismissal.

"Don't be too hard on me," said the Officer, smiling; "I was beating him with a stuffed club."

"Nevertheless," persisted the Chief of Police, "it was a liberty that must have been very disagreeable, though it may not have hurt. Please do not repeat it."

"But," said the Officer, still smiling, "it was a stuffed Thug."

In attempting to express his gratification the Chief of Police thrust out his right hand with such violence that his skin was ruptured at the arm-pit and a stream of sawdust poured from the wound. He was a stuffed Chief of Police.

141. Two Kings

The King of Madagao, being engaged in a dispute with the King of Bornegascar, wrote him as follows:

"Before proceeding further in this matter I demand the recall of your Minister from my capital."

Greatly enraged by this impossible demand, the King of Bornegascar replied:

"I shall not recall my Minister. Moreover, if you do not immediately retract your demand I shall withdraw him!"

This threat so terrified the King of Madagao that in hastening to comply he fell over his own feet, breaking the Third Commandment.

142. The Conscientious Official

While a Division Superintendent of a railway was attending closely to his business of placing obstructions on the track and tampering with the switches he received word that the President of the road was about to discharge him for incompetency.

"Good Heavens!" he cried; "there are more accidents on my division than on all the rest of the line."

"The President is very particular," said the Man who brought him the news; "he thinks the same loss of life might be effected with less damage to the company's property."

"Does he expect me to shoot passengers through the car windows?" exclaimed the indignant official, spiking a loose tie across the rails. "Does he take me for an assassin?"

143. The Moral Sentiment

A Pugilist met the Moral Sentiment of the Community, who was carrying a hat-box. "What have you in the hat-box, my friend?" inquired the Pugilist.

"A new frown," was the answer. "I am bringing it from the frownery — the one over there with the gilded steeple."

"And what are you going to do with the nice new frown?" the Pugilist asked.

"Put down pugilism — if I have to wear it night and day," said the Moral Sentiment of the Community, sternly.

"That's right," said the Pugilist, "that is right, my good friend; if pugilism had been put down yesterday, I wouldn't have this kind of nose to-day. I had a rattling hot fight last evening with —"

"Is that so?" cried the Moral Sentiment of the Community, with sudden animation. "Which licked? Sit down here on the hat-box and tell me all about it!"

144. How Leisure Came

A Man to Whom Time Was Money, and who was bolting his breakfast in order to catch a train, had leaned his newspaper against the sugar-bowl and was reading as he ate. In his haste and abstraction he stuck a pickle-fork into his right eye, and on removing the fork the eye came with it. In buying spectacles the needless outlay for the right lens soon reduced him to poverty, and the Man to Whom Time Was Money had to sustain life by fishing from the end of a wharf.

145. The Politicians

An Old Politician and a Young Politician were traveling through a beautiful country, by the dusty highway which leads to the City of Prosperous Obscurity. Lured by the flowers and the shade and charmed by the songs of birds which invited to woodland paths and green fields, his imagination fired by glimpses of golden domes and glittering palaces in the distance on either hand, the Young Politician said:

"Let us, I beseech thee, turn aside from this comfortless road leading, thou knowest whither, but not I. Let us turn our backs upon duty and abandon ourselves to the delights and advantages beckoning from every grove and calling to us from every shining hill. Let us, if so thou wilt, follow this beautiful path, which, as thou seest, hath a guide-board saying, 'Turn in here all ye who seek the Palace of Popular Attention.'"

"It is a beautiful path, my son," said the Old Politician, without either slackening his pace or turning his head, "and it leadeth among pleasant scenes. But the search for the Palace of Popular Attention is beset with one mighty peril."

"What is that?" said the Young Politician.

"The peril of finding it," the Old Politician replied, pushing on.

146. The Christian Serpent

A Rattlesnake came home to his brood and said: "My children, gather about and receive your father's last blessing, and see how a Christian dies."

"What ails you, Father?" asked the Small Snakes.

"I have been bitten by the editor of a partisan journal," was the reply, accompanied by the ominous death-rattle.

147. The Thoughtful Warden

The Warden of a Penitentiary was one day putting locks on the doors of all the cells when a mechanic said to him:

"Those locks can all be opened from the inside—you are very imprudent."

The Warden did not look up from his work, but said:

"If that is called imprudence I wonder what would be called a thoughtful provision against the vicissitudes of fortune."

148. Treasury and Arms

A Public Treasury, feeling Two Arms lifting out its contents, exclaimed:

"Mr. Shareman, I move for a division."

"You seem to know something about parliamentary forms of speech," said the Two Arms.

"Yes," replied the Public Treasury, "I am familiar with the hauls of legislation."

149. The Broom of the Temple

The city of Gakwak being about to lose its character of capital of the province of Ukwuk, the Wampog issued a proclamation convening all the male residents in council in the Temple of Ul to devise means of defence. The first speaker thought the best policy would be to offer a fried jackass to the gods. The second suggested a public procession headed by the Wampog himself, bearing the Holy Poker on a cushion of cloth-of-brass. Another thought that a scarlet mole should be buried alive in the public park and a suitable incantation chanted over the remains. The advice of the fourth was that the columns of the capitol be rubbed with oil of dog by a person having a moustache on the calf of his leg. When all the others had spoken an Aged Man rose and said:

"High and mighty Wampog and fellow-citizens, I have listened attentively to all the plans proposed. All seem wise, and I do not suffer myself to doubt that any one of them would be efficacious. Nevertheless, I cannot help thinking that if we would put an improved breed of polliwogs in our drinking water, drain our roadways, groom the street cows, offer the stranger within our gates a free choice between the poniard and the potion and relinquish our private system of morals, the other measures of public safety would be needless."

The Aged Man was about to speak further, but the meeting informally adjourned in order to sweep the floor of the temple — for the men of Gakwak are the tidiest housewives in all that province. The Aged Man was the broom.

150. The Critics

While bathing, Antinoüs was seen by Minerva, who was so enamoured of his beauty that, all armed as she happened to be, she descended from Olympus to woo him; but, unluckily displaying her shield with the head of Medusa on it, she had the unhappiness to see the beautiful mortal turn to stone from catching a glimpse of it. She straightway ascended to ask Jove to restore him; but before this could be done a Sculptor and a Critic passed that way and espied him.

"This is a very bad Apollo," said the Sculptor: "the chest is too narrow, and one arm is at least a half-inch shorter than the other. The attitude is unnatural, and I may say impossible. Ah! my friend, you should see my statue of Antinoüs."

"In my judgment," said the Critic, "the figure is tolerably good, though rather Etrurian, but the expression of the face is decidedly Tuscan, and therefore false to nature. By the way, have you read my work on 'The Fallaciousness of the Aspectual in Art'?"

151. A Call to Quit

Seeing that his audiences were becoming smaller every Sunday, a Minister of the Gospel broke off in the midst of a sermon, descended the pulpit stairs and walked on his hands down the central aisle of the church. He then remounted his feet, ascended to the pulpit and resumed his discourse, making no allusion to the incident.

"Now," said he to himself, as he went home, "I shall have, henceforth, a large attendance and no snoring."

But on the following Friday he was waited upon by the Pillars of the Church, who informed him that in order to be in harmony with the New Theology and get full advantage of modern methods of Gospel interpretation they had deemed it advisable to make a change. They had therefore sent a call to Brother Jowjeetum-Fallal, the world-renowned Hindoo human pin-wheel, then holding forth in Hoopitup's circus. They were happy to say that the reverend gentleman had been moved by the Spirit to accept the call, and on the ensuing Sabbath would break the bread of life for the brethren or break his neck in the attempt.

152. The Discontented Malefactor

A Judge having sentenced a Malefactor to the penitentiary was proceeding to point out to him the disadvantages of crime and the profit of reformation.

"Your Honor," said the Malefactor, interrupting, "would you be kind enough to alter my punishment to ten years in the penitentiary and nothing else?"

"Why," said the Judge, surprised, "I have given you only three years!"

"Yes, I know," assented the Malefactor — "three years' imprisonment and the preaching. If you please, I should like to commute the preaching."

153. Father and Son

"My boy," said an aged Father to his fiery and disobedient Son, "a hot temper is the soil of remorse. Promise me that when next you are angry you will count one hundred before you move or speak."

No sooner had the Son promised than he received a stinging blow from the paternal walking-stick, and by the time he had counted to seventy-five had the unhappiness to see the old man jump into a waiting cab and whirl away.

154. The Foolish Woman

A Married Woman, whose lover was about to reform by running away, procured a pistol and shot him dead.

"Why did you do that, Madam?" inquired a Policeman, sauntering by.

"Because," replied the Married Woman, "he was a wicked man, and had purchased a ticket to Chicago."

"My sister," said an adjacent Man of God, solemnly, "you cannot stop the wicked from going to Chicago by killing them."

155. Man and Lightning

A Man Running for Office was overtaken by Lightning.

"You see," said the Lightning, as it crept past him inch by inch, "I can travel considerably faster than you."

"Yes," the Man Running for Office replied, "but think how much longer I keep going!"

156. The Lassoed Bear

A Hunter who had lassoed a Bear was trying to disengage himself from the rope, but the slip-knot about his wrist would not yield, for the Bear was all the time pulling in the slack with his paws. In the midst of his trouble the Hunter saw a Showman passing by, and managed to attract his attention.

"What will you give me," he said, "for my Bear?"

"It will be some five or ten minutes," said the Showman, "before I shall want a bear, and it looks to me as if prices would fall during that time. I think I'll wait and watch the market."

"The price of this animal," the Hunter replied, "is down to bed-rock; you can have him for a cent a pound, spot cash, and I'll throw in the next one that I lasso. But the purchaser must remove the goods from the premises forthwith, to make room for three man-eating tigers, a cat-headed gorilla and an armful of rattlesnakes."

But the Showman passed on in maiden meditation, fancy free, and being joined soon afterward by the Bear, who was absently picking his teeth, it was inferred that they were not unacquainted.

157. A Protagonist of Silver

Some Financiers who were whetting their tongues on their teeth because the Government had "struck down" silver. They were about to "inaugurate" a season of sweatshed, when they were addressed as follows by a Member of their honorable and warlike body:

"Comrades of the thunder and companions of death, I can but regard it as singularly fortunate that we who by conviction and sympathy are designated by nature as the champions of that fairest of her products, the white metal, should also, by a happy chance, be engaged mostly in the business of mining it. Nothing could be more just than that those who from unselfish motives and elevated sentiments are doing battle for the people's rights and interests should themselves be the chief beneficiaries of success. Therefore, O children of the earthquake and the storm, let us stand shoulder to shoulder, heart to heart and pocket to pocket!"

This speech so pleased the other Members of the convention that actuated by a magnanimous impulse they sprang to their feet and left the hall. It was the first time they had ever been known to leave anything having value.

158. The Wooden Guns

An Artillery Regiment of a State Militia applied to the Governor for wooden guns to practice with.

"Those," they explained, "will be cheaper than real ones."

"It shall not be said that I sacrificed efficiency to economy," said the Governor. "You shall have real guns."

"Thank you, thank you," cried the warriors, effusively. "We will take good care of them, and in the event of war return them to the arsenal."

159. The Holy Deacon

An Itinerant Preacher who had wrought hard in the moral vineyard for several hours whispered to a Holy Deacon of the local church:

"Brother, these people know you, and your active support will bear fruit abundantly. Please pass the plate for me, and you shall have one fourth."

The Holy Deacon did so, and putting the money into his pocket waited till the congregation was dismissed, then said good-night.

"But the money, brother, the money that you collected!" said the Itinerant Preacher.

"Nothing is coming to you," was the reply; "the Adversary has hardened their hearts and one fourth is all they gave."

160. The Ineffective Rooter

A Drunken Man was lying in the road with a bleeding nose, upon which he had fallen, when a Pig passed that way.

"You wallow fairly well," said the Pig, "but, my fine fellow, you have much to learn about rooting."

161. A Hasty Settlement

"Your Honor," said an Attorney, rising, "what is the present status of this case—as far as it has gone?"

"I have given a judgment for the residuary legatee under the will," said the Court, "put the costs upon the contestants, decided all questions relating to fees and other charges; and, in short, the estate in litigation has been settled, with all controversies, disputes, misunderstandings and differences of opinion thereunto appertaining."

"Ah, yes, I see," said the Attorney, thoughtfully, "we are making progress —we are getting on famously."

"Progress?" echoed the Judge—"progress? Why, sir, the matter is concluded!"

"Exactly, exactly; it had to be concluded in order to give relevancy to the motion that I am about to make. Your Honor, I move that the judgment of the Court be set aside and the case reopened."

"Upon what ground, sir?" the Judge asked in surprise.

"Upon the ground," said the Attorney, "that after paying all fees and expenses of litigation and all charges against the estate there will still be something left."

"There may have been an error," said His Honor, thoughtfully—"the Court may have underestimated the value of the estate. The motion is taken under advisement."

162. The Poet's Doom

An Object was walking along the King's highway wrapped in meditation and with little else on, when he suddenly found himself at the gates of a strange city. On applying for admittance, he was arrested as a necessitator of ordinances and taken before the King.

"Who are you," said the King, "and what is your business in life?"

"Snouter the Sneak," replied the Object, with ready invention—"pickpocket."

The King was about to command him to be released when the Prime Minister suggested that the prisoner's fingers be examined. They were found greatly flattened and calloused at the ends.

"Ha!" cried the King; "I told you so!—he is addicted to counting syllables. He is a poet. Turn him over to the Lord High Dissuader from the Head Habit."

"My liege," said the Inventor-in-Ordinary of Ingenious Penalties, "I venture to suggest a keener affliction."

"Name it," the King said.

"Let him retain that head!"

It was so ordered.

163. Noser and Note

The Head Rifler of an insolvent bank, learning that it was about to be visited by the official Noser into Things, placed his own personal note for a large amount among its resources, and gaily touching his guitar awaited the inspection. When the Noser came to the note he asked, "What's this?"

"That," said the Assistant Pocketer of Deposits, "is one of our liabilities."

"A liability?" exclaimed the Noser. "Nay, nay, an asset. That is what you mean, doubtless."

"Therein you err," the Pocketer explained; "that note was written in the bank with our own pen, ink and paper, and we have not paid a stationery bill for six months."

"Ah, I see," the Noser said, thoughtfully; "it is a liability. May I ask how you expect to meet it?"

"With fortitude, please God," answered the Assistant Pocketer, his eyes to Heaven raising — "with fortitude and a firm reliance on the laxity of the law."

"Enough, enough," exclaimed the faithful servant of the State, choking with emotion; "here is a certificate of solvency."

"And here is a bottle of ink," the grateful financier said, slipping it into the other's pocket; "it is all that we have."

164. Lion and Rattlesnake

A Man having found a Lion in his path undertook to subdue him by the power of the human eye; and near by was a Rattlesnake engaged in fascinating a small bird.

"How are you getting on, brother?" the Man called out to the other reptile, without removing his eyes from those of the Lion.

"Admirably," replied the serpent. "My success is assured; my victim draws nearer and nearer in spite of her efforts."

"And mine," said the Man, "draws nearer and nearer in spite of mine. Are you sure it is all right?"

"If you don't think so," the reptile replied as well as he then could, with his mouth full of bird, "you'd better give it up."

A half-hour later the Lion, thoughtfully picking his teeth with his claws, told the Rattlesnake that he had never in all his varied experience in being subdued, seen a subduer try so earnestly to give it up. "But," he added, with a wide, significant smile, "I looked him into countenance."

165. The Literary Astronomer

The Director of an Observatory, who, with a thirty-six inch refractor, had discovered the moon, hastened to an Editor, with a four-column account of the event.

"How much?" said the Editor, sententiously, without looking up from his essay on the circularity of the political horizon.

"One hundred and sixty dollars," replied the man who had discovered the moon.

"Not half enough," was the Editor's comment.

"Generous man!" cried the Astronomer, glowing with warm and elevated sentiments, "pay me, then, what you will."

"Great and good friend," said the Editor, blandly, looking up from his work, "we are far asunder, it seems. The paying is to be done by you."

The Director of the Observatory gathered up the manuscript and went away, explaining that it needed correction—he had neglected to dot an m.

166. The Reform School Board

The members of the School Board in Doosnoswair being suspected of appointing female teachers for an improper consideration, the people elected a Board composed wholly of women. In a few years the scandal was at an end; there were no female teachers in the Department.

167. Alderman and Raccoon

"I see quite a number of rings on your tail," said an Alderman to a Raccoon that he met in a zoological garden.

"Yes," replied the Raccoon, "and I hear quite a number of tales on your ring."

The Alderman, being of a sensitive, retiring disposition, shrank from further comparison, and strolling to another part of the garden stole the camel.

168. Cat and King

A Cat was looking at a King, as permitted by the proverb.

"Well," said the monarch, observing her inspection of the royal person, "how do you like me?"

"I can imagine a King," said the Cat, "whom I should like better."

"For example?"

"The King of Mice."

The sovereign was so pleased with the wit of the reply that he gave her permission to scratch his Prime Minister's eyes out.

169. The Man with No Enemies

An Inoffensive Person walking in a public place was assaulted by a Stranger with a Club, and severely beaten.

When the Stranger with a Club was brought to trial, the complainant said to the Judge:

"I do not know why I was assaulted; I have not an enemy in the world."

"That," said the defendant, "is why I struck him."

"Let the prisoner be discharged," said the Judge; "a man who has no enemies has no friends. The courts are not for such."

170. The Flying-Machine

An Ingenious Man who had built a flying-machine invited a great concourse of people to see it go up. At the appointed moment, everything being ready, he boarded the car and turned on the power. The machine immediately broke through the massive substructure upon which it was builded, and sank out of sight into the earth, the aeronaut springing out barely in time to save himself.

"Well," said he, "I have done enough to demonstrate the correctness of my details. The defects," he added, with a look at the ruined brick-work, "are merely basic and fundamental."

On this assurance the people came forward with subscriptions to build a second machine.

171. The Angel's Tear

An Unworthy Man who had laughed at the woes of a Woman whom he loved, was bewailing his indiscretion in sack-cloth-of-gold and ashes-of-roses, when the Angel of Compassion looked down upon him, saying:

"Poor mortal!—how unblest not to know the wickedness of laughing at another's misfortune!"

So saying, he let fall a great tear, which, encountering in its descent a current of cold air, was congealed into a hail-stone. This struck the Unworthy Man upon the head and set him rubbing that bruised organ vigorously with one hand while vainly attempting to expand an umbrella with the other.

Thereat the Angel of Compassion did most shamelessly and wickedly laugh.

172. The City of Political Distinction

Jamrach the Rich, being anxious to reach the City of Political Distinction before nightfall, arrived at a fork of the road and was undecided which branch to follow; so he consulted a Wise-Looking Person who sat by the wayside.

"Take *that* road," said the Wise-Looking Person, pointing it out; "it is known as the Political Highway."

"Thank you," said Jamrach, and was about to proceed.

"About how much do you thank me?" was the reply. "Do you suppose I am here for my health?"

As Jamrach had not become rich by stupidity he handed something to his guide and hastened on, and soon came to a toll-gate kept by a Benevolent Gentleman, to whom he gave something and was suffered to pass. A little farther along he came to a bridge across an imaginary stream, where a Civil Engineer (who had built the bridge) demanded something for interest on his investment, and it was forthcoming. It was growing late when Jamrach came to the margin of what appeared to be a lake of black ink, and there the road terminated. Seeing a Ferryman in his boat he paid something for his passage and was about to embark.

"No," said the Ferryman. "Put your neck in this noose, and I will tow you over. It is the only way," he added, seeing that the passenger was about to complain of the accommodations.

In due time he was dragged across, half strangled and dreadfully be-slubbered by the feculent waters. "There," said the Ferryman, hauling him ashore and disengaging him, "you are now in the City of Political Distinction. It has fifty millions of inhabitants, and as the color of the Filthy Pool does not wash off, they all look exactly alike."

"Alas!" exclaimed Jamrach, weeping and bewailing the loss of all his possessions, paid out in tips and tolls; "I will go back with you."

"I don't think you will," said the Ferryman, pushing off; "this city is situated on the Island of the Unreturning."

173. The Party Over There

A Man in a Hurry, whose watch was at his lawyer's, asked a Grave Person the time of day.

"I heard you ask that Party Over There the same question," said the Grave Person. "What answer did he give you?"

"He said it was about three o'clock," replied the Man in a Hurry; "but he did not look at his watch, and as the sun is nearly down I think it is later."

"The fact that the sun is nearly down," the Grave Person said, "is immaterial, but the fact that he did not consult his timepiece and make answer after due deliberation and consideration is fatal. The answer given," continued the Grave Person, consulting his own timepiece, "is of no effect, invalid, and void."

"What, then," said the Man in a Hurry, eagerly, "is the time of day?"

"The question is remanded to the Party Over There for a new answer," replied the Grave Person, returning his watch to his pocket and moving away with great dignity.

He was a Judge of an Appellate Court.

174. The Poet of Reform

One pleasant day in the latter part of eternity, as the Shades of all the great writers were reposing upon beds of asphodel and moly in the Elysian fields, each happy in hearing from the lips of the others nothing but copious quotation from his own works (for so Jove had kindly bedeviled their ears) there came in among them with triumphant mien a Shade whom none knew. She (for the newcomer showed such evidences of sex as cropped hair and a manly stride) took a seat in their midst and smiling a superior smile explained:

"After centuries of oppression I have wrested my rights from the grasp of the jealous gods. On earth I was the Poetess of Reform and sang to inattentive ears. Now for an eternity of honor and glory."

But it was not to be so, and soon she was the unhappiest of mortals, vainly desirous to wander again in gloom by the infernal lakes. For Jove had not bedeviled her ears, and she heard from the lips of each blessed Shade an incessant flow of quotation from his own works. Moreover, she was denied the happiness of repeating her poems. She could not recall a line of them, for Jove had decreed that the memory of them abide in Pluto's painful domain as a part of the apparatus.

175. The Unchanged Diplomatist

The republic of Madagonia had been long and well represented at the court of the King of Patagascar by an officer called a Dazie, but one day the Madagonian Parliament conferred upon him the superior rank of Dandee. The next day after being apprised of his new dignity he hastened to inform the King of Patagascar.

"Ah, yes, I understand," said the King; "you have been promoted and given increased pay and allowances. There was an appropriation?"

"Yes, your Majesty."

"And you have now two heads, have you not?"

"Oh, no, your Majesty — only one, I assure you."

"Indeed? And how many legs and arms?"

"Two of each, Sire — only two of each."

"And only one body?"

"Just a single body, as you perceive."

Thoughtfully removing his crown and scratching the royal head, the monarch was silent a moment, and then he said:

"I fancy that appropriation has been misapplied. You seem to be about the same kind of damned fool that you were before."

176. An Invitation

A Pious Person who had overcharged his paunch with dead bird by way of attesting his gratitude for escaping the many calamities which Heaven had sent upon others fell asleep at table and dreamed. He thought he lived in a country where turkeys were the ruling class, and every year they held a feast to manifest their sense of Heaven's goodness in sparing their lives, to kill them later. One day, about a week before one of these feasts, he met the Supreme Gobbler, who said:

"You will please get yourself into good condition for the Thanksgiving dinner."

"Yes, your Excellency," replied the Pious Person, delighted, "I shall come hungry, I assure you. It is no small privilege to dine with your Excellency."

The Supreme Gobbler eyed him for a moment in silence; then he said:

"As one of the lower domestic animals, you cannot be expected to know much, but you might know something. Since you do not, you will permit me to point out that being asked to dinner is one thing; being asked to dine is another and a different thing."

With this significant remark the Supreme Gobbler left him, and thenceforward the Pious Person dreamed of himself as white meat and dark until rudely awakened by terror.

177. The Ashes of Madame Blavatsky

The brightest two Lights of Theosophy being in the same place at once in company with the Ashes of Madame Blavatsky, an Inquiring Soul thought the time propitious to learn something worth while. So he sat at the feet of one awhile, and then he sat awhile at the feet of the other, and at last he applied his ear to the keyhole of the casket containing the Ashes of Madame Blavatsky. When the Inquiring Soul had completed his course of instruction he declared himself the Ahkoond of Swat, fell into the baleful habit of standing on his head and swore that the mother who bore him was a pragmatic paralogism. Wherefore he was held in so high reverence that when the two other gentlemen were hanged for lying the Theosophists elected him to the leadership of their Disastral Body, and after a quiet life and an honorable death by the kick of a jackass he was reincarnated as a Yellow Dog. As such he ate the Ashes of Madame Blavatsky, and Theosophy was no more.

178. The Opossum of the Future

One day an Opossum who had gone to sleep hanging from the highest branch of a tree by the tail, awoke and saw a large Snake wound about the limb, between him and the trunk of the tree.

"If I hold on," he said to himself, "I shall be swallowed; if I let go I shall break my neck."

But suddenly he bethought himself to dissemble.

"My perfected friend," he said, "my parental instinct recognizes in you a noble evidence and illustration of the theory of development. You are the Opossum of the Future, the ultimate Fittest Survivor of our species, the ripe result of progressive prehensility — all tail!"

But the Snake, proud of his ancient eminence in Scriptural history, was strictly orthodox and did not accept the scientific view.

179. The Life-Saver

Seventy-five Men presented themselves before the President of the Humane Society and demanded the great gold medal for life-saving.

"Why, yes," said the President; "by diligent effort so many men must have saved a considerable number of lives. How many did you save?"

"Seventy-five, sir," replied their Spokesman.

"Ah, yes, that is one each — very good work — very good work, indeed," the President said. "You shall not only have the Society's great gold medal, but its recommendation for employment at the several life-boat stations along the coast. But how did you save so many lives?"

The Spokesman of the Men replied:

"We are officers of the law, and have just returned from the pursuit of two murderous outlaws."

180. The Australian Grasshopper

A Distinguished Naturalist was traveling in Australia, when he saw a Kangaroo in session and flung a stone at it. The Kangaroo immediately adjourned, tracing against the sunset sky a parabolic curve spanning seven provinces, and evanished below the horizon. The Distinguished Naturalist looked interested, but said nothing for an hour; then he said to his native Guide:

"You have pretty wide meadows here, I suppose?"

"No, not very wide," the Guide answered; "about the same as in England and America."

After another long silence the Distinguished Naturalist said:

"The hay which we shall purchase for our horses this evening—I shall expect to find the stalks about fifty feet long. Am I right?"

"Why, no," said the Guide; "a foot or two is about the usual length of our hay. What can you be thinking of?"

The Distinguished Naturalist made no immediate reply, but later, as in the shades of night they journeyed through the desolate vastness of the Great Lone Land, he broke the silence:

"I was thinking," he said, "of the uncommon magnitude of that grass-hopper."

181. The Pavior

An Author saw a Laborer hammering stones into the pavement of a street, and approaching him said:

"My friend, you seem weary. Ambition is a hard taskmaster."

"I'm working for Mr. Jones, sir," the Laborer replied.

"Well, cheer up," the Author resumed; "fame comes at the most unexpected times. To-day you are poor, obscure and disheartened, but to-morrow the world may be ringing with your name."

"What are you telling me?" the Laborer said. "Can not an honest pavior perform his work in peace, and get his money for it, and his living by it, without others talking rot about ambition and hopes of fame?"

"Can not an honest writer?" said the Author.

182. The Tried Assassin

An Assassin being put upon trial in a New England court, his Counsel rose and said: "Your Honor, I move for a discharge on the ground of 'once in jeopardy': my client has been already tried for that murder and acquitted."

"In what court?" asked the Judge.

"In the Superior Court of San Francisco," the Counsel replied.

"Let the trial proceed—your motion is denied," said the Judge. "An Assassin is not in jeopardy when tried in California."

183. Two Poets

Two Poets were quarreling for the Apple of Discord and the Bone of Contention, for they were very hungry.

"My sons," said Apollo, "I will part the prizes between you. You," he said to the First Poet, "excel in Art—take the Apple. And you," he said to the Second Poet, "in Imagination—take the Bone."

"To Art the best prize!" said the First Poet, triumphantly, and endeavoring to devour his award broke all his teeth. The Apple was a work of Art.

"That shows our Master's contempt for mere Art," said the Second Poet, grinning.

Thereupon he attempted to gnaw his Bone, but his teeth passed through it without encountering resistance. It was an imaginary Bone.

184. The Witch's Steed

A Broomstick which had long served a witch as a steed complained of the nature of its employment, which it thought degrading.

"Very well," said the Witch, "I will give you work in which you will be associated with intellect—you will come in contact with brains. I shall present you to a housewife."

"What!" said the Broomstick, "do you consider the hands of a housewife intellectual?"

"I referred," said the Witch, "to the head of her good man."

185. The Sagacious Rat

A Rat that was about to emerge from his hole caught a glimpse of a Cat waiting for him, and descending to the colony at the bottom of the hole invited a Friend to join him in a visit to a neighboring corn-bin. "I would have gone alone," he said, "but could not deny myself the pleasure of such distinguished company."

"Very well," said the Friend, "I will go with you. Lead on."

"Lead?" exclaimed the other. "What! *I* precede so great and illustrious a rat as you? No, indeed—after you, sir, after you."

Pleased with this great show of deference, the Friend went ahead, and, leaving the hole first, was caught by the Cat, who immediately trotted away with him. The other then went out unmolested.

186. The Bumbo of Jiam

The Pahdour of Patagascar and the Gookul of Madagonia were disputing about an island that both claimed. Finally, at the suggestion of the International League of Cannon Founders, which had important branches in both countries, they decided to refer their claims to the Bumbo of Jiam, and abide by his judgment. In settling the preliminaries of the arbitration they had, however, the misfortune to disagree, and appealed to arms. At the end of a long and disastrous war, when both sides were exhausted and bankrupt, the Bumbo of Jiam intervened in the interest of peace.

"My great and good friends," he said to his brother sovereigns, "it will be advantageous to you to learn that some questions are more complex and perilous than others, presenting a greater number of points upon which it is possible to differ. For four generations your royal predecessors disputed about possession of that island without falling out. Beware, oh, beware the perils of international arbitration! — against which I feel it my duty to protect you henceforth."

So saying, he annexed both countries, and after a long, peaceful and happy reign was poisoned by his Prime Minister.

187. Legislator and Soap

A member of the Kansas Legislature meeting a Cake of Soap was passing it by without recognition, but the Cake of Soap insisted on stopping and shaking hands. Thinking it might possibly be in the enjoyment of the elective franchise, he gave it a cordial and earnest grasp. On letting it go he observed that a portion of it adhered to his fingers, and running to a brook in great alarm, proceeded to wash it off. In doing so he necessarily got some on the other hand, and when he had finished washing both were so white that he went to bed and sent for a physician.

188. The Shadow of the Leader

A Political Leader was walking out one sunny day, when he observed his Shadow leaving him and walking rapidly away.

"Come back here, you scoundrel," he cried.

"If I had been a scoundrel," answered the Shadow, increasing its speed, "I should not have left you."

189. The All-Dog

A Lion seeing a Poodle fell into laughter at the ridiculous spectacle.

"Who ever saw so small a beast?" he said.

"It is very true," said the Poodle, with austere dignity, "that I am small; but, sir, I beg you to observe that I am all dog."

190. A Causeway

A Rich Woman having returned from abroad disembarked at the foot of Knee-deep Street, and was about to walk to her hotel through the mud.

"Madam," said a Policeman, "I cannot permit you to do that; you would soil your shoes and stockings."

"Oh, that is of no importance, really," replied the Rich Woman, with a cheerful smile.

"But, madam, it is needless; from the wharf to the hotel, as you observe, extends an unbroken line of prostrate newspaper men who crave the honor of having you walk upon them."

"In that case," she said, seating herself in a doorway and unlocking her satchel, "I shall have to put on my rubber boots."

191. The Thistles upon the Grave

A Mind Reader made a wager that he would be buried alive and remain so for six months, then be dug up alive. In order to secure the grave against secret disturbance, it was sown with thistles. At the end of three months the Mind Reader lost his bet. He had come up to eat the thistles.

192. Alarm and Pride

"Good morning, my friend," said Alarm to Pride; "how are you this morning?"

"Very tired," replied Pride, seating himself on a stone by the wayside and mopping his steaming brow. "The politicians are wearing me out by pointing to their dirty records with *me,* when they could as well use a stick."

Alarm sighed sympathetically and said:

"It is pretty much the same way here. Instead of using an opera-glass they view the acts of their opponents with *me!*"

As these patient drudges were mingling their tears, they were notified that they must go on duty again, for one of the political parties had nominated a thief and was about to hold a gratification meeting.

193. The Farmer's Friend

A Great Philanthropist who had thought of himself in connection with the Presidency and had introduced a bill into Congress requiring the Government to loan every voter all the money that he needed, on his personal security, was explaining to a Sunday-school at a railway station how much he had done for the country, when an angel looked down from Heaven and wept.

"For example," said the Great Philanthropist, watching the teardrops pattering in the dust, "these early rains are of incalculable advantage to the farmer."

194. Physicians Two

A Wicked Old Man finding himself ill sent for a Physician, who prescribed for him and went away. Then the Wicked Old Man sent for Another Physician, saying nothing of the first, and an entirely different treatment was ordered. This continued for some weeks, the physicians visiting him on alternate days and treating him for two different disorders, with constantly enlarging doses of medicine and more and more rigorous nursing. But one day they accidently met at his bedside while he slept and, the truth coming out, a violent quarrel ensued.

"My good friends," said the patient, awakened by the noise of the dispute, and apprehending the cause of it, "pray be more reasonable. If I could for weeks endure you both, can you not for a little while endure each other? I have been well for ten days, but have remained in bed in the hope of gaining by repose the strength that would justify me in taking your medicines. So far I have touched none of them."

195. The Honest Cadi

A Robber who had plundered a Merchant of one thousand pieces of gold was taken before the Cadi, who asked him if he had anything to say why he should not be decapitated.

"Your Honor," said the Robber, "I could do no otherwise than take the money, for Allah made me that way."

"Your defence is ingenious and sound," said the Cadi, "and I must acquit you of criminality. Unfortunately, Allah has made me so that I must also take off your head—unless," he added, thoughtfully, "you offer me a half of the gold; for He made me weak under temptation."

Thereupon the Robber put five hundred pieces of gold into the Cadi's hand.

"Good," said the Cadi. "I shall now remove only one-half your head. To show my trust in your discretion I shall leave intact the half that you talk with."

196. The Overlooked Factor

A Man that owned a fine Dog, and by a careful selection of its mate had bred a number of animals but a little lower than the angels, fell in love with his washerwoman, married her and reared a family of dolts.

"Alas!" he exclaimed, contemplating the melancholy result, "had I but chosen a mate for myself with half the care that I did for my Dog I should now be a proud and happy father."

"I'm not so sure of that," said the Dog, overhearing the lament. "There's a difference, certainly, between your whelps and mine, but I venture to flatter myself that it is not due altogether to the mothers. You and I are not entirely alike ourselves."

197. A Racial Parallel

Some White Christians engaged in driving Chinese Heathens out of an American town found a newspaper published in Peking in the Chinese tongue and compelled one of their victims to translate an editorial. It turned out to be an appeal to the people of the Province of Pang Ki to drive the foreign devils out of the country and burn their dwellings and churches. At this evidence of Mongolian barbarity the White Christians were so greatly incensed that they carried out their original design.

198. Kangaroo and Zebra

A Kangaroo hopping awkwardly along with some bulky object concealed in her pouch met a Zebra, and desirous of keeping his attention upon himself, said:

"Your costume looks as if you might have come out of the penitentiary."

"Appearances are deceitful," replied the Zebra, smiling in the conscious-ness of a more insupportable wit, "or I should have to think that you had come out of the Legislature."

199. A Matter of Method

A Philosopher seeing a Fool beating his Donkey, said:

"Abstain, my son, abstain, I implore. Those who resort to violence shall suffer from violence."

"That," said the Fool, diligently belaboring the animal, "is what I'm trying to teach this beast — which has kicked me."

"Doubtless," said the Philosopher to himself, as he walked away, "the wis-dom of fools is no deeper nor truer than ours, but they really do seem to have a more impressive way of imparting it."

200. A Man of Principle

During a shower of rain the Keeper of a Zoological garden observed a Man of Principle crouching beneath the belly of the ostrich, which had drawn itself up to its full height to sleep.

"Why, my dear sir," said the Keeper, "if you fear to get wet you'd better creep into the pouch of yonder female kangaroo — the *Saltatrix mackintosha* — for if that ostrich wakes he will kick you to death in a moment!"

"I can't help that," the Man of Principle replied, with that lofty scorn of practical considerations distinguishing his species. "He may kick me to death if he wish, but until he does he shall give me shelter from the storm. He has swallowed my umbrella."

201. The Returned Californian

A Man was hanged by the neck until he was dead. This was in 1893.

"Whence do you come?" Saint Peter asked when the Man presented him-self at the gate of Heaven.

"From California," replied the applicant.

"Enter, my son, enter; you bring joyous tidings."

When the Man had vanished inside, Saint Peter took his memorandum tablet and made the following entry:

"February 16, 1893. California settled by the Christians."

202. The Compassionate Physician

A Kind-Hearted Physician sitting at the bedside of a patient afflicted with an incurable and painful disease heard a noise behind him and turning saw a Cat laughing at the feeble efforts of a wounded Mouse to drag itself out of the room.

"You cruel beast!" cried he. "Why don't you kill it at once, like a lady?"

Rising, he kicked the Cat out of the door and picking up the Mouse compassionately put it out of its misery by pulling off its head. Recalled to the bedside by the moans of his patient, the Kind-Hearted Physician administered a stimulant, a tonic and a nutrient, and went away.

203. A Prophet of Evil

An Undertaker Who Was a Member of a Trust saw a Man Leaning on a Spade, and asked him why he was not at work.

"Because," said the Man Leaning on a Spade, "I belong to the Grave-diggers' National Extortion Society, and we have decided to limit the production of graves and get more money for the reduced output. We have a corner in graves and propose working it to the best advantage."

"My friend," said the Undertaker Who Was a Member of the Trust, "this is a most hateful and injurious scheme. If people can not be assured of graves I fear they will no longer die, and the best interests of civilization will wither like a frosted leaf."

And blowing his eyes upon his handkerchief, he walked away lamenting.

204. Two of the Damned

Two Blighted Beings, haggard, lachrymose and detested, met on a blasted heath in the light of a struggling moon.

"I wish you a merry Christmas," said the First Blighted Being, in a voice like that of a singing tomb.

"And I you a happy New Year," responded the Second Blighted Being, with the accent of a penitent accordeon.

They then fell upon each other's neck and wept scalding rills down each other's spine in token of their banishment to the Realm of Ineffable Bosh. For one of these accursed creatures was the First of January, and the other the Twenty-fifth of December.

205. The Austere Governor

A Governor visiting a State prison was implored by a Convict to pardon him.

"What are you in for?" asked the Governor.

"I held a high office," the Convict humbly replied, "and sold subordinate appointments."

"Then I decline to interfere," said the Governor, with asperity; "a man who abuses his office by making it serve a private end and purvey a personal advantage is unfit to be free. By the way, Mr. Warden," he added to that official, as the Convict slunk away, "in appointing you to this position, I was given to understand that your friends could make the Shikane county delegation to the next State convention solid for—for the present Administration. Was I rightly informed?"

"You were, sir."

"Very well, then, I will bid you good-day. Please be so good as to appoint my nephew Night Chaplain and Reminder of Mothers and Sisters."

206. The Penitent Elector

A Person belonging to the Society for Passing Resolutions of Respect for the Memory of Deceased Members having died received the customary attention.

"Good Heavens!" exclaimed a Sovereign Elector, on hearing the resolutions read, "what a loss to the nation! And to think that I once voted against that angel for Inspector of Gate-latches in Public Squares!"

In remorse the Sovereign Elector deprived himself of political influence by learning to read.

207. Religions of Error

Hearing a sound of strife, a Christian in the Orient asked his Dragoman the cause of it.

"The Buddhists are cutting Mohammedan throats," the Dragoman replied, with Oriental composure.

"I did not know," remarked the Christian, with scientific interest, "that that would make so much noise."

"The Mohammedans are cutting Buddhist throats," added the Dragoman.

"It is astonishing," mused the Christian, "how violent and how general are religious animosities."

So saying he visibly smugged and went off to telegraph for a brigade of cut-throats to protect Christian interests.

208. The Tail of the Sphinx

A Dog of a taciturn disposition said to his Tail:

"Whenever I am angry you rise and bristle; when I am pleased you wag; when I am alarmed you tuck yourself in out of danger. You are too mercurial — you disclose all my emotions. My notion is that tails are given to conceal thought. It is my dearest ambition to be as impassive as the Sphinx."

"My friend, you must recognize the laws and limitations of your being," replied the Tail, with flexions appropriate to the sentiments uttered, "and try to be great some other way. The Sphinx has one hundred and fifty qualifications for impassiveness which you lack."

"What are they?" the Dog asked.

"One hundred and forty-nine tons of sand on its tail."

"And—?"

"A stone tail."

209. The Crew of the Lifeboat

The Gallant Crew at a life-saving station were about to launch their lifeboat for a spin along the coast when they discovered, a little distance away, a capsized vessel with a dozen men clinging to her keel.

"We are fortunate," said the Gallant Crew, "to have seen that in time. Our fate might have been the same as theirs."

So they hauled the lifeboat back into its house and were spared to the service of their country.

210. A Treaty of Peace

Through massacres of each other's citizens China and the United States had been four times plunged into devastating wars, when, in the year 1994, arose a Philosopher in Madagascar, who laid before the Governments of the two distracted countries the following *modus vivendi:*

"Massacres are to be sternly forbidden as heretofore; but any citizen or subject of either country disobeying the injunction is to detach the scalps of all persons massacred and deposit them with a local officer designated to receive and preserve them and sworn to keep and render a true account thereof. At the conclusion of each massacre in either country, or as soon thereafter as practicable, or at stated regular periods, as may be provided by treaty, there shall be a counting of scalps, without regard to sex or age; the Government having the greatest number is to be taxed on the excess at the rate of $1000 a scalp, and the other Government credited with the amount. Once in every decade there shall be a general settlement, when the balance due shall be paid to the creditor nation in Mexican dollars."

The plan was adopted, the necessary treaty made, with legislation to carry out its provisions; the Madagascarene Philosopher took his seat in the Temple of Immortality and Peace spread her white wings over the two nations, to the unspeakable defiling of her plumage.

211. The Nightside of Character

A Gifted and Honorable Editor, who by practice of his profession had acquired wealth and distinction, applied to an Old Friend for the hand of his daughter in marriage.

"With all my heart, and God bless you!" said the Old Friend, grasping him by both hands. "It is a greater honor than I had dared to hope for."

"I knew what your answer would be," replied the Gifted and Honorable Editor. "And yet," he added, with a sly smile, "I feel that I ought to give you as much knowledge of my character as I possess. In this scrap-book is such testimony relating to my shady side as I have within the past ten years been able to cut from the columns of my competitors in the business of elevating humanity to a higher plane of mind and morals—my 'loathsome contemporaries.'"

Laying the book on a table, he withdrew in high spirits to make arrangements for the wedding. Three days later he received the scrap-book from a messenger, with a note warning him never again to darken his Old Friend's door.

"See!" the Gifted and Honorable Editor exclaimed, pointing to that injunction—"I am a painter and grainer!"

And he was led away to the Asylum for the Indiscreet.

212. The Faithful Cashier

The Cashier of a bank having defaulted was asked by the Directors what he had done with the money taken.

"I am greatly surprised by such a question," said the Cashier; "it sounds as if you suspected me of selfishness. Gentlemen, I applied that money to the purpose for which I took it; I paid it as an initiation fee and one year's dues in advance to the Treasurer of the Cashiers' Mutual Defence Association."

"What is the object of that organization?" the Directors inquired.

"When any one of its members is under suspicion," replied the Cashier, "the Association undertakes to clear his character by submitting evidence that he was never a prominent member of any church, nor foremost in Sunday-school work."

Recognizing the value to the bank of a spotless reputation for its officers, the President drew his check for the amount of the shortage and the Cashier was restored to favor.

213. The Circular Clew

A Detective searching for the murderer of a dead man was accosted by a Clew.

"Follow me," said the Clew, "and there's no knowing what you may discover."

So the Detective followed the Clew a whole year through a thousand sinuosities and at last found himself in the office of the Morgue.

"There!" said the Clew, pointing to the open register.

The Detective eagerly scanned the page and found an official statement that the deceased was dead. Thereupon he hastened to Police Headquarters to report progress. The Clew, meanwhile, sauntered among the busy haunts of men, arm in arm with an Ingenious Theory.

214. The Devoted Widow

A Widow weeping on her husband's grave was approached by an Engaging Gentleman who, in a respectful manner, assured her that he had long entertained for her the most tender feelings.

"Wretch!" cried the Widow. "Leave me this instant! Is this a time to talk to me of love?"

"I assure you, madam, that I had not intended to disclose my affection," the Engaging Gentleman humbly explained, "but the power of your beauty has overcome my discretion."

"You should see me when I have not been weeping," said the Widow.

215. The Hardy Patriots

A Dispenser-Elect of Patronage gave notice through the newspapers that applicants for places would be given none until a certain date.

"You are exposing yourself to a grave danger," said a Lawyer.

"How so?" the Dispenser-Elect inquired.

"It will be nearly two months," the Lawyer answered, "before the day that you mention. Few patriots can live so long without eating, and some of the applicants will be compelled to go to work in the meantime. If that kills them, you will be liable to prosecution for murder."

"You underrate their powers of endurance," the official replied.

"What!" said the Lawyer, "you think they can endure work?"

"No," said the other—"hunger."

216. The Humble Peasant

An Office Seeker whom the President had ordered out of Washington was watering the homeward highway with his tears.

"Ah," he said, "how disastrous is ambition! how unsatisfying its rewards! how terrible its disappointments! Behold yonder peasant tilling his field in peace and contentment! He rises with the lark, passes the day in wholesome toil and lies down at night to pleasant dreams. In the mad struggle for place and power he has no part; the roar of the strife reaches his ear like the distant murmur of the ocean. Happy, thrice happy man! I will approach him and bask in the sunshine of his humble felicity. Peasant, hail!"

Leaning upon his rake, the Peasant returned the salutation with a nod, but said nothing.

"My friend," said the Office Seeker, "you see before you the wreck of an ambitious man—ruined by the pursuit of place and power. This morning when I set out from the national capital—"

"Stranger," the Peasant interrupted, "if you're going back there soon maybe you wouldn't mind using your influence to make me Postmaster at Smith's Corners."

The traveler passed on.

217. The Various Delegation

The King of Wideout having been offered the sovereignty of Awayoff, sent for the Three Persons who had made the offer, and said to them:

"I am extremely obliged to you, but before accepting so great a responsibility I must ascertain the sentiments of the people of Awayoff."

"Sire," said the Spokesman of the Three Persons, "they stand before you."

"Indeed!" said the King; "are you, then, the people of Awayoff?"

"Yes, your Majesty."

"There are not many of you," the King said, attentively regarding them with the royal eye, "and you are not so very large; I hardly think you are a quorum. Moreover, I never heard of you until you came here; whereas Awayoff is noted for the quality of its pork and contains hogs of distinction. I shall send a Commissioner to ascertain the sentiments of the hogs."

The Three Persons, bowing profoundly, backed out of the presence; but soon afterward they desired another audience, and on being readmitted said, through their Spokesman:

"May it please your Majesty, we are the hogs."

218. A Harmless Visitor

At a meeting of the Golden League of Mystery a Woman was discovered, writing in a notebook. A member directed the attention of the Superb High Chairman to her, and she was asked to explain her presence there, and what she was doing.

"I came in for my own pleasure and instruction," she said, "and was so struck by the wisdom of the speakers that I could not help making a few notes."

"Madam," said the Superb High Chairman, "we have no objection to visitors if they will pledge themselves not to publish anything they hear. Are you—on your honor as a lady, now, madam—are you not connected with some newspaper or other publication?"

"Good gracious, no!" cried the Woman, earnestly. "Why, sir, I am an officer of the Women's Press Association!"

She was permitted to remain and presented with resolutions of apology.

219. An Inflated Ambition

The President of a great Corporation went into a dry-goods shop and saw a placard which read:

"If You Don't See What You Want Ask For It."

Approaching the shopkeeper, who had been narrowly observing him as he read the placard, he was about to speak, when the shopkeeper called to a salesman:

"John, show this gentleman the earth."

220. The No Case

A Statesman who had been indicted by an unfeeling Grand Jury was arrested by a Sheriff and thrown into jail. As this was abhorrent to his fine spiritual nature, he sent for the District Attorney and asked that the case against him be dismissed.

"Upon what grounds?" asked the District Attorney.

"Lack of evidence to convict," replied the accused.

"Do you happen to have the lack with you?" the official asked. "I should like to see it."

"With pleasure," said the other; "here it is."

So saying he handed the other a check, which the District Attorney carefully examined, and then pronounced it the most complete absence of both proof and presumption that he had ever seen. He said it would acquit the poorest man in the world.

221. Judge and Rash Act

A Judge who had for years looked in vain for an opportunity for infamous distinction, but whom no litigant thought worth bribing, sat one day upon the Bench, lamenting his hard lot and threatening to put an end to his life if business did not improve. Suddenly he found himself confronted by a dreadful figure clad in a shroud, whose pallor and stony eyes smote him with a horrible apprehension.

"Who are you," he faltered, "and why do you come here?"

"I am the Rash Act," was the sepulchral reply; "you may commit me."

"No," the judge said, thoughtfully, "no, that would be quite irregular. I do not sit to-day as a committing magistrate."

222. The Prerogative of Might

A Slander traveling rapidly through the land upon its joyous mission was accosted by a Retraction and commanded to halt and be killed.

"Your career of mischief is at an end," said the Retraction, drawing his club, rolling up his sleeves and spitting on his hands.

"Why should you slay me?" protested the Slander. "Whatever my intentions were, I have been innocuous, for you have dogged my strides and counteracted my influence."

"Dogged your grandmother!" said the Retraction, with contemptuous vulgarity of speech. "In the order of nature it is appointed that we two shall never travel the same road."

"How then," the Slander asked, triumphantly, "have you overtaken me?"

"I have not," replied the Retraction; "we have accidentally met. I came round the world the other way."

But when he tried to execute his fell purpose he found that in the order of nature it was appointed that he himself perish miserably in the encounter.

223. At Large — One Temper

A Turbulent Person was brought before a Judge to be tried for an assault with intent to commit murder, and it was proved that he had been variously obstreperous without apparent provocation, had affected the peripheries of several luckless fellow-citizens with the trunk of a small tree and afterward cleaned out the town. While trying to palliate these misdeeds, the Defendant's Attorney turned suddenly to the Judge, saying:

"Did your Honor ever lose your temper?"

"I fine you twenty-five dollars for contempt of court!" roared the Judge, in wrath. "How dare you mention the loss of my temper in connection with this case?"

After a moment's silence the Attorney said, meekly:

"I thought my client might perhaps have found it."

224. The Divided Delegation

A Delegation at Washington went to a New President, and said:

"Your Excellency, we are unable to agree upon a Favorite Son to represent us in your Cabinet."

"Then," said the New President, "I shall have to lock you up until you do agree."

So the Delegation was cast into the deepest dungeon beneath the moat, where it maintained a divided mind for many weeks, but finally reconciled its differences and asked to be taken before the New President.

"My children," said he, "nothing is so beautiful as harmony. My Cabinet selections were all made before our former interview, but you have supplied a noble instance of patriotism in subordinating your personal preferences to the general good. Go now to your beautiful homes and be happy."

225. Rejected Services

A Heavy Operator overtaken by a Reverse of Fortune was bewailing his sudden fall from affluence to indigence.

"Do not weep," said the Reverse of Fortune. "You need not suffer alone. Name any one of the men who have opposed your schemes, and I will overtake *him.*"

"It is hardly worth while," said the victim, earnestly. "Not a soul of them has a cent. You have already visited them."

226. Deceased and Heirs

A Man died leaving a large estate and many sorrowful relations who claimed it. After some years, when all but one had had judgment given against them, that one was awarded the estate, which he asked his Attorney to have appraised.

"There is nothing to appraise," said the Attorney, pocketing his last fee.

"Then," said the Successful Claimant, "what good has all this litigation done me?"

"You have been a good client to me," the Attorney replied, gathering up his books and papers, "but I must say you betray a surprising ignorance of the purpose of litigation."

227. Politicians and Plunder

Several Political Entities were dividing the spoils.

"I will take the management of the prisons," said a Decent Respect for Public Opinion, "and make a radical change."

"And I," said the Blotted Escutcheon, "will retain my present general connection with affairs, while my friend here, the Soiled Ermine, will remain in the Judiciary."

The Political Pot said it would not boil any more unless replenished from the Filthy Pool.

The Cohesive Power of Public Plunder quietly remarked that the two bosses would, he supposed, naturally be his share.

"No," said the Lowest Depth of Degradation, "they have already fallen to me."

228. Man and Wart

A Person with a Wart on His Nose met a Person Similarly Afflicted, and said:

"Let me propose your name for membership in the Imperial Order of Abnormal Proboscidians, of which I am the High Noble Toby and Surreptitious Treasurer. Two months ago I was the only member. One month ago there were two. To-day we number four Emperors of the Abnormal Proboscis in good standing—doubles every four weeks, see? That's geometrical progression— you know how that piles up. In a year and a half every man in the country will have a wart on his nose. Powerful Order! Initiation, five dollars."

"My friend," said the Person Similarly Afflicted, "here are five dollars. Keep my name off your books."

"Thank you kindly," the Man with a Wart on His Nose replied, pocketing the money; "it is just the same to us as if you joined. Good-bye."

He went away, but in a little while he was back.

"I quite forgot to mention the monthly dues," he said.

229. His Fly-Speck Majesty

A Distinguished Advocate of Republican Institutions was seen pickling his shins in the ocean.

"Why don't you come out on dry land?" said the Spectator. "What are you in there for?"

"Sir," replied the Distinguished Advocate of Republican Institutions, "a ship is expected, bearing His Majesty the King of the Fly-Speck Islands, and I wish to be the first to grasp the crowned hand."

"But," said the Spectator, "you said in your famous speech before the Society for the Prevention of the Protrusion of Nail Heads from Plank Sidewalks that Kings were blood-smeared oppressors and hell-bound loafers."

"My dear sir," said the Distinguished Advocate of Republican Institutions, without removing his eyes from the horizon, "you wander away into the strangest irrelevancies! I spoke of Kings in general."

230. The Pugilist's Diet

The Trainer of a Pugilist consulted a Physician regarding the champion's diet.

"Beef-steaks are too tender," said the Physician; "have his meat cut from the neck of a bull."

"I thought the steaks more digestible," the Trainer explained.

"That is very true," said the Physician; "but they do not sufficiently exercise the chin."

231. Old Man and Pupil

A Beautiful Old Man meeting a Sunday-school Pupil laid his hand tenderly upon the lad's head, saying: "Listen, my son, to the words of the wise and heed the advice of the righteous."

"All right," said the Sunday-school Pupil; "go ahead."

"Oh, I haven't anything to tell you, really," said the Beautiful Old Man. "I am only observing one of the customs of age. I am a pirate."

And when he had taken his hand from the lad's head the latter observed that his hair was full of clotted blood. Then the Beautiful Old Man went his way, instructing other youth.

232. A Forfeited Right

The Chief of the Weather Bureau having predicted a fair day, a Thrifty Person hastened to lay in a large stock of umbrellas, which he exposed for sale on the sidewalk; but the weather remained clear and nobody would buy. Thereupon the Thrifty Person brought an action against the Chief of the Weather Bureau for the cost of the umbrellas.

"Your Honor," said the Defendant's Attorney, when the case was called, "I move that this astonishing action be dismissed. Not only is my client in no way responsible for the loss, but he distinctly forecast the fair weather that caused it."

"That is just it, your Honor," replied the Counsel for the Plaintiff; "by making a correct forecast the defendant fooled my client in the only way that he could do so. He has lied so much and so notoriously that he has no right to tell the truth."

Judgment for the plaintiff.

233. Revenge

An Insurance Agent was trying to induce a Hard Man to Deal With to take out a policy on his house. After listening to him for an hour, while he painted in vivid colors the extreme danger of fire consuming the house, the Hard Man to Deal With said:

"Do you really think it likely that my house will burn down inside the time that policy will run?"

"Certainly," replied the Insurance Agent; "have I not been trying all this time to convince you that I do?"

"Then," said the Hard Man to Deal With, "why are you so eager to have your Company bet me money that it will not?"

The Agent was silent and thoughtful for a moment; then he drew the other apart into an unfrequented place and whispered in his ear:

"My friend, I will impart to you a dark secret. Years ago the Company betrayed my sweetheart by promise of marriage. Under an assumed name I have wormed myself into its service for revenge; and as there is a heaven above us, I will have its heart's blood!"

234. An Optimist

Two Frogs in the belly of a snake were considering their altered circumstances.

"This is pretty hard luck," said one.

"Don't jump to conclusions," the other said; "we are out of the wet and provided with board and lodging."

"With lodging, certainly," said the First Frog; "but I don't see the board."

"You are a croaker," the other explained. "We are the board."

235. Two Footpads

Two Footpads sat at their grog in a roadside resort, comparing the evening's adventures.

"I stood up the Chief of Police," said the First Footpad, "and I got away with what he had."

"And I," said the Second Footpad, "stood up the United States District Attorney, and got away with — "

"Good Lord!" interrupted the other in astonishment and admiration, "you got away with what that fellow had?"

"No," the unfortunate narrator explained, "with a small part of what *I* had."

236. Equipped for Service

During the Civil War a Patriot was passing through the State of Maryland with a pass from the President to join Grant's army and see the fighting. Stopping a day at Annapolis, he visited the shop of a well-known optician and ordered seven powerful telescopes, one for every day in the week. In recognition of this munificent patronage of the State's languishing industries, the Governor commissioned him a colonel.

237. The Basking Cyclone

A Negro in a boat, gathering driftwood, saw a sleeping Alligator and thinking it was a log, fell to estimating the number of shingles it would make for his new cabin. Having satisfied his mind on that point, he stuck his boat-hook into the beast's back to harvest his good fortune. Thereupon the saurian emerged from his dream and, greatly to the surprise of the man-and-brother, took to the water, making a terrible commotion!

"I never befo' seen sech a cyclone as dat," the Negro exclaimed as soon as he had recovered his breath. "It done carry away de ruf of my house!"

238. A Valuable Suggestion

A Big Nation having a quarrel with a Little Nation, resolved to terrify its antagonist by a grand naval demonstration in the latter's principal port. So the Big Nation assembled all its ships of war from all over the world, and was about to send them three hundred and fifty thousand miles to the place of rendezvous, when the President of the Big Nation received the following note from the President of the Little Nation:

"My great and good friend, I hear that you are going to show us your navy in order to impress us with a sense of your power. How needless the expense!

To prove to you that we already know all about it I inclose herewith a list and description of all the ships you have."

The great and good friend was so struck by the hard sense of the letter that he kept his navy at home, saving one thousand million dollars. This economy enabled him to buy a satisfactory decision when the cause of the quarrel was submitted to arbitration.

239. Optimist and Cynic

A man who had experienced the favors of fortune and was an Optimist, met a man who had experienced an optimist and was a Cynic. So the Cynic turned out of the road to let the Optimist roll by in his gold carriage.

"My son," said the Optimist, stopping the gold carriage, "you look as if you had not a friend in the world."

"I don't know if I have or not," replied the Cynic, "for you have the world."

240. The Taken Hand

A Successful Man of Business having occasion to write to a Thief expressed a wish to see him and shake hands.

"No," replied the Thief, "there are some things that I will not take — among them your hand."

"You must use a little strategy," said a Philosopher to whom the Successful Man of Business had reported the Thief's haughty reply. "Leave your hand out some night and he will take it."

So one night the Successful Man of Business left his hand out of a neighbor's pocket and the Thief took it with avidity.

241. Poet and Editor

"My dear sir," said the Editor to the Poet who had called to see about his poem, "I regret to say that owing to an unfortunate altercation in this office the greater part of your manuscript is illegible; a bottle of ink was upset upon it, blotting out all but the first line — that is to say —

" 'The autumn leaves were falling, falling.'

"Unluckily, not having read the poem, I was unable to supply the incidents that followed; otherwise we could have given them in our own words.

If the news is not stale, and has not already appeared in the other papers, perhaps you will kindly relate what occurred, while I make notes of it. 'The autumn leaves were falling, falling.' Go on."

"What!" said the Poet, "do you expect me to reproduce the entire poem from memory?"

"Only the substance of it—just the leading facts. We will add whatever is necessary in the way of amplification and embellishment. It will detain you but a moment. 'The autumn leaves were falling, falling—' Now, then."

There was a sound of a slow getting up and going away. The chronicler of passing events sat through it, motionless, with suspended pen; and when the movement was complete Poesy was represented in that place by nothing but a warm spot on a chair.

242. At the Pole

After a great expenditure of life and treasure a Daring Explorer had succeeded in reaching the North Pole, when he was approached by a Native Galeut who lived there.

"Good morning," said the Native Galeut. "I'm very glad to see you, but why did you come here?"

"Glory," said the Daring Explorer, curtly.

"Yes, yes, I know," the other persisted; "but of what benefit to man is your discovery? To what truths does it give access which were inaccessible before?—facts, I mean, having a scientific value?"

"I'll be Tom scatted if I know," the great man replied, frankly; "you will have to ask the Scientist of the Expedition."

But the Scientist of the Expedition explained that he had been so engrossed with the care of his instruments and the study of his tables that he had found no time to think of it.

243. Party Manager and Gentleman

A Party Manager said to a Gentleman whom he saw minding his own business:

"How much will you pay for a nomination to office?"

"Nothing," the Gentleman replied.

"But you will contribute something to the campaign fund to assist in your election, will you not?" asked the Party Manager, winking.

"Oh, no," said the Gentleman, gravely. "If the people wish me to work for them they must hire me without solicitation. I am very comfortable without office."

"But," urged the Party Manager, "an election is a thing to be desired. It is a high honor to be a servant of the people."

"If servitude is a high honor," the Gentleman said, "it would be indecent for me to seek it; and if obtained by my own exertion it would be no honor."

"Well," persisted the Party Manager, "you will at least, I hope, indorse the party platform."

The Gentleman replied: "It is improbable that its authors have accurately expressed my views without consulting me; and if I indorsed their work without approving it I should be a liar."

"You are a detestable hypocrite and an idiot!" shouted the Party Manager.

"Even your good opinion of my fitness," replied the Gentleman, "shall not persuade me."

244. An Unspeakable Imbecile

A Judge said to a Convicted Assassin:

"Prisoner at the bar, have you anything to say why the death-sentence should not be passed upon you?"

"Will what I say make any difference?" asked the Convicted Assassin.

"I do not see how it can," the Judge answered, reflectively. "No, it will not."

"Then," said the doomed one, "I should just like to remark that you are the most unspeakable old imbecile in seven States and the District of Columbia."

245. Mine-Owner and Jackass

While the Owner of a Silver Mine was on his way to attend a convention of his species he was accosted by a Jackass, who said:

"By an unjust discrimination against quadrupeds I am made ineligible to a seat in your convention; so I am compelled to seek representation through you."

"It will give me great pleasure, sir," said the Owner of a Silver Mine, "to serve one so closely allied to me in — in — well, you know," he added, with a significant gesture of his two hands upward from the sides of his head. "What do you want?"

"Oh, nothing—nothing at all for myself individually," replied the Donkey; "but his country's welfare should be a patriot's supreme care. If Americans are to retain the sacred liberties for which their fathers strove Congress must declare our independence of European dictation by maintaining the price of mules."

246. A Needful War

The people of Kamzembla had an antipathy to the people of Novakatka and set upon some sailors of a Novakatkan vessel, killing two and wounding twelve. The King of Kamzembla having refused either to apologize or pay, the King of Novakatka made war upon him, saying that it was necessary to show that Novakatkans must not be slaughtered. In the battles that ensued the people of Kamzembla slaughtered two thousand Novakatkans and wounded twelve thousand. But the Kamzemblans were unsuccessful, which so chagrined them that never thereafter in all their land was a Novakatkan secure in property or life.

247. Dog and Doctor

A Dog that had seen a Doctor attending the burial of a wealthy patient, said: "When do you expect to dig it up?"

"Why should I dig it up?" the Doctor asked.

"When I bury a bone," said the Dog, "it is with an intention to uncover it later and pick it."

"The bones that I bury," said the Doctor, "are those that I can no longer pick."

248. Legislator and Citizen

A former Legislator asked a Most Respectable Citizen for a letter to the Governor, recommending him for appointment as Commissioner of Shrimps and Crabs.

"Sir," said the Most Respectable Citizen, austerely, "were you not once in the State Senate?"

"Not so bad as that, sir, I assure you," was the reply. "I was a member of the Slower House. I was expelled for selling my influence."

"And you dare to ask for mine!" shouted the Most Respectable Citizen.

"You have the impudence? A man who will accept bribes will probably offer them. Do you mean to—"

"I should not think of making a corrupt proposal to you, sir; but if I were Commissioner of Shrimps and Crabs I might have some influence with the waterfront population, and be able to help you make your fight for Coroner."

"In that case I do not feel justified in denying you the letter."

249. Citizen and Snakes

A Public-spirited Citizen who had failed miserably in trying to secure a National political convention for his city suffered acutely from dejection. While in that frame of mind he leaned thoughtlessly against a druggist's show-window, wherein were one hundred and fifty kinds of assorted snakes. The glass breaking, the reptiles all escaped into the street.

"When you can't do what you wish," said the Public-spirited Citizen, "it is worth while to do what you can."

250. The Rainmaker

An Officer of the Government, with a great outfit of mule-wagons loaded with balloons, kites, dynamite bombs and electrical apparatus, halted in the midst of a desert where there had been no rain for ten years and set up a camp. After several months of preparation and an expenditure of a million dollars all was in readiness, and a series of tremendous explosions occurred on the earth and in the sky. This was followed by a great downpour of rain, which washed the unfortunate Officer of the Government and the outfit off the face of creation and affected the agricultural heart with joy too deep for utterance. A Newspaper Reporter who had just arrived escaped by climbing a hill near by, and there he found the Sole Survivor of the expedition—a mule-driver—down on his knees behind a mesquite bush, praying with extreme fervor.

"Oh, you can't stop it that way," said the Reporter.

"My fellow-traveler to the bar of God," replied the Sole Survivor, looking up over his shoulder, "your understanding is in darkness. I am not stopping this great blessing; under Providence, I am bringing it."

"That is a pretty good joke," said the Reporter, laughing as well as he could in the strangling rain—"a mule-driver's prayer answered!"

"Child of levity and scoffing," replied the other; "you err again, misled by these humble habiliments. I am the Rev. Ezekiel Thrifft, a minister of the gospel, now in the service of the great manufacturing firm of Skinn & Sheer. They make balloons, kites, dynamite bombs and electrical apparatus."

251. Fortune and Fabulist

A Writer of Fables was passing through a lonely forest, when he met a Fortune. Greatly alarmed, he tried to climb a tree, but the Fortune pulled him down and bestowed itself upon him with cruel persistence.

"Why did you try to run away?" said the Fortune, when his struggles had ceased and his screams were stilled. "Why do you glare at me so inhospitably?"

"I don't know what you are," replied the Writer of Fables, deeply disturbed.

"I am wealth; I am respectability," the Fortune explained; "I am elegant houses, a yacht, and a clean shirt every day. I am leisure, I am travel, wine, a shiny hat and an unshiny coat. I am enough to eat."

"All right," said the Writer of Fables, in a whisper; "but for goodness' sake speak lower!"

"Why so?" the Fortune asked, in surprise.

"So as not to wake me," replied the Writer of Fables, a holy calm brooding upon his beautiful face.

252. A Smiling Idol

An Idol said to a Missionary, "My friend, why do you seek to bring me into contempt? If it had not been for me what would you have been? Remember thy creator that thy days be long in the land."

"I confess," replied the Missionary, fingering a number of ten-cent pieces which a Sunday-school in his own country had forwarded to him, "that I am a product of you, but I protest that you cannot quote Scripture with accuracy and point. Therefore will I continue to go up against you with the sword of the Spirit."

Shortly afterwards the Idol's worshipers held a great religious ceremony at the base of his pedestal, and as a part of the rites the Missionary was roasted whole. As the tongue was removed for the high priest's table, "Ah," said the Idol to himself, "that is the sword of the Spirit—the only sword that is less dangerous when unsheathed."

And he smiled so pleasantly at his own wit that the provinces of M'gwana and Scowow were affected with a blight.

253. Philosophers Three

A Bear, a Fox and an Opossum were attacked by an inundation.

"Death loves a coward," said the Bear, and went forward to fight the flood.

"What a fool!" said the Fox. "I know a trick worth two of that." And he slipped into a hollow stump.

"There are malevolent forces," said the Opossum, "which the wise will neither confront nor avoid. The thing is to know the nature of your antagonist."

So saying the Opossum lay down and pretended to be dead.

254. The Boneless King

Some Apes who had deposed their king fell at once into dissension and anarchy. In this strait they sent a Deputation to a neighboring tribe to consult the Oldest and Wisest Ape in All the World.

"My children," said the Oldest and Wisest Ape in All the World, when he had heard the Deputation, "you did right in ridding yourselves of tyranny, but your tribe is not sufficiently advanced to dispense with the forms of monarchy. Entice the tyrant back with fair promises, kill him and enthrone. The skeleton of even the most lawless despot makes a good constitutional sovereign."

At this the Deputation were greatly abashed. "It is impossible," they said, moving away; "our king has no skeleton; he was a stuffed king."

255. A Transposition

Traveling through the sage-brush country a Jackass met a Rabbit, who exclaimed in great astonishment:

"Good heavens! how did you grow so big? You are doubtless the largest rabbit living."

"No," said the Jackass, "you are the smallest donkey."

After a good deal of fruitless argument the question was referred for decision to a passing Coyote, who was a bit of a demagogue and desirous to stand well with both.

"Gentlemen," said he, "you are both right, as was to have been expected by persons so gifted with appliances for receiving instruction from the wise. You, sir," — turning to the superior animal — "are, as he has accurately observed, a rabbit. And you" — to the other — "are correctly described as a jackass. In transposing your names man has acted with incredible folly."

They were so pleased with the decision that they declared the Coyote their candidate for the Grizzly Bearship; but whether he ever obtained the office history does not relate.

256. Six and One

The Committee on Gerrymander worked late into the night drawing intricate lines on a map of the State, and being weary sought repose in a game of poker. At the close of the game the six Republican members were bankrupt and the single Democrat had all the money. On the next day, when the Committee was called to order for business, one of the luckless six mounted his legs, and said:

"Mr. Chairman, before we bend to our noble task of purifying politics in the interest of good government I wish to say a word of the untoward events of last evening. If my memory serves me the disasters which overtook the Majority of this honorable body always befell when it was the Minority's deal. It is my solemn conviction, Mr. Chairman, and to its affirmation I pledge my life, my sacred fortune and my honor, that that wicked and unscrupulous Minority redistricted the cards!"

257. Uncalculating Zeal

A man-eating tiger was ravaging the Kingdom of Damnasia, and the King, greatly concerned for the lives and limbs of his subjects, promised his daughter Zodroulra to any man who would kill the animal. After some days Camaraladdin appeared before the King and demanded the reward.

"But where is the tiger?" the King asked.

"May jackasses sing above my uncle's grave," replied Camaraladdin, "if I dared go within a league of him!"

"Wretch!" cried the King, unsheathing his consoler-under-disappointment; "how dare you claim my daughter when you have done nothing to earn her?"

"Thou art wiser, O King, than Solyman the Great, and thy servant is as dust in the tomb of thy dog, yet thou errest. I did not, it is true, kill the tiger, but behold! I have brought thee the scalp of the man who had accumulated five million pieces of gold and was after more."

The King drew his consoler-under-disappointment, and flicking off Camaraladdin's head said:

"Learn, caitiff, the expediency of uncalculating zeal. If the millionaire had been let alone he would have devoured the tiger."

258. The Honest Citizen

A Political Preferment, labeled with its price, was canvassing the State to find a purchaser. One day it offered itself to a Truly Good Man who after examining the label and finding that the price was twice as great as he was willing to pay spurned the Political Preferment from his door. Then the People said: "Behold, this is an honest citizen!" And the Truly Good Man humbly confessed that it was true.

259. A Creaking Tail

An American Statesman who had twisted the tail of the British Lion until his arms ached was at last rewarded by a sharp, rasping sound.

"I knew your fortitude would give out after a while," said the American Statesman, delighted; "your agony attests my political power."

"Agony I know not!" said the British Lion, yawning; "the swivel in my tail needs a few drops of oil, that is all."

260. Sportsman and Squirrel

A Sportsman who had wounded a Squirrel, which was making desperate efforts to drag itself away, ran after it with a stick, exclaiming:

"Poor thing! I will put it out of its misery."

At that moment the Squirrel stopped from exhaustion, and looking up at its enemy, said:

"I don't venture to doubt the sincerity of your compassion, though it comes rather late, but you seem to lack the faculty of observation. Do you not perceive by my actions that the dearest wish of my heart is to continue in my misery?"

At this exposure of his hypocrisy the Sportsman was so overcome with shame and remorse that he would not strike the Squirrel, but pointing it out to his dog, walked thoughtfully away.

261. Fogy and Sheik

A Fogy who lived in a cave near a great caravan route returned to his home one day and saw, near by, a great concourse of men and animals, and in their midst a tower, at the foot of which something with wheels smoked and panted like an exhausted horse. He sought the Sheik of the Outfit.

"What sin art thou committing now, O son of a Christian dog?" said the Fogy, with a truly Oriental politeness.

"Boring for water, you black-and-tan galoot!" replied the Sheik of the Outfit, with that ready repartee which distinguishes the Unbeliever.

"Knowest thou not, thou whelp of darkness and father of disordered livers," cried the Fogy, "that water will cause grass to spring up here, and trees and possibly even flowers? Knowest thou not that thou art, in truth, producing an oasis?"

"And don't you know," said the Sheik of the Outfit, "that caravans will then stop here for rest and refreshment, giving you a chance to steal the camels, the horses and the goods?"

"May the wild hog defile my grave, but thou speakest wisdom!" the Fogy replied, with the dignity of his race, extending his hand. "Sheik."

They shook.

262. At Heaven's Gate

Having arisen from the tomb, a Woman presented herself at the gate of Heaven, and knocked with a trembling hand.

"Madam," said Saint Peter, rising and approaching the wicket, "whence do you come?"

"From San Francisco," replied the Woman, with embarrassment, as great beads of perspiration spangled her spiritual brow.

"Never mind, my good girl," the Saint said, compassionately. "Eternity is a long time; you can live that down."

"But that, if you please, is not all." The Woman was growing more and more confused. "I poisoned my husband. I chopped up my babies. I—"

"Ah," said the Saint, with sudden austerity, "your confession suggests a very grave possibility. Were you a member of the Women's Press Association?"

The lady drew herself up and replied with warmth:

"I was not."

The gates of pearl and jasper swung back upon their golden hinges, making the most ravishing music, and the Saint, stepping aside, bowed low, saying:

"Enter, then, into thine eternal rest."

But the Woman hesitated.

"The poisoning — the chopping — the — the — " she stammered.

"Of no consequence, I assure you. We are not going to be hard on a lady who did not belong to the Women's Press Association. Take a harp."

"But I applied for membership — I was blackballed."

"Take two harps."

263. Wasted Sweets

A Candidate canvassing his district met a Nurse wheeling a Baby in a carriage and, stooping, imprinted a kiss upon the Baby's clammy muzzle. Rising, he saw a Man, who laughed.

"Why do you laugh?" asked the Candidate.

"Because," replied the Man, "the Baby belongs to an Orphan Asylum."

"But the Nurse," said the Candidate — "the Nurse will surely relate the touching incident wherever she goes, and perhaps write to her former master."

"The Nurse," said the Man who had laughed, "is an illiterate mute."

264. The Catted Anarchist

An Anarchist Orator who had been struck in the face with a Dead Cat by some Respector of Law to him unknown, had the Dead Cat arrested and taken before a Magistrate.

"Why do you appeal to the law?" said the Magistrate — "you who go in for the abolition of law."

"That," replied the Anarchist, who was not without a certain hardness of head, "that is none of your business; I am not bound to be consistent. You sit here to do justice between me and this Dead Cat."

"Very well," said the Magistrate, putting on the black cap and a solemn look; "as the accused makes no defence, and is undoubtedly guilty, I sentence her to be eaten by the public executioner; and as that position happens to be vacant, I appoint you to it, without bonds."

One of the most delighted spectators at the execution was the unknown Respector of Law who had flung the condemned.

265. The Honorable Member

A member of a Legislature who had pledged himself to his Constituents not to steal brought home at the end of the session a large part of the dome of the Capitol. Thereupon the Constituents held an indignation meeting and passed a resolution of tar and feathers.

"You are most unjust," said the Member of the Legislature. "It is true I promised you I would not steal; but had I ever promised you that I would not lie?"

The Constituents said he was an honorable man and elected him to the United States Congress, unpledged and unfledged.

266. The Expatriated Boss

A Boss who had gone to Canada was taunted by a Citizen of Montreal with having fled to avoid prosecution.

"You do me a grave injustice," said the Boss, parting with a pair of tears. "I came to Canada solely because of its political attractions; its Government is the most corrupt in the world."

"Pray forgive me," said the Citizen of Montreal.

They fell upon each other's neck, and at the conclusion of that touching rite the Boss had two watches.

267. An Inadequate Fee

An Ox unable to extricate himself from the mire into which he sank was advised to make use of a Political Pull. When the Political Pull had arrived the Ox said: "My good friend, please make fast to me and let nature take her course."

So the Political Pull made fast to the Ox's head and nature took her course: the Ox was drawn, first, from the mire and next from his skin. Then the Political Pull looked back upon the good fat carcass of beef that he was dragging to his lair and said, with a discontented spirit:

"That is hardly my customary fee; I'll take home this first instalment, then return for the skin."

268. A Statesman

A Statesman who attended a meeting of a Chamber of Commerce rose to speak, but was objected to on the ground that he had nothing to do with commerce.

"Mr. Chairman," said an Aged Member, rising, "I conceive that the objection is not well taken; the gentleman's connection with commerce is close and intimate. He is a commodity."

269. Two Dogs

The Dog as created had a rigid tail, but after some centuries of a cheerless existence, unappreciated by Man, who made him work for his living, he implored the Creator to endow him with a wag. This being done he was able to dissemble his resentment with a sign of affection, and the earth was his and the fulness thereof. Observing this, the Politician (an animal created later) petitioned that a wag might be given him too. As he was incaudate it was conferred upon his chin, which he now wags with great profit and gratification except when he is at his meals.

270. Judge and Plaintiff

A Man of Experience in Business was awaiting the judgment of the Court in an action for damages that he had brought against a railway company. The door opened and the Judge of the Court entered.

"Well," said he, "I am going to decide your case to-day. If I should decide in your favor I wonder how you would express your satisfaction?"

"Sir," said the Man of Experience in Business, "I should risk your anger by offering you one-half the sum awarded."

"Did I say I was going to decide that case?" said the Judge, abruptly, as if awakening from a dream. "Dear me, how absent-minded I am! I mean I have already decided it, and judgment has been entered for the full amount that you sued for."

"Did I say I would give you one-half?" said the Man of Experience in Business, coldly. "Dear me, how near I came to being a rascal! I mean, that I am greatly obliged to you."

271. Return of the Representative

Hearing that the Legislature had adjourned, the people of an Assembly District held a mass-meeting to devise a suitable punishment for their Dishonorable Representative. By one speaker it was proposed that he be disembowelled, by another that he be made to run the gauntlet. Some favored hanging, some thought that it would do him good to appear in a suit of tar and feathers. An Old Man famous for his wisdom and his habit of drooling on his shirt-front suggested that they first catch their hare. So the Chairman appointed a committee to watch for the victim at midnight and take him as he should attempt to sneak into town across-lots from the tamarack swamp. At this point in the proceedings they were interrupted by the sound of a brass band. Their Dishonorable Representative was driving up from the railway station in a coach-and-four, with music and a banner. A few moments later he entered the hall, went upon the platform and said it was the proudest moment of his life. (Cheers.)

272. The Mirror

A silken-eared Spaniel who traced his descent from King Charles the Second chanced to look into a mirror that was leaning against the wainscoting of a room on the ground floor of his mistress' house. Seeing his reflection, he supposed it to be another dog, outside, and said:

"I can chew up any such milksoppy pup as that, and I will."

So he ran out-of-doors and around to the side of the house where he fancied the enemy was. It so happened that at that moment a Bulldog sat there sunning his teeth. The Spaniel stopped short in dire consternation and after regarding the Bulldog a moment from a safe distance said:

"I don't know whether you cultivate the arts of peace or your flag is flung to the battle and the breeze and your voice is for war. If you are a civilian the windows of this house flatter you worse than a newspaper, but if you're a soldier they do you a grave injustice."

This speech being unintelligible to the Bulldog he only civilly smiled, which so terrified the Spaniel that he dropped dead in his tracks.

273. Saint and Sinner

"My friend," said a distinguished officer of the Salvation Army to a Most Wicked Sinner, "I was once a drunkard, a thief, an assassin. The Divine Grace has made me what I am."

The Most Wicked Sinner looked at him from head to foot. "Henceforth," he said, "the Divine Grace, I fancy, will let well enough alone."

274. A Weary Echo

A Convention of female writers, which for two days had been stuffing Woman's couch with goose-quills and hailing the down of a new era, adjourned with unabated enthusiasm, shouting, *"Place aux dames!"* And Echo wearily replied, "Oh, damn."

275. Three Recruits

A Farmer, an Artisan and a Laborer went to the King of their country and complained that they were compelled to support a large standing army of consumers, who did nothing for their keep.

"Very well," said the King, "my subjects' wishes are the highest law."

So he disbanded his army and the consumers became producers also. The sale of their products so brought down prices that farming was ruined and their skilled and unskilled labor drove artisans and laborers into almshouses and highways. In a few years the national distress was so great that the Farmer, the Artisan and the Laborer petitioned the King to restore the standing army.

"What!" said the King; "you wish to support those idle consumers again?"

"No, your Majesty," they replied — "we wish to enlist."

276. The Ancient Order

Hardly had that ancient order, the Sultans of Exceeding Splendor, been completely founded by the Grand Flashing Inaccessible, when a question arose as to what should be the title of address among the members. Some wanted it to be simply "my lord," others held out for "your dukeness," and still others preferred "my sovereign liege." Finally the gorgeous jewel of the order gleaming upon the breast of every member suggested "your badgesty," which was adopted and the order became popularly known as the Kings of Catarrh.

277. A Fatal Disorder

A Dying Man who had been shot was requested by officers of the law to make a statement and be quick about it.

"You were assaulted without provocation, of course," said the District Attorney preparing to set down the answer.

"No," replied the Dying Man, "I was the aggressor."

"Yes, I understand," said the District Attorney; "you committed the aggression—you were compelled to, as it were. You did it in self-defence."

"I don't think he would have hurt me if I had let him alone," said the other. "No, I fancy he was a man of peace and would not have hurt a fly. I brought such a pressure to bear on him that he naturally had to yield—he couldn't hold out. If he had refused to shoot me I don't see how I could decently have continued his acquaintance."

"Good Heavens!" exclaimed the District Attorney, throwing down his notebook and pencil; "this is all quite irregular. I can't make use of such an ante-mortem statement as that."

"I never before knew a man to tell the truth," said the Chief of Police, "when dying of violence."

"Violence nothing!" the Police Surgeon said, pulling out and inspecting the man's tongue—"it is the truth that is killing him."

278. A Talisman

Having been summoned to serve as a juror, a Prominent Citizen sent a physician's certificate stating that he was afflicted with softening of the brain.

"The gentleman is excused," said the Judge, handing back the certificate to the person who had brought it—"he has a brain."

279. An Antidote

A Young Ostrich came to its Mother, groaning with pain and with its wings tightly crossed upon its stomach.

"What have you been eating?" the Mother asked, with solicitude.

"Nothing but a keg of nails," was the reply.

"What!" exclaimed the Mother; "a whole keg of nails, at your age! Why, you will kill yourself that way. Go quickly, my child, and swallow a claw-hammer."

280. Congress and People

Successive Congresses having greatly impoverished the People, they were discouraged and wept copiously.

"Why do you weep?" inquired an Angel who had perched upon a tree near by.

"They have taken all we have," replied the People — "excepting," they added, noting the suggestive visitant — "excepting our hope in Heaven. Thank God, they cannot deprive us of that!"

But at last came the Congress of 1889!

281. Ship and Man

Seeing a ship sailing by upon the sea of politics, toward the Presidency, an Ambitious Person started in hot pursuit along the strand; but the people's eyes being fixed upon the ship no one observed the pursuer. This greatly annoyed him and, recollecting that he was not aquatic, he stopped and shouted across the waves' tumultuous roar:

"Take my name off the passenger list."

Back to him over the waters, hollow and heartless, like laughter in a tomb, rang the voice of the Skipper:

" 'Tain't on!"

And there, in the focus of a million pairs of convergent eyes, the Ambitious Person sat him down between the sun and moon and murmured sadly to his own soul:

"Marooned, by thunder!"

282. The Justice and His Accuser

An eminent Justice of the Supreme Court of Gowk was accused of having obtained his appointment by fraud.

"You wander," he said to the Accuser; "it is of little importance how I obtained my power; it is only important how I have used it."

"I confess," said the Accuser, "that in comparison with the rascally way in which you have conducted yourself on the Bench the rascally way in which you got there does seem rather a trifle."

283. An Ærophobe

A Celebrated Divine having affirmed the fallibility of the Bible, was asked why, then, he preached the religion founded on it.

"If it is fallible," he replied, "there is the greater reason that I explain it, lest it mislead."

"Then am I to infer," said his Questioner, "that *you* are not fallible?"

"You are to infer that I am not pneumophagous."

284. The Thrift of Strength

A Weak Man going down-hill met a Strong Man going up, and said:

"I take this direction because it requires less exertion, not from choice. I pray you, sir, assist me to regain the summit."

"Gladly," said the Strong Man, his face illuminated with the glory of his thought. "I have always considered my strength a sacred gift in trust for my fellow-men. I will take you up with me. Go behind me and push."

285. The Tyrant Frog

A Snake swallowing a frog head-first was approached by a Naturalist with a stick.

"Ah, my deliverer," said the Snake as well as he could, "you have arrived just in time; this reptile, you see, is pitching into me without provocation."

"Sir," replied the Naturalist, "I need a snakeskin for my collection, but if you had not explained I should not have molested you, for I thought you were at dinner."

286. Two Politicians

Two Politicians were exchanging ideas regarding the rewards for public service.

"The reward that I most desire," said the First Politician, "is the gratitude of my fellow citizens."

"That would be very gratifying, no doubt," said the Second Politician, "but, alas! in order to obtain it one has to retire from politics."

For an instant they gazed upon each other with inexpressible tenderness; then the First Politician murmured, "God's will be done! Since we cannot hope for reward let us be content with what we have."

And lifting their right hands for a moment from the public treasury they swore to be content.

287. The Fugitive Office

A Traveler arriving at the capital of a nation saw a vast plain outside the wall, filled with struggling and shouting men. While he looked upon the alarming spectacle an Office broke away from the throng and took shelter in a tomb near to where he stood, the crowd being too intent upon hammering one another to observe that the cause of their contention had departed.

"Poor bruised and bleeding creature," said the compassionate Traveler, "what was your offence?"

"I 'sought the man,'" said the Office.

288. Highwayman and Traveler

A Highwayman confronted a Traveler, and covering him with a firearm, shouted: "Your money or your life!"

"My good friend," said the Traveler, "according to the terms of your demand my money will save my life, my life my money; you imply that you will take one or the other, but not both. If that is what you mean please be good enough to take my life."

"That is not what I mean," said the Highwayman; "you cannot save your money by giving up your life."

"Then take it anyhow," the Traveler said. "If it will not save my money it is good for nothing."

The Highwayman was so pleased with the Traveler's philosophy and wit that he took him into partnership and this splendid combination of talent started a newspaper.

289. The Eligible Son-in-Law

A Truly Clever Person who conducted a savings bank and lent money to his sisters and his cousins and his aunts was approached by a Tatterdemalion who applied for a loan of one hundred thousand dollars.

"What security have you to offer?" asked the Truly Clever Person.

"The best in the world," the applicant replied, confidentially; "I am about to become your son-in-law."

"That would indeed be gilt-edged," said the Banker, gravely; "but what claim have you to the hand of my daughter?"

"One that cannot be lightly denied," said the Tatterdemalion. "I am about to become worth one hundred thousand dollars."

Unable to detect a weak point in this scheme of mutual advantage, the Financier gave the Promoter in Disguise an order for the money and wrote a note to his wife directing her to count out the girl.

290. Statesman and Horse

A Statesman who had saved his country was returning from Washington on foot, when he met a Race Horse going at full speed, and stopped him.

"Turn about and travel the other way," said the Statesman, "and I will keep you company as far as my home. The advantages of traveling together are obvious."

"I cannot do that," said the Race Horse; "I am following my master to Washington. I did not go fast enough to suit him, and he has gone on ahead."

"Who is your master?" inquired the Statesman.

"He is a Statesman who saved his country," answered the Race Horse.

"There appears to be some mistake," the other said. "Why did he wish to travel so fast?"

"So as to be there in time to get the country that he saved."

"I guess he got it," said the other, and limped along, sighing.

291. Policeman and Citizen

A Policeman finding a man who had fallen in a fit said, "This man is drunk," and began beating him on the head with his club. A passing Citizen said:

"Why do you murder a man that is already harmless?"

Thereupon the Policeman left the man in a fit and attacked the Citizen, who after receiving several severe contusions ran away.

"Alas," said the Policeman, "why did I not attack the sober one before exhausting myself upon the other?"

Thenceforward he pursued that plan, and by zeal and diligence rose to be Chief, and sobriety is unknown in the region subject to his sway.

292. Man and Bird

A Man with a Shotgun said to a Bird:

"It is all nonsense, you know, about shooting being a cruel sport. I put my skill against your cunning—that is all there is of it. It is a fair game."

"True," said the Bird, "but I don't wish to play."

"Why not?" inquired the Man with a Shotgun.

"The game," the Bird replied, "is fair as you say; the chances are about even; but consider the stake. I am in it for you, but what is there in it for me?"

Not being prepared with an answer to the question, the Man with a Shotgun sagaciously removed the propounder.

293. Writer and Tramps

An Ambitious Writer distinguished for the condition of his linen was traveling the high road to fame, when he met a Tramp.

"What is the matter with your shirt?" inquired the Tramp.

"It bears the marks of that superb unconcern which is the characteristic of genius," replied the Ambitious Writer, contemptuously passing him by.

Resting by the wayside a little later, the Tramp carved upon the smooth bark of a birch-tree the words, "John Gump, Champion Genius."

294. The Good Government

"What a happy land you are!" said a Republican Form of Government to a Sovereign State. "Be good enough to lie still while I walk upon you, singing the praises of universal suffrage and descanting upon the blessings of civil and religious liberty. In the meantime you can relieve your feelings by cursing the one-man power and the effete monarchies of Europe."

"My public servants have been fools and rogues from the date of your accession to power," replied the State; "my legislative bodies, both State and municipal, are bands of thieves; my taxes are insupportable; my courts are corrupt; my cities are a disgrace to civilization; my corporations have their hands at the throats of every private interest—all my affairs are in disorder and criminal confusion."

"That is all very true," said the Republican Form of Government, putting on its hobnail shoes; "but consider how I thrill you every Fourth of July."

295. Three of a Kind

A Lawyer was retained for the defence of a Burglar whom the police had taken after a desperate struggle with someone not in custody. In consultation with his client the Lawyer asked, "Have you accomplices?"

"Yes, sir," replied the Burglar. "I have two, but neither has been taken. I hired one to defend me against capture and you to defend me against conviction."

This answer deeply impressed the Lawyer, and having ascertained that the Burglar had accumulated no money in his profession he threw up the case.

296. The Lifesaver

An Ancient Maiden, standing on the edge of a wharf near a Modern Swain, was overheard rehearsing the words:

"Noble preserver! The life that you have saved is yours!"

Having repeated them several times with various intonations, she sprang into the water, where she was suffered to drown.

"I am a noble preserver," said the Modern Swain, thoughtfully moving away; "the life that I have saved is indeed mine."

297. From the Minutes

An Orator afflicted with atrophy of the organ of common-sense rose in his place in the halls of legislation and pointed with pride to his Unblotted Escutcheon. Seeing what it supposed to be the finger of scorn pointed at it, the Unblotted Escutcheon turned black with rage. Seeing the Unblotted Escutcheon turning black with what he supposed to be the record of his own misdeeds showing through the whitewash, the Orator fell dead of mortification. Seeing the Orator fall dead of what they supposed to be atrophy of the organ of common-sense, his colleagues resolved that whenever they should adjourn because they were tired it should be out of respect to the memory of him who had so frequently made them so.

298. The Fabulist

An Illustrious Satirist was visiting a traveling menagerie with a view to collecting literary materials. As he was passing near the Elephant that animal said:

"How sad that so justly famous a censor should mar his work by ridicule of persons with pendulous noses — who are the salt of the earth!"

The Kangaroo said:

"I do so enjoy that great man's censure of the ridiculous — particularly his attacks on the proboscidæ; but, alas! he has no reverence for the marsupials, and laughs at our way of carrying our young in a pouch."

The Camel said:

"If he would only respect the sacred Hump, he would be faultless. As it is, I can not permit his work to be read in the presence of my family."

The Ostrich, seeing his approach, thrust her head in the straw, saying:

"If I do not conceal myself, he may be reminded to write something disagreeable about my lack of a crest, or my appetite for scrap-iron; and although he is inexpressibly brilliant when he devotes himself to ridicule of folly and greed, his dulness is matchless when he transcends the limits of legitimate comment."

"That," said the Buzzard to his mate, "is the distinguished author of that glorious fable, 'The Ostrich and the Keg of Raw Nails.' I regret to add, that he wrote also, 'The Buzzard's Feast,' in which a carrion diet is contumeliously disparaged. A carrion diet is the foundation of sound health. If nothing else but corpses were eaten, death would be unknown."

Seeing an attendant approaching, the Illustrious Satirist passed out of the tent and mingled with the crowd. It was afterward discovered that he had crept in under the canvas without paying.

299. A Revivalist Revived

A Revivalist who had fallen dead in the pulpit from too violent religious exercise was astonished to wake up in Hades. He promptly sent for the Adversary of Souls and demanded his freedom, explaining that he was entirely orthodox, and had always led a pious and holy life.

"That is all very true," said the Adversary, "but you taught by example that a verb should not agree with its subject in person and number, whereas the Good Book says that contention is worse than a dinner of herbs. You also tried to release the objective case from its thraldom to the preposition, and it is written that servants should obey their masters. You stay right here."

300. The Debaters

A Hurled-back Allegation which after a brief rest had again started forth upon its mission of mischief met an Inkstand in mid-air.

"How did the Honorable Member whom you represent know that I was coming again?" inquired the Hurled-back Allegation.

"He did not," the Inkstand replied; "he isn't at all forehanded at repartee."

"Why, then, do you come, things being even when he had hurled me back?"

"He wanted to be a little ahead."

301. Two of the Pious

A Christian and a Heathen in His Blindness were disputing, when the Christian, with that charming consideration which serves to distinguish the truly pious from wolves that perish, exclaimed:

"If I could have my way I'd blow up all your gods with dynamite."

"And if I could have mine," retorted the Heathen in His Blindness, bitterly malevolent but oleaginuously suave, "I'd fan all yours out of the universe."

302. The Desperate Object

A Dishonest Gain was driving in its luxurious carriage through its private park, when it saw something which frantically and repeatedly ran against a stone wall, endeavoring to butt out its brains.

"Hold, hold! thou desperate Object," cried the Dishonest Gain; "these beautiful private grounds are no place for such work as thine."

"True," said the Object, pausing; "I have other and better grounds for it."

"Then thou art a happy man," said the Dishonest Gain, "and thy bleeding head is but mere dissembling. Who art thou, great actor?"

"I am known," said the Object, dashing itself again at the wall, "as the Consciousness of Duty Well Performed."

303. The Mourning Brothers

Observing that he was about to die, an Old Man called his two Sons to his bedside and expounded the situation.

"My children," said he, "you have not shown me many marks of respect during my life, but you will attest your sorrow for my death. To him who the longer wears a weed upon his hat in memory of me shall go my entire fortune. I have made a will to that effect."

So when the Old Man was dead each of the youths put a weed upon his hat and wore it until he was himself old, when, seeing that neither would give in, they agreed that the younger should leave off his weeds and the elder give him half the estate. But when the elder applied for the property he found that there had been an Executor!

Thus were hypocrisy and obstinacy fitly punished.

304. A Needless Labor

After waiting many a weary day to revenge himself upon a Lion for some un-considered manifestation of contempt, a Skunk finally saw him coming and posting himself in the path ahead uttered the inaudible discord of his race. Observing that the Lion gave no attention to the matter, the Skunk, keeping carefully out of reach, said:

"Sir, I beg leave to point out that I have set on foot an implacable odor."

"My dear fellow," the Lion replied, "you have taken a needless trouble; I already knew that you are not a rose."

305. A Flourishing Industry

"Are the industries of this country in a flourishing condition?" asked a Trav-eler from a Foreign Land of the first Man he met in America.

"Splendid!" said the Man. "I have more orders than I can fill."

"What is your business?" the Traveler from a Foreign Land inquired.

The Man replied, "I make boxing-gloves for the tongues of pugilists."

306. Patriot and Banker

A Patriot who had taken office poor and retired rich was introduced at a bank where he desired to open an account.

"With pleasure," said the Honest Banker; "we shall be glad to do busi-ness with you; but first you must make yourself an honest man by restoring what you stole from the Government."

"Good heavens!" cried the Patriot; "if I do that, I shall have nothing to deposit with you."

"I don't see that," the Honest Banker replied. "We are not the whole American people."

"Ah, I understand," said the Patriot, musing. "At what sum do you estimate this bank's proportion of the country's loss by me?"

"About a dollar," answered the Honest Banker.

And with a proud consciousness of serving his country wisely and well he charged that sum to the account.

307. The Appropriate Memorial

A High Public Functionary having died, the citizens of his town held a meeting to consider how to honor his memory, and Another High Public Functionary rose and addressed the meeting.

"Mr. Chairman and Gintlemen," said the Other, "it sames to me, and I'm hopin' yez wull approve the suggistion, that an appropriet way to honor the mimory of the deceased would be to erect an emolument sootably inscribed wid his vartues."

The soul of the great man looked down from Heaven and wept.

308. A Defective Petition

An Associate Justice of the Supreme Court was sitting by a river when a Traveler approached and said:

"I wish to cross. Will it be lawful to use this boat?"

"It will," was the reply; "it is my boat."

The Traveler thanked him, and pushing the boat into the water embarked and rowed away. But the boat sank and he was drowned.

"Heartless man!" said an Indignant Spectator. "Why did you not tell him that your boat had a hole in it?"

"The matter of the boat's condition," said the great jurist, "was not brought before me."

309. The Disinterested Arbiter

Two Dogs who had been fighting for a bone, without advantage to either, referred their dispute to a Sheep. The Sheep patiently heard their statements, then flung the bone into a pond.

"Why did you do that?" said the Dogs.

"Because," replied the Sheep, "I am a vegetarian."

310. The Reformed Anarchist

A famous Anarchist wrecked at sea was cast ashore upon the island of Gowqueechy, inhabited by the ancient and powerful tribe of Tumtums. He was found and taken before the Jamgrogrum, who asked him his political faith.

"We ask all strangers that," the Jamgrogrum explained, "in the hope that some day we shall hear of political principles that are superior to ours."

"I am an Anarchist," answered the stranger; "I hold that all government is wicked, all laws are oppressive. I teach that all Jamgrogra should be assassinated."

The monarch called his Prime Minister to his side and giving him some whispered instructions retired.

The next day, when the Prime Minister had presented himself at the palace and had eaten a handful of clay, as court etiquette required, he was asked by the Jamgrogrum for news of the Anarchist.

"May your Majesty's tomb stand forever," said the Prime Minister. "I had him taken to the baths and carefully washed all over."

"Well?"

"When asked, according to your Majesty's instructions, if he were still an Anarchist, he replied that no treatment, however harsh and cruel, could alter his convictions."

"Indeed," exclaimed the Jamgrogrum, with the dejected air of one deprived of a cherished illusion, "then my theory of the unity of dirt and anarchism is overthrown."

"No, your Majesty," said the Prime Minister; "he died ten minutes after the bath."

311. Two Sons

A Man had Two Sons. The elder was virtuous and dutiful, the younger wicked and crafty. When the father was about to die, he called them before him and said: "I have only two things of value — my herd of camels and my blessing. How shall I allot them?"

"Give to me," said the Younger Son, "thy blessing, for it may reform me. The camels I should be sure to sell and squander the money."

The Elder Son, disguising his joy, said that he would try to be content with the camels and a pious mind.

It was so arranged and the Man died. Then the wicked Younger Son went before the Cadi and said: "Behold, my brother has defrauded me of my lawful heritage. He is so bad that our father, as is well known, denied him his blessing; is it likely that he gave him the camels?"

So the Elder Son was compelled to give up the herd and was soundly bastinadoed for his rapacity.

312. The Fortunate Explorer

An Emissary from the President of the United States to the Emperor of Abyssinia was taking leave of that sovereign, who, to attest his regret according to the custom of his country, let fall a flood of tears.

"My fame is assured," said the Emissary; "I have discovered the source of the Nile."

313. The Dutiful Son

A Millionaire who had gone to an almshouse to visit his father met a Neighbor there, who was greatly surprised.

"What!" said the Neighbor, "you do sometimes visit your father?"

"If our situations were reversed," said the Millionaire, "I am sure he would visit me. The old man has always been rather proud of me. Besides," he added softly, "I had to have his signature; I am insuring his life."

314. Widow and Soldier

A Widow whose husband had been hanged in chains was keeping vigil by the corpse the first night and tearfully beseeching the Sentinel who gaurded it to let her steal it.

"Madam," he said, "I can no longer resist your entreaties; your beauty overcomes my sense of duty. I will deliver the body to you and take its place in the cage, where a stroke of my dagger will baffle justice and give me the happiness of dying for so lovely a lady."

"No," said the lady, "I cannot consent to the sacrifice of so noble a life. If indeed you look upon me with favor, assist me and my servants to remove the sacred object to my chateau, where you shall remain in concealment until we can escape from the country."

"Nay," said the Sentinel, "I should surely be discovered and torn from your arms. In three days you can claim the body of your beloved husband; then you can confer upon an honorable soldier such happiness and distinction as you may think his devotion merits."

"Three days!" the lady exclaimed. "That is long for waiting and short for flight. If unincumbered we may reach the frontier. Already the day begins to break—let us leave the body and set out."

315. A Niggardly Offer

Two Soldiers lay dead upon the field of honor.

"What would you give to be alive again?" one asked the other.

"To the enemy, victory," was the reply, "to my country, a long life of disinterested service as a civilian. What would you give?"

"The plaudits of my countrymen."

"You are a pretty tight-fisted bargainer," said the other.

316. Diplomacy

"If you do not submit my claim to arbitration," wrote the President of Omohu to the President of Modugy, "I shall take immediate steps to collect it in my own way!"

"Sir," replied the President of Modugy, "you may go to the devil with your threat of war."

"My great and good friend," wrote the other, "you mistake the character of my communication. It is an antepenultimatum."

317. Two Sceptics

Some heathens whose Idol was greatly weatherworn threw it into a river, and erecting a new one, engaged in public worship at its base.

"What is this all about?" inquired the New Idol.

"Father of Joy and Gore," said the High Priest, "be patient and I will instruct you in the doctrines and rites of our holy religion."

A year later, after a course of study in theology, the Idol asked to be thrown into the river, declaring himself an atheist.

"Do not let that trouble you," said the High Priest—"so am I."

318. A Faulty Performance

A pet Opossum belonging to a Great Critic stole his favorite kitten and was about to kill and eat it when she saw him approaching, and fearing detection she concealed it in her pouch.

"Well, my pretty one," said the Great Critic, with condescension, "what new charms and graces have you to-day?"

Before she could reply the kitten set up a diligent and persistent mewing. When at last the music had ceased the Opossum said:

"I've been dabbling a little in mimicry and ventriloquism; I thought it would please you, sir."

"The desire to please is ever pleasing," the Great Critic answered, not without a touch of professional dignity, "but you have much to learn about the mewing of kittens."

319. Aftermath

"What is that great convulsion of nature?" Neptune asked, turning one ear upward toward the surface of the sea.

"That, sir," replied a Triton, "is a furious engagement by the heroes of the Senegambian Navy."

"So soon again?" said the sea god in surprise. "And whom, pray, are they fighting this time?"

"One another," the Triton explained. "They have fallen out over their recent exploit in sinking the Timbuctonese fleet."

Neptune rose from his couch of coral and paced the ocean's floor with the nervous, irregular strides of one in anger. "See here!" he thundered, "we can't have this kind of thing! When I saw those squadrons fighting I felt that trouble would come of it. A sea fight is pretty to look at, and the music of guns lulls like the evensong of a mermaid in the gloaming, but always the entertainment is prelude to a savage and insupportable uproar among the victors. The next time you see sailors fighting at sea please prevent a disagreeable result by sinking both fleets."

320. The Plaudits of the People

A Man who had been mentioned for high political preferment explained through the newspapers that he was "not a candidate." Thereupon he was lustily cheered by the populace.

"Why do you not cheer?" some one asked a Silent Person standing moodily apart.

"Because," answered the Silent Person, "I understand these plaudits to be given for his humility. Whenever you raise the shout for his knowledge of the English language you can count on the assistance of both my lungs."

"Why, how is that?" asked those who stood nearest.

"A 'candidate' is one who has been nominated," said the Silent Person. "He has not succeeded, as yet, in moving Heaven and Earth sufficiently to procure that distinction."

321. A Half Loaf

Having found the Enemy's fleet in a harbor, the Scourge of the Seas sank a collier in the narrow entrance; and then from his cavernous helmet his merriment rang out over the waters like laughter from a tomb.

"Why this unseemly glee?" the Enemy signaled. "That hulk prevents my coming out."

"I know that, alas!" the Scourge wigwagged back; "but it prevents my going in. That is better than no bread."

322. By the River Marge

Seeing a Politician taking a bath an Observer, curious as to the singular habits of the lower animals, exclaimed:

"What! is nothing left for you to take more valuable than that? Why do you do this thing?"

"I have been in the hands of my friends," replied the Politician.

"Then I should suggest skinning," the Observer said.

"My friend, you are late: somebody suggested it to *them*. I am cleaning the finger marks off my bones."

323. The Main Thing

A Poet proffering his work to an Editor said:

"This is a small poem, but quality is the main thing. I venture to think you'll find it true poetry."

Having read it the Editor put it into a drawer and handing the Poet a ten-cent piece said:

"This is a smallish coin, but I am so bold as to hope that you will be pleased with its purity. It is nearly all silver."

324. The Incredulous Subordinate

A Commanding General retreating after defeat came upon the camp of a Subordinate, who was playing cards with his men.

"Why did you not march to my assistance, sir?" thundered the Commanding General. "Did you not hear the reports of my guns?"

"Reports? O, yes," the Subordinate replied. "I heard them all right, but I did not believe them. I used to be a reporter."

325. The Secret of Happiness

Having been told by an angel that Noureddin Becar was the happiest man in the world, the Sultan caused him to be brought to the palace and said:

"Impart to me, I command thee, the secret of thy happiness."

"O father of the sun and the moon," answered Noureddin Becar, "I did not know that I was happy."

"That," said the Sultan, "is the secret that I sought."

Noureddin Becar retired in deep dejection, fearing that his new-found happiness might forsake him.

326. Atonement

Two Women in heaven claimed one Man newly arrived.

"I was his wife," said one.

"I his sweetheart," said the other.

St. Peter said to the Man: "Go down to the Other Place—you have suffered enough."

327. A Part of the Wages

"Ours is a life of self-sacrifice," said a Clergyman. "While others pursue gain or pleasure we burn the midnight oil in studying how to crack the hardest theological nuts. And all for what earthly reward?"

"Well," said his Parishioner, thoughtfully, "there are, for example, the kernels."

328. Two Parrots

An Author who had made a fortune by writing slang had a Parrot.

"Why have I not a gold cage?" asked the bird.

"Because," said its master, "you are a better thinker than repeater, as your question shows. And we have not the same audience."

329. Twin Intolerables

A Rattlesnake observing the approach of a Man with a Camera crept under a flat stone, leaving nothing exposed but the tip of his nose.

"I was not going to photograph you," the Man with a Camera explained with a touch of sadness in his voice. "Holding the ancient faith in the divine wisdom of serpents, I have come to ask you why I am hated and shunned by all mankind."

"Alas," said the Rattlesnake, "the gods have denied me that knowledge. Can you tell me why I am myself not very much sought after as a companion?"

330. Consolation

A great country having vindicated its courage and prowess by fifteen defeats in which none of its enemy's troops suffered any damage, its Prime Minister sued for peace.

"I'll not be hard on you," said the Victor: "you shall keep everything except your colonies, your liberty, your credit and your self-respect."

"Ah," said the Prime Minister, "you are indeed magnanimous; you leave us our honor."

331. Famine versus Pestilence

"It is hard on you, my gallant friend," said the Victorious Besieger, "but I must say it. Pestilence was among my troops, and if you had not surrendered to me I should have surrendered to you."

"That is what I feared you would do," replied the Vanquished Commander. "My men were eating their belts and cartridge boxes; we could not properly provide for you."

332. The Monarchist Reclaimed

A recreant Citizen of a Great Republic went abroad, hoping to shine in "the fierce light that beats upon a throne." While intriguing to be presented at the court of a fly-speck principality, he fell asleep and dreamed that he was visited by an Angel wearing the robes of a lord high chamberlain.

"Come," said the Angel; "I will present you to all the crowned heads of Europe."

Miraculously conveyed through the air, they arrived at the portal of a vast building. The visitor's name and his rank in the order of the Dukes of Trade were announced, the great iron doors swung open and he found himself in the presence of all the crowned heads of Europe. The bodies had been carted away by the public scavenger.

The royal pageant so disappointed him that he awoke with a sigh, and returning to the land of the free, he plunged into patriotism, became a leader of the Mobocratic party and died an illustrious statesman with both hands in the public treasury.

333. Saint and Soul

St. Peter was sitting at the gate of Heaven when a Soul approached, and, bowing civilly, handed him its card.

"I am very sorry, sir," said St. Peter, after reading the card, "but I really cannot admit you. You will have to go to the Other Place. Sorry, sir, very sorry."

"Don't mention it," said the Soul; "I have been all the month at a watering place, and it will be an agreeable change. I called only to ask if my friend Elihu Root is here."

"No, sir," the Saint replied; "Mr. Root is not dead."

"O, I know that," said the Soul. "I thought he might be visiting God."

334. The Statue at Bumboogle

On a high hill overlooking the ancient city of Bumboogle is a colossal statue, erected by the nation, to the memory of the illustrious Gaaka-Wolwol, "the best and wisest of mankind." A Traveler from a distant country said to the Custodian of the Statue, who is the highest officer of the realm: "The winds of the sea, O Most Exalted, have not blown the fame of your great countryman to my native shores. What did he do?"

"Nothing; that is how we know him to have been good."

"But his wisdom — what did he say?"

"Nothing; that is how we know him to have been wise."

335. Improvidence

A Person who had fallen from wealth to indigence appealed to a Rich Man for alms.

"No," said the Rich Man, "you did not keep what you had. What assurance have I that you will keep what I may give you?"

"But I don't want it to keep," the beggar explained; "I want to exchange it for bread."

"That is just the same," said the Rich Man. "You would not keep the bread."

336. Sheep and Lion

"You are a beast of war," said the Sheep to the Lion, "yet men go gunning for you. Me, a believer in non-resistance, they do not hunt."

"They do not need to," replied the son of the desert; "they can breed you."

337. The Inconsolable Widow

A Woman in widow's weeds was weeping upon a grave.

"Console yourself, madam," said a Sympathetic Stranger. "Heaven's mercies are infinite. There is another man somewhere, besides your husband, with whom you can still be happy."

"There was," she sobbed — "there was, but this is his grave."

338. An Intrusion

Morality put her toe into international politics and it was promptly chopped off.

"A thousand thanks," said Diplomacy, with an engaging bow; "we will keep it in memory of a most distinguished honor."

And Morality has limped a little ever since.

339. The Tolerant Sovereign

The Gamdoodle of Moop summoned his Secretary of War to an audience and said:

"Sir, you cannot be unaware of the great outcry that my loyal subjects are making against you. They say that you are a rascal."

"Your Majesty," replied the Secretary of War, "it is untrue."

"I'm right glad to hear it," the Gamdoodle replied, rising to intimate that the interview was at an end. But observing that the official did not depart, he added: "Is there anything to say?"

"Yes, your Majesty," the Secretary of War answered; "I wish to surrender my portfolio; for while the public outcry is untrue it is not unjust. I am a fool."

At this the Gamdoodle was graciously pleased to smile. "My good man," he said, "return to your duties. I am that way myself."

340. The Mysterious Word

The Chief of a battalion of war correspondents read a manuscript account of a battle.

"My son," he said to its Author, "your story is distinctly unavailable. You say we lost only two men instead of a hundred; that the enemy's loss is unknown, instead of ten thousand, and that we were defeated and ran way. That is no way to write."

"But consider," expostulated the conscientious scribe, "my story may be tame with regard to the number of our casualties, disappointing as to the damage done to the enemy and shocking in its denouement, but it has the advantage of being the truth."

"I don't quite understand," said the Chief, scratching his head.

"Why, the advantage," the other exclaimed — "the merit — the distinction — the profitable excellence — the — "

"Oh," said the Chief, "I know very well the signification of 'advantage'; but what the devil do you mean by 'truth'?"

341. A Born Captain

A Near-Sighted Man in Luzon met one day a Gorgeous Being whom he mistook for the American Commander.

"General," he said, "do you not find the United States volunteers difficult to manage?"

"I might," the Gorgeous Being replied, "if I were their commander; but, no, I am Aguinaldo."

342. Revelation

A Lion was attacked by a pack of famishing Wolves, who circled about him, howling as loud as they could, though none dared approach him.

"These are very useful creatures," said the Lion, as he lay down for his afternoon nap — "they apprise me of my virtues. I never before knew that I was good to eat."

343. Soldier and Vulture

A Soldier struggling through a pestilential morass saw a Vulture perching on the branch of a tree and solemnly snapping its beak.

"What are you?" asked the Soldier, who had never seen a Vulture. "You look like the father of all chickens."

"Men call me all kinds of names," the bird replied, "according to the language that they speak. I call myself an Expansionist."

The soldier grew very grave. "I was that myself until now," he said, "but if you are the thing to be expanded I shall have to think about it."

But when he tried he found that heaven had not supplied him with a thinker.

344. Her Honor the Mayor

A statesman running for Office had the bad luck to fall and break his heart. As he lay bewailing his hard fate the Office of which he had been in pursuit came back to him, keeping just out of reach.

"My poor friend," said the Office, "what was your business with me?"

"I wanted to hold you," the sufferer explained.

"I should think," the Office said, reproachfully, "that it would be much easier to go home and hold the baby."

"Alas," said the unfortunate Statesman, "my home is in Colorado and my wife is Mayor of Maverick—there is no baby."

345. In Advance of His Time

Some rowdies, having savagely beaten an Unoffending Person, were haled before a Judge and prosecuted by their victim. "I seem to remember you," said the Judge to the prosecuting witness. "Did you not make a speech on a street corner recently, denouncing law and tyranny?"

"I did, your Honor."

"The very law to which you now appeal for protection?"

"Yes, your Honor, I hate all law."

"In short, you are an anarchist, are you not?"

"Yes, I am—but not a bigoted one."

"Well, I am not a bigoted enforcer of the law. The prisoners are discharged, and I invite attention to the fact that you are without standing in this court."

Soon afterward the Judge was removed from office, respected by all who knew him.

346. Cause and Effect

A thirteen-inch gun having uttered a projectile relapsed into silence. Then sounded a Far, Faint Voice from beyond the earth's curvature: "Did you damage anything?"

"Did I damage anything?" echoed the portentous tube right scornfully. "If you are envious enough about that to investigate you will find a wide and ragged hole in the public treasury."

"Ah, permit me to introduce myself," said the Far, Faint Voice: "I am that hole. It is a wise child that knows its father—I had supposed myself due to the annual salary warrant of a Rear-Admiral."

347. The Unshrewd Assassin

A convicted Murderer whom a Sheriff was engaged in hanging was asked if he had anything to say.

"Will it do me any good," he inquired, "to say something?"

"That," replied the Sheriff, adjusting the noose, "depends somewhat upon what you say. I thought you might perhaps put yourself into an easier frame of mind by damning the District Attorney."

"How much does he owe you?" the Murderer asked.

"You are not so shrewd as you think yourself," the Sheriff said; "I owe him fifty dollars."

"It is pretty much the same thing," said the Murderer.

"It is altogether the same thing," the Sheriff assented, springing the drop —"to you."

348. Environment

"Prisoner," said the Judge, austerely, "you are justly convicted of murder. Are you guilty, or were you brought up in Kentucky?"

349. A Chained Eagle

A Provincial Statesman newly elected to the parliament of Despotamia declared that he would introduce a resolution censuring the king. As he left the parliament house, he met a Stranger who warned him that if he persisted in his disloyal design he would lose his head.

"That," said he, "would be a smaller privation than the loss of my liberty."

"I do not know that," said the Stranger. "Liberty is something that I cannot rightly appraise, never having had it. I am the king."

350. The Powerless Poet

A Poet whose lines never would scan was summoned before the King and commanded to show cause why he should not be put to death.

"If your ear is imperfect," said the King, "you could count your syllables on your fingers, like an honest workman."

"May your Majesty outlive your Prime Minister by as many years as remain to you," said the Poet, reverently. "I do count my syllables. But observe: my left hand lacks a finger — bitten off by a critic."

"Then," said the King, "why don't you count on the right hand?"

"Alas!" was the reply of the Poet, as he held up the mutilated left, "that is impossible — there is nothing to count with! It is the forefinger that is lacking."

"Unfortunate man!" exclaimed the sympathetic monarch. "We must make your limitations and disabilities immaterial. You shall write for the magazines."

351. From General to Particular

A Man of Candor said to his Wife: "I cannot permit you to think me better than I am. I have many vices and weaknesses."

"That is only natural," said she, smiling sweetly; "none of us is perfect."

Encouraged by her magnanimity, he confessed to a particular falsehood that he had once told her.

"Abominable wretch!" she cried, and clapped her hands thrice.

Thereupon a gigantic Nubian slave appeared and dispatched him with a scimitar.

352. Disappointment

A Dog that had been engaged in pursuit of his own tail abandoned the chase and lying down curled up for repose. In his new posture he found his tail within easy reach of his teeth and seized it with avidity, but immediately released it, wincing with pain.

"After all," he said, "there is more joy in pursuit than in possession."

353. The Merciful Aspirant

A Person who had been made President was walking along a lonely road when he met an Aspirant to Office and called loudly for help. But nobody heard except the Aspirant, who said:

"I have here seven hundred and fifty recommendations for my appointment as National Inspector of Dead Dogs."

The President fell upon his knees and explained that he had a wife and twenty-nine small children. The Aspirant put away the papers, taking some more from another pocket.

"These documents," he said, "are affidavits of my neighbors; they attest my fitness for the office."

The President wrung his hands and wept audibly. He said:

"Eight Cabinet officers are dependent on me for their bread, and most of them are orphans."

The heart of the Aspirant to office was touched at last.

"I spare you," he said, putting away his papers and moving on, "for the sake of those who cannot. Keep your National Inspectorship of Dead Dogs. It shall not be said that I am a hard man to deal with."

The President rose and dusted his knees. "I could not have given it him without breaking my word," he said to himself. "I have promised it to sixteen others."

354. A Discomfited Philosopher

The King of Remotia had a favorite Philosopher to whom he said:

"Thou hast been so faithful a slave that I am desirous to reward thee. Ask of me anything that thou wouldst have."

"Give me," said the Philosopher, "a hair from the head of a man that hath never flattered thee."

The King promised and dismissed him. The next day he summoned him before the throne and handed him a hair.

"Thou art attempting to deceive me," said the Philosopher, carefully scrutinizing the gift. "This hair is from the head of a flatterer who assured thee that he would think it an honor to give thee his head also."

"Thou art not so astute as thou thinkest," the King replied. "That hair is from the head of the only deaf mute in my kingdom."

355. A Monarch Forearmed

The Emperor of Jiam being dissatisfied with himself resolved to make war upon the King of Geylon.

"You'd better not," said the King.

"Why not?" the Emperor inquired, contemptuously — "in my realm every man is a soldier."

"That is why not," the King explained. "In mine every other man is a civilian."

Perceiving that in peace the King had prepared for war, the bellicose Emperor prudently sought a more military antagonist.

356. Wolf and Tortoise

A Wolf meeting a Tortoise said: "My friend, you are the slowest thing out of doors. I do not see how you manage to escape from your enemies."

"As I lack the power to run away," replied the Tortoise, "Providence has thoughtfully supplied me with an impenetrable shell."

The Wolf reflected a long time, then he said:

"It seems to me that it would have been just as easy to give you long legs."

357. A Condition Precedent

The King of Dogs was petitioned by one of his subjects, a reformer, to command that strangers when meeting should treat one another with amity and forbearance. He issued a royal rescript to that effect and ordered the Petitioner to cry it through the world; but whenever the herald appeared he was set upon by the dogs of the locality and cruelly bitten before he could perform his duty.

"Alas!" he said, "I perceive that reform must be preceded by reformation."

358. The Ambitious Statesman

A Man Out of Office applied for relief to the King of the Quakers.

"What can you do?" his Majesty asked.

"I have been a Secretary of War," the Man Out of Office replied, "but I was deposed. That position in your Majesty's Cabinet would, I think, be filled by me very creditably."

The King being greatly pleased by the applicant's manner and appearance, walked across the audience hall to his Prime Minister.

"Tell me how to make a vacancy in the Cabinet," he said.

"Appoint one," said the Prime Minister. "And permit me, Sire, to recommend the one with whom you have just been speaking."

359. The Limit

The King of the Faraway Islands appointed his horse prime minister and rode a man. Observing that under the new order of things the realm prospered, an Aged Statesman advised the king to turn himself out to grass and put an ox upon the throne.

"No," said the sovereign, thoughtfully, "a good principle may be pushed to an injurious extreme. True reform stops short of revolution."

360. As Usual

Annoyed by an Irrelevant Consideration, a Point-at-issue commanded her to get out of his hearing forthwith, but the Irrelevant Consideration gathered up her skirts and trampling him into the mire went her way amidst the plaudits of the populace.

ÆSOPUS EMENDATUS

361. Jupiter and the Baby Show

Jupiter held a baby show, open to all animals, and a Monkey entered her hideous cub for a prize, but Jupiter only laughed at her.

"It is all very well," said the Monkey, "to laugh at my offspring, but you go into any gallery of antique sculpture and look at the statues and busts of the fellows that you begot yourself."

" 'Sh! don't expose me," said Jupiter, and awarded her the first prize.

362. Mercury and the Woodchopper

A Woodchopper who had dropped his ax into a deep pool besought Mercury to recover it for him. That thoughtless deity immediately plunged into the pool, which became so salivated that the trees about its margin all came loose and dropped out.

363. The Penitent Thief

A Boy who had been taught by his Mother to steal grew to be a man and was a professional public official. One day he was taken in the act and condemned to die. While going to the place of execution he passed his Mother and said to her:

"Behold your work! If you had not taught me to steal I should not have come to this."

"Indeed!" said the Mother. "And who, pray, taught you to be detected?"

364. Fox and Grapes

A Fox, seeing some sour grapes hanging within an inch of his nose, and being unwilling to admit that there was anything he would not eat, solemnly declared that they were out of his reach.

365. Farmer and Fox

A Farmer who had a deadly hatred against a certain Fox caught him and tied some tow to his tail; then carrying him to the center of his own grain-field, he set the tow on fire and let the animal go.

"Alas!" said the Farmer, seeing the result; "if that grain had not been heavily insured I might have had to dissemble my hatred of the Fox."

366. Archer and Eagle

An Eagle mortally wounded by an Archer was greatly comforted to observe that the arrow was feathered with one of his own quills.

"I should have felt bad, indeed," he said, "to think that any other eagle had a hand in this."

367. Truth and the Traveler

A Man traveling in a desert met a Woman.

"Who art thou?" asked the Man, "and why dost thou dwell in this dreadful place?"

"My name," replied the Woman, "is Truth; and I live in the desert in order to be near my worshipers when they are driven from among their fellows. They all come, sooner or later."

"Well," said the Man, looking about, "the country doesn't seem to be very thickly settled hereabout."

368. Wolf and Lamb

A Lamb, pursued by a Wolf, fled into the temple.

"The priest will catch you and sacrifice you," said the Wolf, "if you remain there."

"It is just as well to be sacrificed by the priest as to be eaten by you," said the Lamb.

"My friend," said the Wolf, "it pains me to see you considering so great a question from a purely selfish point of view. It is not just as well for me."

369. Grasshopper and Ant

One day in winter a hungry Grasshopper applied to an Ant for some of the food which the ants had stored.

"Why," said the Ant, "did you not store up some food for yourself, instead of singing all the time?"

"So I did," said the Grasshopper; "so I did; but you fellows broke in and carried it all away."

370. Goose and Swan

A Certain rich man reared a Goose and a Swan, the one for his table, the other because she was reputed a good singer. One night when the Cook went to kill the Goose he got hold of the Swan instead. Thereupon the Swan, to induce him to spare her life, began to sing; but she saved him nothing but the trouble of killing her, for she died of the song.

371. Fisher and Fished

A Fisherman who had caught a very small Fish was putting it into his basket when it said:

"I pray you put me back into the stream, for I can be of no use to you; the gods do not eat fish."

"I am no god," said the Fisherman.

"True," said the Fish, "but as soon as Jupiter has heard of your exploit, he will elevate you to the deitage. You are the only man that ever caught a small fish."

372. Wolves and Dogs

"Why should there be strife between us?" said the Wolves to the Sheep. "It is all owing to those meddlesome dogs. Dismiss them, and we shall have peace."

"You seem to think," replied the Sheep, "that it is an easy thing to dismiss dogs."

373. Dame Fortune and the Traveler

A weary Traveler who had lain down and fallen asleep on the brink of a deep well was discovered by Dame Fortune.

"If this fool," she said, "should have an uneasy dream and roll into the well men would say that I did it. It is painful to me to be unjustly accused, and I shall see that I am not."

So saying she rolled the man into the well.

374. Wolf and Shepherds

A Wolf passing a Shepherd's hut looked in and saw the shepherds dining.

"Come in," said one of them ironically, "and partake of your favorite dish, a leg of mutton."

"Thank you," said the Wolf moving away, "but you must excuse me; I have just had a saddle of shepherd."

375. Lion, Cock and Ass

A Lion was about to attack a braying Ass, when a Cock near by crowed shrilly and the Lion ran away. "What frightened him?" the Ass asked.

"Lions have a superstitious terror of my voice," answered the Cock, proudly.

"Well, well, well," said the Ass, shaking his head; "I should think that any animal that is afraid of your voice and doesn't mind mine must have an uncommon kind of ear."

376. Snake and Swallow

A Swallow who had built her nest in a court of justice reared a fine family of young birds. One day a Snake came out of a chink in the wall and was about to eat them. The Just Judge at once issued an injunction, and making an order for their removal to his own house, ate them himself.

377. Victor and Victim

Two Game Cocks having fought a battle, the defeated one skulked away and hid, but the victor mounted a wall and crowed lustily. This attracted the attention of a Hawk, who said:

"Behold! how pride goeth before a fall."

So he swooped down upon the boasting bird and was about to destroy him, when the vanquished Cock came out of his hiding-place and between the two the Hawk was calamitously defeated.

378. Hen and Vipers

A Hen who had patiently hatched out a brood of vipers was accosted by a Swallow, who said: "What a fool you are to give life to creatures who will reward you by destroying you."

"I am a little bit destructive myself," said the Hen, tranquilly swallowing one of the little reptiles; "and it is not an act of folly to provide oneself with the delicacies of the season."

379. Spendthrift and Swallow

A Spendthrift, seeing a single swallow, pawned his cloak, thinking that Summer was at hand. It was.

380. Lion and Thorn

A Lion roaming through the forest got a thorn in his foot and meeting a Shepherd asked him to remove it. The Shepherd did so and the Lion, having just surfeited himself on another shepherd, went away without harming him. Some time afterward the Shepherd was condemned on a false accusation to be cast to the lions in the amphitheatre. When they were about to devour him one of them said:

"This is the man who removed the thorn from my foot."

Hearing this, the others honorably abstained, and the claimant ate the Shepherd all by himself.

381. Fawn and Buck

A Fawn said to its father: "You are larger, stronger and more active than a dog, and you have sharp horns. Why do you run away when you hear one barking?"

"Because, my child," replied the Buck, "my temper is so uncertain that if I permit one of those noisy creatures to come into my presence I am likely to forget myself and do him an injury."

382. Kite, Pigeons and Hawk

Some Pigeons exposed to the attacks of a Kite asked a Hawk to defend them. He consented, and being admitted into the cote waited for the Kite, whom he fell upon and devoured. When he was so surfeited that he could scarcely move the grateful Pigeons scratched out his eyes.

383. Wolf and Babe

A Famishing Wolf passing the door of a cottage in the forest heard a Mother say to her Babe:

"Be quiet, or I will throw you out of the window and the wolves will get you."

So he waited all day below the window, growing more hungry all the time. But at night the Old Man, having returned from the village club, threw out both Child and Mother.

384. Wolf and Ostrich

A Wolf who in devouring a man had choked himself with a bunch of keys asked an ostrich to put her head down his throat and pull them out, which she did.

"I suppose," said the Wolf, "you expect payment for that service."

"A kind act," replied the Ostrich, "is its own reward; I have eaten the keys."

385. Herdsman and Lion

A Herdsman who had lost a bullock entreated the gods to bring him the thief and vowed he would sacrifice a goat to them. Just then a Lion, his jaws dripping with bullock's blood, approached the Herdsman.

"I thank you, good deities," said the Herdsman, resuming his prayer, "for showing me the thief. And now if you will take him away I will stand another goat."

386. War-Horse and Miller

Having heard that the State was about to be invaded by a hostile army, a War-horse belonging to a Colonel of the Militia offered his services to a passing Miller.

"No," said the patriotic Miller, "I will employ no one who deserts his position in the hour of danger. It is sweet to die for one's country."

Something in the sentiment sounded familiar and looking at the Miller more closely the War-horse recognized his master in disguise.

387. Man and Fish-Horn

A Truthful Man finding a musical instrument in the road, asked the name of it and was told that it was a fish-horn. The next time he went fishing he set his nets and blew the fish-horn all day to charm the fish into them, but at nightfall there were not only no fish in his nets, but none along that part of the coast. Meeting a friend while on his way home he was asked what luck he had had.

"Well," said the Truthful Man, "the weather is not right for fishing, but it's a red-letter day for music."

388. Hercules and the Carter

A Carter was driving a wagon loaded with a merchant's goods, when the wheels stuck in a rut. Thereupon he began to pray to Hercules, without other exertion.

"Indolent fellow!" said Hercules; "you ask me to help you, but will not help yourself."

So the Carter helped himself to so many of the most valuable goods that the horses easily ran away with the remainder.

389. Hare and Tortoise

A Hare having ridiculed the slow movements of a Tortoise was challenged by the latter to run a race, a Fox to go to the goal and be the judge. They got off well together, the Hare at the top of her speed, the Tortoise, who had no other intention than making his antagonist exert herself, going very leisurely. After sauntering along for some time he discovered the Hare by the wayside, apparently asleep, and seeing a chance to win pushed on as fast as he could, arriving at the goal hours afterward, suffering from extreme fatigue and claiming the victory.

"Not so," said the Fox; "the Hare was here long ago and went back to cheer you on your way."

390. Lion and Bull

A Lion wishing to lure a Bull to a place where it would be safe to attack him said: "My friend, I have killed a fine sheep; will you come with me and partake of the mutton?"

"With pleasure," said the Bull, "as soon as you have refreshed yourself a little for the journey. Pray have some grass."

391. Old Man and Sons

An Old Man, afflicted with a family of contentious Sons, brought in a bundle of sticks and asked the young men to break it. After repeated efforts they confessed that it could not be done. "Behold," said the Old Man, "the advantage of unity; as long as these sticks are in alliance they are invincible, but observe how feeble they are individually."

Pulling a single stick from the bundle, he broke it easily upon the head of the eldest Son, and this he repeated until all had been served.

392. Wolf and Goat

A Wolf saw a Goat feeding at the summit of a rock, where he could not get at her.

"Why do you stay up there in that sterile place and go hungry?" said the Wolf. "Down here where I am the broken-bottle vine cometh up as a flower, the celluloid collar blossoms as the rose and the tin-can tree brings forth after its kind."

"That is true, no doubt," said the Goat, "but how about the circus-poster crop? I hear that it failed this year down there."

The Wolf, perceiving that he was being derided, went away and resumed his duties at the doors of the poor.

393. Man and Goose

"See these valuable golden eggs," said a Man that owned a Goose. "Surely a Goose which can lay such eggs as those must have a gold mine inside her."

So he killed the Goose and cut her open, but found that she was just like any other goose. Moreover, on examining the eggs that she had laid he found they were just like any other eggs.

394. Dog and Reflection

A Dog passing over a stream on a plank saw his reflection in the water.

"You ugly brute!" he cried; "how dare you look at me in that insolent way?"

He made a grab in the water and getting hold of what he supposed was the other dog's lip lifted out a fine piece of meat which a butcher's boy had dropped into the stream.

395. Man and Eagle

An Eagle was once captured by a Man, who clipped his wings and put him in the poultry yard, along with the chickens. The Eagle was much depressed in spirits by the change.

"Why should you not rather rejoice?" said the Man. "You were only an ordinary fellow as an eagle; but as an old cock you are a fowl of incomparable distinction."

396. Man and Viper

A Man finding a frozen Viper put it into his bosom.

"The coldness of the human heart," he said, with a grin, "will keep the creature in his present condition until I can reach home and revive him on the coals."

But the pleasures of hope so fired his heart that the Viper thawed, slid to the ground and, thanking the Man civilly for his hospitality, glided away.

397. North Wind and Sun

The Sun and the North Wind disputed which was the more powerful and agreed that he should be declared victor who could the sooner strip a traveler of his clothes. So they waited until a traveler came by. But the Traveler had been indiscreet enough to stay over night at a summer hotel, and had no clothes.

398. Crab and Son

A Logical Crab said to his Son, "Why do you not walk straight forward? Your sidelong gait is singularly ungraceful."

"Why don't you walk straight forward yourself?" said the Son.

"Erring youth," replied the Logical Crab, "you are introducing new and irrelevant matter."

399. Jupiter and the Birds

Jupiter commanded all the birds to appear before him, so that he might choose the most beautiful to be their king. The ugly Jackdaw, collecting all the fine feathers that had fallen from the other birds, attached them to his own body and appeared at the examination, looking very gay. The other birds recognizing their own borrowed plumage indignantly protested and began to strip him.

"Hold!" said Jupiter; "this self-made bird has more sense than any of you. He shall be your king."

400. Lion and Mouse

A Lion who had caught a Mouse was about to kill him, when the Mouse said:

"If you will spare my life, I will do as much for you some day."

The Lion good-naturedly let him go. It happened shortly afterwards that the Lion was caught by some hunters and bound with cords. The Mouse, passing that way and seeing that his benefactor was helpless, gnawed off his tail.

401. Lamb and Wolf

A Wolf was slaking his thirst at a stream, when a Lamb left the side of his shepherd, came down the stream and passing ostentatiously round the Wolf, prepared to drink below.

"I beg you to observe," said the Lamb, "that water does not commonly run uphill. My sipping here cannot possibly defile the water where you are; so you have not the flimsiest pretext for slaying me."

"I am not aware," replied the Wolf, "that I need a pretext for liking mutton chops."

End of that small logician.

402. Mountain and Mouse

A Mountain was in labor, and the people of seven cities had assembled to watch its movements and hear its groans. While they waited in breathless expectancy out came a Mouse.

"Oh, what a baby!" they cried in derision.

"I may be a baby," said the Mouse, gravely, as he passed outward through the forest of shins, "but I know tolerably well how to diagnose a volcano."

403. The Bellamy and the Members

The Members of a body of Socialists rose in insurrection against their Bellamy.

"Why," said they, "should we be all the time tucking you out with food when you do nothing to tuck us out?"

So, resolving to take no further action, they went away and looking backward had the satisfaction to see the Bellamy compelled to sell his own book.

404. Cat and Youth

A Cat fell in love with a handsome Young Man and entreated Venus to change her into a woman.

"I should think," said Venus, "you might make so trifling a change without bothering me. However, be a woman."

Afterward, wishing to see if the change were complete, Venus caused a mouse to approach, whereupon the woman shrieked and made such a show of herself that the Young Man would not marry her.

405. Farmer and Sons

A Farmer being about to die, and knowing that during his illness his Sons had permitted the vineyard to become overgrown with weeds while they gambled with the doctor, said to them:

"My boys, there is a great treasure buried in the vineyard. Dig in the ground until you find it."

So the Sons dug up all the weeds, and all the vines too, and even neglected to bury the old man.

OLD SAWS WITH NEW TEETH:
CERTAIN ANCIENT FABLES APPLIED TO
THE LIFE OF OUR TIMES

406. Wolf and Crane

A Rich Man wanted to tell a certain lie, but the lie was of such monstrous size that it stuck in his throat; so he employed an Editor to write it out and publish it in his paper as an editorial. But when the Editor presented his bill the Rich Man said:

"Be content—is it nothing that I refrained from advising you about investments?"

407. Lion and Mouse

A Judge was awakened by the noise of a lawyer prosecuting a Thief. Rising in wrath he was about to sentence the Thief to life imprisonment when the latter said:

"I beg that you will set me free, and I will some day requite your kindness."

Pleased and flattered to be bribed, although by nothing but an empty promise, the Judge let him go. Soon afterward he found that it was more than an empty promise, for having become a Thief he was himself set free by the other, who had become a Judge.

408. Hare and Frogs

The Members of a Legislature being told that they were the meanest thieves in the world resolved to kill themselves. So they bought shrouds and laying them in a convenient place prepared to cut their throats. While they were grinding their razors some Tramps passing that way stole the shrouds.

"Let us live, my friends," said one of the Legislators; "the world is better than we thought. It contains meaner thieves than we."

409. Belly and Members

Some Workingmen employed in a shoe factory went on a strike, saying: "Why should we continue to work to feed and clothe our employer when we have none too much to eat and wear ourselves?"

The Manufacturer, seeing that he could get no labor for a long time and finding the times pretty hard anyhow, burned down his shoe factory for the insurance and when the strikers wanted to resume work there was no work to resume. So they boycotted a tanner.

410. The Piping Fisherman

An Editor who was always vaunting the purity, enterprise and fearlessness of his paper was pained to observe that he got no subscribers. One day it occurred to him to stop saying that his paper was pure and enterprising and fearless, and make it so. "If these are not good qualities," he reasoned, "it is folly to claim them."

Under the new policy he got so many subscribers that his rivals endeav-

ored to discover the secret of his prosperity, but he kept it, and when he died
it died with him.

411. Ants and Grasshopper

Some Members of a Legislature were making schedules of their wealth at the
end of the session, when an Honest Miner came along and asked them to
divide with him. The members of the Legislature inquired:

"Why did you not acquire property of your own?"

"Because," replied the Honest Miner, "I was so busy digging out gold
that I had no leisure to lay up something worth while."

Then the Members of the Legislature derided him, saying:

"If you waste your time in profitless amusement you cannot, of course,
expect to share the rewards of industry."

412. The Dog and His Reflection

A State Official carrying off the dome of the capitol met the Ghost of his predecessor, who had come out of his political grave to warn him that God saw
him. As the place of meeting was lonely and the time midnight, the State Official set down the dome of the capitol and commanded the supposed traveler
to throw up his hands. The Ghost replied that he had not eaten them, and
while he was explaining the situation another State Official silently added the
dome to his own collection.

413. Lion, Bear and Fox

Two Thieves having stolen a piano and being unable to divide it fairly without
a remainder went to law about it and continued the contest as long as either
one could steal a dollar to bribe the judge. When they could give no more an
Honest Man came along and by a single small payment obtained a judgment
and took the piano home, where his daughter used it to develop her biceps
muscles, becoming a famous *pugiliste.*

414. Wolf and Lion

An Indian who had been driven out of a fertile valley by a White Settler, said:

"Now that you have robbed me of my land there is nothing for me to do but issue invitations to a war-dance."

"I don't so much mind your dancing," said the White Settler, putting a fresh cartridge into his rifle, "but if you attempt to make me dance you will become a good Indian lamented by all who didn't know you. How did *you* get this land, anyhow?"

The Indian's claim was compromised for a silk hat and a tin horn.

415. The Ass in the Lion's Skin

A member of the State Militia stood at a street corner, scowling stormily, and the people passing that way went a long way around him, thinking of the horrors of war. But presently, in order to terrify them still more, he strode toward them, when, his sword entangling his legs, he fell upon the field of glory and the people passed over him singing their sweetest songs.

416. Ass and Grasshoppers

A Statesman heard some Laborers singing at their work and wishing to be happy too asked them what made them so.

"Honesty," replied the Laborers.

So the Statesman resolved that he too would be honest and the result was that he died of want.

417. Hare and Tortoise

Of two writers one was brilliant but indolent; the other, though dull, industrious. They set out for the goal of fame with equal opportunities. Before they died the brilliant one was detected in seventy languages as the author of only two or three books of fiction and poetry, while the other was honored in the Bureau of Statistics of his native land as the compiler of sixteen volumes of tabulated information relating to the domestic hog.

418. King Log and King Stork

The People being dissatisfied with a Democratic Legislature, which stole no more than they had, elected a Republican one, which not only stole all they had but exacted a promissory note for the balance due, secured by a mortgage upon their hope of death.

419. Milkmaid and Bucket

A Senator fell to musing as follows: "With the money which I shall get for my vote in favor of the bill to subsidize cat-ranches I can buy a kit of burglar's tools and open a bank. The profit of that enterprise will enable me to obtain a long, low, black schooner, raise a death's-head flag and engage in commerce on the high seas. From my gains in that business I can pay for the Presidency, which at $50,000 a year will give me in four years —" but it took him so long to make the calculation that the bill to subsidize cat-ranches passed without his vote and he was compelled to return to his constituents an honest man tormented with a clean conscience.

420. The Wolf Who Would Be a Lion

A Foolish fellow who had been told that he was a great man believed it and got himself appointed a Commissioner to the Interasylum Exposition of Preserved Idiots. At the first meeting of the Board he was mistaken for one of the exhibits and the janitor was ordered to remove him to his appropriate glass case.

"Alas!" he exclaimed as he was carried out, "why was I not content to remain where the cut of my forehead is so common that it is known as the Pacific Slope?"

421. Monkey and Nuts

A certain city desiring to purchase a site for a public Deformatory procured an appropriation from the Government of the country. Deeming this insufficient for purchase of the site and payment of reasonable commissions to themselves, the Men in Charge of the Matter asked for a larger sum, which was readily given. Believing that the fountain could not be dipped dry, they applied for still more, and more yet. Wearied at last by their importunities the Government said it would be damned if it gave anything at all. So it gave nothing and was damned all the harder.

422. Boys and Frogs

Some editors of newspapers were engaged in diffusing general intelligence and elevating the moral sentiment of the public. They had been doing this for some time, when an Eminent Statesman stuck his head out of the pool of politics and speaking for the members of his profession said:

"My friends, I beg you will desist. I know you make a great deal of money by this kind of thing, but consider the damage you inflict upon the business of others!"

FABLES IN RHYME

423. The Sleeping Lion

A Bull, the angel of the wild,
A Bull as gentle as a child,
A pleasant mannered Bull that lay
Upon a hill at break of day
And munched his cud, observed a gleam
Of crimson on the world's extreme
Where the Dawn-Spirit had released
His flaring banner in the east.
The Bull, a flame in either eye
That frightened the offending sky,
Rose, pawed the earth until his skin
Was dun with dust from tail to chin,
And lowering his horrid brows,
Roared out: "How dare you thus arouse
The sleeping lion in my breast!"
Then, like a storm from out the west,
He blindly charged, and without check,
Went o'er a cliff and broke his neck!
A Tiger, calm, serene, sedate,
Administered on his estate,
And as he turned him into chyle

Remarked with a contented smile:
"That sleeping lion in his breast
Was just an ass that needed rest."

424. In Dogland

A Man who fared along a road
That passed a yellow Dog's abode
Incurred a paralyzing bite
From that incarnate appetite,
Creation's joy and hope and crown—
The pride and terror of the town!
The Man in anger went before
The nearest Magistrate and swore
A warrant out for the Dog's Master,
As author of the dire disaster.
Haled into court, that citizen
Employed attorneys, eight or ten,
Who as one man arose, and O,
The kind of things they said were so!
All honest souls, a crowd immense,
Were witnesses for the defence,
And when they came to testify
Of that bad plaintiff—my, O my!
Defendant rose and gravely swore
The Dog had never bit before.
"How could I know, till he transgressed,
The serpent lurking in his breast?"
And all the people cried: "That's so!
How could he know? How could he know?"

That won—Defendant left the place
On shoulders of the populace.
The miserable Plaintiff slunk
Away and soon was dead or drunk,
Tradition says not which; I think
Death is inferior to drink.
But that's irrelevant: what now

Concerns us is the bow and wow
Made by the snapdogs of that region
(Their name, tradition says, was Legion)
When, with a sound of trumpets blown,
The great decision was made known
From Sweetpotatoville to Pone.
They said, the dogs did, that the law
Was good — *pro bonos mores* (Latin
That dogs and lawyers mostly chat in).
They said, the while their bosoms burned
With ardor, that their souls discerned
"The dawn of a new era," which
They promptly "hailed" at concert pitch!

As dogs had now the legal right
To trouble Man for one free bite
'Twas voted that they would. They did:
That land, from Glorypool to Squid,
With snarl and yelp and snap of teeth
(Flashing like falchions from the sheath)
Was vocal till each cur beneath
The sun had fleshed his maiden fang
In some one of the human gang!
True, all the dogs whose heads were frosted
With age had long before exhausted
Their awful privilege, and these
Died of chagrin among their fleas;
But there were pups enough at heel
Of every human leg to deal
Out floods of hydrophobia's sap
And wash that country from the map.

425. A Pair of Opposites

A Fabulist of wide repute,
Whose laugh was loud and wit was mute —
Whose grammar had the grace of guess,
And language an initial S —

Whose tireless efforts, long sustained,
Proved him far better brawned than brained,
Once met a Toad. "My son," said he,
" 'Twould jar you to get onto me!
You're swell, but I'm the dandy guy
That slings the gilt-edged lullaby.
Dost tumble? What I'm shouting, see,
Is, you're the antithesis of Me."
"That compliment," the Toad replied,
"Is grateful to my foolish pride:
It seems to mean that though I hop
Right awkwardly I sometimes stop."
The gods, whom long the Fabulist
Had plagued (the Toad had only hissed)
Emitted loud Olympian snorts
Of joy to hear the King of Warts
Administer a mental pang
To the Protagonist of Slang.
So Jove appointed him to be
Chief Jester by divine decree,
And ne'er another joke made he.

426. The Degenerate

Two Horses that had always chewed
The bitter grain of servitude —
Between their meals had ever felt
The bit in mouth and lash on pelt —
Once, as they drew the creaking wain,
Saw a wild Zebra of the plain,
Unknown to halter, stall or cage.
Cried one: "Good Lord! this is an age
Of miracle!" "Not so," said t'other,
"That vision is a horse-and-brother.
Degraded as he is by sin,
He has an equine soul within,
Albeit Law, with stern reproof,
Has laid on him the heavy hoof.

Those stripes but show he's 'serving time'
In punishment of some great crime."
The other thought an hour's span,
Then said: "Perhaps he stole a man."

427. The Vain Cat

Remarked a Tortoise to a Cat:
"Your speed's a thing to marvel at!
I saw you as you flitted by,
And wished I were one-half so spry."
The Cat said, humbly: "Why, indeed
I was not showing then my speed —
That was a poor performance." Then
She said exultantly (as when
The condor feels his bosom thrill
Remembering Chimborazo's hill,
And how he soared so high above,
It looked a valley, he a dove):
" 'Twould fire your very carapace
To see me with a dog in chase!"
Its snout in any kind of swill,
Pride, like a pig, will suck its fill.

428. A Socialist

"You're keeping me poor — I have only this egg.
All rich men are rascals!" said Impycu Dregg.
Couponicus Pigg said: "Your thanks, then, are due
To me for not making a rascal of you."
But Impycu Dregg all the same flung his egg,
Which burst in the wig of Couponicus Pigg.

429. The Co-defendants

A Jackass by a Lion chased
Had made so admirable haste
That his pursuer, far behind,

Had, long before, his hope resigned
And gone to sleep; but still poor Jack
Pressed on, nor ventured to look back.
"Why, what's the matter?" cried a Steer,
Obstructing him in his career.
"Out of the way and let us pass!"
Roared the still apprehensive Ass.
" 'Us'? Why, my friend," the Steer replied,
"I see but you, and none beside."
"I'm but the foremost," answered Jack —
"The woods are full of us 'way back.
Behold, he clawed me here and here;
See how he tore my precious ear!
Believe me, sir, your count's at fault —
No one escapes that cat's assault."
To let them limp along, the Steer
Backed off in wonder and in fear.
The Ass evanished like a flame,
But not another donkey came.
Then said the Steer: "I've saved — well done! —
All jackasses beneath the sun,
Rolled into one, rolled into one."

430. In Consequence of Applause

"What makes you so round?"
Said an indolent Hound
To a Tiger that looked
As if he had booked
All the pilgrims of earth
For an inside berth.
Said the Tiger: "I strayed
To the edge of a glade
Where a man on a stump,
Sleek, handsome and plump,
His notions expounded
To those who surrounded
Him there with their ears

Erected like spears
For the words that he flung
From his flickering tongue."
"Yes, yes, my good cat,
But what of all that?
That statesman, I swear,
Had enough and to spare
Of the breezes that blow
Out of heaven, but, O
'Tis remarkably odd he
Could blow up your body
And make you so poddy."
"By-and-by the man stopped,
And his forehead he mopped,
And his scalp — which was bald.
Then somebody called
For three cheers — " "Hully Gee!
I'm beginning to see."
"And a tiger. That's me."

UNREPRINTED FABLES FROM

FANTASTIC FABLES (1899)

431. Two in Trouble

Meeting a fat and patriotic Statesman on his way to Washington to beseech the President for an office, an idle Tramp accosted him and begged twenty-five cents with which to buy a suit of clothes.

"Melancholy wreck," said the Statesman, "what brought you to this state of degradation? Liquor, I suppose."

"I am temperate to the verge of absurdity," replied the Tramp. "My foible was patriotism; I was ruined by the baneful habit of trying to serve my country. What ruined you?"

"Indolence."

432. The Power of the Scalawag

A Forestry Commissioner had just felled a giant tree when, seeing an honest man approaching, he dropped his ax and fled. The next day when he cautiously returned to get his ax, he found the following lines pencilled on the stump:

"What nature reared by centuries of toil,
A scalawag in half a day can spoil;
An equal fate for him may Heaven provide —
Damned in the moment of his tallest pride."

433. The Seeker and the Sought

A Politician seeing a fat Turkey which he wanted for dinner, baited a hook with a grain of corn and dragged it before the fowl at the end of a long and almost invisible line. When the Turkey had swallowed the hook, the Politician ran, drawing the creature after him.

"Fellow-citizens," he cried, addressing some turkey-breeders whom he met, "you observe that the man does not seek the bird, but the bird seeks the man. For this unsolicited and unexpected dinner I thank you with all my heart."

434. The Ingenious Blackmailer

An Inventor went to a King and was granted an audience, when the following conversation ensued:

Inventor. — "May it please your Majesty, I have invented a rifle that discharges lightning."

King. — "Ah, you wish to sell me the secret."

Inventor. — "Yes; it will enable your army to overrun any nation that is accessible."

King. — "In order to get any good of my outlay for your invention, I must make a war, and do so as soon as I can arm my troops — before your secret is discovered by foreign nations. How much do you want?"

Inventor. — "One million dollars."

King. — "And how much will it cost to make the change of arms?"

Inventor. — "Fifty millions."

King. — "And the war will cost — ?"

Inventor. — "But consider the glory and the spoils!"

King. — "Exactly. But if I am not seeking these advantages? What if I decline to purchase?"

Inventor. — "There is no economy in that. Though a patriot, I am poor; if my own country will not patronise me, I must seek a market elsewhere."

King (to Prime Minister). — "Take this blackmailer and cut off his head."

435. The Massacre

Some Holy Missionaries in China having been deprived of life by the Bigoted Heathens, the Christian Press made a note of it, and was greatly pained to point out the contrast between the Bigoted Heathens and the law-abiding countrymen of the Holy Missionaries who had wickedly been sent to eternal bliss.

"Yes," assented a Miserable Sinner, as he finished reading the articles, "the Heathens of Ying Shing are deceitful above all things and desperately wicked. By the way," he added, turning over the paper to read the entertaining and instructive Fables, "I know the Heathenese lingo. Ying Shing means Rock Creek; it is in the Province of Wyo Ming."

436. The Self-Made Monkey

A Man of humble birth and no breeding, who held a high political office, was passing through a forest, when he met a Monkey.

"I take it you are one of my constituents," the Man said.

"No," replied the Monkey; "but I will support you if you can urge a valid claim to my approval."

"I am a self-made man," said the other, proudly.

"That is nothing," the Monkey said. And going to a digger pine, he rose by his own unaided exertions to the top branch, where he sat, all bedaubed with the pitch which that vegetable exudes. "Now," he added, "I am a self-made Monkey."

437. The Thief and the Honest Man

A Thief who had brought a suit against his accomplices to recover his share of the plunder taken from an Honest Man, demanded the Honest Man's attendance at the trial to testify to his loss. But the Honest Man explained that as he was merely the agent of a company of other honest men it was none of his affair; and when the officers came to serve him with a subpoena he hid himself behind his back and wiled away the dragging hours of retirement and inaction by picking his own pockets.

ÆSOPUS EMENDATUS

438. The Man and the Dog

A Man who had been bitten by a Dog was told that the wound would heal if he would dip a piece of bread in the blood and give it to the Dog. He did so.

"No," said the Dog; "if I were to accept that, it might be thought that in biting you I was actuated by improper motives."

"And by what motives were you actuated?" asked the Man.

"I desired," replied the Dog, "merely to harmonise myself with the Divine Scheme of Things. I'm a child of Nature."

439. The Cat and the Birds

Hearing that the Birds in an aviary were ill, a Cat went to them and said that he was a physician, and would cure them if they would let him in.

"To what school of medicine do you belong?" asked the Birds.

"I am a Miaulopathist," said the Cat.

"Did you ever practise Gohomœopathy?" the Birds inquired, winking faintly.

The Cat took the hint and his leave.

440. The Lion and the Boar

A Lion and a Boar, who were fighting for water at a pool, saw some vultures hovering significantly above them. "Let us make up our quarrel," said the Boar, "or these fellows will get one of us, sure."

"I should not so much mind that," replied the Lion, "if they would get the right one. However, I am willing to stop fighting, and then perhaps I can grab a vulture. I like chicken better than pork, anyhow."

FABLES FROM

THE DEVIL'S DICTIONARY

441. Cunning

A Bear accosted once a Fox,
  And the two stopped a Rabbit.
Said Bruin: "I have found a box
  Of honey; let us bag it!"

The Fox said: "That is well enough
  For you, but why should we fight?
I like full well the pleasant stuff,
  But do not love the bee-fight."

Thus he, dissembling all his glee.
  "Nay," said the Rabbit, feigning
Assent; "as strong a force are we
  As ever went campaigning.

"All warlike virtues we unite,
  Our character completing;
Fox to manoeuvre, Bear to fight,
  And Rabbit for retreating.

"The prizes of the war we'll share,
Like conquerors in story:
Sweets to the Fox, stings to the Bear,
And I content for glory!"

442. Fable

A statue of Eve and the Apple was accosted by a hippopotamus on a show-bill.

"Give me a bite of your apple," said the hippopotamus, "and see me smile."

"I would," said Eve, making a rough estimate of the probable dimensions of the smile, "but I have promised a bite to the Mammoth Cave, another to the crater of Vesuvius, and a third to the interval between the lowest anthropoid Methodist and the most highly organized wooden Indian. I must be just before I am generous."

443. Head

Heavenly-Blowing-Ear-Bird was Tycoon, and he condemned to decapitation his great captain, Lily-Oh-Awful-Long-Augustness-Camphor-Boat. Soon after the hour appointed for the execution, what was his Majesty's surprise when he saw calmly approaching the throne the man who should by that time have been ten minutes dead!

"Seventeen hundred and twenty-five impossible dragons!" shouted the enraged monarch. "Did I not sentence you to stand in the marketplace and have your head struck off by the scimitar of the public executioner at exactly three o'clock this afternoon; and"—here the mighty Heavenly-Blowing-Ear-Bird consulted his watch—"is it not now 3:10?"

"Son of a thousand illustrious fathers," answered Lily-Oh-Awful-Long-Augustness-Camphor-Boat, "all that you say is so true that truth is a lie to it. But your Majesty's sunny and vitalizing wishes have been pestilently disregarded. With joy I ran and placed myself in the center of the marketplace. The executioner appeared with his bare scimitar, ostentatiously whirled it and then, touching me but lightly on the neck, strode away, hissed and pelted by the populace—with whom I was ever a favorite. I came here to pray for justice upon his own treasonous head."

"Which regiment of executioners did the black-boweled caitiff belong to?" asked the sovereign.

"The Ninety-eight Hundred and Thirty-seventh," was the reply. "I know the very man; his name is Gentle-Rice-Tooth-Erratic-Great-Great-Youth-of-the-Thunder."

"Let him be summoned before me," said the monarch, adressing an attendant.

A half-hour later the culprit stood in the incandescent Presence.

"Thou son of a seven-legged hunchback with prehensile thumbs!" roared Heavenly-Blowing-Ear-Bird, "why didst thou but lightly tap the neck which it was thy duty, and should have been thy pleasure, to bisect?"

"Lord of Cranes," replied Gentle-Rice-Tooth-Erratic-Great-Great-Youth-of-the-Thunder, smiling grimly, "command him to blow his nose with his fingers."

Being commanded, Lily-Oh-Awful-Long-Augustness-Camphor-Boat laid hold of his proboscis with a powerful grip and trumpeted like a wounded elephant, the Tycoon and whole court expecting to see his severed head flying violently from him. Nothing of the kind occurred; the nose-blowing prospered peacfully to the end, the head remaining firmly in place. All eyes were now turned on the executioner, who was as a spectacle to see. He was as pale as the snow on the summit of Fujiyama, his knees trembled and his breath *sakhemenl oka sumi remichi fee* (untranslatable).

"Several thousand spike-tailed brass lions!" he cried. "I am a ruined and disgraced swordsman. I struck the villain feebly because in flourishing the scimitar I had accidentally passed it through my own neck. Father of Slaughter, I resign my office."

So saying, Gentle - Rice - Tooth - Erratic - Great - Great - Youth - of - the - Thunder lifted his arm, grasped his topknot and, lifting off his head, advanced to the throne and laid it humbly at the Tycoon's feet.

444. Looking-Glass

The King of Manchuria had a magic looking-glass, whereon whoso looked saw, not his own image, but only that of the king. A certain courtier who had long enjoyed the king's favor and was thereby enriched beyond any other subject of the realm, said to the king: "Give me, I pray, thy wonderful mirror, so that when absent out of thine august presence I may yet do homage before thy visible shadow, prostrating myself night and morning in the glory of thy benign countenance, as which nothing has so divine splendor, O Noonday Sun of the Universe!"

Please with the speech, the king commanded that the mirror be conveyed to the courtier's palace; but after, having gone thither without apprisal, he found it in an apartment where was naught but idle lumber. And the mirror was dimmed with dust and overlaced with cobwebs. This so angered him that he fisted it hard, shattering the glass, and was sorely hurt. Enraged all the more by this mischance, he commanded that the ungrateful courtier be thrown into prison, and that the glass be repaired and taken back to his own palace; and this was done. But when the king looked again on the mirror he saw not his image as before, but only the figure of a crowned ass, having a bloody bandage on one of its hinder hooves — as the artificers and all who had looked upon it had before discerned but feared to report. Taught wisdom and charity, the king restored his courtier to liberty, had the mirror set into the back of the throne and reigned many years with justice and humility; and one day when he fell asleep in death while on the throne, the whole court saw in the mirror the luminous figure of an angel, which remains to this day.

445. Opposition

The King of Ghargaroo, who had been abroad to study the science of government, appointed one hundred of his fattest subjects as members of a parliament to make laws for the collection of revenue. Forty of these he named the Party of Opposition and had his Prime Minister carefully instruct them in their duty of opposing every royal measure. Nevertheless, the first one that was submitted passed unanimously. Greatly displeased, the King vetoed it, informing the Opposition that if they did that again they would pay for their obstinacy with their heads. The entire forty promptly disemboweled themselves.

"What shall we do now?" the King asked. "Liberal institutions cannot be maintained without a party of Opposition."

"Splendor of the universe," replied the Prime Minister, "it is true these dogs of darkness have no longer their credentials, but all is not lost. Leave the matter to this worm of the dust."

So the Minister had the bodies of his Majesty's Opposition embalmed and stuffed with straw, put back into the seats of power and nailed there. Forty votes were recorded against every bill and the nation prospered. But one day a bill imposing a tax on warts was defeated — the members of the Government party had not been nailed to their seats! This so enraged the King that the Prime Minister was put to death, the parliament was dissolved with a battery of artillery, and government of the people, by the people, for the people perished from Ghargaroo.

446. Satan

Being instated as an archangel, Satan made himself multifariously objection-able and was finally expelled from Heaven. Halfway in his descent he paused, bent his head in thought a moment and at last went back. "There is one favor that I should like to ask," said he.

"Name it."

"Man, I understand, is about to be created. He will need laws."

"What, wretch! you his appointed adversary, charged from the dawn of eternity with hatred of his soul — you ask for the right to make his laws?"

"Pardon; what I have to ask is that he be permitted to make them himself."

It was so ordered.

447. Ultimatum

Having received an ultimatum from Austria, the Turkish Ministry met to con-sider it.

"O servant of the Prophet," said the Sheik of the Imperial Chibouk to the Mamoosh of the Invincible Army, "how many unconquerable soldiers have we in arms?"

"Upholder of the Faith," that dignitary replied after examining his memo-randa, "they are in numbers as the leaves of the forest!"

"And how many impenetrable battleships strike terror to the hearts of all Christian swine?" he asked the Imaum of the Ever Victorious Navy.

"Uncle of the Full Moon," was the reply, "deign to know that they are as the waves of the ocean, the sands of the desert and the stars of Heaven!"

For eight hours the broad brow of the Sheik of the Imperial Chibouk was corrugated with evidences of deep thought: he was calculating the chances of war. Then, "Sons of angels," he said, "the die is cast! I shall suggest to the Ulema of the Imperial Ear that he advise inaction. In the name of Allah, the council is adjourned."

UNCOLLECTED FABLES

448.

An office-seeker whom the Governor hated was recommended for an office in that functionary's gift by such influential men that the latter did not dare deny it to him. So he appointed the fellow and then put the best face upon the matter that he could by saying: "I dismissed the rascal from private life for cause." But the offender bore the disgrace with a sweet and saintly fortitude that disarmed the rancor of needy patriots and froze the sneers upon their lips.

449.

A colonel was cleaning the spittoons of a fashionable drinking saloon for his morning cocktail, when the barkeeper playfully pushed him off his feet, seating him squarely in a cuspidore that had not as yet received his intelligent attention. He arose with dignity and while sponging the after convexity of his trousers before a mirror, was seized with vertigo and fell dead. Many early patrons of the place were deeply affected the next morning on seeing their old friend's duties performed by a strange colonel.

450.

When a friend of the people was asked, the other day, to define his position
with reference to protection and free trade, he said his views would be more
concisely and accurately stated in the platform adopted by the national convention of his party next year than he could state them himself.

451.

When an opposing candidate's friend called on a conscientious editor and
offered him one thousand dollars to "let up," the conscientious editor readily
accepted the bribe. But in the next issue of the paper he was worse than ever,
besides exposing "a villainous attempt to corrupt the purity of the press with a
paltry bribe of fifty dollars," which had been flung in the face of the man offering it, but on second thought was tacitly accepted and given to the directors of
the orphan asylum — whose card of thanks was appended to the article. There
is a nine-hundred-and-fifty-dollar coolness between the opposing candidate
and the former friend who negotiated the bribe.

452.

A benevolent lady who looked after the needs of deserving charities called on a
truly good man for a donation to the training school for broken-backed idiots.
The truly good man gave her one hundred dollars on the condition that she
was to acknowledge through the public press the receipt of five hundred dollars from him. The benevolent lady acknowledged through the public press
the receipt of ten dollars from the truly good man, which sum she duly paid
in. Their mutual esteem soon ripened into a warmer sentiment, which could
only be allayed by marriage.

453.

Forgetting that he had taken a bribe from the plaintiff, a just and upright judge
took also a bribe from the defendant. Reminded of his oversight by the clerk
of the court, "I must do the best I can," said he. So he gave judgment for the
plaintiff, who hadn't the ghost of a case, and instructed the defendant how to
have it set aside. "But why did you not give *me* judgment?" protested the defendant. "My dear fellow, I did not dare to brave public opinion: the plaintiff
is my wife's cousin."

454.

A lady of irreproachable character vehemently denounced her lover as a faithless wretch, and in a storm of tears said to him: "I saw you on the Oakland ferry-boat flirting with your wife." "But, my dear," said the devoted husband, "it was merely ———". "Don't talk to me, sir; you know well enough what that kind of thing leads to."

455.

A dying Christian said: "I die in the sure and certain hope of a speedy resurrection and a blessed immortality in communion and fellowship with the Holy Spirit." Having said this he immediately expired. A moment later the body opened its eyes an instant and said: "Sold again!"

456.

A Pot surrounded by a number of Potkins was sitting on a hearth near a Kettle in the midst of Kettlings. Suddenly the Potkins, looking blackly at the Kettle, cried out: "Smutty-face!"

There was no reply, but the Kettle made a mute appeal to the Pot to call off its dogs; but this was contemptuously disregarded. Finding their argument unanswered, the Potkins said to one another: "Now we have got this thing all our own way"; and with added zeal they cried out again and again: "Smutty-face! Smutty-face! Smutty-face!"

At last one of the Kettlings — an impulsive soul — threw a glance of defiance at the Pot and shouted: "Smutty-face too!"

Then the Potkins all boiled with rage, and the Pot, slopping over, instructed the Tongs to bring an action for libel and to get as many Potkins on the jury as possible.

457.

One day a number of Rowdies blackguarded a Gentleman who was passing, and said all manner of disagreeable things about him; but the Gentleman did not heed them and passed on about his business and the Rowdies said: "He dares not reply!"

Pretty soon the Gentleman's Companion came along, and some one asked him if the charges against his friend were true.

"It is all nonsense," said the Companion.

Then the Rowdies set up a terrible cry and said: "How undignified for any one who enjoys the companionship of gentlemen to notice anything *we* say!"

458.

A Straw engaged in showing which way the wind blew was struck by a cyclone and driven furiously out of sight beyond the Political Horizon.

"I fear I shall have some difficulty," said the Straw, dejectedly, "in defining my position."

"That is unfortunate," answered the Political Horizon; "there will be a good many applicants for it pretty soon."

459.

A Volcano that was throwing stones all over the landscape was accosted by a Politician who, after eying the performance awhile, said:

"I can beat you at that, old man."

"Prove it," thundered the Volcano, defiantly throwing more stones.

"Proof is superfluous," said the Politician, drily — "I live in a glass house."

460.

A Man Who Was Running for Office was hindered by a Political Opponent, who stood in his way and attempted to force him back, but fearing he should be unsuccessful, opened a box that he carried and let out a rattlesnake which bit the Man Who Was Running for Office and made him so lame that he could no longer run.

"Do you think it fair," said the cripple, sitting down and moodily nursing his wounded leg, "to bite me with a snake in order to let your friend pass me?"

"O, never mind," said the Political Opponent; "I would not do you any real injustice: that is only a campaign snake."

"And what remedial name have you for this rapidly spreading mortification?" asked the patient, exhibiting his swollen and blackening leg.

"This is nothing but political effect."

461.

A Gallantry meeting a Bribe asked:

"Whom do you serve? I do not understand the pine cone on your livery."

"Never mind," was the proud reply; "it is more important how I serve him. I have made my master rich."

"And I will make mine President of the United States," said the Gallantry, with superior pride.

462.

A Pusillanimous Liar having spoken was called to account by an Infamous Slanderer.

"As the challenged party," said the Pusillanimous Liar, "I have the choice of weapons. I choose mud."

After fighting for some hours they had to be separated, for it was no longer possible to say which was the Pusillanimous Liar and which the Infamous Slanderer.

463.

A Record Without a Blot and an Escutcheon Without a Stain resolved to marry, for each was the last of its race; but the banns were forbidden by an Unimpeachable Integrity, on the ground that it would itself be left without the possibility of mating and with no hope of posterity.

464.

An Eminent Jurist meeting a Grasping Monopoly said: "Get thee behind me, Satan!" and looked upon the Grasping Monopoly with so severe a virtue that all thought of tempting him was instantly abandoned. So the Grasping Monopoly got behind the Eminent Jurist. And there, too, was the Eminent Jurist's right hand, palm upward and fingers significantly twiddling.

465.

A Libel, seeing itself pursued by a Retraction, laughed loud and long and said: "The old girl is so slow that I can take a nap and still beat her a league."

Before he woke the Retraction had passed him, and the people along the route, admiring her graceful waddle and her undeviating course and charmed by her voice, took a lively interest in what she had to tell them and wondered what the devil it all meant. In the meantime the Libel, having wakened and found himself distanced, loped nimbly away in a hundred other directions overlaying the land with a system of the most lovely curves and loops, and filling it with the music of his tale.

466.

A Uniformed Club wielded by a Rich Candidate accidentally came in contact with the cheek of a partizan editor, and glancing off, struck the Rich Candidate himself for five hundred dollars.

467.

A Young Man who had absently trodden on the corns of a Schoolma'am made an honest woman of her by secretly giving her a yellow dog. Years afterward, when the Young Man was an old war-horse and the yellow dog an old man, a Moral Person said:

"See what a scoundrel! He ought to have given her the yellow dog first. The villain has been guilty of reparation!"

Then the Moral Person contemplated with tender satisfaction three bushels of photographs of young women upon whose toes he had danced multitudes of hornpipes, paying never a yellow dog.

468.

In defining his position a Defeated Candidate-elect said:

"I favor freedom of the ballot, an honest currency and the principles of personal liberty."

This was said in the presence of a Voter Who Had Never Heard It Before, but he said not a word in praise of the noble sentiment.

The Voter Who Had Never Heard It Before was a Deaf Mute.

469.

A Statesman who, in the home of a Wise Man, was confidently predicting the success of his party, was taken by the ear and led out of doors.

"Parting is such sweet sorrow," said the Wise Man, "that I would fain prolong it; but business is business."

And the Wise Man kicked the Statesman on the end of the back, and the Statesman absented himself thence.

"The man who cannot see," said the Wise Man, "that it is wiser and decenter to show that his party ought to succeed than to predict that it will, is a kiln-dried idiot, and shall not enter my house. Besides, we are going to win this election ourselves."

Turning to reënter his house, the Wise Man found that the wind had closed the door, and a spring-bolt had fastened it.

470.

The Child of an Indian Brave and a Brilliant Peroration having been born, the Indian Brave said:

"What shall we name this terror of the plains that paints his nose pea-green and brings the raging buffalo in thunder to the ground?"

The Brilliant Peroration said she thought that Demosthenes Cicero Patrick Pitt O'Connell would be about the terror's size.

"No," the Indian Brave replied, folding his arms with dignity, "he is the son of a warrior and shall be named in the manner of my tribe. I will look out of the window and the first thing I see, that shall be his name."

He looked out of the window and said:

"Let the heir of the Red Man and devourer of hop toads be called Candidate-with-His-Pockets-Hanging-Out-Escaping from a Saloon."

471.

A Candidate for Office who had made it a point of honor to maintain the incorruptibility of the press, and was now shunned by all who knew him, applied to a Bloated Capitalist for a small Loan to start an opposition paper with; but the Loan clung convulsively to the Bloated Capitalist's breast, sobbing so piteously that he said:

"You see how it is—I really have not the heart. But I'll tell you what I'll do. Take my vote and influence at ten per cent. less than the regular market price. On the discount you ought to be able to start a pretty good campaign paper."

472.

An Office Holder who had taken a bribe was confronted by the receipt in the hands of a Political Opponent, and so strong was his terror that his liver turned white in a single night.

473.

A Democratic Member of the Legislature, walking in a cemetery, saw sticking out of the earth the end of a Gray Hair which he had brought down in sorrow to the grave. Pulling it out, he laid it on the sleeve of his coat and regarding it with filial tenderness, expressed the hope that it had had a big funeral.

"Yes, my son," said the Gray Hair, "I was followed to the sepulchre by the execrations of all who hate you."

"And the Gray Hairs of my father," said the Democratic Member of the Legislature, "have I brought them also down with sorrow to the grave?"

"No, he is a Democrat himself," was the reply. "Besides, he wears a wig."

474.

When Young-Man-Afraid-of-His-Record had been nominated to the chieftaincy of his tribe he was visited in his wigwam by the Big Medicine Man of Tammany, and was so overcome with apprehension that for some moments his guest was left standing. At last a young brave in attendance spread a bear-skin for him and said:

"Your great father desires you to be seated."

"My father!" repeated the Big Medicine Man, with great dignity. "The slobber-champing rhinaughty curious is my father; this white-faced impostor is only an old woman. I will repose on her bosom."

So he sat down upon Young-Man-Afraid-of-His-Record, and the impression is there to this day.

475.

A Silver Spoon met a Workingman's Moses and poured out upon him a copious flow of bitter reproach.

"What!" cried the Workingman's Moses; "have you no gratitude? Did I not in your early spoonhood remove you from a household where for three years you had suffered the indignity of stirring a rebel widow's rye-coffee, and convey you to a place where for the remainder of your life you could enjoy the felicity of assisting to compound an honest gentleman's fragrant punches of good New England rum? But if kind words and gentle means will not reclaim the wicked they must be dealt with in a severer manner."

So the Silver Spoon, with five of its mates, was given away as a bridal present and pilloried in the glare of publicity, with the donor's card attached to its neck by a string.

476.

A Political Boss was secretly removing the coins from the eyes of a dead body and biting them (the coins) to ascertain if they were good, when a Molar of the *maxilla superior* protested through the Eustachian tube that the incisors and bicuspids were getting all the good eating.

"It is a merely sentimental advantage they get out of it," replied the Political Boss; "there isn't any divvy in it. Your claim shall be recognized as soon as I begin upon the corpse."

477.

A Civil-Servant going home from a grand rally, with his torchlight extinguished, overtook a Voluntary Contribution and expressed his gratification at having company; but when they had arrived at the loneliest part of the road his affable companion halted, threw off his cloak and stood revealed as a Compulsory Assessment.

478.

A Gentlemen whose existence had offended a Thrifty Patriot was ordered by the latter to keep his distance. He answered:

"I hope to be able to: I have observed that the farther away from you I get, the more things I can keep."

479.

A Stanch Democrat who had voted at every presidential election since he came of age, and every time for Jackson, was instilling the principles of constitutional government into the mind of an Alien, who had given formal notice of his intention to become a citizen. The Alien listened long and patiently to the doctrines of the Democratic party, and then went to consult a lawyer, to learn if he could be sued for breach of promise in case he should swear allegiance to the Ahkoond of Swat.

480.

A Tariff for Revenue Only
Was feeling uncommonly lonely;
    He sighed: "It appears
    (And therefore these tears)
The country's about to postpone me."

Protection said: "Sir, your averment
Is mild — something worse than deferment
    Awaits you: remember
    The Fourth of November
Is set for your decent interment."

481.

An Old Professional Candidate whose sands of life were nearly run out discovered a New Lease of Life and was about to avail himself of its advantages.

"Alas!" said the New Lease of Life; "why should I be devoted to so unworthy a purpose as prolonging an existence that has already exceeded the allotted span? Pray bestow me upon Governor Cleveland."

"That would do no good," replied the Old Professional Candidate: "he has to die next month anyhow."

"I know that," was the rejoinder, "but at the last moment he could bequeath me to his memory."

"He won't want to be remembered," said the Old Professional Candidate.

482.

The Irish Vote was lying in a hod, and the hod was on the shoulder of a man, and the man was on the top of a ladder. The Irish Vote was considering how it should be thrown. Presently the American Hog, passing that way, paused and putting his broad shoulder against the ladder, closed his eyes in sleepy satisfaction, as he scratched his hide. Then the Near Future said:

"It looks to me—though I'm a little near-sighted—as if the Irish Vote would be thrown by the same old party."

483.

A Candidate Who Loved the People was one day talking to a Wicked Millionaire, who said:

"The public be damned!"

By this heartless remark the Candidate Who Loved the People was thrown into such acute distress that it was for some time thought he was a Green Cucumber; but the Green Cucumber that the Candidate Who Loved the People was thought to be pointed out the difference by saying:

"He is crookeder than I am and a good deal deadlier."

Finding that he could not conceal his identity, the Candidate Who Loved the People threw off all disguise, smiled right cheerfully and damned the public a little himself.

484.

An Officeholder who had been remarkably successful in stocks was heard to remark that if the appropriation for his department had not unluckily been exhausted without advantage to the public he would have consented to serve till the end of his term, and should not have seen "the palms and temples of the south."

485.

An aged and experienced Public Character one day called his sons about him and said to them:

"My children, the time has now arrived for you to go out into the world and shift for yourselves in the neighborhood of the public treasury. It is a give-and-take kind of life, the secret of which is to give as little as you can spare and take as much as you can get. There will be a good deal of calumniation, and as we are all vulnerable it has been said that those who live in glass houses should not throw stones. I do not go so far as that, my sons; I only say that I hope no child of mine living in such a house will ever be insensible to the advantage of going out of doors to throw them."

486.

A Democrat ambitious to serve his country in the hauls of legislation kept a Standing army which he uniformed at his own expense. One day he visited the Standing Army at its headquarters and asked:

"Have you any suggestions to make about your uniform?"

"Yes," said the Standing Army, "I find that the most logical red cotton for capes cannot be had at ten cents a yard, but will cost twelve. We ought to have the best. In order to convince the erring Republican there should be more brass braid on the tunic; and it is proved by experience that white trousers are less argumentative than red. There is also a dangerous concession to the principles of a protective tariff in a tin spear with an unpainted handle."

"But, my noble embattled host," said the Candidate, "the changes you suggest will cost several thousand dollars. How can I afford the expense?"

"Excellent Commander-in-Chief," replied the Standing Army, "you wander from the subject. In order entirely to establish the soundness of your views on local questions of importance, the regulation helmet should have a horsehair plume and a brass buckle to the chin-strap."

The Candidate said reflectively as he turned away to give the necessary orders:

"It would have been almost as cheap for me to have had a clear judgment, an honorable record and a good personal character."

487.

A Diver going up met the American Navy coming down.

"What!" said the Diver, "have they been putting you in the water again?"

"I don't so much mind that," replied the American Navy, "I bid defiance to the elements; but whenever I start out to make the flag respected a three-masted schooner ensues, and rams me."

"It is all right, my friend," said the Diver, "every three-masted schooner along the coast flies the flag."

488.

A Broken Pledge applied to a Campaign Document to set its bones.

"No," said the Campaign Document, coldly, "it is not my business to set bones, but traps."

489.

A Rousing Speech meeting a Frothy Harangue said:

"Defend yourself—this is a good place to settle our difference."

"What *is* our difference?" inquired the Frothy Harangue, sadly.

"It consists, mainly," said the Rousing Speech, with a humorous twinkle in his eye, "in the politics of the newspapers which report us. It is the newspapers that have set us against one another—we who are twins."

490.

A Democratic Candidate for Treasurer, who had exchanged coats with a scarecrow, was congratulated on his new prosperity.

"Yes," he said, "it is another striking illustration of the advantages of Free Trade."

491.

Prowling about in a school-house, a Political Boss found an English Grammar, and throwing off his coat, got a neck hold of it and was about to vanquish it; but the book, slipping nimbly from his grasp, was on top of him in an instant, pressing both his shoulders to the floor.

492.

A Scavenger who had been nominated by acclamation explained that it was the proudest moment of his life.

"When I embraced my present profession," he added, "I did not think that it would so cordially return the embrace."

493.

"I was told," said the Dismantled Mendicant, "that the man should not seek the office, but the office should seek the man. I waited twenty years for the office to do its duty in this matter, but it would not. So I sought the office."

"Well, then, what are you snuffling and blubbering about?" tenderly inquired the Opulent Ragpicker.

"Because," replied the Dismantled Mendicant, shivering in the sharp east wind—"because when I sought the office I had the misfortune to find it."

494.

A Record belonging to a Democratic candidate for the presidency attempted to secure the services of a Sponge.

"That is all very well," said the Sponge, shrinking to half its former size, "but whose services could *I* secure afterward?"

A by-standing Wool-Scourer said:

"You might get Niagara Falls to hit you a few times."

495.

A Democratic Statesman addressing a popular meeting, inadvertently mentioned the name of James G. Blaine; then, perceiving his mistake, lifted his hand hastily, to command silence.

"You may beat Lulu Hurst at her little game," said the Audience, "but you are not strong enough to hold down this cheer."

496.

A Pork-Packer who had been nominated for Mayor met an Educated Pig, who looked at him intently for a moment and then said:

"You can pack *me* an make a profit on me, but I'll be pickled if any political party can afford to pack *you!*"

497.

A Goat passing along the street near the residence of a family that was moving, approached a mirror standing against a wagon-wheel, and seeing his image in it, backed a few paces away, lowered his head and made a leap at it. The mirror was shattered into fragments and the goat caught between the spokes of the wheel behind it. On being released some minutes later, he ran round to the other side of the wagon, gazed across the fields, and shaking his head despondently, explained that if he had not been detained by an accident that ugly rascal would not have had time to run away.

"My dear fellow," said an Old Politician who had observed the battle, "the ugly rascal was not an issue in this campaign."

498.

A Torch-Light Procession met a Red-Headed Girl and was extinguished in the superior effulgence.

"I think my candidate need give himself no further uneasiness in the matter," said the Red-Headed Girl, passing in at the door of her house.

But the moment the door was closed the Torch-Light Procession became visible again, as brilliant as before, and the contest had to be settled with ballots, just as if God hadn't made any Girl and the Devil hadn't made any Procession.

499.

A Candidate with one foot in his Political Grave predicted a triumphant election.

"What makes you think so?" inquired a Political Grave, cautiously reaching upward along the leg and extending a new drift to undermine the other foot.

"It is my duty to think so," said the candidate, proudly.

"My good friend," said the Political Grave, taking in the other leg and rising up about the neck, "since your reason is at the service of your sentiments and your judgment is tributary to your conscience, you do not appear to have much use for brains. I'll take that head if you please."

The spot is still pointed out to the traveler.

500.

A Pile of *Examiners* met an *Alta* sailing o'er life's troubled main. "Hello, little one! What are you doing here?" shouted the Pile of *Examiners*, and its voice, through the bars of its helmet, rang hoarsely out across the waste of waters like laughter in a tomb. "Oh, I'm lying-to," said the *Alta,* with far-heard whisper o'er the deep.

" *'Too?'* " repeated the Pile of *Examiners,* thoughtfully, " *'too?'* I wonder what other sins the pestilent little pirate is committing."

501.

The Hump of a Camel was introduced to a Prominent Citizen, hated and shunned by all who knew him. "Ah, your Prominency," said the Hump of a Camel, wearily and sadly, shaking his no head, "life, doubtless, is all bread and honey to *you:* the sorrows of the saddle are to you but the vague rumor of a fanciful disadvantage. You don't know what it is to be sat upon."

"O, don't I, though?" cried the Prominent Citizen, with sudden animation. "My friend," he added, with gravity, "you live in a land of Arabs, I in a land of editors. I'm sat upon 'more harder and more frequently' than you."

502.

A Boss said to a Candidate for the Nomination: "Let us dine together."

"You do me a very great honor," said the Candidate for the Nomination, eagerly, "and I gladly adopt the suggestion. I will be the host."

"I have planned it differently," said the Boss, with a bleak light in his eye; "you will be the dinner."

503.

A Piece of Presumption met a Dog's Tail. "My sorrowing friend," said the Piece of Presumption, "your bereavement touches me with the tenderest compassion. How did you lose your dog?"

"I tried to wag him," was the reply, "and he broke off."

"It served you mighty well right!" said the Piece of Presumption, with sudden coldure. "A Fellow who doesn't know his place can't expect to have it very long."

"The value of a rebuke," wagged the Dog's Tail, reflectively, "is to be found not in its applicability to the offence of him who receives, but in its accordance with the practice of him who administers."

"Jesso," said the Piece of Presumption, walking deeply away.

504.

A *Chronicle* which had been thrown out of a house was trying to decide which way it would be blown along the street, but found some difficulty in preferring one direction to another. On one hand lay the offal dump of a slaughter-house, and the paper naturally yearned for the companionship of congenial abhorrences. But the breeze moving in that direction had passed over fields of new-mown hay and was disagreeably sweet and wholesome. The fastidious journal shrank from its touch and could not make up its own mind to embark upon it; whereas the occasional puffs from the offalry were most inviting. Unable at last to deny itself a transient delight for a permanent advantage, it mounted the current of its choice, was carried into a flower garden whence it was unable to escape, and died of disgust amidst the screaming odors of heliotrope and mignonette.

505.

There was a man named Daly, and he drank. One day he came home strikingly drunk, and when his wife suggested that he change his boots and go to bed he took a portion of a forest and brained her. He then brained John and Jerry and Patrice, in the order here set down, and afterward threw the baby into the fire. The dog, believing that these actions portended trouble in the household, crept under the floor, the pig expired of apprehension in the parlor, and he kicked the cat up the chimney. Then rearing his form to its full stature, he looked upon the ruin he had wrought, and smiling a dark significant smile said: "I am the 'Monarch of the Dalys!'"

506.

A Person who had had a Chastened Spirit was accosted by a Woe of Ireland, which laid hold upon both his ears. The Person who had a Chastened Spirit shook himself free, and in the ensuing remarks laid broad and deep the foundations of a new and startling system of profanity.

507.

A Grave with a Simple Headstone approached a Man About to Write a Story and said: "Sir, I have come to do my duty; you will need me to put your fool in."

The Man About to Write the Story replied: "I don't know what you mean."

"I mean your hero," explained the Grave with a Simple Headstone.

"Then," said the other, "you are all wrong; the hero lives and becomes famous, but ever at the approach of twilight, when—"

"Ah! I understand," said the mound, nodding with all its grasses; "but it is quite the same; I hold sheroes as well; I'll stay within call."

508.

The Rev. Dr. Stebbins is a good and wise man, but he is not beautiful. Being in Hollister one day, he was invited to attend a hanging, the local parson having declined on the ground of prejudice: his wife had been the victim of the murder. Many strangers attended, and as the procession, headed by the man of God, appeared at the jail door to cross the inclosure to the scaffold, it halted, leaving him just outside with a Deputy Sheriff visible behind him. "What a vicious countenance!" said a spectator. "Yes," said another, "his lawyer didn't have no fair show."

509.

A Dull, Sickening Thud loitering by the wayside was approached by a Loathsome Contemporary traveling with strange haste. "Sir," said the loiterer, "you are about to have the honor to fall in with a no less distinguished person than myself."

"I have fallen in with you already," said the other surprised, hastening on and casting a look of terror behind. Pretty soon he was overtaken by a Monarch of the Dailies, and at the same moment found himself on the brink of the Gulf of Dark Despair. Looking about him with mad disquietude he perceived the Dull, Sickening Thud still at his side and fell in with him, as predicted.

510.

A Boned Turkey was proceeding weakly along the street on crutches, when he was seized from behind by a Late Reveler and devoured with avidity. An hour afterward the Late Reveler saw a Horrible Specter and shrieked "Who art thou?"

"I am the Fourth of July," replied the Horrible Specter, producing a case of instruments of torture.

"But I thought you were not to be celebrated this year," protested the sufferer.

"Not publicly," explained the apparition; "this is a private celebration. You are asleep."

"Permit me to introduce also your sainted Mother-in-Law," murmured the Boned Turkey.

The spot is still pointed out to the traveler.

511.

A Dog whose sands of life were nearly run out lay helpless at his master's door. "Alas!" he whined, "age has robbed me of the power to fulfill the purpose of my being and the functions of my race. My voice is so impaired and my teeth are so infrequent that I can no longer adequately terrify the incautious passer-by nor properly mangle the hardy visitor. Thank heaven," he added, reverently, "the older I grow the more offensive I am to the eye and nose, and the more I scatter plenty (of fleas) o'er a smiling land."

512.

A Federal Judge was engaged in setting aside an Act of Congress, when his Grandfather, who was Clerk of his court, explained that there was more money to be made in fees by enforcing it. Thereupon the Federal Judge made a decision sustaining the law, and was afterward appointed a Custodian of Morals and lived respected by all who knew him.

513.

A Piece of Cold Cheek at the corner of Bush and Kearny streets last Sunday morning was overheard to remark: "If Dr. Josselyn and the other persons implicated with him were the only ones concerned, society would not need bother itself about the result of the investigation which must follow this indictment, if it is prosecuted, as *we propose to see that it shall be*." "Ah!" said an Arctic Explorer, who was passing by, "this is, indeed, truly polar!" And shivering in his furs, he produced from his pocket a quart flask of train oil and drained it to the last drop. An expedition equipped with dog-sledges is about to start in search of his remains.

514.

A Silurian Editor met a Large and Increasing Circulation, and looking at it in astonishment said:

"What are you? I never saw anything like you before — at least not close to."

"I am a fisherman," the Large and Increasing Circulation answered. "I catcha da small adda."

"I will take a dozen small adders," said the Silurian Editor: "I want to study their methods of controversy. In the mean time I shall skirmish round and see if I can catch a few short advertisements."

But he did not catch any.

515.

A Soul which had been an hour in Hades cried aloud to St. Peter, saying:

"What are the water rates here?"

St. Peter, not knowing whence the voice came, asked:

"Are you a large consumer?"

"Not as large as I was," the Soul replied, "being already considerably shriveled; but I am willing to become a consumer — at present I am one of the consumed."

"What was your business on earth?" inquired the Saint.

"I was President of a water company," the Soul said.

516.

A Goucher meeting a Camel who seemed about to sink under the weight of his hump, exclaimed:

"My good ship of the desert, that is a pretty heavy deck load that you carry."

"Yes," said the Camel, "this is my Meany."

517.

A Monarch of the Dailies, walking arm in arm with Public Opinion, saw a small black-and-white animal directly in the path.

"Let us turn out and go around it," said Public Opinion.

"Surely we need not fear so contemptible an object," said the Monarch of the Dailies. "I shall go ahead and kick the creature out of the way."

"As your Majesty's Prime Minister," Public Opinion persisted, "I must beg you to do no such thing. No doubt you could kick the creature clear across the equator, but for the next five years the royal robes would be telling of the encounter."

"Why, what kind of beast is it?" the Monarch of the Dailies was graciously pleased to inquire.

"It is called," replied the Prime Minister, "a Pickering."

518.

The Private Secretary to a ruined and disgraced Governor fell asleep and dreamed that he saw an Angel walking in the Garden of Eden, where a serpent was in stealthy conversation with a woman. The woman soon moved away in the direction of a distant fruit tree, and the Angel approaching the Serpent said with a frown:

"What right have you, monster, to come in here and speak to the woman?"

And the Serpent answered: "I am her Private Secretary."

519.

A Cloud which had long been darkening the fortunes of a certain State Senator saw him rise in his place and begin weeping to a question of privilege. The touching spectacle so affected the sensibilities of the Cloud that it wept copiously in sympathy. Wherefore the farmers were jubilant.

520.

A Lone Legislator who had tarried at the State capital after his fellows had gone home to be hanged by their constituents met His Record, and not recognizing it, said:

"Get out of my way, you Gam-doodled nigger!"

His Record stepped aside, and as the Lone Legislator passed on, remarked in his ear:

"See you later."

Then the Lone Legislator was filled with remorse and said: "Alas! I can no longer point to you with pride."

"No," said His Record, "I will henceforth do the pointing myself."

521.

A Vrooman who had had a millstone hung about his neck and been cast into the sea was joined at the bottom by all his Personal and Political Friends.

"How came you here?" said the Vrooman.

"The people are casting out devils up there," said the Personal and Political Friends, "and — and — we ran down a steep place."

522.

Perceiving that the Earth had stopped revolving and all the heavenly bodies were holding their breath, an Astronomer was greatly alarmed and begged that things might go on as usual.

"That is impossible at present," said the Earth. "Senator Goucher has declared that his future course with regard to the press will depend upon the answer which he gets to a telegram. We are waiting to learn the answer."

523.

A newly appointed Yosemite Valley Commissioner arrived at the scene of his labors, and taking a bucket of tar from beneath his gaberdine dipped a stick in it and began discharging his official duties by daubing upon the face of El Capitan the words: "The Pope's Irish."

Exhausted by the effort he fell asleep, when another Commissioner passing that way took the stick and wrote below the other inscription: "So am I," and contemplating the personal pronoun with profound emotion was overcome also.

An Artist passing that way and finding them deep asleep, coated the forefingers of their right hands with some of the tar and then tickled their noses with a spear of grass; whereat, half awaking, they vigorously rubbed those organs with the coated fingers, and the Artist said the effect was "finer than a fiddle."

When the Board presented its accounts to the Controller, at the end of the year, one of the items read as follows: "To improving the valley by substituting an Effect for a Fiddle, $7,000."

524.

A Governor who had a Boruck for Private Secretary was overheard by the State to swear that he would not serve again for one million dollars.

"I have more money than that," said the State, "but perhaps we can arrange a compromise. Suppose you don't serve!"

525.

A Governor's Private Secretary was observed standing on a step-ladder beneath the dome of the Capitol, bare-headed.

"It does not appear to fit," said an Irreverent Spectator.

"It fitted well enough," said the Private Secretary, "before I got my hair cut."

"Don't you mean," asked the Irreverent Spectator, "before you got your comb cut?"

The reply was unfit for publication.

526.

Some Political Aspirations, which had long lodged in a cave, said:

"Why should we consort longer with bats and reptiles? Let us get out of this."

So they moved into the head of an Honest Man, who at once mounted a stump and told the people he had no Political Aspirations. So the people, charmed by his unselfishness, elected him Inspector of Dead Dogs on Vacant Lots.

527.

A great multitude of loafers and fishers had surrounded a New President and were clamoring to be fed. The New President seeing that he had not enough loaves and fishes to feed one in a thousand of them beat his breast in despair, for he expected to be torn to pieces by the disappointed crowd.

"Well," he said, "I will at least do a just act before I die. There is a Modest Man standing on the outskirts of the crowd who has asked for nothing; let him be brought forward."

When the Modest Man was brought before him the New President said to him:

"My friend, I have observed your forbearance and it touches me deeply. Now you may have anything that I can give you. Speak up."

"Your Excellency," replied the Modest Man, "I want nothing but what is left after the others are served. Give me the fragments of the feast."

The New President, mistaking him for a madman, thought it prudent to humor him and said:

"Certainly; how will you carry them away?"

The Modest Man said: "Give yourself no uneasiness as to that; I have brought seven baskets."

528.

A Sugar King was pointing with pride to some samples of his art.

"It was made from the beet-root," he said.

"It is not half as sweet as I am," said a Dude, removing the head of a walking-stick from his mouth, "and I'm a product of the juice of the cane."

529.

A Secretary of State said to a Lexicographer:

"Now that I am in power we shall have a more vigorous foreign policy, for I am a fighter."

"What was your rank in the civil war?" asked the Lexicographer.

"I—I—was a plumed knight," was the hesitating reply, "but I favored a vigorous prosecution of the war."

Then the Lexicographer took out his notebook and wrote:

"FIGHTER, *n*. A person who instigates other persons to fight."

530.

Two ingrates sat in the taproom of a wayside inn near the gates of Hades, recounting their exploits.

"*Ma Foi!*" said he whom men call the Christmas Gift; "it was a good day's work: I have made a pauper of my maker!"

"And I?" said he who is known as the New Year's Resolution — "have I spared mine? To his vices have I not added crime? Behold him — a perjurer!"

Then the two ingrates, pledging one another in bumpers of sack, said: "Pleasant dreams to you," and retired for the year.

531.

A Governor Waterman whom a cyclone had lifted to the Summit of His Ambition said to that peak: "I should like to remain with you always, my friend: the view is magnificent!"

"You can't stay here all the time," replied the Summit of His Ambition: "I don't keep a hotel."

"But can't I come again some time?" the Governor Waterman asked.

"Well, yes — if the wind is favorable," said the Summit of His Ambition; "but not on a calm day. And now, sonny, it is pretty nearly time for you to go down."

At that moment a strange apparition came forward and stood beside the Governor Waterman.

"Who are *you?*" that worthy person inquired.

"A Dull Sickening Thud," replied the apparition. "I am ready for duty — I shall be with you when you descend."

532.

A Prison Warden was diligently writing letters one evening and marking them "Confidential," preparatory to throwing them into the public highway in the morning, when he heard a Voice saying: "I thought I would drop in and see if we could do some business together."

"Happy to hear you," said the Prison Warden cordially. "Whom have I the honor to address?"

"Political Capital," replied the Voice.

"I thought that was capital I," the Prison Warden said, thoughtfully.

Heedless of the interruption, the Voice continued: "You are always trying to make me, and now I've come to be made. Existence hasn't done any great things for *you*, but I am willing to try it."

"No," said the Prison Warden, drearily, "my last and most strenuous effort to make you has been meanly baffled by the State Controller. You will have to apply to a more able-bodied creator."

The Voice, retiring in a whisper, vanished with a sigh which extinguished the candle, and the Prison Warden was left in the darkness, alone with his identity!

533.

A Monarch of the Dailies who had saved the life of a shipwrecked fisherman was sitting in his sanctum, writing up the details of a dog fight in Madagascar, when an Evening Silurian thrust his face in at the window, saying: "If you think that saving human lives is legitimate journalism you are greatly mistaken. *I* don't do it."

"I know you don't," said the Monarch of the Dailies, pleasantly, "but you are trying very hard to save your own, and here's a dollar to assist you."

The Evening Silurian clutched the money and began to move dreamily away, but the Monarch of the Dailies called him back and said: "I don't know but you may be right about my saving the fisherman: perhaps it really was not legitimate journalism—I haven't thought much about that. Suppose we leave it to the fisherman."

But the Evening Silurian, overcome by the sudden accession to his wealth, was already celebrating it by falling asleep.

534.

A Frightful Epidemic which had desolated the cities of two continents came to a country hotel and engaged board and lodging. A few moments later it saw an Emaciated Person and said to him: "I shall have, perhaps, a little business with the guests; it may take a week or more to transact it. I suppose I shall be made pretty comfortable while here."

"I suppose so," said the Emaciated Person; "I have been here from the start, and I'm comfortable."

Immediately after dinner the Emaciated Person saw the Frightful Epidemic, grip-sack in hand, leaving the place.

"What! so soon?" said the Emaciated Person.

"Yes," said the Frightful Epidemic, "I have recollected an engagement elsewhere; if I didn't keep it I should be sick. What kind of ostrich are you, to be comfortable here?"

"My name," said the Emaciated Person, "is Loss of Appetite."

535.

A Yosemite Valley Commissioner, who had placed one hundred million tons of dynamite against the base of El Capitan, was scratching a match upon the end of his back when he saw a hard-featured Woman passing by. Fearing detection, he struck his match and holding it between his hands pretended to be lighting his pipe.

"You need not dissemble," said the Woman: "I entirely approve what you are about to do."

For the first time in his life the Yosemite Valley Commissioner felt a thrill of joy which he could not trace to an expectation of gain. He gazed with admiration upon her whose favor could so powerfully affect him and inquired: "Who are you, madam?"

"I am your conscience," was the reply.

"Conscience, conscience?" he repeated, interrogatively, with a puzzled expression. "O yes," he cried, with the light of a sudden revelation suffusing his face — "on my mother's side, I suppose. I knew I had relations somewhere in this part of the State."

Lifting his coat-skirts with his left forearm, he struck another match and fired the dynamite. She stepped back to avoid the explosion and he never saw her again.

536.

A Chiropodist accosted a Lame Person and offered to remove his corns. "What!" exclaimed the Lame Person, "remove my corns and expose the country to the horrors of unexpected rainstorms? What do you take me for?"

"Who *are* you?" asked the Chiropodist, backing away.

"An officer of the Signal Service," the Lame Person replied.

537.

A Foreign Nobleman who had married a Rich American Girl was discovered in the act of breaking her heart.

"Why do you break her heart?" asked the Discoverer.

"Because," replied the Foreign Nobleman, "the law does not permit me to break her head."

538.

A Rich American Girl who had married a Foreign Nobleman was seen weeping by the roadside.

"Why do you weep, my good girl," a Passing Traveler asked.

"Because my husband has broken my heart," answered the Rich American Girl.

"Indeed!" exclaimed the Passing Traveler, absently. "And what, pray, did you expect?"

"I expected," was the reply, accompanied by a fresh burst of tears, "to break his."

539.

A Bulldog whose master had put a muzzle on him met a Mastiff.

"I think this ornament very becoming to me," said the Bulldog, secretly trembling; "it is the handsomest in town."

"Before we part," said the Mastiff, closely scanning the muzzle, "you will think it too loose."

"How so?" asked the Bulldog.

"If it had been tighter," the Mastiff replied, "you would have had to keep your mouth shut about it, and I should not have observed it."

So saying he set upon the Bulldog and thrashed him with impunity.

540.

A Famous Pugilist who had refused to fight for a purse of $15,000 was seen by a Friend some years afterward coming out of a low boarding-house, badly lacerated in the face and with several bald places on his head.

"Well, John," said the Friend cheerfully, "the grass is pretty short with you now, isn't it?"

"Yes," replied the Famous Pugilist, "prices have fallen. I fight for my board now."

"With whom?" asked the Friend, eager to see a match.

"With my landlady," the Famous Pugilist replied.

541.

A Candidate for re-election met a Constituent and shaking him heartily by the hand said: "How do you do, Mr. Smith?"

"My name is Jones," the Constituent said, solemnly.

"Ah, yes, I see," said the Candidate; "I mistook you for your brother. I hope Mrs. Jones is well."

"You have struck a streak of hard luck," said the Constituent, "and I am very sorry for you. I buried Mrs. Jones yesterday."

542.

A Teetotaler was singing a beautiful temperance song containing the sentiment,

> Water, sweet water, bright water for me,
> And wine for the trembling debaucheeee!

As he finished he saw before him a Melancholy Remain.

"Sing of the devil," said the Teetotaler, "and you'll see him in the audience."

"It is true," said the Melancholy Remain, in a voice sadly sweet, such as when winds and harp strings meet; "I *am* a trembling debaucheeee."

"Why not leave the wine cup and drink water?" the Teetotaler asked with humane solicitude.

"Drink water is it?" exclaimed the Melancholy Remain. "Why, I drink nothing else; that is how I became as you see me. I live in Oakland."

543.

A Gentleman Dog of the Mexican breed, who was bald-headed from the point of his nose to the tip of his tail, met a Lady Dog of the Setter sort and said, "What a beautiful creature! — what lovely hair!"

"It used to be much thicker and longer," said the Lady Dog, modestly, "before I had a fever and it came out."

"Ah, yes," said the Gentleman Dog, "I thought so. I was myself pretty hairy, too, at one time."

"And what became of your Hyperian locks?" the Lady Dog inquired, with deep feeling.

"All went to make wigs for chestnuts," answered the native of the Sister Republic.

544.

As a condemned murderer was about to mount the scaffold he looked upward and said, thoughtfully:

"The cross-beam at the top appears too slender. I can hardly make up my mind to trust it."

"It is all right," said the Sheriff; "you can depend upon it."

A few moments later the condemned murderer was depending.

545.

A Citrus Belt said to a Thermal Belt which had long inhabited the same breezy altitude on a mountain side: "Whither away so fast, pretty maid?"

"I cannot maintain my footing, on account of the ice and snow," replied the Thermal Belt, moving on down toward the valley. "I am following the thermometer."

"Well," said the Citrus Belt, packing his grippe, "there's no living without you."

And he joined the procession.

546.

A Policeman hearing a succession of sharp shrieks ran to the spot whence they seemed to come and found the Collectorship of the Port gesticulating with an umbrella, her hair down and with a general appearance of hysteria.

"What's the racket, you holy terror?" said the Policeman, with the characteristic tenderness which distinguishes his calling from that of the pirate of the Spanish Main.

"Colonel Jackson attempted to put his hands on me," said the Collectorship of the Port, sobbing, "and — and his hands are not clean!"

"Appearances are deceitful," said Colonel Jackson next day, when asked to explain them. "I give you my sacred word I did not come within a mile of her."

547. The Fire-Fiend and the Bursted Hose

A Fire-Fiend on Professional Business in an Overgrown Village with Metropolitan Aspirations, stumbled over a length of Burst Hose worth 85 cents a foot. Whereupon the Hose made an Abject Apology. To which the Fire-Fiend responded:

"Don't mention it; you have not Put me Out at all."

This Fable teaches — but no; it ought to, but it doesn't.

548. The City Hall Job and the Rotten Brick Work

A City Hall Job which had never been Discovered, fell in with a section of Rotten Brick-Work exposed to the Bright Sunlight of Publicity.

"You ought to be ashamed of this Exposure," remarked the Job, with contempt. "Do you not understand the necessity of Keeping Dark?"

"I do not as yet," replied the Unabashed Section, "but I shall no doubt Tumble in the Near Future."

This fable is another that doesn't teach anything.

549. The Rolling Stone and the Silurian Bowlder

A Rolling Stone which was engaged in Procuring a New and Efficient Fire Apparatus for a Progressive Town was hailed by a Silurian Bowlder, deeply imbedded in the ground and covered with a fine, rich growth of green moss.

"Do you not know," said the Silurian Bowlder, "that if you keep on in this way you will gather no moss? Look at me; I have not moved in 1,100 years."

"I can readily believe it," replied the Rolling Stone; "but, if you will permit a prophecy, it is my opinion that you will get a move on you when you least expect it."

That very night the Silurian Bowlder was distributed over 300 square miles by a charge of Dynamite of the Public Opinion Brand, and the Rolling Stone was elected to fill the vacancy.

This Fable teaches us that gathering moss is not such a snap as we have been led to suppose.

550. The Enterprising Publican and the Licentious Press

An Enterprising Publican who had Incorporated Himself as an Athletic Club was reproached by a Licentious Press with the Fact that Athletics formed no part of his Curriculum.

"You are mistaken," replied the Publican; "if you will drop in any evening I will show you a fine exhibition of Tumblers on the Horizontal Bar."

551. The Body-Snatcher and the Inquisitive Policeman

A Body-Snatcher, returning at midnight from a Professional Visit, saw an Inquisitive Policeman advancing in his General Direction.

"This Policeman probably wishes to converse with me upon matters of Grave Importance," said the Body-Snatcher to himself, "and as I am in no mood for argument I will Drop the Subject in advance." This he did, in a thicket of bushes near by, and then passed the Policeman with a polite "good evening."

This Fable teaches that a Body in the Bush is worth two in the Hand.

552. The Indignant Populace and the Grasping Monopoly

An Indignant Populace which had been seriously injured in attempting to board a cable dummy complained bitterly to a Grasping Monopoly which owned this Modern Juggernaut. To which the Grasping Monopoly replied: "You do not understand the subject of cable dummies at all; as soon as you Catch On you will have no further cause of complaint."

The Grasping Monopoly then proceeded to Declare a Dividend out of the Damages that the Indignant Populace had not received, while the Populace retired to nurse the Damages it had.

553.

An Ass hearing some grasshoppers chirping in a meadow was charmed with the song.

"How did you acquire such beautiful voices?" he asked.

"By dining upon thistles," replied the disingenuous insects.

"Thistles don't do it for me," said the Ass, sadly; "I'm no singer."

"The only trouble with you," said the kind-hearted Grasshoppers, "is that you have no ear."

554.

A Swallow engaged in trying to make a summer was joined by a Crow and the two disputed about their plumage.

"Your fine feathers are very good in the spring," said the Crow, "but mine protect me from the winter."

"But not from the farmer," said the Swallow.

555.

A Fight to a Finish was tranquilly pursuing the evil terror of its way, when a Chief of Police commanded it to surcease.

"Why, what is the matter with me?" inquired the Fight to a Finish, innocently.

"You incite to violence," replied the Chief of Police, with tart asperity — "your conduct is calculated to provoke a breach of the peace."

"I should like to know what is more peaceful than *that*," said the Fight to a Finish. And it pointed to a heavily gloved gentleman resting quietly upon the back of his head, with the lower jaw flung carelessly across his left shoulder.

556.

A Wit thrust his hand into a jar of chestnuts and grasped so many that he could not pull it out. Unwilling to lose his means of livelihood, yet unable to withdraw the hand, he wept bitterly and wished that he had learned another trade.

"Drop some of the chestnuts," exclaimed a by-stander.

So the Wit let go of all but these, and found that he could quite easily pull his hand out of the jar and put it in his editor's pocket.

557.

A Shepherd of a facetious turn of mind once cried: "Wolf! Wolf!" and his Neighbors, running to assist him and finding no wolf, beat him cruelly for deceiving them. Soon afterward his flock was attacked by a lion and the Shepherd cried out: "Wolf! Wolf!" as before. The Neighbors said: "That rascal is trying to fool us again, and we will cudgel him as before."

But when they had come to the spot the lion ate them and the humorous Shepherd was greatly pleased with the success of his stratagem.

558.

An old and infirm Lion being unable to pursue his prey lay down in his den
and gave it out that he was ill. Thereupon the other animals made him visits
of condolence in the hope of finding him so helpless that they could kill him
and eat him. But it was just the other way. By and by a Fox appeared and was
invited to enter.

"No, said the Fox, "I see too many footprints going in and not enough
coming out."

"I am surprised and pained by your want of sagacity," said the Lion. "Do
you not know that I am held in so profound respect that all animals back out
of my presence when taking leave?"

Being thus reassured the Fox entered and was eaten like a radish.

559.

The female Beasts were in controversy as to which of them brought forth the
greatest number of young at a birth, and agreed to leave the matter to the
Lioness.

"By the way," they said, after stating their question, "how many do you
yourself give birth to?"

"Only one," said the Lioness proudly, "but a rug made of his skin is worth
a great deal of money."

Thereupon they paid her the honors due to a Merchant Princess.

560.

"I beg to observe," said a Cock, who had been caught by a Cat, "that in crowing when men are asleep I am actuated by a pious regard for their best interest,
so you have not the slightest pretext for putting me to death."

"I was not aware that I needed one," said the Cat, eating him.

561.

A Tortoise was complaining of his hard life in being unable to fly, when an
Eagle, overhearing him, offered to take him up into the sky. The Tortise con-
senting, the Eagle grasped him in his talons, and rising to a great height in the
air, dropped him, saying: "That will teach you contentment."

"On the contrary," said the Tortoise, descending toward a stony soil, "it distinctly emphasizes my natural disadvantages. I never felt the need of wings so keenly as I do at this moment."

562.

A man and a lion traveling together fell to boasting of their power, each contending that his was the greater. While disputing, they passed a group of statuary in which a Californian sculptor had embodied his conception of Europa and the Bull.

"See," said the man, "how my views are confirmed by the first object that we pass!"

"That is so," said the lion, "the man does seem to be having rather the better of the lion."

A work of genius teaches more lessons than its author had in mind.

563.

Two Men traveling together met a Bear, whereupon one of them climbed a tree, but the other, being unable to climb, threw himself upon the earth and pretended to be asleep.

"How lucky!" said the Bear, lifting a mouthful of tendons out of the man's leg. "It is really too warm to exert oneself in killing game; but when the Lord provides it I would be wicked to refuse."

Cunning slays more (of the cunning) than the sword.

564.

A Wolf disguised in sheep's clothing pastured all day with the flock and at night permitted himself to be shut up in the fold.

Pretty soon the Shepherd, in quest of mutton, came with a knife and laid hold of the Wolf, but the sheepskin came off and the beast stood revealed in his true character.

"It seems to me," said the shepherd, backing away, "that you are not so fat as I had thought."

565.

A Trap, having snapped off the tail of a Fox, said to him:

"Never mind, my son; I shall do as much for a lot of your fellows before I have done."

"I beg you will not," said the Fox earnestly. "I am a prominent citizen now, but if other citizens were equally gifted I should lose my distinction."

566.

A flying Pigeon suffering from thirst saw a goblet of water painted on a panel by Mr. Samuel Brookes and was dashing down upon it with a force that would surely have broken her neck, when something caused her to stop and reflect.

"I don't believe that is real water," she said, eyeing it more critically; "it looks too wet."

The by-standers who had naturally expected to pick up the disabled Pigeon were so enraged that they set upon Mr. Brookes and tore him into small children.

567.

A Dog lying in a manger would not suffer an Ox to approach.

"What a selfish Dog!" said the Ox to himself: "he cannot eat the hay, yet he will not let me eat it."

"What an inconsiderate Ox," soliloquized the Dog; "he cannot lie in this manger, yet he wishes to make me get out of it."

568.

Some Boys were throwing stones at the Frogs in a pool, when an old Frog who had sat unmoved during the performance said: "My children, I can no longer keep selfishly silent without doing violence to the most generous instincts of my nature. I earnestly advise you to desist, for throwing stones makes the arm ache, and no boy was ever known to hit anything that he threw at. It is fun for us, but it is death to you."

569.

The oxen once sought to destroy the butchers, whose trade they considered contrary to good morals. They assembled on a certain day to devise plans for carrying out their purpose, and when all but one had spoken they called on him to give his views. "Gentlemen," he said, "I have but a single question to ask. Do you prefer to be eaten alive?"

570.

An astronomer used to go out at night to gaze at the stars. One night while his attention was fixed upon the sky he stumbled over a bank of earth, dislodging some lumps of gold. The next day he went back to the place, and, seeing the gold, located a mining claim, and grew enormously rich, and seven cities fight for the honor of his birth; for he is esteemed the most practical man and sagacious prospector that ever lived.

571.

Some Frogs who had maintained a republican form of Government besought Jupiter to give them a king. So Jupiter sent a log; whereupon, with true republican freedom, they set to and gnawed all the bark off it, and then asked him to depose the log and send them a stork.

"No," said Jupiter, "you would not leave a feather of him. You will have to restore the Republic and live upon one another, as before."

572.

A Kid standing on the thatch of a cottage reviled a Wolf who was passing below.

"O come off the roof," said the Wolf, indifferently.

But the Kid preferred to remain gloved.

573.

A pious Country Woman had two Hired Girls and a disagreeable habit of making them rise in the morning at the first crowing of the cock. So they resolved to assassinate that ancient bird; but, going out to execute their plan, they found that their mistress had already killed it for the preacher.

574.

A Sheep seeing a wounded wolf lying in his lair, said to him: "If I fetch you some water from the brook you will, I suppose, agree not to eat me?"

"With pleasure," replied the Wolf; "but it is only fair to notify you that a wolf's word is a sandy foundation to build upon."

"Sir," said the Sheep, "your frankness inspires me with added confidence in you; but unfortunately I have nothing to bring the water in."

575.

A fisherman engaged in his calling, made a very large catch, and was delighted; but when he reflected that nobody would believe him, he was less hilarious.

576.

An Ass who had long shocked the ears of all other animals with his bray put on a lion's skin. Thenceforward they called his note a roar, and encored him whenever he lifted up his voice.

577.

The Peacock complained to Juno that he was unable to sing.

"True," said Juno, "but see how gorgeous your plumage is!"

"That is all very well," replied the fowl, "but I should prefer to be more soberly fledged and have a softer voice."

"My child," said Juno, "be content. To each is allotted some gift fitting him for his station in life. You are intended for the opera bouffe."

578.

Some Dogs, finding the skin of a Bear, fell upon it with great gallantry and tore it into shreds and patches.

"Ah, you are very brave," said the Bear, "but if I had had it on, you would — "

Here the Bear was interrupted by a fit of sneezing, for he was too lightly clad for that climate.

579.

The She-goats having petitioned Jupiter for beards, obtained them—which greatly incensed the He-goats.

"Never mind," said Jupiter—"having beards they will now all want to be shaved. Perhaps it is needless to point out the effect upon what I may call tonsorial loquacity as an art."

The He-goats, glowing with the happiness of anticipation, said they had not thought Jupiter so clever.

580.

An Indian performing the Ghost Dance was asked by a Newspaper Man to explain it.

"It is very simple," said the Indian; "the Agency people starve me until I am nothing but a ghost, and my hunger makes me dance."

"Then you are not expecting any Messiah?" the Newspaper Man asked—"you don't want one?"

"No," said the Indian; "not unless he will bring his own grub."

Then the Newspaper Man telegraphed to his editor that the Indians were trying to dance their fat off, so as to be in condition for the war-path, and had set out a banquet for the Messiah.

581.

A Campaign Lie, wounded, was writhing in pain and dying among its worshipers, when Truth passed that way.

"When I am crushed to earth," she said, "I rise again; the eternal years—"

"I guess you'll see me pretty active myself about the next campaign," was the reply. "Don't imagine that I am really departing this life: I am only studying for the stage under Clara Morris."

582.

One morning as Protection to American Industry stood leaning on her spear she saw a cheerful person going by to his work, whistling.

"You seem unreasonably happy," said she. "For my part, I don't see how any one can honestly refuse to be dismal when thinking of the woes of American Industry."

"That is so," said the cheerful one; "but I never think of them except when some one directs my attention to them. I am American Industry."

"Indeed!" exclaimed she. "Then permit me to unload my shield on you."

So she hung it upon his neck and he staggered away, no longer needing to be reminded of his woes.

583.

A Bacillus of Tuberculosis was sitting by the wayside lunching on lung when he was accosted by a Quantity of Lymph, who said: "O come off!"

"If you think you can make me come off," replied the Bacillus, haughtily, "just come on."

The Quantity of Lymph was about to spring upon him, when a good old Physician passing that way said: "My children, you should not quarrel. You are both members of a learned and honorable profession."

"But how am I to be useful if I don't choke him off?" asked the Quantity of Lymph.

"By making him eat slowly; moderation is conducive to health — his moderation to my health."

And executing a slow, significant wink, the good Physician withdrew.

584.

A Distinguished Statesman while running for office was accosted by a Bitter Opponent of having written a compromising letter. He denied it.

"I will make him confess after election," said the Bitter Opponent.

"As soon as the voting is over," said the Distinguished Statesman, "I will compel him to retract his charge."

When the election had been decided an Intending Suicide, acting as go-between, obtained their assent to a time and place of meeting to settle the letter business on a staying basis.

"Why have you taken so much trouble in the affair?" the Intending Suicide was asked.

"In the interest of solitude," he replied. "At the appointed time I shall go to the appointed place and cut my throat. Naturally, I wish to be alone."

585.

A Member-elect of the Legislature saw a Bribe coming his way, and being terrified turned and ran into the arms of a larger Bribe approaching from the opposite direction.

"How unhappy is the lot of man," sighed the Member-elect of the Legislature, ceasing to struggle and bending his gaze upon the other Members-elect: "in avoiding Scylla he falls into Charybdis!"

"Is that so?" said the other Members-elect in one breath.

And then they all rushed up the road to meet Scylla.

586.

Two Giraffes ran a race and one of them won by a neck; whereupon a sporting correspondent telegraphed to his paper as follows:

"Mudswan won in 3:51 without effort. In fact, Stuckup wasn't in it."

587.

A Lady meeting a Man in a lonely spot where his screams would not be heard thanked him politely for giving up his seat to her in a street car. The Man's physician having warned him that any excitement might be fatal he had the Lady indicted for an attempt to produce the most deplorable consequences.

588.

The Governor of California pardoned a Convict who to show his gratitude stole a Yellow Dog and presented it to his illustrious benefactor. One day the Owner of the Yellow Dog saw his property lying by the Gubernatorial Chair exchanging looks with the Private Secretary. The Owner of the Yellow Dog whistled and patted his leg in vain.

"Alas, your Excellency," he said, "I did not think that *his* Excellency's memory of a good master would be so soon effaced by low and evil associations."

589.

A Druggist was about to fill a prescription for nervousness when the paper that it was written on was blown into the street and striking an Agnostic who was driving by so startled him that he lost control of his horse. So the horse ran away, smashing the vehicle, killing itself and severely injuring the Agnostic. Limping back to the drug store to have his wounds dressed, the Agnostic picked up the prescription and found that it was one for himself, which he had that morning sent to the drug store.

"Surely," he said, falling upon his knees, "there is some benign Power that intervenes in the interest of the foolish."

From that day there was not in seven provinces so devout a man as he.

590.

A Young Woman who had chopped off her lover's head for infidelity, he having winked at his wife, was tried on a charge of murder. The jury stood Eleven for acquittal and One for conviction.

"Why do you persist in impoliteness to a lady?" asked the Eleven.

"Because she has removed my sweetheart's only means of support," said the One, weeping. "I refer to the widow of the deceased, whom I shall now have to marry."

This unhappy predicament so touched the sympathies of the Eleven that they changed their views and the Young Woman was convicted. But the Judge set aside the verdict on the ground that it was not in accordance with the testimony of the prisoner.

591.

During a lull in a thunder storm a Woman who was visiting a neighbor thought she would go home, and taking her pet dog in her arms was about to step into the street, when a Priest who was passing said to her: "My daughter, do not go out where the Lightning can get a fair fling at you with that dog in your arms."

So the woman put down the dog, but the Lightning had seen all, through a window, and when she stepped out it struck her dead.

592.

The Lady Respondent in a recent celebrated divorce case was reading of the unhappy dissensions amongst the Liberals and Home-Rulers.

"Alas!" she exclaimed, "I fear that nothing will ever go right until Woman is given her fair share of political power."

593.

Said a Plate of Hash: "I slay more than the sword."

"That," said the Sword, "is because people eat you. Suppose they should eat *me!*"

Hearing this, a professional Sword-swallower seized the sword and was about to thrust it down his gullet.

"What!" exclaimed the Plate of Hash — "without vinegar or mustard?"

594.

A Deer which was attacked by a dog said: "You take a coward's advantage. Don't you see that I have shed my horns."

"We are more evenly matched than you think," replied the dog, "for I have shed my tail."

595.

A Wealthy Young Man who wanted to be a Senator could find no toga for sale in his own State, changed his political convictions and moved into the State adjoining. The people of that commonwealth, "irrespective of party affiliations," fell, first upon his neck, and then upon his property. But the Wealthy Young Man got no toga and in despair he rent even the garments that he had.

596.

Two millionaires were fighting in the Venada Bank when a Terrier which had been calmly regarding the fray from beneath its eyebrows turned to the President of the Bank and said: "It seems a pity that they should be worrying one another in this way. Have you no rats about the place?"

597.

Some of the least benevolent of Nature's agencies were disputing their several claims to supremacy.

Said the Tempest: "I do but sigh and the seashore is strewn with wrecks of the world's navies, while on land the forests bend in homage to my power."

The Earthquake said: "When I turn in my sleep cities are thrown down upon the heads of those who dwell in them. The earth cracks open between the feet of the pedestrian, imparting a certain animation to his style."

"When I walk at noonday," said the Pestilence, "my footprints are graves. I undo the closest and tenderest ties — and part the debtor from his creditor."

"And I," said the Church Maiden, "sell tickets for charity concerts, and —"

The rest of her speech was drowned in the acclamations declaring her the Queen of Evils.

598.

A cab containing a Great and Good Man and his Private Secretary was upset by collision with a street car and the Great and Good Man was flung out and stood upon the back of his neck. "Behold," he exclaimed in that thrilling instant, "the modern Atlas! I support the whole world!"

"So you ought," said the Private Secretary, disentangling himself from the wreck; "the whole world has long supported you."

599. The Bundle of Sticks

A Boss went into the chamber of the Board of Supervisors carrying twelve sticks, which he threw upon the floor and challenged the Mayor to break them. The Mayor broke three, one after another, when the Boss, binding the remaining nine into a solid bundle, defied him to break that, which he was unable to do. The lesson was not lost upon the Supervisors.

600. The Cock and the Jewel

A Lawyer rummaging about among the articles exposed at a sale of "old horse" found a Conscience. "If," said he, "the man who lost this had found it he would doubtless have hugged it to his bosom, forgetting the fate of the man who warmed the viper; but, as for me, I would rather have the personal friendship of one Judge than all the consciences in the church."

601. The Farmer and the Viper

Frank M. Pixley finding Robert W. Waterman shivering with obscurity set him in the sunshine of political prosperity and he became Governor. No sooner had he grown comfortable in the Gubernatorial chair than he turned fiercely upon Mr. Pixley and fatally denied him the office of Park Commissioner.

602. Hercules and the Wagoner

A Pauper stricken down with a painful disease entreated a Physician to prescribe for him. "No," said the Physician, after searching the Pauper's pockets, "a man who will not take the trouble to prescribe for himself appeals to me in vain."

603. The Mountain in Labor

The courage and chivalry of the ages, the romantic traditions of the field of honor, the history of the ordeal of combat—all the influences and suasions that spring from the duello and go broading through the thoughts and lives of men, to stir them to words of courtesy and deeds of daring in assertion of the right and its enforcement by feats of arms, centered their purposes and converged their powers and benign energies to the production of a champion who should restore the ancient and honorable régime. The World stood afar off, holding its breath, and Expectation fastened her eyes upon the luminous focus of those streams of spirit. And slowly thence evolving in visible genesis, lo, that son of thunder, Preskie Belknap!

604. The Wolf in Sheep's Clothing

A Silurian pretended to be a human being in order to secure the Chairmanship of a Local Improvement Club so as to thwart its efforts. Seeing that while earnestly advocating improvement in the abstract he vigorously opposed any particular measure that promised a good result the Members of the Club fell upon him and killed him all over. His dead body then became the editor of the *Bulletin*.

605. The Fox Who Had Lost His Tail in a Trap

A Politician who had retired from an important office short in his accounts and destitute of self-respect went to a foreign country in order that his offence might be forgotten. As life was too short for that, he returned to the scene of his disgrace and aspired to political control, for which, he explained, his lack of self-respect eminently fitted him. "I advise you all," he continued, "to get rid of yours and follow me."

606. The Shepherd's Boy and the Cry of "Wolf"

For many years the press of a certain State warned the people at the convening of each new Legislature that the members were about to carry away the river upon whose banks was the capital. As the Legislature never did, the people grew indifferent and heedless of the warning. But at last came the Legislature of 1891.

607. Belling the Cat

Some merchants grievously oppressed by a Railroad held an indignation meeting and resolved to assert their rights in the courts. But no one was ambitious to be the plaintiff, and the first suit has yet to be brought.

608. The Distended Fox

A poor Lawyer having taken service with a great Corporation was so generously rewarded that he became rich and wished to retire and set up for himself. "Then," he said, "I shall regain the approval of the good and the respect of the wise, while my wealth will assure me a continuance of the fool's favor and the rogue's admiration."

But when he presented his resignation the President of the Corporation said: "You have been a faithful servant, but in serving us you have had to break all the Ten Commandments, and in the interest of morality I shall have to work you into the penitentiary if you leave us."

He remained.

609. The Fox and the Grapes

A Justice of the Supreme Court who, although the people had retired him without a pension, was nevertheless a pen-shunner, was asked if he would not like to go back upon the Bench.

"No," he said, "not as long as wicked little newspaper boys are permitted to place bent pine upon it."

610. The Owl and the Grasshopper

An Excellent Journal was disturbed in its Olympian repose by the senseless bluster of a Loathsome Contemporary eternally denouncing the "tax eaters." Since the Loathsome Contemporary could not be laughed into silence, the Excellent Journal sent its Fighting Editor over to the other shop, and he did most disastrously and consummately trounce the editors of the offending sheet. Thus a great good which could not be accomplished by coarse and obvious means was wrought by finesse and indirection.

611. The Estee and the Engine

An Estee who had planted his feet between the metals of a Railway, saw a train approaching and, bracing himself against his back, butted it as hard as he could. His brain remained plastered upon the front of the engine, but his other fragment was projected into space, and at the date of this writing fondly hopes to come down in Washington and receive the applause of the nation.

612. The Thrifty Artist

An Artist who had painted a portrait of a Distinguished Man invited the Distinguished Man's Mother to come to his studio and see it. As she entered the studio the picture arrested her attention, and she stood before it a long time, too full of emotion for utterance. At last she reluctantly withdrew her eyes and said: "Ah, you paint archangels beautifully indeed; and now please show me the portrait of my son."

613. The Wicked Granger

An Auctioneer engaged in selling a seat in the United States Senate cried out: "What do I hear, gentlemen, what do I hear?"

"I guess," said an old Granger standing by — "I guess, pardner, it's the noise o' them Vigilantes a callin' the roll."

The Auctioneer was so struck by the possibilities suggested by the remark that he accepted a bid for less than the seat was really worth and left in such haste that he neglected to divide the money amongst the owners.

614. An International Episode

Some Patagonians who had removed to Nova Zembla and become naturalized were incensed by the treatment that other Patagonians received at the hands of certain native Nova Zemblans. So they held an indignation meeting and passed a resolution asking the Prime Minister of Nova Zembla to punish the offenders.

"I will look into the matter," said the Prime Minister.

"You'd better," said the Chairman of the indignation meeting, over the wire, "for we have sent another petition to the Prime Minister of Patagonia, asking him to compel you."

"O you have, have you?" replied the Nova Zemblan official. "Well, that is treason."

So he caused them all to be brought before the High Court of Instantaneous Conviction, and when dismissed from that tribunal each was shorter by a head.

615. The Balancing Bear

The animals in a show had been forbidden to ask for gratuities from visitors, but the bear was observed sitting up and making a lap whenever any one passed by, munching peanuts. "Did I not forbid you to cadge for tips?" said the Keeper, frowning and thoughtfully fingering a pointed iron rod.

"My dear sir," answered the Bear, "you mistake the character of the phenomenon which it has been your privilege to observe. I was adding to the attractions of this show one of the most remarkable studies in equilibration that have ever been offered to the public. I believe I am the only living creature that can sit upon the end of the back without falling over."

"A most ingenious and surprising performance," assented the Keeper, inserting the pointed rod between the bars of the cage, "but, for myself, I do not find it nearly so interesting as the exhibition of general agility which you are now about to give."

616. Immunity

A Person of Consequence met an Unconsidered Trifle and was unkind enough to upbraid it for its low degree in the scale of being.

"I am not a particularly high and mighty personage, that is very true," said the Unconsidered Trifle, "but the position has its advantages."

"What are they?" the Person of Consequence asked, with a sneer.

"The newspapers do not call me a 'prominent citizen,'" was the proud reply.

617. The Tail and the Dog

Observing his tail in violent agitation a Dog said:

"This is a striking example of unconscious emotion: I must be deliriously happy, to do that, yet the apparent gravity of my mood is but faintly reflected by the absolute immobility of my body."

But the phenomenon that he observed had a simpler explanation: at various times in the preceding week he had had the indiscretion to commend his Tail, and that member, fired with a sense of its importance in the combination, was trying to wag him.

618. The Assassin's Punishment

A Distinguished Member of the Mafia was diligently polishing a pair of boots when the Man in the Boots, finding that his pistol hurt his hip, took it out to relieve the pressure. Thereupon the Distinguished Member of the Mafia desisted from his work, fell upon his knees and cried for mercy. He proceeded to explain that the Mafia was a mutual benefit society and did not kill American citizens.

"I don't care a cent how many American citizens it kills," said the Man in the Boots, accepting the character of avenger, "but why does it harp and fiddle on the ferry-boats when I want to talk?"

No sufficient explanation being given, the Man in the Boots covered the wretched being with his weapon and retired without paying for his shine.

619. The Soul and the Body

The Body complained that while the Soul was immortal, itself was doomed to perish without the hope of a blessed resurrection.

"That is fair," said the Soul; "you have your innings in this world."

"But you," said the Body, "live here and hereafter too."

"It is true," the Soul assented, "that I drag out a miserable kind of semi-existence here below, but you have all the fun."

620. Hunger and Thrift

Said Faith to a Hungry Man: "Shut your eyes and open your mouth."

This was obediently done and a Thrifty Person approaching thrust between the Hungry Man's teeth certain pellets of sawdust-and-treacle.

"That," said the Thrifty Person, "is the bread of life, and it comes high."

So saying he took the Hungry Man's purse and went on his way rejoicing. But when it was time for the bread of life to digest, the Hungry Person had to open his eyes in order to take a view of life appropriately serious.

621. The Bear and the Jackass

Having made the acquaintance of a Bear, a young Jackass was deeply gratified and promised himself great pleasure in the communion of souls. In the mean time the Bear had told his wife that he had met a very pleasant fellow who had, however, a pair of criminally long ears and a voice that incited to misdemeanor. A rat in the Bear's den heard these disparaging remarks and the ears of the Jackass soon came to them, and loudly and somewhat unmelodiously he lamented the perfidy of his false friend. "I shall let bears alone henceforth," he exclaimed; "they are not restrained, it seems, by considerations of decency and good faith."

"Why," said an Owl who, being within a marine league, had overheard his complaint—"why should you bewail the natural consequence of your own folly? Your treacherous friend has not disparaged you because he is a bear, but because he is married. Did you expect to enjoy the friendship of a married

animal on the same easy terms as that of an unmarried? Learn, then, from me
this great central, basic and eternal truth: No Man Is a Hero to His Friend's
Wife."

622. The Thief's Tracks

A Giant Thief who was compelled to cross a bed of clay was observed carefully
covering up his tracks with sand from a bag which he carried for the purpose.

"Why do you do that?" he was asked by an Officer who was idling near by.

"Because," he answered, "I scorn the cheap notoriety of present detection, caring only for posthumous fame."

Twenty centuries afterward, when some degenerate workmen of the period were excavating for the penitentiary which with great propriety was to be
erected on the spot they found his tracks, the sand having blown away and the
clay hardened to stone. A scientist promptly christened him *Homo Nevadensis*
because he had been so big a thief.

623. The Model Legislator

A Dead Dog whom an intelligent constituency had elected to represent them
in the hauls of legislation did nothing during the session but emit a disagreeable odor. On adjournment his record was so much cleaner than that of his
associates that he was received at home with the most distinguishing honors.
Perceiving this the members chosen at the next election all emitted disagreeable odors and were known as the Legislature of a Thousand Flowers. But the
fragrance of a living politician is so much more deleterious than that of a dead
dog that on returning to their constituencies they were all shot.

624.

A Philosopher observing a Manufacturer prostrating himself before the President, asked him why he did so. "I thought," said the Philosopher, "that the
President was our servant."

"So he is," replied the Manufacturer, taking another lick at the dust where
the President had stood, "but he represents the power and glory of our
Nation."

A little later the Manufacturer's foreman passed by.

"Why don't you prostrate yourself before that fellow?" asked the Philosopher. "He represents the power and glory of your factory."

"That," said the Manufacturer, contemptuously, "is nobody but Smith."

625.

Once there was a McKinley, and the McKinley attended a protective tariff banquet and made a speech.

"I am proud to belong," said the McKinley, "to a party advocated by such men as Webster, Clay, Lincoln, Grant, Hayes, Garfield and Harrison."

Then the spirits of Hayes, Garfield and Harrison (for all were dead, politically and otherwise) said: "We are proud to have the approval of the McKinley."

But the spirits of Webster, Clay, Lincoln and Grant maintained so cold a silence that the angels all shivered.

626.

The First Lady of the Land having launched a war-ship by touching an electric button, the crowd made a rush to obtain the button as a trophy. When removed it was found to have been wholly unconnected with any kind of apparatus for launching the ship.

"But when she touched it the ship really moved down the ways," said an Intelligent Spectator, with a disquieting sense of the supernatural.

"Yessir," replied a Workman, "w'en I seen her tetch it I jest waved my handkercher, an' my mates they split out the last blocks. The wonders of modern science is 'way up!"

627.

A Pale Person applied for admittance to a public hospital.

"It will be necessary," said the Resident Physician, "for you to undergo a medical examination."

When the examination had been made the Resident Physician said: "I am very sorry, sir, but you are by no means a sound and able-bodied man. You are, in fact, so ill that you are likely to die any day. We cannot admit you."

628.

A Dog that was on exhibition at the Kennel Club's show became hungry and going into the audience ate a child. Seeing his child eaten the Father complained to the Manager of the show demanding reparation.

"It cannot be denied," said the Manager, "that you have a good case. Heaven forbid that I should deny justice to the meanest of God's creatures! Over there in the corner is a cage of valuable pups. Choose one and eat it."

629.

The Pastor of a certain church which had been decorated in anticipation of the visit of an illustrious worshiper took his Little Boy to see the beautiful spectacle.

"Please, papa," said the Little Boy when he had looked his fill, "I should like to come again when it is decorated for God. I suppose it will be much finer then."

"Yes, I suppose so," said the Pastor, thoughtfully — "if he comes in the flower season."

630.

"I am not long for this world now," said the Old Man, lifting his glass to his lips, "my sands of life are nearly run out."

"That, I suppose," the River Pilot said, thoughtfully, "is why there is usually a bar at your mouth."

631.

A Truly Good Man who had bought a high office for $400,000 was traveling with the Illustrious Person who sold it, when they came to a Sunday School and entering were invited by the Superintendent to address the pupils, which they did, to their own great spiritual profit. When they had finished, the Superintendent rose and said: "If Brother Elwood Bruner is here the children would be pleased to hear a few remarks from *him*."

632.

A Woman who had cut off her husband's head was uncertain what she ought to do with it. In her perplexity she applied for advice to the Chief of Police.

"What is the matter with it?" asked the Chief of Police.

"Nothing is the matter with it," the woman replied; "it is a good head."

"Then why not use it for the purpose you had in mind when you removed it?"

"I had no purpose in mind further than to cause his death."

"Ah, in that case," said the Chief of Police, rubbing his hands with delight to think how cleverly he had elicited a confession of crime, "I shall have to arrest you."

633.

A Patriot who had fallen among snakes and worms was about to be put to death by the public executioner, a Rattlesnake of uncommon power, when he bethought him to appeal his case to the King of the Reptiles. As soon as His Majesty heard the name of the prisoner he said:

"Let him be at once released; there is some mistake. He is no man, but a reptile like ourselves. I saw him at his President's reception crawling on his belly."

When this was reported to the Patriot he said: "I refuse my freedom; I crawled on my belly, not as a reptile but as a loyal American citizen testifying my respect for the President's high office. Bring on your Rattlesnake."

But that public functionary declined to perform his duty, saying that he had some respect for his own high office and would not bite anything of that kind.

634.

An Eminent Pig was appointed Minister to the Bears and started to his post of duty. When half way to Bearland he received a letter from the Premier of Pigonia recalling him.

"The Emperor of the Bears," said the letter, "refuses to receive you, on the ground that you are not fat enough."

"I may not be very fat," said the rejected diplomatist, turning back; "but," he added, proudly, "I am all pig."

635.

A Poor and Humble Person whose business was writing fables was standing in a crowd, when a Distinguished Man passed by in a gold carriage and the people all threw up their hats. But the Poor and Humble Person remained covered.

"Why don't you throw up your hat?" shouted the People, menacingly. "How dare you be so disrespectful?"

"My good friends," said the Poor and Humble Person, "I beg you will not consider me lacking in respect, but this is the only hat I have, and I know my luck. If I should throw it up I feel certain that it would never come down."

636.

An Elephant about to cross a frail bridge requested the Mahout astride his neck to dismount.

"Arrah, now," said the Mahout with true Oriental obstinacy, "wud ye be havin' me walk across wid ye an' make two uv us on the bridge at wance?"

Perceiving that bulk was the same thing as brains, the Elephant hid away his feelings in his trunk and moved on.

637.

An Old Man whose sands of life were nearly run out saw a Fair Youth entering a saloon and endeavored to dissuade him.

"Beware, my son, beware of this perilous place," said he; "for here lurks the Enemy of Souls!"

But the Fair Youth, unheeding, pushed gaily by him and entered to collect the rent. The Old Man wept and still attempting to reclaim him followed him in. Whereupon, the Enemy of Souls came from behind the bar in a white apron, and the Old Man whose sands of life were nearly run out was himself run out, the Enemy of Souls explaining with heat that the free-list was suspended!

638.

An Ass visiting Santa Cruz as the guest of the Humming Bird was offered by his host a sip of dew from the heart of a honeysuckle.

"No," said the Ass, with the delicacy and tact which served to distinguish him from a professor of deportment; "that stuff is fit for nobody but swillionaires and abandoned hens. Gimme a thistle."

Whereupon the thistle was put under his tail, and his plunges were a great convulsion of nature.

639.

Said a Bishop to a Layman:

"It is important that you have correct views regarding the fundamental truths of religion. For example, you should understand the proposition of Thomas Aquinas that angels can go from point to point without passing through the intermediate space."

"I think," said the Layman, scratching his head, "that I understand it well enough for every practical purpose. They go a long way around."

His ashes were surrendered to his family.

640.

Summoned before a Grand Jury to say what he did with the fragments of the Decalogue, a Dickchute refused to attend, on the ground that the Grand Jury was an illegal body, the clerk of the court who swore them in having been imperfectly naturalized by a Judge whose appointment was obtained by misrepresentation.

When threatened with arrest the Dickchute applied for a writ of *noli me tangere,* and a Danmurphy was about to grant it, but was bitten by one of God's rattlesnakes and dying was damned. His successor was a decent man, and when the application came before him said:

"Let him take a writ of *vamoscat rancho* instead."

Thereupon the Dickchute departed out of that country attended by a great number of dead cats.

641.

A Vagrant Theosophist was expounding the doctrine of universal re-incarnation.

"All shall live again," he cried, kindling with enthusiasm and consuming himself in the flame of his own felicity; "all the creatures of the Creator shall pass, without loss of identity, into other bodies — every living thing that God has made!'"

"It's a bad outlook for me," said an adjacent Mule, sadly shaking his head: "I'm not in it. God made all other living creatures but I am the work of an ass."

"So is Theosophy," said a Miscreant Observer.

And the Mule was comforted.

642.

A dead Boodler was awakened by an Angel and told to prepare himself for trial.

"Before whom?" he asked, rubbing his eyes and yawning.

"The Ruler of the Universe," the Angel replied, in a low, reverential tone.

"I deny the legality of the tribunal," said the Boodler, with animation. "Please be so good as to take me to Judge Murphy."

"Excuse me," said the Angel; "you'll get there soon enough, but I can't take you. There would be nothing left of me but an odor of burnt features. Judge Murphy is dead, too."

643.

A Citizen seeing a Policeman walking his beat crossed over the street and accosted him, saying:

"I beg your pardon, but I really have forgotten whose turn it is. Do you happen to remember?"

The Policeman reflected a moment, and then replied:

"I believe the last man to perish in this feud was one of the Force, the slayer, if I mistake not, being an actor."

"You are right, you are right," the Civilian assented, returning to his hip-pocket the firearm that he had drawn. "Since it is not my inning I wish you a good evening and trust you will pardon me for stopping you."

"Don't mention it," said the Policeman, civilly, shooting him dead — "always glad to be reminded of my rights. After all," he added, thoughtfully, "I'm not quite sure but it was after the Curtis affair that Policeman Kelly killed Citizen Dwyer."

644.

An American Adventurer, who thought it time to turn the tables, went to England and boldly declared himself a "scion of nobility."

"What kind of a thing is that?" inquired English Society. "Never heard of it."

"My friends," said the Adventurer, gazing upon English Society with the compassionate contempt of a magnanimous nature fortified by superior advantages, "it is clear that you do not read the American newspapers."

645.

When a Lexicographer who was writing a dictionary had got as far as the word "Commissioner" he paused in deep thought, unable to invent a satisfactory definition for the word. While he was racking his brain he looked out of his study window and saw passing along the street, in a gold carriage and clad in cloth-of-diamonds, a Person whom the King of that country had appointed to select a site for the royal postoffice. Inspired by the gorgeous pageant, the Lexicographer seized his pen and dashing at his manuscript, wrote, with inconceivable vivacity, as follows: —

"COMMISSIONER, *n.* One who gets a commission."

"It is thus," said the Lexicographer, thoughtfully wiping his pen with his ear, "that from the darkness of a nation's calamity may shine a blessed light to illuminate the path of genius."

646.

A Reporter accosted the Foreman of a Grand Jury and said: —

"I saw a political boss coming out of your Star Chamber looking unblest. May I inquire if he has been doing something?"

"Yes, sir," promptly replied the Foreman of the Grand Jury; "we have ascertained from himself and fifty other witnesses that he fired a pistol at a hackman when there was a policeman within easy range. We have indicted him for perversion of the means of doing good."

"Did he hit the hackman?" the Reporter inquired.

"I really do not know," the Foreman of the Grand Jury answered; "we did not go into that."

647.

An Eminent Shipbuilder openly advocated the payment of more than a million dollars for a sanded bog upon which to rear a great public building.

"Tell me, your Eminence, quite confidentally, as between two thieves," said a Rising Young Pickpocket, "why you favor that absurd site."

Taking that seeking soul aside into a solitary place, the Eminent Shipbuilder whispered into his ear: —

"I expect to get the contract for building the hull."

648.

"Now that we have abandoned polygamy," said the Bell-Wether of the Mormon flock, "I trust that your Honor will restore to our Church all the property that has been taken from us for violation of the *ex post facto* law against plural marriages."

The suggestion was made to a Federal Judge distinguished for the purity of his character and his great attainments.

"I would most willingly do so," he replied, "but for one thing, which makes the surrender problematically legal and moral."

"What is that?" inquired the Bell-Wether, deeply disappointed.

"The magnitude of the sum involved. The morality of giving up three millions of dollars is open to the gravest doubt. Why, that is a larger sum than the diligent and painstaking pirate could hope to acquire by plunder in the most favorable season."

"There is a precedent, your Honor," said the petitioner. "Jay Gould, a thief, so illustrious that this honorable court pales in comparison, surrendered more than that amount to the shareholders of the Erie Railway."

"True," said the Federal Judge, reflectively — "I had overlooked that. Mr. Gould is an authority for whom the United States entertain the profoundest respect. I will take the matter under advisement."

649.

A Boundless Blackguard, who was what the newspapers are pleased to call a "co-respondent" in a divorce case in a country where there is no co-responsibility, took the witness-stand and committed perjuries until the Defendant's Counsel deemed the number sufficient. To his surprise and infinite relief the

Plaintiff's Attorney let him go without cross-examination. For this the B. B. had the indiscretion to express his gratitude out of court.

"My dear fellow," said the Plaintiff's Attorney, "I know my business. I was not fool enough to make you tell the truth."

"Why," said the B. B., scratching his nowl, "what you consider the truth was just what you needed, was it not?"

"Not much, my downy pelican — not from *you*."

The spot where that miserable person's countenance fell is still pointed out to the traveler.

650.

A Morrisestee being asked by a Man Who Was Not President if he would consent to join the Cabinet replied: —

"That depends. How many vacancies is it proposed to make for me?"

"Why, only one, I suppose," said the Man Who Was Not President.

"Then, sir," said the Morrisestee, "I shall not squeeze in."

651.

A Statesman who had a Goose which laid a gold egg every day of the week and two on Sunday was dissatisfied with the character of the output.

"I shall never really prosper," he said to the Goose, "until you lay, also, some silver eggs."

"No," she replied, "I cannot conscientiously do that. I am a single-standard goose; if you are a double you may do it yourself."

Soon afterward the Statesman was observed to be so poor that he was unable to obtain any office in the gift of the people: his Goose was cooked.

652.

A Conscientious Man went to a Lawyer and said: —

"I wish your advice. I love my wife devotedly, but once in an illucid interval I wrote an indiscreet letter to the wife of my twin brother. How can I get it back?"

"Why, confound you!" said the Lawyer — "if your relations with her are what you said they were when you came yesterday about the divorce I don't see why you should want it back. Didn't you say she had consented to run away with you?"

"I? — I never before laid eyes on you! What the devil do you mean, sir?"

"Ah, I see," said the Lawyer blandly — "pray calm yourself; no harm done. I mistook you for your brother."

The spectacle of the Conscientious Man calming himself drew a considerable crowd of the curious.

653.

Finding that however he shifted his position he was always in the shadow of his Secretary of State, who stood looking curiously down upon him, a certain President directed his Little Boy to sneak around behind the obscuring functionary and "let daylight through him" with a toy pistol. It is thought at the hospital that one of the Little Boy's fingers may be saved as far as the second joint, but owing to the thoroughfare for bullets between the giant Secretary's legs the old man is indubitably dead.

654.

An Officer of the Law standing in a crowd felt a Bruner picking his pocket. Grasping the Bruner by the wrist he slipped a handcuff upon it and then linked it to his own.

"Now," said the Officer of the Law, "you can explain to the populace that you put your hand in my pocket for the purpose of trapping me; then bid me march, and I will accompany you to the police station without resistance."

"I pray you," said the Bruner, diligently weeping, "do not taunt me with the sins of my early crookhood. I have reformed, and in this case shall pursue a less ingenious and more ingenuous course."

"For example?"

"I shall accept the situation like a gentleman, and jump my bail."

655.

A Brevet Son who at enormous expense was trying to break his Unmother's last illwill and contestament got a decision against him.

"Just what we wanted!" cried his Attorneys, triumphantly in chorus —

"just what we wanted! *Now* let them look out! — we *can at last* TAKE an AP-PEAL!"

Thereupon the Brevet Son cheered up and drew some more checks.

656.

A Traveler in a far country came to a large city, where he saw many men and women killing one another. For a long time he looked on from a secure place on the wall of the city, then sighed and turned away, saying to himself: "How sad that Allah should send the scourge of civil war to so great a people!"

"It is not a battle that you see," said an Inhabitant of the City; "these are but the ordinary incidents of our civilization: they are murders."

"Surely," said the Traveler, "it would be better to forbid murder. It cannot be good for trade."

"Nay, there you are wrong," the Inhabitant of the City said, smiling; "business is very good indeed, and there is plenty of money."

"How wonderful!" the Traveler exclaimed. "When I tell my countrymen that they will say: 'The man is a liar, or he dreams.' May Allah put it into your heart to give me your honored name, that I may put them to confusion by saying from whom I had the tale."

"I am known as Hassan the Tomb-builder."

657.

As the Recording Angel reclined upon a cool cloud, gently fanning himself with his right wing, his Deputy flew in from the office in a state of terrible excitement and stammered out:

"If you please, sir, come to the desk at once: I don't know what to do. Twenty-four hours have passed in San Francisco without a murder, and there is no place to record the fact: we have for more than forty years been using the credit side of that city's account to figure up the vote at elections in Spitzbergen."

"Good Lordy, man!" exclaimed the Recording Angel, petulantly — "you come bothering me about such a thing as that? Return to your duties at once — I hear Elwood Bruner swearing in Sacramento. Won't San Francisco's bloodless day count for her in the sum of her debits, idiot?"

"That's so," said the Deputy, thoughtfully scratching his head; "I didn't think of that. The silence of the revolvers down there has rattled me."

658.

A Student of Politics from Patagascar visited Montreal, and while there wrote in his notebook as follows:

"This country has a treaty of extradition with the Kingdom of California, an island in the Pacific ocean. A treaty of extradition is one whereby each of the two high contracting Powers agrees to receive the criminals of the other."

On returning to his own country he was appointed to the Regius Professorship of Foreign Institutions in the University of Gakwak.

659.

A Philosopher who was musing upon the vanity of life was disturbed by the sound of the pistol-shots in the streets and houses.

"I could think with better effect in a more quiet atmosphere," he said. "It would be to the advantage of philosophy if we could have a suspension of hostilities."

"A more advantageous thing to have just now," said a Practical Man, looking up at a dusty and decaying gallows, "would be a suspension of hostiles."

660.

The Alumni of Snail College held views of the merit of their *alma mater* which the Alumni of Barnyard University found themselves unable to approve, while themselves entertaining opinions unacceptable to the others, regarding their own institution's greatness and worth. In order to ascertain which place of learning was really the better they agreed to kick an inflated Ball. The first time it was kicked the Ball exclaimed:

"If you were not more puffed up with conceit than I with air you would perceive that the question which divides you does not divide me. It has no interest to me, and I am absolutely impartial. Why, then, are you dissatisfied with my decision as Umpire?"

"You are not Umpire," said an Alumnus of Snail, and, "You have made no decision," added an Alumnus of Barnyard.

"Then what the devil are you kicking about?" said the Ball.

This fable teaches that an empty globe is not necessarily devoid of sense because there is no alumnus attached.

661.

A Cyclone which had vainly attacked the White House was leaving Washington in deep disappointment when it met the Democratic Party coming in.

"Hello!" exclaimed the Democratic Party—"what are you doing so far from your native West?"

"Trying to give that fellow Harrison a blowout," replied the Cyclone, dejectedly. "But I think he is there to stay."

The Democratic Party smiled prophetically and with an air of deep intention passed on in silence.

662.

Three Men in an Oakland restaurant were casting lots to decide which of them should die to keep life in the others, when they were rescued by an expedition from San Francisco.

"Could you find nothing to eat in the restaurant?" the Captain of the Expedition asked.

"O plenty to eat," replied one of the reviving sufferers, faintly; "but we could find nobody to eat it."

663.

A Home Missionary seeing a Little Man who looked like a heathen in his blindness accosted him and began to exhort.

"My friend," he said, "I trust that you have a living sense of the Creator's goodness in providing for you such a beautiful world, so excellent in all its features and so well adapted to your needs."

"No," said the Little Man, "I can't say that my sense of that is particularly lively just now. One of my needs, for example, is to stand on my feet—one walks so much more comfortably that way. I like, too, to be, as a general thing, free from contact from falling building material of the heavier sorts. Of the various features of this world I admire least of all the fissures that emit boiling water when I wish to be roasted. In short, sir, I just came over from Nagoya, Japan."

In snatching a brand from the burning it is important to know how to lay hold of it.

664.

An Unspeakable who was summoned before a grand jury to testify to his own misdeeds became so severely afflicted with loss of memory that when asked his name he replied: "Stephen Gage."

Loss of memory proved contagious, for no sooner had the Foreman of the grand jury heard the name than he so far forgot himself as to put his hand in his pocket and get a good grip upon his purse.

665.

A City by the Sea, which was absently scanning the ground in every direction, was asked by a Neighboring Village if it had lost anything.

"Yes," said the City by the Sea, "I have lost a political convention."

"Never mind," the Neighboring Village said, "you will always have your hope in Heaven."

"I'm not so sure about that," was the reply — "there is to be a convention of newspaper men here next summer."

This fable teaches that consolation should be based upon a knowledge of all the facts.

666.

A Woman having fallen into the water was engaged in drowning when a Man sprang in and swam out to her.

"Madam," he said, "before taking further action in this matter I should like to know if you are married."

"No," said the Woman, preparing to go down for the third and last time, "I am not."

"In that case," the Man said, turning round in his own length and striking out for dry land, "I must let nature take her course. I am unmarried myself."

Thereupon the Woman waded ashore; but as the noble preserver had not given her a very strong claim upon him she was content to be a sister to him.

667.

A Philosopher was conversing with a Woman.

"The woman whom I shall marry," said the Philosopher, "has a great advantage in store for her."

"Ah," exclaimed the Woman, "you have a very good opinion of yourself, truly. Is it, then, a great advantage to marry you?"

"That is not what I mean, madam," said the Philosopher — "I refer to the advantage of birth. She is as yet unborn."

668.

A bald and bent and feeble Old Man hobbled up to the gate of heaven.

"My venerable friend," said St. Peter, "it is evident that we have done a good deal for you already; you were not punished by an early death."

"No," said the Old Man, "I was spared a long time. I died of old age."

"That implies a pretty large sum-total of sins," the Saint said, thoughtfully twirling his key on his forefinger. "What have you to say for yourself?"

"I am a member," said the venerable applicant, "of the Young Men's Christian Association."

669.

An Aeronaut, who was being driven across California by a violent east wind, was seen by a Reporter, who ran to an army signal station and asked him in the flag language what he thought of the State.

"It seems to be moving," replied the Aeronaut with his hat.

"I regard California as one of the most progressive countries in the world," is how it appeared in the "interview" published the next morning.

670.

A Good Woman who had a Domestic Husband presented him with a gold latchkey set with rubies and emeralds. In order to show that he was worthy of that touching token of confidence he went out of an evening many times a month and came home early in the morning, entirely sober. One day he entered a jeweler's shop and saw there a Dear Friend. The Dear Friend was giving the jeweler instructions how to attach a latchkey to a watch-chain so that it could be easily removed for use. When the Domestic Husband saw the latchkey in the Dear Friend's hand and observed that it was a duplicate of his own he was so overcome by the coincidence that he never spoke again — to him.

671.

A Young Man in Moderate Circumstances said to a Millionaire: —

"Teach me how to become rich."

"With pleasure," assented the Millionaire, "and" — he added to himself — "with profit. You have only to follow my lead in all investments."

At the end of a few months the Young Man in Moderate Circumstances had vanished from the scene and his place was occupied by a Youth to Fortune and to Fame Unknown, who answered to the same name.

"You observe," said the Millionaire — "the property which was once yours is now mine. I teach by example."

672.

A Boy asked his Father to tell him the difference between a politician and a statesman.

"Subtract the politician's price from the statesman's price," replied the Father, "and the remainder is the difference."

673.

In a competitive examination at St. Petersburg, to determine which of the Foreign Newspaper Correspondents should have dominion during the ensuing mendacial year, the Judges were for a long time unable to agree. They were about to declare the confraternity a republic of kings, free and equal, when He of the London *Daily News* mounted his latter legs and said: —

"Your Excellencies, I will withdraw every example of my skill that I have submitted in this examination if I may substitute a single statement with which I have just been inspired."

There being no objection He read from a dispatch which he had prepared for his paper as follows: —

"The Minister of the Interior, in declining the proposition of a deputation of rich Moscow merchants to form a society for the relief of the victims of the famine in the stricken districts, declared that anybody attempting to visit the districts where the famine prevailed for any such object as that described would be arrested."

The reading evoked a tempest of applause, and bringing forth the starry diadem they crowned Him king of all.

674.

Three Commissioners to Select a Site for a Postoffice sat one night about a table in a wayside inn. A single candle's feeble ray scarcely served to reveal the scarred and swarthy faces underneath the brims of the slouch hats and make points of light on the metal of the weapons and flagons on the table.

"Od zounds!" said the Eldest of the three, as the tavern clock was heard striking thirteen — "it is an eerie hour and eke an unholy! Methinks it were a fitting time to hale before us that vagrant scholar snoring in the tap-room and constrain him to tell us a saint story."

At this suggestion the two others looked uneasily behind them into the gloom and visibly shuddered.

"Satan send there be no saints come here," said the Youngest Commissioner, devoutly crossing himself, "nor anything good and fair!"

"Amen!" fervently exclaimed the Commissioner who had not spoken, and "Amen!" repeated the Eldest.

At that moment a gentle breeze wafted in through the open casement the song of a nightingale blended with the fragrance of a Castilian rose, and with exclamations of horror and disgust, mingled with fierce oaths blown through their beards, the Three Commissioners took to horse and were not seen in all that region for many a long day.

675.

Said a Philosopher to a Physician:

"Do you not wish that you could cure folly?"

"Yes," the Physician replied, "but I should be sorry if any other man could."

"Why?"

"Because he might do so — unless he were a physician."

"And then there would be no more medicine?"

"Nor philosophy."

676.

A Holy Man hearing the Mate of a Steamboat cursing a deck-hand said: —

"My son, do you not know that it is wicked to use such language as that?"

"O, that's nothing," said the Mate of the Steamboat — "You should hear me when we're coalin'."

"But," persisted the Holy Man, "the Bible says: 'Swear not at all.' "

"Just so, sir, just so," assented the offender, cheerfully: "they don't all need it this mornin' — only that dam galoot with the cropped head."

677.

Two friendly nations having been brought to the verge of war, from which they were saved with difficulty, an inquiry was set afoot for the persons who had created the inharmony. After a brief search they were found hiding behind their own backs and promptly hanged. The following lines were inscribed upon the stone that reluctantly marked the place of their burial:

> Here Matta and Harrison, lying at rest
> (Republics ungrateful their throttles attest),
> Are waiting God's judgment on work of their pens,
> Who says — as He smiles in approval of men's:
> "To mortals the fruit of their work and their worth, —
> These madmen I'll give what they raised when on earth!"

678.

Two society men who were enemies having sailed from Europe on the same ship, their native land (which is the Home of the Brave) was in dire consternation lest they kill each other and set the ocean on fire to conceal the crime. When the ship arrived at the Home of the Brave, and the excited Populace rushed aboard to learn the harrowing details of the tragedy from the white lips of survivors, nobody had heard of the presence of the two enemies. Diligent search discovered them, nearly dead of hunger, exposure and exhaustion — One clinging to the tip of the jibboom, the Other astride the rudder. The skipper said he had observed that the ship had not answered the helm rightly during the voyage, but what it was that the helm had asked her the Populace did not stay to ascertain.

679.

The People of Pataskatka having a grievance against the People of Novagascar, demanded reparation, which being withheld was enforced by an ultimatum. Thereupon the People of Kamazemblagonia, a powerful nation, said:

"Novagascar is a feeble folk, like the conies of Scripture, the Pataskatkans are bullying them. They would not dare talk so to us."

Presently, in another matter, the Pataskatkans talked so to the Kamazemblagonians.

"Ah," said the Kamazemblagonians, smiling blandly without actual dislocation of the face, "they don't mean a word of it, don't you know — it's quite too jolly absurd."

And the *modus vivendi* was prolonged.

680.

Darkness fell upon the face of the earth, the vail of the Temple was rent in twain and the dead came forth!

"What is that great convulsion of nature about, down your way?" Saint Peter asked of a newly arrived soul.

"General European war," replied the disembodied reporter. "Let me in, please."

"Not yet," the Saint said. "Your record up to the time of your death is all right, but I'm in doubt about that European war story. Just stand apart until I confirm it."

The next soul interrogated promptly replied: "The married daughter of a millionaire suspended her vows."

"Ah," said the Saint, "that is more like. You see, my friend," he added, turning to the Reporter, "you can't run in any of your fakes here. Begone!"

The Reporter bewent.

681.

A Silurian walking in the suburbs came to a pile of Bricks by the wayside and immediately flew into a great rage.

"How dare you intrude yourselves into the architecture of this city!" he cried. "As if wood and adobe were not good enough building materials!"

"You wrong us, sir," replied one of the Bricks. "We have nothing to do with architecture, being too soft. We are material for paving your streets."

The Silurian humbly begged their pardon, kissed his hand to them and passed on, in maiden meditation fancy free.

682.

A Bald Old Man seeing a Young Fellow looking despondent, said to him:

"My son, impart to me the nature of thy trouble that the wisdom of experience may be a lamp to the feet of youth."

"Right gratefully will I avail myself of your superior light," replied the Young Fellow, "for assuredly I walk in the valley of the shadow of indecision. I am a druggist and wish to know how to make a good hair restorative."

But the Bald Old Man was up and away.

683.

A Plain Person and a Man of Imagination saw a pig inhumed in mire, weltering in it and unutterably happy.

"See that filthy beast wallow!" said the Plain Person, disgusted.

"My dear sir," said the Man of Imagination, "you err. That animal is not wallowing."

"Not wallowing?" exclaimed the other. "What, then, is it doing?"

"It is serving," the Man of Imagination explained, "as a member of a Government Commission to select a site for a Postoffice."

684.

Some Statesmen saw a Man with a Sack get off a train at Ramento of that ilk. They followed him with the deepest solicitude into the State Capitol, where he entered the Assembly Chamber and depositing the Sack on the Speaker's desk began fanning himself with his hat.

"What have you in the Sack, my worthy man?" said the Speaker.

"Sack?" replied the Man—"I don't see any Sack!"

"And what do you call this?" the Speaker said, touching it cautiously with the tip of his forefinger—which he immediately wiped with a handkerchief.

"That, sir," was the reply, "is the Will of the People."

Hearing this, a number of defeated candidates who were present, soliciting janitorships from their successful competitors, came forward and solemnly bowed to it.

685.

A McAllister who had betrayed his master was found hanging to a tree with thirty pieces of silver in his pocket.

"A buy-metallist, clearly," said a Roman Centurion, sententiously, as he transferred the coins to his own pocket.

"No," said a Jewish Rabbi standing near, exploring his robes for the business card of a brother in the armor trade, "I fancy he favored the surcingle standard: he was evidently a cincher from Swayback."

686.

A Supervisor of the City and County of Squedunk, who had accepted office in order to make his town the Paris of America, was seen one afternoon at the end of his term wading in one of the principal streets.

"What are you doing in there?" asked the Statesman who had enjoyed the contract of paving the street.

"I want to get on the other side," the Supervisor said, trying to carry his coat-skirts in one hand and hold up both legs of his trousers with the other.

"Look here, my good man," said the Statesman, absently rattling the loose diamonds in his pockets, "the two banks of this street are exactly alike; it can't make much difference to you which one you are on."

"It makes this difference," was the reply: "my boy is plowing over there in the Place de l'Opera, and I want to tell him it is time to knock off and drive home the cows, which are grazing in the Boulevard des Italiens."

A vagrant zephyr strayed over from the glue factory in the Champs Elysées and put an end to the conversation.

687.

While Dr. Bartlett, the celebrated naturalist of the *Bulletin,* was on a hill overlooking a dense forest a giraffe, which had escaped from a show, thrust its head up from among the trees and began to browse on the tops of them. The next day the *Bulletin* was enriched with an editorial on the California tree-climbing goat (*Capricornus shinupsus*) with valuable suggestions to the horticulturist as to its possible usefulness in pruning.

688.

A Bill which had been referred to the Committee on Public Morals returned to the Assembly, like the dove to the ark, and complained to the Speaker that it had been sent on a fool's errand.

"What, what!" said the Speaker, "is it possible that I have neglected to appoint a Committee on Public Morals? Good gracious! where will this State go when it dies!"

"O, the Committee is all right enough," the Bill explained; "but you have forgotten to appoint any public morals."

689.

A Minister of the Gospel, meeting a Young Man in the street, said to him:

"My young friend, I am summoned to yonder house to be present at the passing of a pure soul from this world of sin. Would you like to see a Christian die?"

"Of what denomination?" the Young Man inquired.

"One of my congregation," the minister explained with some surprise—"a Presbyterian."

"Wouldn't miss it for the world," said the Young Man, with great vivacity; "all my wife's relations are that way."

690.

While an Honorable Member of the State Senate was addressing the house his eye happened to fall upon the clock. At this he abandoned the point of his remarks "where he was at," and explaining that he had a Stephen Gagement with Colonel Mazuma, legged it for the door, followed by the entire Senate.

The spot is still shown to the traveler.

691.

An Old Man fondling a brass instrument sat sunning himself upon the edge of a wharf, when a Woman with wild eyes and unstudied hair rushed up to him and said:

"Ah, kind sir, you too are a musician: be kind then to one of your profession—a sister of your art. I beseech you, sir, go to John Bunby, of 321 Kneedeep street, and say to him that Elizabeth Julia, his wife, is no more. Say to him that you saw her die, and that he is free. Say to him — O, I pray you fail not to say to him that I died an innocent woman, blessing him with my latest thought."

So speaking, the Woman sprang into the sea. The old man got upon his feet, and as the unhappy Woman's head rose for an instant above the surface she saw him put the instrument to his ear, and through the roar of the water in her own ears heard him exclaim: "Hay?"

692.

One night a man-eating Tiger met the ghost of one of his victims on its way to frighten its mother-in-law. The Tiger sprang upon the Ghost, with open jaws, intending to crush its head, whereupon the Ghost vanished. The animal was somewhat surprised, and after moving his jaws a while, and licking his lips, he soliloquized as follows:

"That fellow went down easier than anybody that I ever ate, but I can't say that I particularly relish him. He tastes too much like tiger."

693.

An Attorney-General who had wrested from the State's reluctant debtors a large sum of money and kept it for his honesty was passing through a wood, when he saw what he took to be a lion, sleeping by the wayside. At the same time he met a Constable, who shouted:

"What have you done with that money?"

Observing that the Constable's voice had roused the wild beast, the Attorney-General was filled with terror. But the Constable gave the animal no attention and continued:

"I should like you to divide."

At that the beast dropped its nose between its forepaws and slept again.

When the two men had finished their business together the Attorney-General said:

"Did you not observe the lion?"

"That, my friend," replied the Constable, "was your conscience; but it will not molest you now. It wakes in the presence of justice, but when that is satisfied" — here the Constable placed a bank-note in his pocket-book — "it again falls asleep."

694.

The Queen of the Flyspeck Islands having been driven from her throne applied to the President of All-out-of-Doors for relief.

"Upon what grounds, madam?" the President inquired.

"Justice," the Queen replied: "the gentlemen who deposed me are mostly All-out-of-Doorians."

"Madam," said the President, laying his hand upon his heart and bowing profoundly, "you unseal the vials of my compassion. Pray consider yourself again upon the throne."

"But," said the Queen, "is not that a rather illusory reinstatement?"

"It may be," replied the President of All-out-of-Doors, "but it is the only statement that I have to make."

695.

A Serious Young Lady, deeply in love with a gentleman of God who was a minister, complained of ill-health.

"Yes," said a Frivolous Worldling of her sex, "I have observed that you suffer from pulpitation of the heart."

Yet Heaven's great mercy embraces even the Frivolous Worldling.

696.

Seeing his wife wearing a hoop-skirt a Man said:

"My dear, I am going out to purchase a plug hat. If on my return I find you still wearing that thing I shall take the trouble to slice off your ears."

Returning, he found her still wearing it, and sliced off her ears.

The next day the Woman was again wearing the offensive garment.

"Madam," said the Man, "I am astonished!"

"At what?" said she. "Did you suppose that hoop-skirts were suspended from the ears?"

697.

A Member of the Legislature was returning to his constutients at the end of the session, when he was met by a Stranger from Afar.

"What are you doing, my friend," said the Stranger from Afar, "with the big gilt umbrella when it is not raining?"

"This is not an umbrella," said the Member of the Legislature; "this is the dome of the capitol."

"Ah, I see," the Stranger said. "But why did you not bring the rest of the building too, my good man?"

"Sir!" exclaimed the Member of the Legislature indignantly, "do you take me for a hog? I expect to be re-elected."

698.

One night at a ball a little dog belonging to the hostess broke into the throng of waltzers and engaged in an earnest pursuit of its own tail. Upon this the dancers all stood still and laughed immoderately, and the musicians ceased playing to enjoy the sport.

"Strike up, strike up!" cried the Leader of the Orchestra—"with the morality of this dog's performance you have nothing to do. Do you suppose that music is necessary to the devil only? Strike up!"

699.

With heart bowed down and a tear rilling either slope of his nose, a lezinsky was bewailing his hard fortune.

"Ah, unhappy me!" he soliloquized. "Would that I had been content with the fame and popularity of silence, abstaining from the oblivion of publication. But I listened to the voice of the tempter and published an illuminated edition of my 'Poetical Address to an Ailing Liver'—since when I am unknown, even to my creditors; and when as now I am without the book, to refer to the title-page, I am myself in ignorance of my name."

Seeing a russell approaching the lezinsky accosted him, saying:

"My dear sir, if you know me I beg to you to tell me who I have the bad luck to be. What is my name?"

And the russell answered him, coldly, with a strong accent on the second syllable:

"Damfino!"

"Ah, yes, that sounds familiar," cried the lezinsky—"that must be the name. Thank you, thank you, kind stranger!"

And he grasped, effusively, both hands of the russell—who, after a hurried scrutiny of the unhappy man's face, removed one hand and put it on his purse.

700.

At a high jinks of the Bohemian Club a Fable being requested to come forward and read itself cheerfully complied.

"But where is the moral?" the Sire asked.

"The moral came here with me," answered the Fable, "but it felt pretty lonely in this crowd. I fancy it went over to the rooms of the Women's Press Association."

"It will find plenty of congenial company, certainly," said the Sire; "morals are compulsory there."

"Yes, indeed," said the Jokemaster-General of the evening, pensively. "But there is nothing about them in the constitution and by-laws."

701.

Voltaire and some gentlemen of the Court were traveling in a wild country, and put up one night at a wayside inn. Their surroundings suggested stories of robbers, and each told one in his turn. When Voltaire's turn came he said: "Once upon a time there will be, in a place called California, a Forestry Commissioner named Walter Moore."

702.

A Young Man who, through no fault of his, was about to be married was calling on the Girl to whom he was betrothed.

"I am going to show you something that should interest you," said the Girl, unlocking a drawer and taking out a photograph. "This is I — as the California Venus."

Taking the picture from her hand the Young Man glanced at it and laying it down, back upward, rose to his feet and bent upon her a Look!

"What!" she exclaimed — "you think me improper? Gustavus, you do not love me."

"Yes," he replied, "I love you, but also I am an officer of the Society for the Suppression of Vice."

"Spare me, O spare me!" the Girl cried, falling on her knees and embracing him.

"Well, yes," he said, thoughtfully, possessing himself of his hat and moving toward the door — "I fancy you can be spared."

She sleeps in the valley.

703.

A Governor who had signed a bill that had not been passed by the Legislature was arraigned at the bar of Public Opinion and requested to explain.

"I have a complete defense," he said, calmly.

"Yes, but what is it?" demanded the Prosecuting Press.

"I am a fool," the Governor replied.

Judgment for the defendant.

704.

Having admitted a Hawaiian leper into a crowded hospital, a certain Physician went before the gods and demanded a reward for his compassionate action.

"Take it," said Jupiter: "I decree that you shall have a sincere manifestation of goodwill from every Hawaiian leper that you meet."

And thenceforth every Hawaiian leper that the good Physician met came forward and rubbed noses with him.

705.

A Collector of Infernal Revenue charged with the delicate duty of enforcing a law for the deportation of all Chinese without tags was engaged in vaporing of what he intended to do, without considering whether anybody intended to let him.

"What a swashbuckler!" said a Disgusted Citizen overhearing.

"No," said a Discriminating Philosopher, reflectively, "not quite that. Observe the head of him: he's a kind of squashbuckler."

706.

An Artist was observed shedding tears at a tomb.

"For whom do you weep, my friend?" inquired the Observer.

The mourner explained that his grief was over the California Venus.

"Of what," said the Observer, "did the poor girl die?"

"Of mumps, rickets and elephantiasis," replied the Artist, with a fresh outburst of grief as the words recalled the image of the deceased — "all chronic and congenital."

"And had she also that 'tired feeling'?"

"No, O, no—that is what ailed everybody else. Hers was an unattired feeling."

707.

A Board of Mismanagement of a World's Fair had under discussion the question of opening it on Sundays, and a Wicked Member had made a speech favoring that action.

"What!" shouted a Holy Member, "do you not believe that God has appointed a day of rest—one day in seven?"

"What I don't believe," the Wicked Member explained, "is that God has appointed this Board to assist Him in enforcing His views and wishes."

708.

A wealthy Philanthropist, who had made partial restitution by founding a university, wanted a good man to stand and deliver lectures on law, promote international arbitration and assist God in setting up the millennium.

"I know the very man for the job," said the Horse-Trainer-in-Chief, "but he is an ex-President of the United States."

"He can live that down," said the Philanthropist.

709.

A Chief of the Weather Bureau who had predicted that it would rain cats and dogs was espied sauntering across the country quite unconcerned and in holiday attire.

"Ah-ha!" exclaimed the Populace, "if it is going to storm why the silk hat and the no umbrella?"

"My friends," the Chief of the Weather Bureau answered, "it pains me to think that you should suspect me of improvidence. This hat belongs to my brother."

"And the no umbrella," said the Populace, "how about the no umbrella?"

"That," he explained, with austerity, "is my own. If I choose to expose it to the risk of damage it is no business of yours."

So he passed on, "in maiden meditation"—it was his first attempt at thinking.

710.

The Director-General of the Columbian Exposé was summoned before the Representatives of All Nations.

"Sir," they said, severely, "this is the first day of May, and your show is not ready. What falsehood have you to urge in explanation of your criminal tardiness?"

"I thought it no use to be in a hurry," said the Culprit—"the principal exhibit cannot be procured for more than two months yet."

"To what have you the caitiff hardihood to refer?" they asked him.

"To the Fourth of July," he replied.

711.

An Elderly Dude named John P. Irish was diligently engaged in charming a Bright Young Woman, when she innocently addressed him as "Mister."

"I beg your pardon, my dear young lady," said the Elderly Dude; "that title sounds rather harsh to me—I have been called Colonel for so long."

"How long?" inquired the Bright Young Woman.

"All my life," he replied.

"Dear me," said the Bright Young Woman, thoughtfully; "I had no idea that promotion was so slow!"

712.

The Parliament of Novaya Zemlia having an appropriation bill before it, summoned the Estimator of Pensions and inquired what sum would be needed in his department for the ensuing two years.

"It is impossible to say with accuracy," that official replied, "for we are threatened with a great epidemic, which nevertheless may not arrive. If we estimate the mortality among old soldiers on a cholera basis we should provide for largely augmented payments. With a normal death rate the annual increase will be less."

713.

The Spirit of Christopher Columbus having set out from Heaven and sailed an inconceivable distance through space, arrived at a country whose inhabitants were worshiping what appeared to be an image of one of themselves.

"God o' my soul!" cried the Spirit of Christopher Columbus; "I have discovered a new Stupidity! When I relate this on my return to Heaven I shall be loaded with honors."

But when the Great Discoverer drew nearer to the idol and saw that it was an image bearing his own name he wept aloud.

"For what do you weep?" one of the natives asked, not recognizing him.

"Alas!" the Spirit explained, "I shall not dare to report the full magnitude and glory of my feat. Not a soul would believe me!"

714.

A Miserable Man was passing along a street when his attention was arrested by a sign which hung in front of a place where agricultural implements grew. "Baker & Hamilton, Tiger Mowers," the sign shouted.

Entering the implementery, the Miserable Man said to an Attendant:

"Please send a good workman up to my house: I have a tiger that needs mowing."

"What do you mean?" asked the surprised Attendant.

"My wife," the man said.

715.

While driving his locomotive at the rate of 112½ miles an hour an Engineer of the Future was overtaken by a Constable on a flycycle.

"Come, now, you," said the Constable, poking his head into the cab, "I can't have you dawdling along this way, obstructing the country roads. Get a move on you."

"But," protested the Engineer of the Future, "I'm ahead of time."

"O, you are ahead of Time," sneered the Constable. "Well, my good man, he will run over you, sure."

At that moment the engine came into collision with an immense rock which had rolled down a mountain side and thoughtlessly placed itself upon the track.

"It is lucky we were going at a snail's pace," said the Passengers of the Future. "We might have been badly shaken up by the like o' that."

716.

A Distinguished Official of the Southern Pacific Company was descanting upon the wisdom with which his company's affairs were managed.

"Why, sir," said he, "it would amaze you to get an insight into our methods!"

"O no it wouldn't," replied his Patient, gravely: "I'm a thief myself."

717.

"Papa," said the Daughter of the House, "I saw the new lodger standing on his head."

"Indeed!" replied the Landlady's Husband; "and have you observed any other suspicious actions?"

"O, yes, Papa; he makes mouths at himself in the hall mirror, and bites the heads off mice."

"My daughter, this is very serious; go tell your mother to count the silver. I fear we have taken in a poet."

718.

A Police Sergeant who had for many years been clothing his ribs with fat fried out of fallen women was called upon by the Commissioners for an accounting.

"It is estimated," he explained, "that my accretion of adipose matter from that source amounts to forty-five pounds. What are you going to do about it?"

"Remove you," said the Commissioners, "from your adisposition."

719.

A Thief who had stolen a newspaper man's watch, plainly inscribed with the owner's name and profession, wore it with great advantage and satisfaction for many years, but at last it stopped.

"I cannot afford to learn the watchmaker's trade," said the Thief, "although it is so nearly allied to my own; and if I take this timepiece to another person for repairs he will read the inscription and think me a member of the press. That would cover me with shame as with a garment and bring down the gray hairs of my parents with sorrow to the grave."

So he secretly returned the watch to its rightful owner, who thenceforth kept it for his honesty.

720.

A Chinaman in America, who had failed to register and was about to experience the disaster of living in his native land, was bewailing his hard lot.

"Then why do you not register?" inquired a sympathetic Bystander.

"Because," replied the unfortunate man, "the Six Companies charged with the duty of looking after my welfare told me not to do so."

721.

An Indigent Tinker engaged in making zinc pockets for Police Sergeants was approached by a Sleek Respectable who requested a few moments' conversation with him.

"My friend," said the Sleek Respectable, when they were alone, "I should weep to disparage your skill as a workman, but you really must be more careful. Those pockets leak."

"Alas," cried the Indigent Tinker, "to what impudence my poverty and weakness expose me. What interest have you in this matter?"

"One-third of ten per cent.," the Sleek Respectable replied, with great composure: "I am a Police Commissioner."

722.

"The Spanish Infanta," cried a Leader of Fashion, with clasped hands and eyes rapturously uprolled, as one having a divine revelation, "has six pages to carry her trains!"

"Madam," said the Monarch of the Dailies, "I have sometimes one hundred and twenty pages, and my trains carry them."

Whereat the Leader of Fashion dashed out her brainie against a pillow and was gathered to her feathers.

723.

A Merchant who had invested his entire fortune in a ship and a cargo of gray-blue cats set sail for Malta, where he expected to dispose of his goods at a great profit. On the third day out the ship was overtaken by a long, low, black schooner, which brought her to by firing a gun across her bows. As soon as the merchantman had lain to, her owner observed the schooner running up a black flag bearing a death's-head and crossed bones in red, and saw that her deck was swarming with C. P. Huntingtons. Every Huntington, naked to the waist, had a cutlass in his teeth and a sheet of paper under his left hand; in his right he brandished a loaded pen. At the word of command from their black-bearded Leader they all fell to writing letters to W. H. Mills, affirming the depravity of competing lines of traffic and the desirability of more factories. One after another the ill-fated Merchant and his crew fell dead upon the deck of their ship, which was then boarded by a boat-load of the Huntingtons, to take possession of the cargo. Unluckily the cats had been shipped in bulk, and their military spirit had locked them so tightly together by the claws and teeth that all were dead.

"Behold," said the head Huntington, "the injurious effects of competition! A single cat would have been an harmonious cargo."

724.

It being thought expedient to hold a World's Fair in the State of Washifornegon immediately after the close of the one at Porkago, the people of the various cities and towns rose in enthusiastic support of the scheme and subscribed abundantly. When after three months of hard work cheerfully performed the Canvassing and Finance Committee made its report it was found that the contributions amounted to no less a sum than 760 sites and ten dollars in cash. The sites are still pointed out to the traveler.

725.

Some Murphys bickering about the will of the man who had been guilty of them were warned by the Parlor Pig.

"If you do not cease disgracing me," said the Pig, "I must look for another situation."

"I don't care if you do," said a she Murphy, tartly; "you are nothing but a low-bred American, anyhow."

"I confess," the Pig explained, "that I am of that nationality, and am afflicted with such imperfect manners as are not inconsistent with a general tendency to put both forefeet in the trough, while visibly destitute of those graces, epistolary and other, which come of handing round hash in a mealery; but I beg you to remember that although a pig I am no hog—I never caused you a pain in the stomach by defiling the grave of my parents."

"How could that cause me a pain in the stomach?" the she Murphy asked, forgetting impertinence in her curiosity.

"That's where they were buried," the Pig explained—"along with their beans."

726.

The President of Doosnoswair and the Czar of Dontgivitaway negotiated an extradition treaty.

"Why, you scoundrel!" cried the Doosnoswairians when the treaty had been proclaimed—"you have included political offences!"

"Yes," replied the President, "I was unable to see how the disruption of a Czar is a lesser crime than the taking off of a moujik. Besides," he added, thoughtfully, "it seemed, from my point of view, desirable to secure some protection for Presidents. Two of them, you know, have been already—"

But the sound of his voice was lost in shouts of "Down with tyrants!"

"That," said the President, under his breath, "depends."

727.

The State Capital at Sacramento being told that it was to be removed to San Jose asked why.

"Because," was the reply, "Sacramento is a wicked town."

"True," said the State Capital, "but it does not follow that if I'm to leave Sacramento I should be taken to San Jose, where J. J. Owen is. What ails Hades?"

"Imminence of J. J. Owen," was the reply.

728.

A Popular Actor having had it pointed out to him that successful pugilists became successful actors, said it was a poor rule that would not work both ways. So he challenged one of the foremost of the seventeen Champions of the World, and backed himself with a year's salary as the Prince of Denmark. He was afterward observed to utter the two important truths following, together with a double-handful of teeth:

1. "It is a poor rule that will not work both ways."
2. "The poor we have always with us."

729.

The Editor of a newspaper wished to publish an interview with a Poet of the Sierras in his native wild, but every reporter whom he detailed to do the work told so woeful a tale about a dependent family that the Editor had not the heart to send any of them upon the perilous errand. At last he telegaphed his wishes to a noted Bandit, who was passing the summer near the place infested by the Poet of the Sierras. The Bandit not only interviewed the outlaw, but converted him from the errors of poesy to the eternal truths of assassination.

730.

A Man was on trial for murder. During a lull in the defence he fancied he heard a drawing of revolvers, and raising his head he saw everybody in the courtroom taking aim at somebody else.

"I beg that you will desist, gentlemen," he said: "some of you are aiming in the direction of the only unarmed man present. I have an aversion to bloodshed."

Thereupon all desisted, and the District Attorney moved that the case be dismissed.

"A person so peaceably disposed," he said, "cannot have committed murder."

731.

A Preacher, who was about to be hanged for declaring that a fire in which a score of brave and dutiful firemen had perished was a "judgment" upon certain Sabbath-breakers not present at the fire, was offered his freedom on condition that he atone for his stupid blasphemy by one sensible utterance.

"What God hath joined together," said that conscientious martyr, feeling his neck and the noose, "let no man put asunder."

Thereupon the weeping hangman released him according to promise, and he departed out of that land.

732.

"Do you know, Willie," said the Sunday-School Teacher, "why in slaying the three thousand Philistines Samson used the jawbone of the editor of the Fresno *Expositor?*"

" 'Cause he had saw that it had slayed the editor hisself," replied Willie; and the Sunday-School Teacher handed him three blue tickets and a red one.

733.

An indigent Old Man who was unable to work and unwilling to starve went to live with his wealthy Son.

"Now my boy," said the Old Man, "you will have opportunity to pay off our debt of gratitude by doing for me what I did for you."

"Hardly," the Son replied, — "at least I shall have to take you to my villa in the country. There are not switches enough growing about here."

734.

A Lady engaged in cooking with vitriol the countenances of her various male acquaintances was accosted by the Law and requested to explain her conduct.

"Very little explanation is needed," she said. "They all bear in their attire and in their beards the damning evidence of their sex."

"True," said the Law; "their guilt is obvious."

So she passed on, in maiden premeditation, fancy free.

735.

An Old Soldier applied for a pension.

"Upon what ground?" the Commissioner inquired.

Said the Old Soldier: "I was shot all to pieces."

"And are the other pieces in receipt of pensions?" inquired the Commissioner, looking kindly upon the fragment before him.

"O no," said the Old Soldier cheerfully, "they get nothing: they have no votes."

736.

A Man of God on his way to the temple paused to observe a Muscular Worldling chastising a member of an erring sect.

"My energetic fellow-worm," said the Man of God, at the close of the rite, "wherefore the admonition?"

"No dam galoot," replied the Muscular Worldling, resuming his outer raiment, "shall deny the efficacy of baptism while I have a sinew left that will work."

"Go," said the Man of God — "go and sinew more."

737.

"It is not the staring that I object to," said the Comet to Professor David-son — "it is rather flattering to be an object of interest to you fellows; but the attentions of the press are distinctly disagreeable."

"How so?" the Professor asked. "I find the newspapers very helpful."

"It is not the same way with you," the "celestial visitor" explained. "Let me ask you how you would like to have the various stages of your progress (along your cocktail route, for example) charted on the old diagrams that served, years ago, to illustrate Shaeffer's remarkable shots at billiards?"

The Comet paused for a reply, but the great diagrammarian, blushing deeply with a consciousness of guilt, had slunk away and hidden his shame in the penumbra of his observatory.

738.

A Soul applied for admittance at the Gate of Heaven.

"I was a soldier of the Salvation Army," said the Soul.

"We do not take in anybody here for what he was," Saint Peter explained, "but for what he did."

"I sang," the Soul said, "and thereby reclaimed many."

"Well, well," the Saint said. "I must not permit my personal prejudices to affect the performance of my duty. Just wait a moment."

So saying, he rang a bell, and when an Angel appeared in answer to the summons said:

"Is the late Mr. Shea inside — the architect who designed the tower for the City Hall in San Francisco?"

"He was," the Angel replied, "but that was one of your mistakes. It was corrected by pitching him out over the rear wall. No other architect has come here in the past three hundred years."

"Ah, I remember," said the Saint. "Well, hunt up one of the mediæval chaps and have him build a hymnarium for this person and his kind, who are not to sing elsewhere. See that the walls are well padded with a three-ply cloud."

"It shall be as you say, sir," said the Angel, moving away.

"I wish you good morning," said Saint Peter to the Soul, handing down a gold harp from a shelf at his side. "Follow the bird."

739.

An Unfortunate Man who had been appointed Superintendent of a Mint was flying from his pursuers when he met a Native.

"Why do you not make a stand?" said the Native; "you might be able to beat them off."

"Alas," replied the hapless outlaw, "I am unarmed."

"Here, take this Winchester rifle," the Native said, "and give them fits!"

The hunted man shook his head sadly. "No, my generous friend," said he. "I must away. A rifle would be of small service against their superior armament; they are equipped with the deadly recommendation!"

"Unknown but engaging fugitive," said the Native, thrusting his hand into the hip-pocket of his breechclout, "you shall have the means of meeting at least one of them on equal terms. I have here a recommendation. It is for a position in the Mint."

The flight was resumed.

740.

"I observe that Mackinder is defending you against the slanders of a certain Fabulist," said a Superserviceable Person to a railroad company's Fixer of the Press.

"What is a Mackinder?" the Fixer of the Press asked.

"Editor of the St. Helena *Liver Complaint*," was the reply.

"Responsible editor?" inquired the Fixer, trying to recollect.

"No—liable editor."

"O, I remember it now: I met it once and as there was plenty of daylight, and I was not alone with it on a blasted heath, I made rather a study of it."

"Doubtless," said the Superserviceable Person, "it wishes to be fixed."

"You do it an injustice, I'm sure," said the Fixer of the Press, thoughtfully. "If I can read character the Mackinder is not corrupt, only vain—not avaricious, but ambitious: he seeks not wealth, but distinction, glory."

"Well?"

"He does not really care to be fixed; he wants it thought that he has been already fixed—that he was worth fixing. We must do something to help the poor devil into better society. Go, my friend, and cause it to be published that I paid him $2."

741.

Sweeping the horizon with his glass, the Skipper of a tugboat saw the Governor of Colorado navigating a mule in blood to the bridle, and put out to rescue him. "Mule ahoy!" hailed the Skipper.

"I, I, sir," the Governor shouted back in the Seamanese tongue.

"What mule is that?" asked the Skipper.

"The Davis H. Waite, Junior, of Aspen," was the proud reply.

"Ah, I see," the Skipper shouted, meditatively, through his trumpet. "Shall I pass you a hee-hawser?"

"No," replied that ancient mariner, turning his prow seaward and setting all ears; "I like this."

And so he sailed away into the sunset, singing: "A Life on the Ocean Wave!"

742.

A stranger in a great city saw a gorgeous procession with a brass band, and a man mauling a big drum.

"What is it all about?" he asked a Bystander.

"That is for the opening of the Midwinter Fair," was the reply. "I know, for I hire the band."

"But," said the stranger, "this is not Midwinter—the Fair cannot be open yet."

"No, certainly not," the Bystander replied, absently waving his handkerchief at the procession; "that is the way to get it open."

"You must be a very public spirited citizen," said the stranger, reverently—"to pay for the band."

"Indeed I am," said the other—"I expect to get the contract for putting a gridle-cake roof on the Temple of Mechanical Futility and Satanic Arts."

743.

A Woman engaged in cowhiding a person of whose sex she was unable to approve was accosted by an Enthusiastic Spectator, who said:

"Madam, if the matter is not too urgent for delay you could accomplish your purpose more effectively, not to say artistically, by first removing the malefactor's nether habiliment."

"Sir," replied the Woman between two blows of the cowhide, "your suggestion is insulting! I am too much of a lady to do that."

744.

A Warm-tempered Person who was about to be tried on a charge of murdering a policeman who had arrested him told his Attorney tht he thought it could be shown that he did not kill the officer.

"If they should force an intelligent jury upon us," said the Attorney, "such evidence as that would hang you. No, we must try to show that the officer whom you killed was one of the Chief's most trusted subordinates and in high favor with the Commission. The jury will not then dare to defy public opinion by convicting you."

745.

A Pious and Temperate Man who had for many years conducted a bank on Sunday-school principles went to the other side of the continent, and while he was there he was told that his bank had failed.

"Dear me!" he said, edging a little nearer to the sea; "this is quite unexpected. Are you very sure about it?"

Being informed that there was no doubt of it, and that the Sheriff was in possession, he rolled his eyes heavenward, spread his erected hands and said with unspeakable sadness:

"He smokes!"

Then bowing his venerable head until the visor of his halo struck his stomach, he added, in a more cheerful tone:

"I have been young and devout, and am now old and holy, yet have I never seen the righteous without a nest-egg, nor his seed shadowing snipes."

746.

Believing that change is the great law of nature, the Gray Gabler of Buzzard Bay called before him the Collector of Internal Revenue for the Second District of California and cut off his head.

"What am I to do with this thing?" said the Collector, picking up the head and curiously examining it. "What use can I make of it?"

"That is not relevant to the occasion," the Gray Gabler remarked with exceeding gravity. "A more pertinent question would be — What use *have* you *been* making of it? As to that, you can have an investigation if you desire."

The sufferer reflected awhile, scratching his neck thoughtfully, as if trying to understand the untoward event, but finally, taking the head in both hands, shook it negatively and walked away into the obscurity of private life, saying that he would let bad enough alone if it would let him alone.

747.

The Ghost of a Deposed Emperor met the President who had succeeded him by the grace of Revolution, and said:

"Your Excllency, I observe certain mutterings of discontent amongst my former subjects. Surely they are not dissatisfied with the new regime!"

"No," replied the President, "the mutterings that you hear are merely hold-overs from your reign. The people are quite happy now."

Just then a huge shell, thrown from a war-ship in the harbor, passed over their heads and exploded in the Executive Mansion.

"An echo of the recent revolution, I presume," said the Ghost of a Deposed Emperor, acridly.

"For a denizen of another world to sneer at mischances occurring in this," said the President, "is in execrable taste."

748.

A Writer engaged in enriching his vocabulary looked up from his work and asked his Wife if there were any news.

"Yes," she replied, after thoughtfully throwing the *Morning Call* out of the window and running her eye over the *Examiner;* "the President has decided not to enforce the Geary law."

"Good Heaven!" shouted the Writer, in great excitement. "That decision is the most disastrous that ever was made!"

"Are the Chinamen so very mischievous then?" asked the Wife, astonished at her phlegmatic husband's earnestness.

"O, the Chinamen are harmless enough," the Writer explained, "but consider the loss to the language! If the President had done his duty we should have had the noun 'deporture,' with 'deport' as an intransitive verb — 'Seven hundred Celestials took their deporture by yesterday's steamer' — 'The distinguished Chinese house-servant, Ah Gum, has deported for Hongkong,' etc. That Cleveland is an unspeakable scoundrel, dear."

749.

The Jiamese Public was eagerly searching the columns of a newspaper to find an account of the latest official disemboweling of foreign importers and the list of winning numbers in the Patagonian lottery; but there was nothing in the paper but insufferable stuff about the birth of a mewling brat at the Executive Mansion in the Capitol. "This is the first birth," said the newspaper, "that ever took place in the Black House."

"By Jupiter!" cried the Jiamese Public, jumping up and cracking his heels together — "it shall be the last!"

With that he added to the Constitution an amendment making married women ineligible to the Presidency.

750.

The Gakwak of Bapootra was making a speech. It was at a celebration of the centennial anniversary of the founding of their Capitol.

"If the Gailutes who assembled here to make laws for others," said the Gakwak, "forget the duty of um-um and er-er patriotism, and legislate in such a way as to deprive me of the happiness of approval, the time when the corner-stone of this building was laid and the circumstances surrounding it won't be worth a—"

Here the Gakwak paused with lifted arms and a great silence fell upon the people, as darkness falls from Heaven.

"His Exalted Obesity is about to swear," cried the Superior Pea-Green Indispensable of the Fish-Hooks, coming forward and waving his wand of office — "let the nation shudder!"

Thereupon the nation shuddered, and the Gailutes excreted beads of icy perspiration.

"——— is not worth," concluded the Gakwak, bringing down his arms and folding them under his coat-skirts, "an Olney."

The people breathed again: an olney is the smallest Bapootran coin.

751.

A Pixley testifying in court said:

"I have no respect for the newspapers. I am on oath, and would like that to go into the record of the court—I have no respect for the newspapers."

Then the editors of all the newspapers excepting the Pixley's held a meeting and unanimously passed the following resolution:

"WHEREAS the Pixley has made oath that he does not respect us, be it

"*Resolved* that in this dictum we gratefully recognize a divine intimnation that we are at liberty to respect ourselves."

752.

A lecturer on Phrenology having invited his audience to come forward and have their heads examined, a C. R. Bennett gravely advanced to the platform and gravely submitted his dome of thought to manipulation. No sooner had the Professor of Phrenology run his fingers over that shining globe than he said:

"Ladies and gentlemen, this depraved and dangerous person should be commended to the attention of the Executive Officer of the Society for the Suppression of Vice."

This harsh judgment greatly astonished the audience, and a Prominent Citizen rose, saying:

"Sir, the person you have before you is the Executive Officer of the Society for the Suppression of Vice."

"The devil he is!" cried the Professor of Phrenology, unhanding the villain. "If I had known that of him I would not have touched him—not with a fishing rod!"

753.

Two distinguished Italians having quarreled at a "banquet" in Chicago, one of them was carried out of the room by his friends.

"He called me a liar!—he called me a liar!" the other shouted in great excitement.

"O bother," said a Civilized Human Being, "can't you find something worse than that to get mad about? Just look at that bill of fare!"

754.

A Human Head having washed ashore at Sausalito, the Coroner of Oakland made a formal application for it.

"I want it," he explained, "to wash the shore of Oakland."

755.

The Inhabitants of a Sister City had an epidemic of starvation and died so rapidly that it was feared there would not be enough of the living to bury the dead. That apprehension proved unfounded, for what the living lacked in numbers they made up in proficiency with shovel and spade: their skill was surprising.

"What makes the Inhabitants of the Sister City so skillful in excavating?" inquired a Stranger in the Land.

"Their habit," replied a Dweller in Pulicosa, "of putting in most of their time digging for buried treasure."

"And what has caused the famine?"

"The same."

756.

An Illustrious Traveler was sent to a lunatic asylum despite the fact that he had discovered Noah's Ark in a seaworthy condition on the summit of Mount Arrarat.

"Behold, my son," said the Superintendent of the lunatic asylum, "the vanity of the advantages of travel—the futility of storing the mind with the riches of observation."

And the Illustrious Traveler said that if ever again he reached his native village his longest excursion would not reach beyond his own door by ten miles.

757.

An Anarchist engaged in charging a bomb was accosted by a Chief of Police, who inquired what he was doing.

"Preparing a plea for the Rights of Man," the Anarchist replied.

"Among them," said the Chief of Police, "do you count the right of immunity from assassination?"

"O dear, no," replied the Anarchist, putting in another handful of dynamite; "that would be incompatible with the right to assassinate."

"You are so very logical," the officer said, "that I hardly venture to engage in controversy with you, but I cannot forbear to invite your attention to a consideration that you seem to have overlooked. It is this."

So saying, he drew forth his club.

758.

A President sitting in the place of state was informed that the candidate of his party had been beaten, whereupon he smiled broadly so that his jowls were tremulous with delight and the mouth of him cavernous to see.

"Bring me yonder pen," he gave orders to an attendant, which having been done he proceeded to indite a Thanksgiving Proclamation setting forth the gratitude that possessed his soul. "I violate no confidence," he said later to the hired advisers gathered about him, "in stating that my belief that there is none really worthy but myself alone in the party has been fully sustained."

Those hearing gave no dissent, for the stipend they received was seemly, and they had no contracts by which to hold the jobs.

759.

Deeming himself fair to look upon and of a mighty brain that throbbed with noble thoughts, a Shortridge importuned that he be invested by the people with a toga of distinction. But the people demurred, asking of him: "Who art thou?"

Drawing himself to a towering height at which one of small feet could with difficulty have maintained a balance, he replied: "Truly it is said of me that I am brother to an editor who speaks for all."

"Say no more," responded with people with one accord. "Your honors are already great enough. The toga goes elsewhere. See?"

760.

After having clamored for a vindication a candidate for Congress found himself snowed under by the votes of those who loved decency. Working his way from under the pile of ballots he caught his breath and announced that he had been duly vindicated.

"I do not quite see," said an observer, "how you arrive at this conclusion. Will you kindly explain?"

"Certainly," replied the candidate. "It is true that my right to be called an honest man got the worst of the contest, but as to my right to be called an ass, the vindication is complete."

761.

A lady having received the promise of a man that he would vote to grant to her the right of suffrage went her way rejoicing. But upon election day he voted otherwise, and the lady, smarting under defeat, reproached him with tears. But he made answer that what he had done was out of the kindness of his heart. "For," he reasoned, "you were made happy for a time by my promise. But for the promise your unhappiness would have been as keen and had an earlier start."

So he left her wondering, but of her subsequent remarks no record was made.

762.

After having been elected to serve the people a Johnson man made the mistake of conducting himself as the servant of a notable wrongdoer who thrived by preying upon his fellows, so that the people were wroth and made hostile ado.

Yet the Johnson man besought that they send him again to office, saying that his work was not yet done, and that there was great need of him in Congress.

But they failed to see the point, replying: "Your nerve is so extraordinary that we choose to keep you among us as a curio. Also, it is better to have you where the police are within easy call."

Thus it happened that Huntington was grieved, and that necessity arose for him to hire a new agent.

763.

With eyes downcast a murderer paced his cell communing with himself.

"Alas," he murmured, "that I should have been condemned to death by a California court."

Hearing him and being touched to pity his cell-mate made inquiry as to the cause of the manifest grief.

"Do you not know what that sentence means?" responded the murderer. "I do not dread the gallows. But to have my case monkeyed with until old age shall carry me off is mighty tough."

The cell-mate acknowledged that it was in the nature of a hardship.

764.

Having a contract to furnish his government with armor plate a Carnegie supplied a quality thereof pitted with blow holes, and exceeding frail. Being called to task for his dereliction he made ready explanation. "Your point is not well taken," he stated blandly. "It is true that in resistance the blow holes are not formidable, but think of the extra buoyancy they give the craft."

Palpably chagrined the objectors withdrew and the Carnegie straightway endowed a Sunday-school.

765.

After occupying the executive chair for eight years a President waxed fat so that he let out his waistband notably and the size of him was as a mountain.

"I am greater than all the people," quoth the fat President, as he spat on a freshly baited hook.

"Do not deceive yourself," timidly suggested an adviser. "I once knew a museum giantess that individually could have given you cards and spades and beaten you on any fair scales."

But the fat President perceiving himself to be misunderstood deemed it not seemly to pursue the conversation further.

766.

The people of an island having long been robbed arose in rebellion and smote their oppressors, whereupon the oppressors arrived in swarms as if they would devour the rebels bodily. Seeing they were in great straits the islanders appealed to a great nation nearby for countenance, but the head of the nation bade them begone. Yet to their oppressors he said: "I am a merciful man and do not like the lingering torture you inflict on these helpless ones. I pray you kill them quickly and have some style about you. Pardon my brevity. I go now to shoot ducks."

767.

An actress wishing to receive some advertising sought out a manager and to him made known her desire. He listened patiently and then observed: "The people are weary of the divorce story and the stolen pearls. There is one desperate recourse for you if you are bent on creating a sensation."

"I am ready for anything," responded the actress eagerly.

"My advice," concluded the manager, "is that you learn how to act and then act."

Thereupon the actress fled, not having intent to essay the impossible.

768.

"I hear that you are versed in law and have prospered greatly," said one upon meeting a friend of his youth.

"As to that," responded the friend, "I am not certain, but you overestimate me. I do not know much law, but I have got fastened to a fat estate, which is better."

It was upon this showing that the other made bold to strike him for a loan.

769.

A beggar meeting a prosperous citizen he sought of him a small advance, but the prosperous citizen said nay. Much put out by this treatment the beggar smote the next citizen he met and took from him without asking lief. "How much better it is," he said as he turned the pockets of his victim, "to be independent and not get into a position to be jeered at by wealth."

However, a policeman appeared just then and remarked that the explanation, while lucid and interesting, didn't go.

770.

Two pugilists disputing as to the possession of a certain purse for which they had fought appeared in court to have the matter adjudicated, but the court, after listening to them, threw both into the street. "Not only is pugilism disgraceful," remarked the Judge, climbing back upon the bench, "but the people with whom conversation is a profession ought to pay some attention to grammar. Call the next case."

771.

An ancient thief whose respectability took the form of great wealth, hoping further to loot the people, went with a gang of lobbyists to the capital of the nation. Having arrived he called the lobbyists about him and made speech. "Do not err," he said, "in offering to purchase people by naming too small a sum. These statesmen are apt to be sensitive and hold themselves in high esteem."

Whereupon he dismissed his lobbyists with a wink, and they whiled away time by picking each others' pockets.

772. The Conservative Employer

A Woman with seven dependent children was permitted to work for a Benevolent Gentleman for a wage of four dollars a week. One day she ventured to ask him for a little money.

"Why, no," he said; "I owe you only six weeks' wages, whereas it is a rule of my business to be always two months in arrears. Money given to you now would be in the nature of an advance, a loan. What security could you give?"

"My daughter has a small insurance on my life," the Woman replied. "The policy could be assigned to you."

"God forbid!" said the Benevolent Gentleman. "That would break down a sacred tradition of my class. No, I cannot for a possible private gain consent that it shall make any difference to me whether an employee lives or dies."

773. The Secret of Success

An Astronomer who had gained a wide renown as Director of a great observatory was asked to what he attributed his success.

"To my regular habits," he replied — "especially the habit of going to bed early and sleeping late. Men who turn night into day never become really distinguished. Look at my subordinate astronomers, for example."

774. The King and the Genius

A genius who had built an airship was asked by the king why he did not send it up.

"Alas!" he replied, sighing; "having lived a blameless life, I have no means to man it. Perhaps your Majesty will supply a captain and crew from among your own enemies."

"But," said the king. "I too am destitute of enemies."

"I beg your Majesty to forgive me," the genius said. "I spoke without reflection. You also have lived a blameless life."

"Well, no," said his Majesty, thoughtfully scratching the royal head where it did not itch; "that is not just the way of it. The fact is, my enemies have all died a blameless death."

775. The Man-Eating Sergeant

Calling the roll of his soldiers after a battle, a Captain observed that there was no response to the name of Sergeant Thundermuzzle.

"Go seek him," said he to a Corporal.

"Yes, sir," assented the Corporal, "but can you give me any notion of the direction in which I am most likely to find him?"

"Direction?" thundered the Captain—"direction? Why, sir, there can be but one direction in which to look for Sergeant Thundermuzzle while the foemen are not entirely exterminated. He swore this morning that he would eat them."

The Corporal started away toward the field of battle.

"Go back to the supply train, you fool!" shouted the Captain. "You'll find him negotiating with the Commissary of Subsistence. Do you suppose he would eat those fellows without salt?"

776. The Two Actors

Seeing himself imitated in his strut by an Ape an Actor visiting a zoölogical garden rebuked the animal severely for bad manners.

"Do you not know," said he, "that it is extremely vulgar and offensive to imitate another?"

"Another what?" said the offender.

The Actor reflected, long, seriously and profitably.

"Another Ape," he said.

777. The Knights of Envy

A Knight who had liberated a maiden from the den of a dragon and was listening to the plaudits of the populace suddenly lifted his mailed hand, commanding silence.

"I thought," he explained, that I heard a discordant note."

> " 'Twas musical, but sadly sweet,
> Such as when files and saw-teeth meet
> And take a long unmeasured tone
> To mortal minstrelsy unknown."

"Doubtless it was the evensong of a distant jackass," said Sir Viper Belittlemuch, moving in a sidelong fashion toward the outskirt of the throng; "that songster has a fairly good voice, but no ear."

"I'm inclined to think," said Sir Yappet de Sparage, looking furtively over his shoulder at the right foot of the nearest man behind him, "that it was the voice of a plate-armor factory intoning its love to the moon."

"If this assembly were polled," said an aged Courtier, thoughtfully, "there would be found as many explanations of that discordant note as there are knights to whose friendly offices a captive maiden would prefer the dragon."

778. The Vigilant Guardian

Listening at the front door of a fine mansion, a Policeman overheard the owner murdering his wife in the parlor.

"Justice," said the Policeman, "may be slow, but she sometimes manages to arrive."

So saying, he went round to the back door, entered the house, and while the owner was preoccupied with his task carried away the family silver.

779. The Studious Official

A Police Commissioner Who Had Been Abroad studying how to have an efficient force provoked a violent quarrel with the Chief.

"In which of the great European cities did you learn to do that?" the Chairman of the Board asked.

The Police Commissioner Who Had Been Abroad was pained.

"You might treat me with common civility," said he.

"What for?" asked the Chairman of the Board, who was a Utilitarian.

The book in which the answer is not recorded is held in high esteem by philosophers.

780. The Ignorant Ass

A Professor in a University having uttered certain convictions, a mass-meeting was called to consider them. When it had convened in the great banqueting hall of a newspaper the several speeches showed such a preponderance of dissent that it was again called to order, as an indignation meeting, and passed resolutions of censure. As the meeting was about to adjourn an Old Man, renowned for wisdom and worth, entered the hall, leading a small yearling donkey. Pausing at the edge of the speaker's platform he drew a club from under his coat and beat the small beast unmercifully until compelled to desist.

"Why did you do that?" the Chairman asked — "what is the matter with the poor little creature?"

"Ignorance," the Old Man replied — "invincible insupportable ignorance! The propositions of the University Professor are not known to this infernal jackass as obvious elementary truths!"

"Indeed!" said the Chairman, with mock respect, "and may this meeting venture to ask how you ascertained that?"

"I heard him inveighing against them," said the wise and worthy Old Man.

781. The Unusual Manager

A Gentleman who through an erroneous estimate of his character had been put in charge of a political campaign was asked on the evening of election day what he thought were the chances of his candidate having won.

"I know nothing about it," said he.

"What!" exclaimed the Inquiring One, "you do not claim a victory?"

"I do not know what you mean by 'claim'," the Gentleman replied; "it is not my habit to claim anything that is not certainly mine unless my claim would help me to obtain it."

"Then you concede this election to our opponents?" asked the other, in manifest astonishment.

"I cannot 'concede' anything that is not in my control," was the reply.

"Well," said the other, in deep disgust, "it is plain that we need a man at the helm whose heart is in the voyage."

"What you need, individually," the Gentleman said, "is a good dictionary and the sense to understand it."

782. The Lady and the Tiger

A Benevolent and Fat Old Lady observing a Tiger in a cage was moved by compassion to say:

"Poor, dear creature! I am so sorry that you cannot get out."

"I don't want to get out," said the Tiger, his cavernous mouth drenched and dripping with the waters of desire; "what plunges me into a gulf of dark despair is that you cannot get in."

783. Characters Three

The Oldest Inhabitant accosted Any Schoolboy, saying:

"Being fond of reading controversial literature I have always been greatly impressed with the variety and scope of your knowledge. Will you kindly tell me how you learned the many things which such a multitude of persons rush into print without having ascertained?"

"It would do no good to tell you," replied Any Schoolboy; "a person of your astonishing inexperience would not profit by anything told him."

The colloquy was overheard by the Fiend in Human Shape, who sighed to think how easily these persons had won their distinction, whereas his own renown was the niggard reward of a diligent activity.

784. The Recandidate

A Man Who Had Been a President continued to beget children, which being observed repeatedly and at great length by a Reader of the Newspapers that person was thrown into an unamiable frame of mind.

"If the expiration of his term is to give us no relief," said he, "we may as well put him back into office."

The next day he read in a newspaper that the Man Who Had Been a President was "prominently mentioned for reëlection."

785. Murderers' Row as a Health Resort

A convicted Murderer dying of old age in the seclusion of his cell was approached by the Ghost of his victim.

"Aha," said the Ghost, with a sepulchral chuckle, "I have my revenge at last."

"True," the Murderer gasped, "but I beg you to observe that it is the revenge of my choice. Your vengeance on the rest of the population of the world—with here and there an exception—has been a good deal swifter in the past, and will be in the future. By the way, what did they do to you?"

"I've nothing against any body but you," replied the Ghost.

"Then I'm greatly obliged to you," the Murderer said with a wan smile: "Your disfavor is not only a great distinction, but it is uncommonly wholesome. Exercise, sunshine and air are fairly good makeshift aids to health, but if poor Methuselah, with his splendid constitution, had known the hygienic advantages of a tranquil life in the shadow of the gallows we might have had him with us to this day."

786.

Compelled by fear of public opinion to confer military rank upon a distinguished political rival, the President (of Labragascar) considered what to do next.

"If I send him against the enemy," he mused, "he may return at the close of the war with such glory that I shall be quite extinguished in it; if I keep him in camp there is no hope of his getting shot."

In his perplexity he consulted the Secretary of Re-election, who, having duly perpended the matter, delivered judgment as follows:

"May it please your Excellency, there is but one way out of this dilemma, and although it is so full of peril that I hardly dare to suggest it, yet I pray you remember that in great emergencies great men accept great risks. We must make peace."

They made peace.

787.

A Spanish General having surrendered without resistance was honored by his American Conqueror with a grand review. As corps after corps of the victorious army marched past the reviewing stand the captive's delight grew visibly and audibly.

"I do not understand," said the American General, "how you can find matter of joy in the vast number of your enemies. I had hoped that it would plunge you into the deepest dejection."

"My friend, you must pardon me for disappointing a just expectation," said the Spanish General, courteously repressing his hilarity; "but, naturally, the adversity of your country does not appeal to my compassion."

"Adversity?"

"Consider the pensions."

788.

An Oppressed People, loudly proclaiming the brotherhood of man and the fatherhood of God, made its moan to the Land of the Free for deliverance from the tyrant's chain. The Land of the Free sent her sons to liberate the Oppressed People. In doing so they had the good fortune to capture the tyrant's chain, which they valued highly as a trophy of the chase. After returning to their own country the lightness of their luggage suggested an inspection, when it was discovered that the tyrant's chain had been stolen by the Oppressed People, who whiled away the tedious hours of the ensuing centuries of independence by fitting it to one another's neck.

789. From Darkest Georgia

A Gentleman from Georgia having drifted over to the African coast was captured by the Blacks, who decided to skin him alive—whereat the Gentleman from Georgia did most significantly smile.

"Why does the prisoner smile?" inquired the King, of his Head Interpreter. But all the arts and charms of that functionary elicited no explanation of the phenomenon, and the Gentleman from Georgia was left in the hands of the Royal Decorticator, who was equipped with the most effective skinning apparatus that human ingenuity could devise. At the end of three weeks that dread official reported to the King as follows:

"Father of the Rivers and the Hills, spit upon thy slave. I send you the hair, teeth and claws of the white dog from over the sea, with certain small rolls of cuticle; but the true skin I and my seven assistants have so far been unable to reach. Superposed on it, and lying immediately beneath the cuticle, we found the outer one of seventeen layers of indurated barbarism. Be pleased, O Brother to the Earthquake and the Piano, to trample thy slave into the mire and say what further he shall do."

To which the King made answer thus:

"Surrender your office to the illustrious stranger and bid him count the kinks in your small intestine."

790. A Weak Attachment

A political boss, who having been eschewed by his party, was appointed to the highest office in the gift of its official leader, met a dog's tail, which was in an attitude of dejection between the animal's hinder legs.

"My unhappy friend," said the deposed boss, "what is the matter with you, and where does it hurt?"

"This ungrateful dog," answered the tail, "has thrown me off—that is where it hurts."

"But," said the other, "you are not off; you are on."

"Only stuck on," the tail explained, cautiously attempting a deprecatory wag. "The beast's master did that."

Ever thereafter, when dethroned statesmen listened for the voice of hope, he heard only that of despair, reminding him that he was only stuck on.

791. On Second Thoughts

"I calculate," said a Veteran Officer, "that in my forty years of military service I have taken twenty thousand lives; yet I am only a brigadier-general! My country is indeed ungrateful."

"Yes," assented the Chaplain of the brigade, as in duty bound, "but there is a Greater than the President. I shall this day beseech Him not to overlook you."

"Thank you," said the Veteran Officer; "you are a holy and righteous man."

So saying he walked away, indulging his dream of promotion. Later in the day he returned and taking the Chaplain aside said:

"O, about that petition to the Throne of Grace. Would you mind putting it on the ground of my piety, and saying nothing about those twenty thousand dead? I don't like to bother God with mortuary statistics."

792. An Unequal Strife

A Lion and a Tiger had a bet on a giraffe race, but the Tiger was unable to attend.

"You lost," said the Lion when they met; "my animal won by a neck."

"H'm," murmured the Tiger reflectively, "I don't mind losing, but I'll be skinned if I didn't think it would be a closer race than that!"

793. The Threatening Weather

At an out-of-door meeting a demagogue was making a passionate plea for monkey suffrage, when an angel looked down from heaven and wept upon him. He lifted his eyes to the sky for a moment, then observing the husband of his laundress occupying a seat on one platform, said to him in an earnest whisper,

"Run home and tell your wife to take in all her washing from the drying line — I am about to advocate the initiative, the referendum, and the recall."

794. A Literary Violet

A Common Libeler said to a Superior Person:

"The liberties of the people are threatened with destruction and republican institutions topple to their fall! The Legislature has passed a law compelling me to father every lie that I write about another. I have to put my name to all my censorious articles."

"Why," said the Superior Person, with the smile of his kind, "I have done that all my life and find it no great hardship."

"Ah, but you have an unfair advantage," protested the Common Libeler; "you know whom to vilify."

"Yes," assented the Superior Person, with a certain gracious dignity, "I flatter myself that I am not altogether devoid of knowledge concerning the rudiments of my business."

Nodding a tolerant good-day to the Common Libeler in his despair, the Superior Person seated himself at his own feet, where he found abundant inspiration for countless Fables and Anecdotes, the wisdom whereof transcended expression.

795.

A General who was conducting a war in a distant island wrote to the Agricultural Department of his Government to ship him a ton of acorns. When asked what he intended to do with them he replied:

"There is no shade in our trenches, and the troops suffer from heat. A growth of large oaks will add much to the comfort of the men in the firing line."

He would have said more, but his attention was arrested by a burst of song from a neighboring jungle.

"Ah," he sighed, "that is a round robin."

And he walked sadly away.

796.

By becoming a subject of the Queen of Muldoodle a citizen of Gom incurred the hatred of the Gommeaux, who rose as one man and called him rascal.

"Your courts are kept pretty busy naturalizing immigrants," he retorted. "You have a great many rascals if it is rascally to forswear one's allegiance."

"It is only rascally," replied the Gommeaux, "to renounce one's allegiance to *us.*"

797. Bullet and Bone

A Dum-Dum Bullet having arrived at the Thigh Bone of a soldier said:

"I am about to smash you into splinters of uncommon fineness, instead of making a clean perforation and passing on about my business."

"Then I venture to remind you," replied the Bone, with great austerity, "that you have been prohibited by the Peace Congress as a needlessly cruel device. You will have the goodness to withdraw."

"Do you think that as one of the horrors of war I ought to forego this admirable opportunity to promote peace by making war odious?" asked the Bullet. "I pause for a reply," it added, flattening itself in a shower of bone-dust against an adjacent rock.

798. The Interlocutors

"You are making a good deal of noise in the world," said a Fortified Place to a Furious Bombardment.

"Naturally you do not like it," replied the Furious Bombardment. "You have weak ears, I suppose."

"What, I? My friend, you misunderstand my interest in the matter. It is merely friendly curiosity — you would not hurt a fly."

And the Fortified Place, smiling a sweet, sad smile, fell to thinking of other things.

799. An Attractive Warrior

A Wounded Soldier opened his eyes and asked: "Where am I?"

"On the operating table," answered a Surgeon, putting away the chloroform bottle. "We have taken out of you a fragment of shell, a grapeshot, two rifle bullets and the point of a bayonet."

"Just my luck!" mused the Wounded Soldier. "Everything goes against me."

"It seems to me," the Surgeon said, "that everything comes your way."

800. The Escaping Garrison

The Governor-General of a blockaded island collected a vast army in his capital, which he fortified with so gigantic works that nobody could get in and nobody could get out; but Spring sizzled into Summer and Summer boiled into Autumn, and the enemy came not.

"Very well," said the Governor-General, "if I cannot fight I can proclaim."

So he flung upon the city so many proclamations attesting the courage and devotion of his troops that his loftiest ramparts were snowed under and the garrison escaped.

801. He Had Them

A Civilian having applied for a commission in the army the President asked him:

"What are your qualifications?"

"Qualifications?" the Civilian repeated — "what's them?"

"That is what I am trying to find out," replied the President — "what yours are."

"Well, well," said the Civilian, "this floors me! For ten years I've run the party in my ward, and I never before — "

"Hold!" said the President; "you've answered my question. Be a Lieutenant-Colonel and Quartermaster."

His name stands high upon the roll of heroes. It is John Smith.

802.

An Admiral, who had won a great victory off the coast of Madagascar while absent from the battle, was boasting of the exploit.

"I don't think it a very remarkable feat," said one of the audience, "considering your numerical superiority in Commanders-in-Chief."

"What do you mean by that?" the Admiral asked, doubtfully; "there was only one of me. It was a great one," he added under his breath.

"My estimate," said the other, "is that there were about fifteen hundred millions of you in command of that fleet, not counting the inhabitants of Madagascar and the mainland contiguous to it, who manifestly belong in another class. Your advantage was all the greater if we reckon the population of the planets and such of the fixed stars as may be cool enough to grow Commanders-in-Chief."

The Admiral was greatly incensed and, being afflicted with aphasia, thundered, "God bless your body!"

803.

The King of Novagonia being desirous of a mighty navy sent for a Distinguished Foreigner to advise him.

"The first thing to be done," said the Distinguished Foreigner, "is to organize a Bureau of Navigation."

"What!" exclaimed the King — "before we have anything to navigate?"

"Your Majesty is a favorite in Heaven and the hope of the world," was the reply, "but worm of the dust as I am I must say that the royal comprehension of purposes is imperfect and the royal faith in established but unfamiliar methods distinctly faulty."

So the Bureau of Navigation was set up, and began at once to attest the worth of its personnel by vilifying everybody else, and this it continued to do while there remained in all the land a reputation undefiled. And the entire country rang with the scandal of it.

One day the Head of the Bureau was surprised and pained by a visit from the King.

"I implore your Majesty's mercy!" cried the officer, prostrating himself at the royal feet. "Spare my life and I will at once disband the Bureau of Navigation!"

"No," said the King, "I should be sorry to have a navy irregularly constituted. But my good name is to me sweeter than honey and more precious than pearls. I have come to solicit a place in the Bureau."

804.

A naval officer had testified before a court of inquiry that a measured distance of three miles was fifteen. After the court had adjourned a civilian called his attention to the error.

"Error?" said the witness — "I am not aware that an error was committed. In what did it consist?"

"In the untruth," replied his critic — "in what we landlubbers in our coarse speech call a" — hesitating — "a lie!"

"O, that's all right," said the officer, smiling; "let the thing have its true name, that's all I ask. A lie is always a lie, but whether it is an error depends. Doubtless you did not observe on which side I was testifying."

805.

"I am justly entitled to all the glory of that great naval victory," said His Absency, "for I was the highest officer in those seas."

"I am not so sure of all that," said the Horizon, thoughtfully. "You may have outranked everybody else, but you were a long way below me."

806. A Faulty Rigging

A Donkey famous throughout Gambesia for pious devotion to the god of his imagination was trying to convert a Mole.

"Your make-up and habits," said the Donkey, "give a significant hint of your fate if you do not embrace the truth and worship the Hoot Owl of our fathers. In the life to come, as in this, your course will be downward to the dark."

"And you will fly upward to the light, I suppose," the Mole replied.

"Certainly; it is for that that I am pious."

"Ah," said the Mole, absently beginning a tunnel at the root of a valuable tulip, "it will be a performance worth seeing—with your wings set so far forward."

807. A Welcome Immigration

A lion dining on a man was asked by a passing jackal what the man had done to displease him.

"Nothing at all," was the reply; "on the contrary he has given me great pleasure. Men of his trade are much needed in this country and should not be made to feel themselves unwelcome."

"His trade?" said the jackal. "What was his trade?"

"He was a lion-hunter," said the king of beasts.

808. The Judicial Mind

A Judge of the Court of Technicality and Presumption, at Ghargaroo, received a letter from a lady in Ballybazoo, whom he had known a long time before. The lady asked him if he had any knowledge of her son, of whom she had heard nothing for twenty years. In reply he assured her he had and begged to remain her obedient servant.

The anxious mother at once went to Ghargaroo for tidings of her son. Replying to her questioning, the Judge informed her that he had met the boy at her house in Ballybazoo before his disappearance, and had observed that the lad had a wart on the left side of his nose.

"And you suffer me," said the lady, "to make a long and costly journey just to learn *that*—all of which I knew before!"

"Ballybazoo is outside my jurisdiction," the Judge explained, "I could not serve you with a writ of ne exeat regno."

"But why," persisted the lady, "did you not tell me that was all you knew?"

"Madam, you asked me if I had any knowledge of him—there was no other question before me. You did not ask me what my knowledge of him was."

A president who had overheard the conversation was so impressed by the Judge's most judicial answer that he appointed him an Associate Justice of the Supreme Court and inviting his attention to an important case then pending directed him to decide against the appellant.

809. The Penitent Benefactor

A Millionaire who had founded many public libraries died in the consciousness of merit and the faith of eternal renown. While waiting for Charon to ferry him over the Styx he fell into conversation with an Author similarly circumstanced.

"It gives me great pleasure, sir," said the Millionaire, "to meet one for whose profession I have done so much."

"You are the architect of your own pleasure," said the Author. "It was you that brought me here. If you had not made it easy for a hundred persons to read one copy of my works I might have sold enough of them to give me a living, and need not have cut my throat to appease my hunger."

"I never thought of it in just that way before," said the Millionaire, in deep meditation. "Perhaps my merit is less great than it seemed; but at least I am sure of my fame, posterity will not concern itself with the wrongs of authors."

"It is authors that you call posterity," the other soul explained. "Their voice is known as the judgment of posterity — that is its nickname. None but they and those whom they are willing to quote can get a hearing."

At this the Millionaire was so sorry for what he had done that he tried to come back to Pittsburg to lead a different life. But Charon had other views, and at last accounts the good man was in Elysium, lying on a bed of amaranth and moly and singing "The Star-Spangled Banner."

810. The Two Wine Bottles

Two wine bottles were talking of women.

"They are very excellent and virtuous," said the bottle that was full.

"One judges by what one hears," said the other; "I hold a different opinion."

"That," said the full one, "is all that you do hold."

"Yes," assented the other, "I attended a stag dinner."

811. The Wolves and the Jackals

The wolves of the mainland swam over to an island and undertook to subdue the jackals there. Being unable to do so, they were in danger of losing their reputation for power. In this emergency they sought advice from the king of the foxes, renowned for wisdom.

"Do the jackals fight as hard as ever?" the king asked.

"I grieve to confess that they do," replied the ambassador of the wolves.

"Call them remnant bands of irresponsible ladrones," said the king of the foxes.

The wolves acted on the suggestion and their military prestige was unimpaired.

812. The People That Were Hard to Suit

The manager of a trust called the people together and said: "My friends, I am going to raise the price of grindstones."

"You scoundrel!" said the people; "have you no compassion for us miserable consumers?"

"Did I say 'raise' the price?" cried the manager of the trust — "I mean that I am about to lower it."

"Yes, villain, to kill off competition," they roared — "to bring ruin upon independent dealers!"

"Ah, my friends," said he, "you are a little difficult to please to-day. Will you be good enough to tell me what to do?"

"Get off the earth," the people answered. So he went to Kalamazoo.

813. A Benefactor

A squirrel who had buried a number of hickory nuts forgot the place, and before he found it the nuts had sprouted and were unfit to eat. Summoning the other squirrels to the spot, he pointed out the young shoots and said with great solemnity: "My friends, we live too selfishly. Behold, I have done a little something for the future. From this grove posterity will gather abundant food."

At this they declared him a great benefactor and loaded him with honors, which he bore modestly till he was shot for a stew and the young hickory trees made into hoop poles.

814. The Different Circumstances

A rich man who lay at the point of death offered his physician his entire fortune if he would cure him.

"You are late in your liberality," said the physician. "Why did you not make me that offer five years ago, when you had typhoid fever? You were just as sure that you were going to die as you are now."

"The circumstances are very different," the patient explained. "My fortune was much larger then."

815. Threes

The greatest man in a congressional district met a pig and had the condescension to say, "Good-morning, my humble friend."

"I beg your pardon," said the pig austerely, "I am the greatest hog in all this region!"

As the two passed on, a philosopher was heard to murmur, "One small pair."

Nature, who had just created a politician, an ass and a dog, replied: "Not good."

816. The Publisher and the Skull

A publisher engaged in the traditional occupation of sipping champagne out of an author's skull imposed upon himself the privation of pausing to remark: "If this improvident gentleman had been blacksmith as well as author, I might have had to wait a long time for my flagon. One should have another trade in addition to writing."

Said the skull: "You do not seem to need another trade in addition to publishing."

817. The Bird and the Cat

A bird that was about to be devoured by a cat said: "Surely you will not destroy so harmless a creature as I!"

"Not wantonly," said the cat, with a mouthful of feathers. "I don't care particularly for bird, but very much for the fine nutty flavor imparted to it by many generations of my friends the worms."

818. The Blameless Reptile

"Why do you punish me?" said a snake that was undergoing a clubbing. "I cannot help being a snake."

"I am assisting you to help it," replied the power at the other end of the club. "My preference is for a grease-spot."

819. The Philosopher and His Dog

A philosopher who had tied a heavy stone to his dog's tail and was about to throw him into the water to drown him stumbled into the water himself. The dog sprang to the rescue and, the stone having slipped off, brought the philosopher ashore.

"Alas," said the dog, sorrowfully, "I must look for another master."

"Don't bother about that," said the philosopher, pulling a cord from his pocket; "I will look for another stone."

820. The Qualified Candidate

A man desirous of political preferment went to the leader of his party and made known his wish.

"Are your personal opinions in harmony with those of the party?" the leader inquired.

"I think there will be no trouble in securing a virtual conformity," the aspirant explained; "for five years I have been working as an echo at a mountain watering place."

821. The Testimony of Science

A cave bat was describing the outside world.

"It is a much larger cavern than this," he said. "The walls are of onyx, the roof is of lead, the floor is probably silver. Gold stalactites depend from above and copper stalagmites rise below. We don't know the exact age of these formations. There is a river that flows up-hill and has fishes that are parallelopipedons. They are believed to have eyes."

"Fishes with eyes!" squeaked the other bats; "that is manifestly impossible!"

"Science has no answer to the caviling of ignorance. The bats there are seven feet long, cheerful in disposition—and most amiably spotted with blue. They are very wise and do not die."

"None of us has ever been out there, none of them has ever been in here," cried a bat from the darkest and most distant chamber of the cave; "how is all this learned?"

"By the scientific method of inevitable inference," was the reply.

822. The Man and the Sword

"You take life seriously," said the duelist, wiping the blood from his blade.

"Yes," assented the weapon, "but consider what I have gone through."

823. The New Method

A citizen whose property had been taken by political thieves was bewailing his untoward fate.

"You used to meet them socially, did you not?" inquired an observant neighbor.

"Their crime is all the greater for that," was the reply.

"Possibly," said the observant one; "but it is also the easier. Henceforth, whenever you take the hand of a thief, a decent regard for the interest of your pockets requires that you keep it."

Always afterward, when the citizen took the hand of a thief, he was so reluctant to let go that all thieves thought he loved them, and, by way of adding the charm of ingratitude to the advantages of thrift, they plundered him with a special and particular assiduity.

824. The Defective Beauty

A man was pointing out with pride and delight the charms of his bride.

"I do not observe that she has any rattles," said a rattlesnake.

"Nor any bristles," said a pig.

"Where are her horns?" said the ox.

"And her warts," said the toad.

"No one is perfect," said the man, thoughtfully scratching his head, "even the devil has not a fine head of hair."

825. King and Parrot

A King whose trusted Prime Minister had been detected in conspiracy against the throne entered the criminal's dwelling and passing in deep dejection through a private apartment heard a Parrot shouting: "I want to be a queen, I want to be a queen!"

"Aha!" exclaimed the King, "in seeking reasons for the act of a married man they reckon ill who leave out the wife."

Returning to the palace he issued a royal rescript, providing for maintenance of a parrot in the household of every officer of the kingdom.

826. A Tale of Two Tails

A dog's tail diligently engaged in a vain endeavor to wag the dog was about to desist in despair and let nature take her course when it heard a monkey's tail saying, from an adjacent tree: "In order to do that you must first secure a firm grasp on some important principle of action."

Looking upward it saw the monkey's tail tightly wound about a limb and energetically swinging the monkey through wide arcs of oscillation.

"The great," mused the dog's tail, "are the prehensile. There is an aristocracy of birth; monkey-tails are born to the purple."

827. The Traveler from the Shades

A wicked man who had been dead, but was restored to life, was asked how he felt.

"My health is not so bad," he replied, "but it will require some time to get me acclimated. I am wearing three overcoats at present."

"What form of government have they in — abroad, you know — where you were?"

"It was formerly an absolute monarchy, but as the sovereign wished to pass most of his time on earth he gave his subjects civil and religious liberty, with the elective franchise. Thereby each becomes a part of the apparatus, assisting to carry out the purpose of the founder of the colony."

"May I ask if you acquired the language of the country?"

"All languages are spoken there, but chiefly those of southeastern Europe."

The inquirer turned sadly away. "Alas," he sighed, "to secure so small a change of conditions it is hardly worth while to die."

828.

A man who wished to be Grand Panjandrum of the Republic of Gakwak was so reticent that he was known as "the silent candidate." As the country had for years been suffering from loquacity in high station, this taciturn aspirant was exceedingly popular with the religious element that attended daily mass for the repose of the Executive tongue. One morning it was discovered that some one had set up in the great public square of the capital city a wooden image of a man without a head. On the pedestal was this inscription: "The Silenter Candidate."

The other gentleman was not nominated.

829.

A newspaper war correspondent who had sent to his paper a series of telegrams recounting the most rapid marches known to military history received from his editor one day a map of the theatre of war, printed on the roughest paper that he had ever seen. An accompanying note informed him that the newspaper had adopted a more conservative policy, and it was thought best that he use a map supplying inferior facilities for the movement of troops and wagon trains. Unable to carry out his strategical combinations on so resistant a surface, he threw himself into the thick of the fray, and, taking poison, was soon dead upon the field of honor.

830.

A person who had been a great political leader, but had retired to private life followed by the execrations of his country, was observed frothing at the mouth and declaring that twice two were a parallel of latitude.

"The poor man has gone unusual," said his party; "we must put him in an asylum."

When arrested he was found to have upon him a detailed plan for converting old boots into watch-springs and the outlines of a method of intercepting nothing in particular until there is enough of it to make a President of the United States.

He passed the remainder of his life looking out of a grated window and awaiting his party's return to sanity.

831.

On the eve of a great battle some scouts captured the general of one of the armies and took him before their own commander, who promptly ordered him to the rear as a prisoner of war.

"But, General," said the crafty captive, "I am a chaplain."

"Oh, I see," said the other commander; "and did you pray for the success of your army?"

"My holy office compelled me," was the reluctant answer.

"Did you pray very loud and hard?"

"Surely I could do no less."

"Turn to the light and let us have a good look at you."

After a long scrutiny of the captive's face the other general said to an officer of the staff: "Give the fellow whatever he needs and turn him loose. Send away six divisions of infantry and ten batteries of artillery; we shall not require them."

832.

A famous orator pointed out to his fellow members of the 'Mbongu Parliament that by not insisting on their rights they were forfeiting their power, their dignity and their self-respect.

"Gentlemen," he exclaimed in impassioned tones that stirred the sleeping echoes of a thousand previous debates to irrelevant interruptions, "if you permit the King to trample you under foot — to walk upon you! — what are you?"

And a distinguished member of the craven majority shouted: "We are good walking."

They were.

833.

A Political Boss met a man wandering aimlessly about the country and asked him who he was. As the man made no reply the Boss said:

"This fellow is a mute; I must ask my question otherwise."

Taking paper and pencil from his pocket, he wrote: "What is your name?"

The stranger took the writing, turned it upside down, considered it a while, and with a solemn shake of the head handed it back. He was obviously unable to read.

The Boss was delighted. "At last," he said, "I have found God's best gift to man — an available candidate!"

834.

A hen that had hatched out a brood of ducklings said to them: "My children, listen to the words of age and heed the counsels of experience. Just beyond that hill lies a pond of water. Never go near it, lest you fall in and be drowned."

She had scarcely ceased speaking, when the ducklings raced away from her, over the hill, and, launching themselves upon the pond, sailed away to parts unknown. Wearied by her futile attempts at rescue and reclamation, the hen returned to the barnyard and related the awful incident to her mate.

"Foolish bird," said he, "did you not know that the only safeguard of goodness is ignorance of sin?" After a moment's reflection he added, softly to himself: "The conduct of those chickens is insupportable. They shall be no longer children of mine!"

835.

An Infamous Allegation which had been hurled back lay gasping and bleeding at the feet of its author.

"I beg your pardon," said its author, "it was not my intention that you should make the round trip."

"You forget with whom you are dealing," replied the Infamous Allegation. "The fellow that takes the single-trip ticket is known as the Friendly Service."

836.

A man who had been in exalted station was accused of having entertained negroes.

"That is the second time that charge has been made against me," he thundered, "pray tell me when I did it?"

"When you denied it the first time," replied his accuser.

837.

A victorious general pursuing his beaten enemy was cautioned by a friendly editor not to be rash.

"The further you advance into your enemy's country," said the literary strategist, "the longer and more precarious will be your line of communication, the shorter and more secure his. He is trying to draw you on."

"And I," replied the veteran campaigner, "am trying as hard as I can to be drawn on."

The spectacle of two souls with but a single thought was so affecting that the friendly editor fell upon his own neck and wept.

838.

A violet softly sighed,
    A hollyhock shouted above.
In the heart of the violet, pride;
    In the heart of the hollyhock, love.

839.

A man who had insured his life experienced a quickening of the conscience and sought the president of the company.

"I am told," said he, "that over and above your legitimate profits from the game you have an immense surplus. It seems to me that it belongs to the policy-holders."

"I don't know about that," the president replied, "but rather than have a controversy I would willingly give you your proportion right now."

"Then why don't you?" the man said.

"My friend," replied the king of finance in a low tone, looking cautiously ahead, "there is a question of delicacy. The money is tainted."

840.

When a certain man was buried, the widow, standing at the graveside, did not weep. "Vulgar creature!" said a neighbor — "she has no manners."

"Be charitable," said a keener observer; "she has forgotten her handkerchief."

841.

A thief was carrying away a red-hot stove.

"Why do you not set it down to cool?" asked an officer of the law.

"Because," said the thief, "I fear that you would arrest it."

842.

A famous statesman traveled to an unknown country whose inhabitants, divining his character, implored him to give them wise counsel.

"Make your nation a republic," he said, "and you will have liberty."

"We already have liberty," they replied — "what is a republic?"

Greatly disconcerted, he left them and went into another land; and there also the people sought advice of his wisdom.

"Make your nation a republic," he said, as before, "and you will have liberty."

"This," they answered, "has been long a republic — what is liberty?"

843.

"Madam," said the magistrate, "your refined manner and rich attire are not suggestive of poverty as an aggravation of your crime; this court is indisposed to harshness in dealing with one of so evident respectability. Go home and sin no more."

"Alas," replied the prisoner, "I am president of the Married Women's Domesticity Club and have no home."

"Then return to your elegant residence and sin no more."

844.

A member of his Majesty's Opposition in the Patagascarene parliament was seen coming out of the palace of the Grand Panjandrum, whither he had been summoned.

"Have you anything to say for publication?" asked a reporter.

"Not very much," replied the statesman absently. "I have joined the Majority."

"Good heavens!" the reporter cried; "is that possible?"

"Yes," said the statesman, "he has called me a liar."

The spot is still pointed out to the traveler.

845.

A man having the Kairnagy medal for heroism was asked to relate the feat by which he had earned it.

"I sometimes save human life," he said modestly.

"But the particular instance that the medal attests?"

"I am a sheriff. Heading a posse of citizens in pursuit of a notorious bandit and his gang, I came to a fork in the road, where he had led his rogues to the left. I led mine to the right."

846. A Hope of Reform

"A sea-serpent has washed ashore in France," said a Man reading a Newspaper.

"I shall try to obtain it," said a Great Philanthropist; "perhaps it can be persuaded to wash the shores of America."

COMMENTARY

Abbreviations

A	*Argonaut* (San Francisco)
Ae	Fables of Aesop, as cited in the Appendix to *Babrius and Phaedrus*, ed. Ben Edwin Perry (Cambridge, MA: Harvard University Press; London: William Heinemann, 1965)
CW	*Collected Works* (1909–12; 12 vols.)
CL	*Current Literature* (New York)
Co	*Cosmopolitan* (New York)
F	*Fun* (London)
FF	*Fantastic Fables* (1899)
MT	*Mark Twain's Library of Humor*, ed. William Dean Howells (New York: Charles L. Webster & Co., 1888)
NYA	*New York American*
NYJ	*New York Journal*
OT	*Oakland Daily Evening Tribune*
SFE	*San Francisco Examiner*
TMS	Typed manuscript
UVa	University of Virginia
W	*Wasp* (San Francisco)

The Fables of Zambri, the Parsee

"The Fables of Zambri, the Parsee" first appeared in *Fun* in two series, the first from 13 July to 28 September 1872, the second from 23 November 1872 to 8 March 1873. All the fables were reprinted in *Cobwebs from an Empty Skull* (London: George Routledge & Sons, 1874), from which the text and sequence are derived.

Prefacing the first group of fables in *Fun* (13 July 1872) is the following note:

> TO THE EDITOR OF FUN.
>
> SIR, — I have translated from the Persian of Zambri, the Parsee, a contemporary of Zoroaster, and a much better man, the following fables, which I think quite equal to the worst of those written by the late Mr. Æsop. I have a lot more on hand, and shall continue to translate as long as you will stand it.
>
> Dod Grile.

A Parsee is a Zoroastrian descended from Persian refugees settled in India.

1) *F* (27 July 1872): First Series, No. 13; rpt. *MT*, pp. 425–26 (as "The Nobleman and the Oyster"). In *F* the oyster is described as a "small American oyster."

2) *F* (13 July 1872): First Series, No. 1; rpt. *A* (22 April 1877); *CL* (July 1888); *Anti-Philistine* (15 June 1897).

3) *F* (13 July 1872): First Series, No. 2; rpt. *A* (28 April 1877); *CL* (August 1888). In *F* the penultimate paragraph reads: "And he had him in a fricasee."

4) *F* (13 July 1872): First Series, No. 3. *Swop* is an archaic variant of *swap*. In *F* "How clever!" reads "Smarty!"

5) *F* (13 July 1872): First Series, No. 4; rpt. *Anti-Philistine* (15 June 1897).

6) *F* (13 July 1872): First Series, No. 5; rpt. *Anti-Philistine* (15 June 1897). Cf. Ae 155 (The Wolf and the Lamb).

7) *F* (27 July 1872): First Series, No. 12. In *F* the third paragraph reads: "Up to this point, this fable teaches that it is easier to say go home than to go." The definition of "Life" is from Herbert Spencer (1820–1903); it was first propounded in rudimentary form in *The Principles of Psychology* (1855) and in definitive form in *The Principles of Biology* (1864–67), Part 1, chs. 4–5. It is quoted again in Bierce's "Moxon's Master" (1895) by Moxon as a proof of the lack of fundamental distinction between a living creature and a sophisticated machine.

8) *F* (20 July 1872): First Series, No. 6. In *F*, before the last paragraph is the paragraph: "He had at last the pleasure of being denied a desire." *Haec fabula docet* is Latin for "This fable teaches."

9) *F* (20 July 1872): First Series, No. 7; rpt. *A* (22 April 1877); *CL* (August 1888).

10) *F* (20 July 1872): First Series, No. 9; rpt. *A* (8 April 1877); *MT*, p. 196; *CL* (February 1889) (both as "The Dog and the Bees").

11) *F* (20 July 1872): First Series, No. 8; rpt. *A* (28 April 1877); *CL* (July 1888); *CW* 6 ("Fables from *Fun*").

12) *F* (20 July 1872): First Series, No. 10. In *F*, in the penultimate paragraph "everything" is italicized.

13) *F* (20 July 1872): First Series, No. 11.

14) *F* (3 August 1872): First Series, No. 16; rpt. *A* (28 April 1877); *CL* (August 1888).

15) *F* (17 August 1872): First Series, No. 21; *CW* 6 ("Fables from *Fun*").

16) *F* (3 August 1872): First Series, No. 15. The *Zend-Avesta* is a significant work of Zoroastrianism, a commentary on the Avestan texts that dates to around the 9th century C.E.

17) *F* (17 August 1872): First Series, No. 22; rpt. *A* (8 April 1877).

18) *F* (24 August 1872): First Series, No. 25; rpt. *A* (8 April 1877).

19) *F* (17 August 1872): First Series, No. 20; rpt. *A* (5 May 1877); *MT*, p. 348 (as "The Man and the Goose"); *CL* (May 1889); *CW* 6 ("Fables from *Fun*"). In *F* there is an additional paragraph at the end: "This narrative proves that it is right to pluck living geese."

20) *F* (17 August 1872): First Series, No. 23.

21) *F* (24 August 1872): First Series, No. 26; rpt. *A* (21 July 1877); *CL* (May 1889); *CW* 6 ("Fables from *Fun*"). In *A* the last two paragraphs are omitted.

22) *F* (24 August 1872): First Series, No. 27; rpt. *A* (2 June 1877); *CL* (August 1888).

23) *F* (31 August 1872): First Series, No. 30; rpt. *A* (2 June 1877).

24) *F* (31 August 1872): First Series, No. 29; rpt. *A* (21 July 1877). Bierce is probably using "corn" in the British sense, referring to any type of grain (see the change from "corn" to "wheat" in 68A). In *A* the second sentence of the penultimate paragraph and the final paragraph are omitted.

25) *F* (31 August 1872): First Series, No. 31; rpt. *A* (15 April 1877); *CL* (July 1888).

26) *F* (31 August 1872): First Series, No. 28. In *F* the first paragraph reads as follows: "Some one described as a *savant* at Margate, who had got beyond his depth, called lustily for succour." After "Margate" is a footnote: "I don't believe this.— TRANSLATOR." After "depth" is a footnote: "This I believe. — TRANSLATOR."

27) *F* (31 August 1872): First Series, No. 32; rpt. *A* (15 April 1877); *CL* (August 1888). In *F* "pike" reads "salmon."

28) *F* (17 August 1872): First Series, No. 19. In *A* "a domestic rat" reads "the cat" (and so on through the rest of the fable).

29) *F* (31 August 1872): First Series, No. 33. In *F* the conclusion reads:

> . . . snake's tail; and it had the desired effect.
>
> The moral is that an effect desired by one may not be agreeable to another, differently situated.

30) *F* (31 August 1872): First Series, No. 34; *CW* 6 ("Fables from *Fun*"). The point is that lawyers charge outrageous fees for performing small services for their clients.

31) *F* (7 September 1872): First Series, No. 35; rpt. *A* (30 June 1877); *CL* (May 1889).

32) *F* (7 September 1872): First Series, No. 36.

33) *F* (7 September 1872): First Series, No. 37; rpt. *A* (2 June 1877); *CL* (August 1888). Cf. Ae 53 (The Farmer's Sons). See also 391.

34) *F* (7 September 1872): First Series, No. 38; *CW* 6 ("Fables from *Fun*"). In *F* there is an additional paragraph at the end: "The moral of this fable is too deep for me."

35) *F* (7 September 1872): First Series, No. 39. In *F* there is an additional paragraph at the end: "This fable teaches so questionable a morality it may properly be left to interpret itself." Cf. Ae 486 (The Kite and the Doves). See also 382.

36) *F* (10 August 1872): First Series, No. 18. The reference in the third paragraph is to Aeneas's lifting his father Anchises on his shoulders and bearing him away from fallen Troy (Vergil, *Aeneid* 2). In the penultimate paragraph, the "sketch" in both *F* and *Cobwebs* depicts a variety of snakes lying on the ground, these being the "dead branches" the father is referring to. *Fabula ostendit* is Latin for "The fable shows."

37) *F* (7 September 1872): First Series, No. 40.

38) *F* (7 September 1872): First Series, No. 41.

39) *F* (14 September 1872): First Series, No. 43.

40) *F* (14 September 1872): First Series, No. 47.

41) *F* (14 September 1872): First Series, No. 44.

42) *F* (21 September 1872): First Series, No. 49.

43) *F* (14 September 1872): First Series, No. 45; rpt. *A* (8 April 1877); *CW* 6 ("Fables from *Fun*"). In *F* there is an additional paragraph at the end: "This fable teaches nothing whatever."

44) *F* (14 September 1872): First Series, No. 46; rpt. *A* (22 April 1877); *CL* (August 1888). In *F* there is a footnote to the word "Fabian": "The Fabulist seems here to have employed that favourite figure termed 'anachronism.' — TRANSLATOR." "Fabian" is a reference to the Fabian Society, founded in 1884 and devoted to the gradual adoption of socialism. The name is derived from the Roman general and dictator Q. Fabius Maximus, nicknamed "Cunctator" (the Delayer). Cf. Ae 400 (The Bees and the Shepherd).

45) *F* (14 September 1872): First Series, No. 48. In *F* there is an additional paragraph at the end: "The moral of this story has got dropt out somehow."

46) *F* (10 August 1872): First Series, No. 17; rpt. *A* (2 June 1877).

47) *F* (21 September 1872): First Series, No. 52.

48) *F* (21 September 1872): First Series, No. 51. The moral is from La Fontaine: "Ventre affamé n'a point d'oreilles." *Fables*, Book 9 (1678–79), fable 17. See also Introduction, p. x and note.

49) *F* (21 September 1872): First Series, No. 53. In *F*, since it follows 47, the fable begins: "Another snake . . ."

50) *F* (21 September 1872): First Series, No. 50; rpt. *A* (5 May 1877). In *F* "a pinch of snuff" reads as "a chew of tobacco."

51) *F* (28 September 1872): First Series, No. 54. In *F* there is an additional paragraph at the end: "This fable has been variously interpreted."

52) *F* (28 September 1872): First Series, No. 55; rpt. *A* (5 May 1877). A "mahout" is an elephant driver.

53) *F* (23 November 1872): Second Series, No. 2; rpt. *A* (15 April 1877); *CL* (July 1888).

54) *F* (28 September 1872): First Series, No. 56. In *F* there is an additional paragraph at the end: "You cannot nearly always predict the state of the market."

55) *F* (28 September 1872): First Series, No. 57.

56) *F* (3 August 1872): First Series, No. 14. In *F* there is an additional paragraph at the end: "This fable ought to have been made to teach that this is true only of *involuntary* burdens."

57) *F* (23 November 1872): Second Series, No. 3. In *F* there is a footnote to the word "ghost": "In Persian *spook;* I have rendered it 'ghost' for FUN. — *Translator.*"

58) *F* (28 September 1872): First Series, No. 58; rpt. *MT*, p. 542 (as "The Boy and the Tortoise"). In *F* there is an additional paragraph at the end: "Fire is quickening to the intellect — so the Ghebers affirm." Ghebers (or Guebers) are an ancient Persian sect of fire worshipers.

59) *F* (23 November 1872): Second Series, No. 4. In *F* "malice" (paragraph 5) reads as "disposition."

60) *F* (30 November 1872): Second Series, No. 6.

61) *F* (30 November 1872): Second Series, No. 5.

62) *F* (30 November 1872): Second Series, No. 7; rpt. *A* (2 June 1877). For "Zend-Avesta," see note on 16.

63) *F* (30 November 1872): Second Series, No. 8; rpt. *A* (5 May 1877).

64) *F* (30 November 1872): Second Series, No. 9; rpt. *A* (21 July 1877).

65) *F* (7 December 1872): Second Series, No. 11; rpt. *MT*, p. 558 (as "The Camel and the Zebra"); *CL* (May 1889).

66) *F* (24 August 1872): First Series, No. 24.

67) *F* (7 December 1872): Second Series, No. 12; rpt. *A* (21 July 1877). In *F* there is an additional paragraph at the end: "This tale seems to imply the falsity of certain accepted beliefs. [It is, therefore, insulting. — *Translator.*]" Arimanes or Ahriman is the Persian devil.

68) *F* (7 December 1872): Second Series, No. 13; rpt. *A* (8 April 1877); *MT*, pp. 339–40 (as "The Ant and the Grain of Corn"); *CL* (February 1889) (as "The Ant and the

Grain of Corn"); *CW* 6 ("Fables from *Fun*"). In *F* there is an additional paragraph at the end: "Nevertheless, this fable does *not* teach that social observances are always — or even commonly — grounded in good sense. If it did, that would make it true."

69) *F* (7 December 1872): Second Series, No. 14. In *F* the last paragraph begins: "Many a subtle philosopher has failed to solve that knotty problem, himself, owing . . ."

70) *F* (14 December 1872): Second Series, No. 15; rpt. *A* (22 April 1877); *CL* (July 1888). The footnote is omitted in *A* and *CL*.

71) *F* (14 December 1872): Second Series, No. 16.

72) *F* (14 December 1872): Second Series, No. 18; rpt. *A* (28 April 1877); *CL* (May 1889).

73) *F* (14 December 1872): Second Series, No. 17. In *F* there is an additional paragraph at the end: "No moral."

74) *F* (14 December 1872): Second Series, No. 19; rpt. *A* (15 April 1877); *CL* (August 1888).

75) *F* (21 December 1872): Second Series, No. 21.

76) *F* (21 December 1872): Second Series, No. 20. In *F* there is an additional paragraph at the end: "The best olives are put up by CROSSE and BLACKWELL." Crosse & Blackwell is a brand name for a variety of British food products.

77) *F* (21 December 1872): Second Series, No. 22; *CW* 6 ("Fables from *Fun*"). In *F* there is a footnote to the word "Cicero": "Our author's anachronistic liberty is degenerating into licence. At the time he wrote, Cicero had no reputation — to speak of. — *Translator.*"

78) *F* (21 December 1872): Second Series, No. 23. Bierce was relentless in his criticism of the manifest failings — needlessly orotund language, sensationalism, and the utterance of outright falsehoods, among others — of newspaper reporters.

79) *F* (21 December 1872): Second Series, No. 25.

80) *F* (21 December 1872): Second Series, No. 24; rpt. *A* (2 June 1877); *CL* (May 1889).

81) *F* (4 January 1873): Second Series, No. 31.

82) *F* (4 January 1873): Second Series, No. 32. In *F* "Deuce" reads as "Eblis" (the Islamic Hell). Cf. Ae 130 (The Stomach and the Feet). See also 409.

83) *F* (4 January 1873): Second Series, No. 33.

84) *F* (4 January 1873): Second Series, No. 34; rpt. *A* (30 June 1877); *CL* (May 1889). The final paragraph is omitted in *A*.

85) *F* (28 December 1872): Second Series, No. 26. In *F* there is an additional paragraph at the end: "Moral: The business of writing a fable to a woodcut prepared for another purpose is a most melancholy industry. It is a depressing pursuit." The reference is to the illustration (appearing only in *F*) of a bear swimming in water with a monkey and a mouse on its back.

86) *F* (23 November 1872): Second Series, No. 1.

87) *F* (4 January 1873): Second Series, No. 35; rpt. *A* (2 June 1877).

88) *F* (4 January 1873): Second Series, No. 36.

89) *F* (28 December 1872): Second Series, No. 27.

90) *F* (28 December 1872): Second Series, No. 28; rpt. *A* (2 June 1877).

91) *F* (28 December 1872): Second Series, No. 29; rpt. *A* (30 June 1877); *CL* (May 1889). Bierce turns this trope into a tale of terror in "The Man and the Snake" (1890), in which a man dies of terror at what he fancies to be a snake under his bed, but which proves to be a toy.

92) *F* (4 January 1873): Second Series, No. 37. Ispahan (now spelled Isfahan or Esfahan) is a large city in Persia (Iran) about 200 miles south of Teheran.

93) *F* (11 January 1873): Second Series, No. 38; *CW* 6 ("Fables from *Fun*").

94) *F* (11 January 1873): Second Series, No. 39; rpt. *A* (30 June 1877). The fable is one of Bierce's many attacks on the religious "argument from design." Cf. "Prattle," *W* No. 347 (24 March 1883): 5.

95) *F* (11 January 1873): Second Series, No. 42.

96) *F* (11 January 1873): Second Series, No. 41; rpt. *A* (8 April 1877).

97) *F* (11 January 1873): Second Series, No. 40.

98) *F* (14 September 1873): First Series, No. 42.

99) *F* (18 January 1873): Second Series, No. 44. In *F* there is an additional paragraph at the end: "This fable, like many others, inculcates revenge; but as revenge presupposes an injury or insult, the lesson is superfluous."

100) *F* (18 January 1873): Second Series, No. 46; rpt. *A* (21 July 1877).

101) *F* (18 January 1873): Second Series, No. 47.

102) *F* (18 January 1873): Second Series, No. 48; rpt. *MT*, pp. 129-30 (as "The Robin and the Woodpecker").

103) *F* (25 January 1873): Second Series, No. 50.

104) *F* (25 January 1873): Second Series, No. 49; rpt. *A* (15 April 1877).

105) *F* (18 January 1873): Second Series, No. 45; rpt. *A* (15 April 1877). In *A* "A salmon" becomes "An Oregon salmon."

106) *F* (25 January 1873): Second Series, No. 51.

107) *F* (25 January 1873): Second Series, No. 52.

108) *F* (18 January 1873): Second Series, No. 43.

109) *F* (25 January 1873): Second Series, No. 53; rpt. *A* (15 April 1877); *CW* 6 ("Fables from *Fun*").

110) *F* (1 February 1873): Second Series, No. 54; rpt. *Anti-Philistine* (15 June 1897); *CW* 6 ("Fables from *Fun*").

111) *F* (1 February 1873): Second Series, No. 57; rpt. *A* (2 June 1877); *CL* (May 1889).
In *F* there is an additional paragraph at the end: "The lesson of this narrative is too
obvious to require statement."

112) *F* (1 February 1873): Second Series, No. 55.

113) *F* (1 February 1873): Second Series, No. 56; rpt. *A* (5 May 1877); rpt. *Anti-
Philistine* (15 June 1897).

114) *F* (1 February 1873): Second Series, No. 58; rpt. *A* (28 April 1877); *CL* (August
1888).

115) *F* (8 February 1873): Second Series, No. 59; rpt. *A* (5 May 1877). Cf. Ae 598
(Wasp and Spider).

116) *F* (8 February 1873): Second Series, No. 60; rpt. *A* (22 April 1877).

117) *F* (8 February 1873): Second Series, No. 61; rpt. *A* (28 April 1877); *CL* (July
1888).

118) *F* (8 February 1873): Second Series, No. 63; rpt. *A* (22 April 1877). The footnote
is omitted in *A*.

119) *F* (8 February 1873): Second Series, No. 62; rpt. *A* (5 May 1877); *CL* (July 1888).
Bierce's scorn of the notion of trial by jury was of long standing; see the satire "The
Jury in Ancient America" (*Co*, August 1905; later incorporated into "Ashes of the
Beacon" *CW* 1.17–88).

120) *F* (7 December 1872): Second Series, No. 10; *CW* 6 ("Fables from *Fun*"). In *F*
there is an additional paragraph at the end: "MORAL: As above."

121) *F* (15 February 1873): Second Series, No. 64.

122) *F* (15 February 1873): Second Series, No. 65.

123) *F* (15 February 1873): Second Series, No. 66; rpt. *A* (22 April 1877); *CL* (August
1888).

124) *F* (22 February 1873): Second Series, No. 67.

125) *F* (22 February 1873): Second Series, No. 70.

126) *F* (22 February 1873): Second Series, No. 68; rpt. *A* (21 July 1877). In *A* everything after "exasperatingly cool" is omitted.

127) *F* (22 February 1873): Second Series, No. 69. *Crede experto* is Latin for "Believe
one who has experienced it" (cf. *credite experto* in Vergil, *Aeneid* 11.283).

128) *F* (1 March 1873): Second Series, No. 71; rpt. *A* (21 July 1877).

129) *F* (8 March 1873): Second Series, No. 74; *CW* 6 ("Fables from *Fun*"). A reference
to naval battles using ironclads. Ironclads were first devised jointly by the French and
the English in 1855 during the Crimean war. They became popular when the *Monitor*
and the *Merrimack* battled in 1862, during the Civil War, but their failure during the
siege of Fort Sumter in 1863 led to their eventual disuse.

130) *F* (4 January 1873): Second Series, No. 30.

131) *F* (1 March 1873): Second Series, No. 72.

132) *F* (1 March 1873): Second Series, No. 73. See also note on 7.

133) *F* (8 March 1873): Second Series, No. 75.

134) *F* (8 March 1873): Second Series, No. 76; *CW* 6 ("Fables from *Fun*").

135) *F* (8 March 1873): Second Series, No. 77.

Fables from *Fun*

When preparing his fables for the sixth volume of his *Collected Works* (1911), Bierce included revised versions of fifteen of the Zambri fables. A note prefacing the fables reads: "(These fables appeared in the London 'Fun' in 1872-73. They have been slightly revised.)" In the manuscript that served as the typesetting copy for *CW* (now at the Huntington Library and Art Gallery, San Marino, CA), Bierce initially affixed titles to some fables, but later crossed them out. These titles are included in brackets in the text.

Fantastic Fables

Fantastic Fables was first published by G. P. Putnam's Sons in 1899. This edition was reprinted by Dover Publications in 1970. In 1911 a revised and expanded edition was included (along with *The Monk and the Hangman's Daughter*) in the sixth volume of Bierce's *Collected Works*. This volume was reprinted as *The Monk and the Hangman's Daughter and Fantastic Fables* by Boni & Liveright (New York) in 1925 and by Jonathan Cape (London) in 1927. The sections "Æsopus Emendatus" and "Old Saws with New Teeth" were included in the first edition and were reprinted without material alteration in the edition of 1911; the section of "Fables in Rhyme" is found only in the edition of 1911. Most of the fables in *FF* were first published in *SFE* between 1887 and 1893, and usually appeared without title; titles were first added in *FF* and in many cases slightly amended (usually by the elimination of the articles "A" and "The") in *CW*. The fifty-nine fables added in the edition of 1911 were in large part first published in *SFE* between 1897 and 1904 and in *Co* in 1905-7.

136) *SFE* (22 August 1891) (untitled); *FF* (as "The Moral Principle and the Material Interest"); *CW* 6.

137) *SFE* (24 October 1891) (untitled); *FF*; *CW* 6. In *SFE* there are the following variants: (1) after "fidelity" is the phrase "for according to our holy religion a married man seeking admittance at the gate of Heaven is required to swear that he has never defiled himself with an unworthy woman." (2) "Crimson candle" reads "large wax candle." (3) The conclusion reads:

> . . . holding a lighted candle, as was the custom; but before the village Flamen had half finished his solemn chant there was an explosion which wrecked everything and killed all!
>   The cause of the explosion is unknown.

138) *SFE* (20 March 1891) (as "The Escutcheon and the Ermine"); *FF* (as "The Blotted Escutcheon and the Soiled Ermine"); *CW* 6. In *SFE* there are two variants: (1) For "the honorable member" the text reads "the member from Bruner." (2) There is an additional paragraph at the end: "Having so spoken the member from Armstrong sat down amid the plaudits of the House." Elwood Bruner was a California assemblyman who was accused of selling positions in the police department. J. W. Armstrong was a former judge of the Superior Court of Sacramento County. Bierce discusses the two of them in "Prattle," *SFE* (15 March 1891): 6. *Mustela maculata* ("soiled ermine") is Bierce's coinage; the family of *mustelae* denotes a variety of weasels, skunks, ermines, ferrets, and the like.

139) *SFE* (30 October 1891) (untitled); *FF; CW* 6. In *SFE* "the Emperor of Bang" reads "the Emperor of Boombang." Cf. "Prattle," *SFE* (26 July 1896): 6: "Mr. Joel H. Justin has invented a battle bolt that will penetrate the armor of a thunder junk before releasing its latent lightning to surprise and pain the crew. When the Government shall have paid Joel a good round price for the use of his invention he will naturally contrive a kind of armor that will baffle that missile, and the Government will be compelled to purchase that also, or he will sell it to some other nation. It would be cheaper to confront this thrifty patriot with some practitioner of the gentle art of assassination and let nature take its course." See also note on 434.

140) *SFE* (15 June 1887) (untitled); *FF* (as "An Officer and a Thug"); *CW* 6.

141) *SFE* (30 January 1892) (untitled); *FF; CW* 6. In *SFE* the fable concludes: ". . . feet and broke his record."

142) *SFE* (28 November 1891) (untitled); *FF; CW* 6. Bierce's anger over the frequency of railway accidents was of long standing.

143) *SFE* (13 January 1890) (untitled); *FF; CW* 6. In *SFE* "Pugilist" is "Slogger."

144) *SFE* (12 December 1890) (untitled); *FF; CW* 6.

145) *SFE* (13 January 1890) (untitled); *FF; CW* 6. In *SFE* and *FF* "Popular Attention" reads "Political Distinction."

146) *SFE* (4 June 1887) (untitled); *FF; CW* 6.

147) *SFE* (7 March 1889) (untitled); *FF; CW* 6.

148) *SFE* (7 March 1889) (untitled); *FF* (as "The Treasury and the Arms"); *CW* 6. The concluding pun is one Bierce made on many occasions in his columns.

149) *SFE* (15 April 1893) (untitled); *FF; CW* 6. In *SFE* the last sentence reads: "The last speaker was the mop." "Oil of Dog" (1890) is a story in Bierce's "The Parenticide Club" (*CW* 8.163–70).

150) *SFE* (11 April 1891) (as "A Work of Art"); *FF; CW* 6. This account of Antinoüs and Minerva does not correspond to any known Greco-Roman myth.

151) *SFE* (2 January 1892) (untitled); *FF; CW* 6. In *SFE* "Hindoo" reads "Madagascerene"; "Hoopitup's circus" reads "Sell's Circus."

152) *SFE* (3 October 1891) (untitled); *FF; CW* 6. In *SFE* "ten years" reads "four years."

153) *SFE* (14 January 1893) (untitled); *FF; CW* 6.

154) *SFE* (6 May 1893) (untitled); *FF; CW* 6. In *SFE* "by running away" reads "by the way of Ogden and Omaha."

155) *SFE* (3 October 1891) (untitled); *FF* (as "The Man and the Lightning"); *CW* 6. In *SFE* "A Man Running for Office" reads "A Political Boss."

156) *FF; CW* 6.

157) *SFE* (16 July 1893) (untitled); *FF; CW* 6. The reference in the first paragraph is to Grover Cleveland's leading the campaign to repeal the Sherman Silver Purchase Act. The repeal (which occurred on 1 November 1893) and the United States' subsequent return to the gold standard was hailed by businessmen.

158) *SFE* (16 July 1893) (untitled); *FF; CW* 6. Bierce's scorn of state militias was unrelenting: ". . . it is a ten-thousand-times-demonstrated fact that militia will not fight. In the war of Independence nearly every disaster to the American arms was caused by the militia running away. In the war of the Rebellion they never marched upon an enemy, never defended their homes, never failed to disperse when menaced. In the railroad riots of a few years ago they never fired on a mob till cornered, and were invariably whipped when they did not fraternize with their persecutors; they left their armories only to be pelted and pursued. They ran like deer." "Prattle," *W* No. 312 (22 July 1882): 453.

159) *SFE* (20 August 1893) (untitled); *FF; CW* 6.

160) *SFE* (12 December 1890) (untitled); *FF; CW* 6.

161) *SFE* (6 May 1893) (untitled); *FF; CW* 6.

162) *SFE* (22 August 1891) (untitled); *FF; CW* 6. In *SFE* "This is a poet" reads "This is Adair Welcker, of Berkeley, formerly known as the Sacramento Shakspeare." Welcker was a poet whom Bierce repeatedly lambasted in his columns.

163) *SFE* (20 May 1893) (untitled); *FF* (as "The Noser and the Note"); *CW* 6.

164) *SFE* (11 April 1891) (as "Two Fascinators"); *FF* (as "The Lion and the Rattlesnake"); *CW* 6.

165) *SFE* (20 May 1893) (untitled); *FF; CW* 6. In *SFE* "moon" reads "sun." The fable is probably directed toward Professor E. S. Holden, director of the Lick Observatory, at whom Bierce frequently poked fun.

166) *SFE* (15 April 1893) (untitled); *FF; CW* 6. For the name Doosnoswair, see 74.

167) *SFE* (22 January 1890) (untitled); *FF* (as "The Alderman and the Raccoon"); *CW* 6. In *SFE* "an Alderman" reads "a San Francisco Supervisor"; "in a zoological garden" reads "at Woodward's Garden [*sic*]." Woodward's Gardens was a pioneer amusement park in San Francisco, on Mission Street between Duboce Avenue and 14th Street.

168) *FF* (as "The Cat and the King"); *CW* 6.

169) *SFE* (20 August 1893) (untitled); *FF; CW* 6.

170) *SFE* (3 April 1891) (as "The Clipper of the Clouds"); *FF; CW* 6.

171) *SFE* (30 October 1891) (untitled); *FF; CW* 6.

172) *SFE* (20 March 1891) (as "The Isle of the Unreturning"); *FF; CW* 6. In *SFE* "Jamrach the Rich" is "Prosperity" throughout the fable. "Jamrach" is a name Bierce uses frequently; Jamrach Holobom is the narrator of the sketch "His Waterloo" (*OT*, 16 August 1890) and the reputed author of two poems, "At the Close of the Canvass" and "Election Day," included in "The Passing Show," *SFE* (4 November and 11 November 1900, respectively).

173) *SFE* (2 January 1892) (untitled); *FF; CW* 6.

174) *SFE* (13 October 1891) (untitled); *FF* (as "The Poetess of Reform"); *CW* 6. Bierce's hostility to "reform" and to didacticism is evident in his letters to Blanche Partington in 1892: "You want to 'reform things,' poor girl — to rise and lay about you, slaying monsters and liberating captive maids. You would 'help to alter for the better the position of working-women.' You would be a missionary — and the rest of it. Perhaps I shall not make myself understood when I say that this discourages me; that in such aims (worthy as they are) I would do nothing to assist you; that such ambitions are not only impracticable but incompatible with the spirit that gives success in art; that such ends are a prostitution of art; that 'helpful' writing is dull reading. . . . Literature (I don't mean journalism) is an *art;* — it is not a form of benevolence. It has nothing to do with 'reform,' and when used as a means of reform suffers accordingly and justly." *The Letters of Ambrose Bierce* (San Francisco: Book Club of California, 1922), pp. 3-4.

175) *SFE* (15 April 1893) (untitled); *FF; SFE* (16 October 1905) (untitled); *CW* 6. In the second *SFE* appearance Bierce quotes the fable in his column "Views of One," preceded by the paragraph: "In 'diplomatic circles' it is reported that Minister Takahira of Japan is to be elevated to the rank of Ambassador." The names of the countries are of course a play on Patagonia and Madagascar.

176) *SFE* (28 November 1891) (untitled); *FF; CW* 6. In *SFE* the fable appeared two days after Thanksgiving. The final word there is "decapitation."

177) *SFE* (13 October 1891) (untitled); *FF; CW* 6. In *SFE* the fable opens: "The two shiningest lights of Theosophy, Col. H. S. Olcott and Mr. William Q. Judge, being in San Francisco at once, in company with the Ashes of Madame Blavatsky, an Inquiring Soul. . . ." Bierce has here named three of the leading figures who founded the Theosophical Society in 1875: Henry Steel Olcott (1832-1907), William Q. Judge (1851-96), and Helena P. Blavatsky (1831-91), author of *Isis Unveiled* (1877), *The Secret Doctrine* (1888), and many other works. For Bierce's opinion of Theosophy, see "Prattle," *SFE* (15 May 1892): 6: "I am in receipt of a kind invitation to join the Theosophical Society, whose main object, it appears, is 'the practical realization of Universal Brotherhood.' I must be excused — that is about the last thing that I could wish to bring about. . . . The Society may tickle its ears with fantastic phrases babbled in gorgeous dreams until it is drunken with words, but I shall not join the debauch."

Blavatsky died on 8 May 1891 and was cremated three days later. Her ashes were divided into three portions. One part was taken by Olcott, who buried it beneath a statue of Blavatsky at Adyar, India; another was taken by Judge, who took it to New York (it is now in the keeping of the Theosophical Society in Pasadena, California); a third was taken by Annie Besant (1847-1933), another leading theosophist, who took it to India and dropped it into the Ganges. For the Ahkoond of Swat, see note on 479.

178) *SFE* (11 April 1891) (as "The Orthodox Serpent"); *FF; CW* 6. In *SFE* there is an additional sentence at the end: "As once in the Fall of Man, so now he was concerned in the Fall of Opossum."

179) *SFE* (6 May 1893) (untitled); *FF* (as "The Life-Savers"); *CW* 6. In *SFE* "two murderous outlaws" reads "Evans and Sontag." Chris Evans and John Sontag (a.k.a. John Contant) robbed a train near Collis on 3 August 1892. A posse was sent to capture them, but it failed to do so. The robbers were caught the following summer by gunmen hired by the state police; Sontag was killed and Evans seriously injured.

180) *SFE* (29 March 1892) (untitled); *FF; CW* 6. In *SFE* the words "of the California Academy of Sciences" is appended to "A Distinguished Naturalist."

181) *SFE* (14 January 1893) (untitled); *FF; CW* 6. A pavior is one who lays pavements.

182) *SFE* (12 December 1890) (untitled); *FF; CW* 6. In *SFE* "New England" reads "Oregon."

183) *SFE* (24 January 1890) (untitled); *FF* (as "The Two Poets"); *CW* 6.

184) *SFE* (11 April 1891) (as "Promotion of the Humble"); *FF; CW* 6.

185) *SFE* (29 March 1892) (untitled); *FF; CW* 6.

186) *SFE* (20 August 1893) (untitled); *FF; CW* 6. For the names of the countries, see note on 175. For Bierce's view on arbitration, see the essay "Arbitration" (*CW* 11.130-41), culled from two "Prattle" columns, *SFE* (15 July 1894) and (22 July 1894).

187) *SFE* (4 June 1887) (untitled); *FF* (as "The Member and the Soap"); *CW* 6. The word "Kansas" was added only in *FF*. In *SFE* there is an additional sentence at the end: "Then the Cake of Soap went on its way, saying: 'I am one subject that these chaps don't usually handle without gloves.'"

188) *SFE* (29 March 1889) (untitled); *FF; CW* 6. In *SFE* "Political Leader" reads "Boss."

189) *FF; CW* 6.

190) *SFE* (7 May 1893) (untitled); *FF; CW* 6.

191) *SFE* (20 August 1893) (untitled); *FF; CW* 6. In *SFE* the text reads: "A Mind Reader made a wager of ten thousand dollars that he would be buried alive and remain so for three months, then be dug up alive. In order to assure the grave against secret disturbance it was sown with barley. Unluckily a thistle sprang up amongst the barley, and at the end of three weeks the Mind Reader came up to eat it, and so lost his money." The idea is that the mind reader is a jackass, since jackasses like thistles.

192) *SFE* (14 January 1893) (untitled); *FF; CW* 6.

193) *SFE* (12 December 1890) (untitled); *FF; CW* 6. Possibly a reference to the controversy raised by Andrew Carnegie (1835-1919), who published two articles in the

North American Review, "Wealth" (June 1889) and "Best Fields for Philanthropy" (December 1889), which recommended that wealthy individuals donate the bulk of their assets into philanthropic efforts to benefit the poor, especially in the creation of free public libraries, art galleries, and the like. Of course Carnegie made no such proposal in Congress as Bierce here states.

194) *SFE* (11 April 1891) (as "The Two Physicians"); *FF; CW* 6.

195) *SFE* (11 April 1891) (as "The Robber and the Cadi"); *FF; CW* 6. A cadi is a civil judge among the Arabs.

196) *SFE* (3 October 1891) (untitled); *FF; CW* 6. In *SFE* "You and I" reads "We."

197) *SFE* (20 August 1893) (untitled); *FF; CW* 6. In *SFE* "an American town" reads "a Californian town." Bierce was a longtime critic of the violence and prejudice directed against Chinese immigrants.

198) *SFE* (11 April 1891) (as "The Cruel Retort"); *FF* (as "The Kangaroo and the Zebra"); *CW* 6.

199) *SFE* (14 January 1893) (untitled); *FF; CW* 6; rpt. in "Unpublished Fables," *Biblio* 4, No. 11 (July 1925): 827 (see also 685 and 688). None of the three fables printed in *Biblio* was unpublished; all three were taken from this fable column in *SFE*.

200) *SFE* (28 November 1891) (untitled); *FF* (as "The Man of Principle"); *CW* 6.

201) *SFE* (20 May 1893) (untitled); *FF; CW* 6. In *SFE* the first paragraph reads: "A Man who had committed murder was seized by an Officer, and when tried and convicted of the offense was hanged by the neck until he was dead." There is also an additional paragraph at the end: "But the man was from New Jersey."

202) *SFE* (24 January 1890) (untitled); *FF; CW* 6.

203) *SFE* (3 January 1890) (untitled); *FF; CW* 6. For Bierce's lenient view of "trusts" (monopolies) and his hostility to labor unions, see "In the Infancy of 'Trusts' " (1899), in *CW* 9.191–99.

204) *SFE* (3 January 1890) (untitled); *FF; CW* 6.

205) *SFE* (30 October 1891) (untitled); *FF; CW* 6.

206) *SFE* (12 December 1890) (untitled); *FF; CW* 6.

207) *SFE* (20 August 1893) (untitled); *FF; CW* 6. In *SFE* the penultimate paragraph has additional text: "Everywhere in the world the devotees of each local faith abhor the devotees of every other, and abstain from murder only so long as they do not dare to commit it. And the strangest thing about it is that all these religions are erroneous and mischievous excepting mine. Mine, thank God, is true and beneficial—at least my sect of it is."

208) *SFE* (14 January 1893) (untitled); *FF; CW* 6.

209) *SFE* (6 May 1893) (untitled); *FF; CW* 6. On this same theme, see 179 (which appeared in the same issue of *SFE* as this fable).

210) *SFE* (3 October 1891) (untitled); *FF; CW* 6.

211) *SFE* (6 August 1893) (untitled); *FF; CW* 6. Also printed in *Figaro* (Chicago) No. 181 (17 August 1893): 421 (in "Fables without Morals"). In *SFE* the fable concludes ". . . the Lately Indiscreet."

212) *SFE* (15 April 1893) (untitled); *FF; CW* 6.

213) *SFE* (24 September 1893) (untitled); *FF; CW* 6. Also printed in *Figaro* (Chicago) No. 188 (5 October 1893): 77 (as "A Fable").

214) *FF; CW* 6.

215) *SFE* (10 June 1893) (untitled); *FF; CW* 6. In *SFE* "A Dispenser-Elect of Patronge" reads "A New Superintendent of the Mint." Bierce worked for the U.S. Mint in San Francisco in 1875–77.

216) *SFE* (20 May 1893) (untitled); *FF; CW* 6.

217) *SFE* (7 May 1893) (untitled); *FF; CW* 6. In *SFE* "Awayoff" reads "Wayoff."

218) *SFE* (14 November 1891) (untitled); *FF; CW* 6. A few weeks before the first publication of this fable Bierce had launched a vicious diatribe against the Pacific Coast Women's Press Association; see "Prattle," *SFE* (4 October 1891): 6.

219) *SFE* (22 January 1890) (untitled); *FF; CW* 6. In *SFE* "a great Corporation" reads "the Spring Valley Water Works." The *Wasp* was owned by the Spring Valley Water Company for much of Bierce's tenure on it.

220) *SFE* (1 August 1891) (untitled); *FF; CW* 6. In the final sentence *SFE* and *FF* read "oldest" for "poorest."

221) *SFE* (22 August 1891) (untitled); *FF* (as "The Judge and the Rash Act"); *CW* 6.

222) *SFE* (3 April 1891) (as "The Slander and the Retraction"); *FF; CW* 6.

223) *SFE* (30 January 1892) (untitled); *FF; CW* 6. In *SFE* "a Judge" reads "a Judge-murphy." Daniel Murphy was a San Francisco judge frequently attacked by Bierce. "I do not know Judge Murphy, and never to my knowledge saw him, but I deem it singularly fortunate that always when I am looking about for some conspicuous instance of judicial tyranny or stupidity something moves him to supply it." "Prattle," *SFE* (19 August 1888): 4.

224) *SFE* (15 March 1889) (untitled); *FF; CW* 6. In *SFE* and *FF* there is an additional paragraph at the end: "It is not recorded that the Depegation was happy." The fable appeared in *SFE* less than two weeks after the inauguration of President Benjamin Harrison.

225) *SFE* (7 March 1889) (untitled); *FF; CW* 6. In *SFE* and *FF* the final paragraph reads: " 'I beg you will not,' said the victim earnestly: 'There is not a soul of them who has a cent!' "

226) *SFE* (18 January 1890) (untitled); *FF* (as "The Deceased and His Heirs"); *CW* 6.

227) *SFE* (7 March 1889) (untitled); *FF* (as "The Politicians and the Plunder"); *CW* 6.

228) *SFE* (22 January 1890) (untitled); *FF* (as "The Man and His Wart"); *CW* 6.

229) *SFE* (6 December 1890) (untitled); *FF; CW* 6. In *SFE* and *FF* the fable concludes: ". . . Kings in the abstract." The Flyspeck Islands was Bierce's derisive name for Hawaii (see "Prattle," *SFE* [3 May 1891]: 6). See also 692. Bierce frequently derided Americans' sycophancy in the presence of visiting royalty or nobility. See "The American Sycophant," *CW* 11.296–309.

230) *SFE* (29 March 1892) (untitled); *FF; CW* 6. In *SFE* "chin" reads "jaw."

231) *SFE* (30 January 1891) (untitled); *FF* (as "The Old Man and the Pupil"); *CW* 6.

232) *SFE* (30 January 1892) (untitled); *FF; CW* 6. See 681.

233) *SFE* (1 August 1891) (untitled); *FF; CW* 6. For Bierce's dim view of insurance, see "Insurance in Ancient America" (*Co,* September 1906; incorporated into "Ashes of the Beacon" [*CW* 1.17–88]).

234) *SFE* (30 January 1891) (untitled); *FF; CW* 6.

235) *SFE* (22 August 1891) (untitled); *FF; CW* 6. In *SFE* "the Chief of Police" reads "Chief of Police Crowley"; "District Attorney" reads "District Attorney Garter." Patrick Crowley was the Chief of Police in San Francisco. Charles A. Garter was the U.S. District Attorney for the Northern District of California.

236) *SFE* (7 June 1887) (untitled); *FF; CW* 6. In *SFE* "a Patriot" reads "Mr. Frank Pixley." Pixley (1824–95), founder and editor of the *Argonaut,* became the object of Bierce's undying wrath when he failed to rehire Bierce upon the latter's return from his Black Hills Expedition of 1880–81.

237) *SFE* (1 August 1891) (untitled); *FF; CW* 6.

238) *SFE* (14 November 1891) (untitled); *FF; CW* 6. Perhaps a reference to the United States' troubles with Chile at this time (see 676).

239) *SFE* (22 August 1891) (untitled); *FF* (as "The Optimist and the Cynic"); *CW* 6. In *SFE* there are two additional paragraphs at the end:

> "Well," said the Optimist, with the modesty that distinguishes his tribe from the violets of the field, "I don't say that it is the best world ever made, but it is a fairly serviceable one, as worlds go — I think I may say that much without vanity."
>
> And the gold carriage rolled on, leaving the Cynic to re-write the first verse of the first chapter of Genesis in the light of the new revelation.

240) *FF; CW* 6.

241) *OT* (4 October 1890) (in article, "Words and Things"); *FF* (as "The Poet and the Editor"); *CW* 6.

242) *SFE* (14 November 1891) (untitled); *FF; CW* 6.

243) *SFE* (4 April 1889) (untitled); *FF* (as "The Party Manager and the Gentleman"); *CW* 6. Bierce had given an abstract of his political principles, very much in line with this fable, in two "Prattle" columns in *SFE* (8 July 1888 and 28 October 1888).

244) *SFE* (30 January 1892) (untitled); *FF; CW* 6. Bierce was a fervent proponent of the death penalty.

245) *SFE* (6 August 1893) (untitled); *FF* (as "The Mine Owner and the Jackass"); *CW* 6.

246) *SFE* (2 January 1892) (untitled); *FF; CW* 6. In *SFE* and *FF* "Kamzembla" reads "Madagonia." Another reference to the Chilean affair (see 676).

247) *SFE* (13 January 1890) (untitled); *FF* (as "The Dog and the Physician"); *CW* 6.

248) *SFE* (20 March 1891) (as "The Indignant Respectable Citizen"); *FF* (as "The Legislator and the Citizen"); *CW* 6. In *SFE* and *FF* there is the following at the end:

> So he took his pen, and, some demon guiding his hand, he wrote, greatly to his astonishment:

> Who sells his influence should stop it,
> For honest men do only swap it.

249) *SFE* (14 November 1891) (untitled); *FF* (as "The Citizen and the Snakes"); *CW* 6. See 664.

250) *SFE* (22 August 1891) (untitled); *FF; CW* 6.

251) *SFE* (4 June 1887) (untitled); *FF* (as "Fortune and the Fabulist"); *CW* 6. In *SFE* "A Writer of Fables" reads "A Newspaper Writer" throughout the fable.

252) *SFE* (20 March 1891) (as "The Sword of the Spirit"); *FF; CW* 6. In the final paragraph *SFE* and *FF* add the name "Ghargaroo" to the list of provinces. The omission was probably made because Bierce had already used the name in a chapter of "The Land Beyond the Blow" (*CW* 1.151–57).

253) *SFE* (15 January 1890) (untitled); *FF; CW* 6.

254) *SFE* (15 January 1890) (untitled); *FF; CW* 6. In *SFE* "Some Apes" reads "Some Brazilian apes."

255) *SFE* (3 October 1891) (untitled); *FF; CW* 6.

256) *SFE* (29 March 1892) (untitled); *FF; CW* 6.

257) *SFE* (2 January 1892) (untitled); *FF; CW* 6.

258) *SFE* (20 March 1891); *FF; CW* 6.

259) *SFE* (4 April 1889) (untitled); *FF; CW* 6. In " 'Agony I know not!' " reads " 'Agony your grandmother!' "

260) *SFE* (24 October 1891) (untitled); *FF* (as "The Sportsman and the Squirrel"); *CW* 6.

261) *SFE* (15 January 1890) (untitled); *FF* (as "The Fogy and the Sheik"); *CW* 6. In *SFE* "Fogy" reads "Silurian" throughout the fable. Silurian was a frequently used slang term of the period derived from the geological epoch of that name, hence referring to someone old-fashioned or out-of-date.

262) *SFE* (3 October 1891) (untitled); *FF; CW* 6. In *SFE* the fifth paragraph concludes: "I — I wanted to kiss Adolph Sutro." Sutro was an important businessman and the mayor of San Francisco from 1894 to 1896. For the Pacific Coast Women's Press Association, see note on 218.

263) *SFE* (12 June 1887) (untitled); *FF; CW* 6. In *SFE* and *FF* the final phrase reads: " '. . . an inmate of the Institution for the Illiterate Deaf and Dumb.' "

264) *SFE* (20 March 1891) (as "The Cond——d Cat"); *FF; CW* 6.

265) *SFE* (30 January 1891) (untitled); *FF* (as "The Honourable Member"); *CW* 6.

266) *SFE* (24 October 1891) (untitled); *FF; CW* 6. In *SFE* the fable opens: "A Boss who had gone from San Francisco to Montreal was taunted by a resident of the latter city with having fled . . ."

267) *SFE* (22 August 1891) (untitled); *FF; CW* 6.

268) *SFE* (24 October 1891) (untitled); *FF; CW* 6. In *SFE* "A Statesman" reads "A Stuffed Colonel."

269) *SFE* (13 October 1891) (untitled); *FF; CW* 6.

270) *SFE* (13 October 1891) (untitled); *FF* (as "The Judge and the Plaintiff"); *CW* 6.

271) *SFE* (3 April 1891) (as "The Returning Brave"); *FF; CW* 6.

272) *SFE* (30 January 1892) (untitled); *FF; CW* 6.

273) *SFE* (14 November 1891) (untitled); *FF; CW* 6.

274) *SFE* (13 October 1891) (untitled); *FF; CW* 6. The French phrase means "A place for the ladies!" See 218 and 262.

275) *SFE* (30 January 1892) (untitled); *FF; CW* 6.

276) *SFE* (24 October 1891) (untitled); *FF; CW* 6.

277) *SFE* (6 May 1893) (untitled); *FF; CW* 6.

278) *SFE* (14 November 1891) (untitled); *FF; CW* 6. See note on 119.

279) *SFE* (15 January 1890) (untitled); *FF; CW* 6.

280) *FF* (as "The Congress and the People"); *CW* 6. See 606.

281) *SFE* (16 July 1893) (untitled); *FF* (as "A Ship and a Man"); *CW* 6. In *SFE* there are the following variants: (1) "ship" reads "United States Senatorship"; (2) "an Ambitious Person" reads "a William H. Mills"; (3) in the second paragraph there is an additional clause: " — I travel by rail!" For Mills, see note on 723.

282) *SFE* (22 August 1891) (untitled); *FF; CW* 6. In *SFE* the fable begins: "An eminent Associate Justice of the Supreme Court of Patagascar was accused of having obtained his appointment by causing a lying telegram to be sent to the President of that republic."

283) *SFE* (2 January 1892) (untitled); *FF; CW* 6. In *SFE* "pneumophagous" reads "aerophagous."

284) *SFE* (2 January 1892) (untitled); *FF; CW* 6.

285) *SFE* (22 March 1889) (untitled); *FF; CW* 6. In *SFE* the final paragraph begins: " 'It cannot make much difference to you, Monsieur,' " replied the Naturalist. "I need a . . ."

286) *SFE* (30 January 1891) (untitled); *FF; CW* 6. In *SFE* the penultimate paragraph concludes: " 'Since we cannot hope for reward let us be content with the offices and perquisites.' " There is also an additional sentence at the end: "The spot is still pointed out to the traveler."

287) *SFE* (15 March 1889) (untitled); *FF; CW* 6. In *SFE* and *FF* the penultimate paragraph concludes: " '. . . what misfortune caused you to be so far away from the source of power?' "

288) *SFE* (1 August 1891) (untitled); *FF* (as "The Highwayman and the Traveller"); *CW* 6.

289) *SFE* (1 August 1891) (untitled); *FF; CW* 6. In *SFE* and *FF* "A Truly Clever Person" reads "A Truly Pious Person" throughout the fable.

290) *SFE* (29 March 1889) (untitled); *FF* (as "The Statesman and the Horse"); *CW* 6. In *SFE* "A Statesman" reads "A Republican Statesman" throughout the fable; in the second paragraph "as far as my home" reads "as far as San Francisco."

291) *SFE* (15 January 1890) (untitled); *FF* (as "The Policeman and the Citizen"); *CW* 6.

292) *SFE* (15 January 1890) (untitled); *FF* (as "The Man and the Bird"); *CW* 6.

293) *SFE* (7 June 1887) (untitled); *FF* (as "The Writer and the Tramps"); *CW* 6.

294) *SFE* (22 March 1889) (untitled); *FF; CW* 6. In *SFE* "a Sovereign State" reads "a Golden State."

295) *SFE* (13 January 1890) (untitled); *FF; CW* 6. In *SFE* and *FF* "A Lawyer" reads "A Lawyer in whom an instinct of justice had survived the wreck of his ignorance of law."

296) *SFE* (29 March 1889) (untitled); *FF* (as "The Life-Saver"); *CW* 6.

297) *SFE* (30 January 1891) (untitled); *FF; CW* 6. In *SFE* "An Orator" reads "A Goucher." For Goucher, see note on 516.

298) *SFE* (22 March 1889); *FF* (as "The Fabulist and the Animals"); *CW* 6. In *SFE* and *FF* "An Illustrious Satirist" reads "A wise and illustrious Writer of Fables."

299) *SFE* (29 March 1889) (untitled); *FF; CW* 6. In *SFE* "A Revivalist" reads "A Sam Jones." The Rev. Sam Jones was a local preacher frequently criticized by Bierce.

300) *SFE* (13 October 1891) (untitled); *FF; CW* 6. In *SFE* there is an additional paragraph at the end: "And the Inkstand hurried forward to perform its immemorial work in the hands of legislation."

301) *SFE* (30 October 1891) (untitled); *FF; CW* 6.

302) *SFE* (15 March 1889) (untitled); *FF; CW* 6.

303) *SFE* (2 January 1892) (untitled); *FF; CW* 6.

304) *SFE* (1 August 1891) (untitled); *FF* (as "A Needless Labour"); *CW* 6. In *SFE* "Skunk" reads "Polecat"; the conclusion reads, " '. . . I knew you were a Polecat before.' "

305) *SFE* (4 April 1889) (untitled); *FF; CW* 6.

306) *SFE* (14 November 1891) (untitled); *FF* (as "The Patriot and the Banker"); *CW* 6. In *SFE* "A Patriot" reads "A Statesman and Patriot."

307) *SFE* (30 January 1891) (untitled); *FF; CW* 6.

308) *Co* (April 1907) (untitled); *CW* 6.

309) *SFE* (22 March 1889) (untitled); *FF; CW* 6.

310) *NYJ* (2 November 1901); *SFE* (8 November 1901); *CW* 6. In *NYJ* and *SFE* "Jamgrogrum" reads "Panjandrum" throughout the fable; the final phrase reads: " '. . . after we put him into clean clothing.' "

311) *Co* (September 1905) (untitled); *CW* 6.

312) *NYA* (17 April 1904) (untitled); *SFE* (1 May 1904) (untitled); *CW* 6.

313) *SFE* (30 January 1892) (untitled); *FF; CW* 6.

314) *NYA* (17 April 1904) (untitled); *SFE* (1 May 1904) (untitled); *CW* 6. Cf. Ae 543 (The Widow and the Soldier).

315) *NYA* (10 May 1904) (untitled); *CW* 6. In *NYA* the last paragraph reads: " 'You are a hard man to do business with, you tight-fisted rascal!' " The fable is not reprinted in the analogous column (22 May 1904) in *SFE*.

316) *Co* (September 1905) (untitled); *CW* 6. In *Co* "Omuhu" and "Modugy" read "Patagascar" and "Madagonia," respectively. "Antepenultimate" means "third to last"; Bierce used the word "Antepenultimata" as the title for *CW* 11, although he interpreted it to mean that "the stuff does not profess to be 'the last word' on any subject, nor even the next-to-the-last." Bierce to Walter Neale, 3 January 1912 (ms., Huntington Library and Art Gallery).

317) *Co* (September 1905) (untitled); *CW* 6.

318) *SFE* (30 April 1899); *CW* 6.

319) *NYJ* (20 October 1901); *Cleveland World* (20 October 1901); *SFE* (25 October 1901) (untitled); *CW* 6.

320) *SFE* (7 November 1897); *CW* 6.

321) *NYJ* (20 October 1901); *Cleveland World* (20 October 1901); *SFE* (25 October 1901) (untitled); *CW* 6. In the newspaper appearances the second paragraph concludes: " 'That hulk is not enough to prevent my coming out.' " There is an additional paragraph at the end: "By this quotation from the 'Proverbial Philosophy' of the late Mr. Tupper the enemy was greatly disheartened." The reference is to a local poet, Martin Farquhuar Tupper, whom Bierce repeatedly attacked.

322) *SFE* (7 November 1897) (as "By the River's Marge"); *CW* 6.

323) *SFE* (7 November 1897); *CW* 6.

324) *SFE* (12 May 1901); *CW* 6.

325) *Co* (September 1905) (untitled); *CW* 6.

326) *Co* (September 1905) (untitled); *CW* 6.

327) *SFE* (7 November 1897); *CW* 6.

328) *Co* (March 1907) (untitled; in section "Negligible Epigrams"); *CW* 6. Bierce exhibited a longstanding hostility toward the use of slang and dialect in literature. See "Some Sober Words on Slang" (*Co*, July 1907).

329) *SFE* (7 November 1897) (as "Two of a Kind"); *CW* 6. In *SFE* "Camera" reads "Kodak."

330) *SFE* (12 May 1901); *CW* 6.

331) *SFE* (12 May 1901); *CW* 6.

332) *Co* (July 1907) (untitled); *CW* 6. The quotation (properly "that fierce light which beats upon a throne") is from Tennyson's *Idylls of the King*, Dedication, line 26.

333) *SFE* (13 August 1899) (untitled); *CW* 6. In *SFE* "Elihu Root" reads "Chauncey Depew." Chauncey Depew (1834-1928) was a Republican senator from New York (1899-1911). Elihu Root (1834-1937) became President McKinley's secretary of war in 1899 upon the resignation of General R. A. Alger (see note on 358). He was later secretary of state under Theodore Roosevelt (1905-9) and senator from New York (1909-15).

334) *NYA* (10 May 1904) (untitled); *SFE* (22 May 1904) (untitled); *CW* 6. In *NYA* and *SFE* "Bumboogle" reads "Otumwee"; "by the nation" reads "by decree of the Grand Panjandrum of the nation."

335) *NYA* (10 May 1904) (untitled); *SFE* (22 May 1904) (untitled); *CW* 6.

336) *Co* (September 1905) (untitled); *CW* 6.

337) *Co* (April 1907) (untitled); *CW* 6.

338) *NYA* (2 October 1903); *SFE* (17 October 1903) (in "A Spread of Quick-Lunch Wisdom for Busy Readers"); *CW* 6.

339) *SFE* (30 April 1899) (as "Two of a Kind"); *CW* 6. See 358.

340) *SFE* (12 May 1901); *CW* 6.

341) *SFE* (13 August 1899) (untitled); *CW* 6. Luzon is a city in the Philippines. Emilio Aguinaldo was a Filipino revolutionary who established the Malolos Republic in 1898 and set up a provisional government in Luzon; although initially supported by the United States and assisting in the overthrow of Spanish rule in the Philippines, he eventually proved to be a thorn in the side of the United States and was captured in March 1901.

342) *NYA* (10 May 1904) (untitled); *SFE* (22 May 1904) (untitled); *CW* 6.

343) *SFE* (13 August 1899) (untitled); *CW* 6.

344) *NYJ* (2 November 1901); *SFE* (8 November 1901) (as "The Statesman and His Hopes"); *CW* 6. In *NYJ* and *SFE* "Colorado" reads "Wyorado." Wyoming and Colo-

rado were two of the earliest states to grant suffrage to women, Wyoming doing so in 1869 (while it was still a territory) and Colorado in 1893. The fable is oddly prescient in that in November 1911, about six months after the appearance of *CW* 6, Susan Wisser attracted national attention by becoming the mayor of Dayton, Wyoming — apparently the first woman mayor in the United States.

345) *NYA* (17 April 1904) (untitled); *SFE* (1 May 1904) (untitled); *CW* 6.

346) *SFE* (12 May 1901); *CW* 6.

347) *SFE* (30 April 1899); *CW* 6.

348) *NYJ* (17 November 1901); *SFE* (24 November 1901) (as "A Justifiable Homicide"); *CW* 6. In *NYJ* and *SFE* there is the following after the first paragraph:

> "If it please Your Honor," replied the Prisoner, "I will relate the circumstances, and as to my guilt will be guided to a decision by your opinion. The gentleman who is no more, a resident of New York City, came to me at my home and said: 'The overthrow of Tammany is a striking proof of the wisdom and virtue of the masses, a memorable demonstration of the value of the universal suffrage in municipal affairs, a sharp rebuke to Mr. Hewitt.'
>
> "I admit, Your Honor, that I killed the man the moment he had done speaking."
>
> "Where is your home?" the Judge asked, not unsympathetically; "where did this occur?"
>
> "An untoward fate," replied the Prisoner, "compels me to live in Philadelphia."
>
> "Let the Prisoner go," said the Judge, and the Prosecuting Attorney left the court without a stain upon his reputation.

Abram S. Hewitt was a congressman from New York from 1874 to 1887 and mayor of New York City from 1887 to 1889. He devoted much of his political career to overthrowing Tammany.

349) *Co* (April 1907) (untitled); *CW* 6.

350) *NYJ* (17 November 1901); *SFE* (24 November 1901) (as "A Poet and the King"); *CW* 6.

351) *Co* (April 1907); *CW* 6.

352) *Co* (July 1907) (untitled); *CW* 6. In *Co* the final paragraph reads: " 'After all,' he said, 'in seeking gratification of an imaginary appetite there is more joy in pursuit than in possession.' "

353) *SFE* (13 August 1899) (untitled); *CW* 6.

354) *Co* (April 1907) (untitled); *CW* 6.

355) *SFE* (30 April 1899); *CW* 6.

356) *NYA* (17 April 1904) (untitled); *SFE* (1 May 1904) (untitled); *CW* 6. In *NYA* and *SFE* there are the following paragraphs at the end:

> "And then," said the tortoise, "what would become of the tortoise-shell comb industry?"
>
> "Nonsense!" the wolf said; "that shell of yours is celluloid."
>
> Through the mouth of that humble quadruped spake "the commercial spirit of the age."

357) *Co* (September 1905) (untitled); *CW* 6.

358) *SFE* (13 August 1899) (untitled); *CW* 6. In *SFE* "Out of Office" reads "Out of a Job." The third paragraph opens: " 'I have been working lately as a Secretary of War,' the Man Out of a Job replied, 'but I was Rooted out.' " The reference is to General Russell Alexander Alger, secretary of war from 1895 to 1899, who resigned at the request of President McKinley because of the furor he created over his tactical and financial mismanagement during the Spanish-American War of 1898. He was replaced by Elihu Root (see note on 333).

359) *Co* (July 1907) (untitled); *CW* 6.

360) *Co* (April 1907) (untitled); *CW* 6.

361) *OT* (26 July 1890) (untitled); *FF*; *CW* 6. In *OT* "offspring" reads "tootsy-wootsy." Cf. Ae 364 (The Ape Mother and Zeus).

362) *OT* (9 August 1890) (untitled); *FF*; *CW* 6. Cf. Ae 173 (Hermes and the Woodcutter).

363) *OT* (26 July 1890) (untitled); *FF*; *CW* 6. In *OT* "public official" reads "thief." Cf. Ae 200 (The Thief and His Mother).

364) *OT* (2 August 1890) (untitled); *FF* (as "The Fox and the Grapes"); *CW* 6. Cf. Ae 15 (The Fox and the Grapes out of Reach).

365) *OT* (2 August 1890) (untitled); *FF* (as "The Farmer and the Fox"); *CW* 6. In *OT* and *FF* "deadly" reads "deadly and implacable." Cf. Ae 283 (The Fire-Bearing Fox).

366) *OT* (2 August 1890) (untitled); *FF* (as "The Archer and the Eagle"); *CW* 6. Cf. Ae 276 (The Wounded Eagle).

367) *OT* (9 August 1890) (untitled); *FF* (as "Truth and the Traveller"); *CW* 6. Cf. Ae 355 (The Wayfarer and Truth).

368) *OT* (9 August 1890) (untitled); *FF* (as "The Wolf and the Lamb"); *CW* 6. Cf. Ae 261 (The Wolf and the Lamb).

369) *OT* (12 July 1890) (untitled); *FF* (as "The Grasshopper and the Ant"); *CW* 6. Cf. Ae 373 (The Cicada and the Ant).

370) *OT* (2 August 1890) (untitled); *FF* (as "The Goose and the Swan"); *CW* 6. Cf. Ae 399 (The Swan That Was Caught Instead of a Goose).

371) *OT* (2 August 1890) (untitled); *FF* (as "The Fisher and the Fished"); *CW* 6. In

OT "he will elevate you to the deitage" reads "he will promote you." Cf. Ae 282 (Little Fish Escape the Net).

372) *OT* (26 July 1890) (untitled); *FF* (as "The Wolves and the Dogs"); *CW* 6. In *OT* and *FF* there is an additional sentence at the end: " 'Have you always found it so?' " Cf. Ae 342 (The Wolves and the Dogs).

373) *OT* (2 August 1890) (untitled); *FF* (as "Dame Fortune and the Traveller"); *CW* 6. Cf. Ae 174 (Fortune and the Traveller by the Well).

374) *OT* (2 August 1890) (untitled); *FF* (as "The Wolf and the Shepherds"); *CW* 6. Cf. Ae 365 (The Shepherd About to Enclose a Wolf in the Fold).

375) *OT* (2 August 1890) (untitled); *FF* (as "The Lion, the Cock, and the Ass"); *CW* 6. Cf. Ae 82 (Ass, Cock, and Lion).·

376) *OT* (26 July 1890) (untitled); *FF* (as "The Snake and the Swallow"); *CW* 6. Cf. Ae 227 (The Swallow Nesting on the Courthouse).

377) *OT* (26 July 1890) (untitled); *FF* (as "The Victor and the Victim"); *CW* 6. In *OT* "destroy" reads "thrash" and "defeated" reads "done up." Cf. Ae 281 (The Fighting Cocks).

378) *OT* (9 August 1890) (untitled); *FF* (as "The Hen and the Vipers"); *CW* 6. In *OT* and *FF* the second paragraph opens: " 'I am a little bit on the destroy myself,' . . ." Cf. Ae 192 (The Hen and the Swallow).

379) *OT* (9 August 1890) (untitled); *FF* (as "A Seasonable Joke"); *CW* 6. Cf. Ae 169 (The Prodigal Young Man and the Swallow).

380) *OT* (9 August 1890) (untitled); *FF* (as "The Lion and the Thorn"); *CW* 6. In *OT* "honorably abstained" reads "respectfully fell back"; "claimant" reads "Lion who had spoken." Cf. Ae 563 (The Lion and the Shepherd) and 563a (Androclus [*sic*] and the Lion).

381) *OT* (12 July 1890) (untitled); *FF* (as "The Fawn and the Buck"); *CW* 6. In *OT* "father" and "Buck" read "mother." Cf. Ae 351 (The Calf and the Deer).

382) *OT* (26 July 1890) (untitled); *FF* (as "The Kite, the Pigeons, and the Hawk"); *CW* 6. In *OT* "scratched out his eyes" reads "tore him to pieces." Cf. Ae 486 (The Kite and the Doves).

383) *OT* (9 August 1890) (untitled); *FF* (as "The Wolf and the Babe"); *CW* 6. In *OT* "threw out both Child and Mother" reads "threw the child out of the window." Cf. Ae 158 (The Wolf and the Old Woman Nurse).

384) *OT* (12 July 1890) (untitled); *FF* (as "The Wolf and the Ostrich"); *CW* 6. Cf. Ae 156 (The Wolf and the Heron). See also 406.

385) *OT* (12 July 1890) (untitled); *FF* (as "The Herdsman and the Lion"); *CW* 6. Cf. Ae 49 (The Herdsman Who Lost a Calf).

386) *OT* (26 July 1890) (untitled); *FF* (as "The War-Horse and the Miller"); *CW* 6. The sentence at the end of the second paragraph is of course a translation of Horace's *dulce et decorum est pro patria mori* (*Odes* 3.2.13). Cf. Ae 320 (The Soldier and His Horse).

387) *OT* (12 July 1890) (untitled); *FF* (as "The Man and the Fish-Horn"); *CW* 6. Cf. Ae 11 (The Fisherman Pipes to the Fish).

388) *OT* (12 July 1890) (untitled); *FF; CW* 6. Cf. Ae 291 (The Ox-Driver and Heracles).

389) *OT* (12 July 1890) (untitled); *FF* (as "The Hare and the Tortoise"); *CW* 6. In *OT* "to cheer you on your way" reads "to encourage you." Cf. Ae 226 (The Tortoise and the Hare). See also 417.

390) *OT* (9 August 1890) (untitled); *FF* (as "The Lion and the Bull"); *CW* 6. Cf. Ae 143 (The Lion and the Bull).

391) *OT* (12 July 1890) (untitled); *FF* (as "The Old Man and His Sons"); *CW* 6. Cf. Ae 53 (The Farmer's Sons). An adaptation of 33.

392) *OT* (9 August 1890) (untitled); *FF* (as "The Wolf and the Feeding Goat"); *CW* 6. In *OT* the second sentence of the second paragraph begins: " 'Down here where I am the broken-bottle vine grows in abundance, the paper collar blossoms as the rose, . . ." Cf. Ae 157 (The Wolf and the Goat).

393) *OT* (2 August 1890) (untitled); *FF* (as "The Man and His Goose"); *CW* 6. Cf. Ae 87 (The Goose That Laid the Golden Eggs).

394) *OT* (12 July 1890) (untitled); *FF* (as "The Dog and the Reflection"); *CW* 6. In *OT* "insolent way" reads "tone of voice." Cf. Ae 133 (The Dog with the Meat and His Shadow). See also 412.

395) *OT* (9 August 1890) (untitled); *FF* (as "The Man and the Eagle"); *CW* 6. Cf. Ae 275 (The Eagle Who Had His Wings Cropped).

396) *OT* (12 July 1890) (untitled); *FF* (as "The Man and the Viper"); *CW* 6. Cf. Ae 176 (The Man Who Warmed a Snake) and 617 (The Serpent in a Man's Bosom).

397) *OT* (9 August 1890) (untitled); *FF* (as "The North Wind and the Sun"); *CW* 6. Cf. Ae 46 (The North Wind and the Sun).

398) *OT* (26 July 1890) (untitled); *FF* (as "The Crab and His Son"); *CW* 6. Cf. Ae 322 (The Crab and His Mother).

399) *OT* (26 July 1890) (untitled); *FF; CW* 6. Cf. Ae 101 (The Jackdaw in the Borrowed Feathers).

400) *OT* (12 July 1890) (untitled); *FF* (as "The Lion and the Mouse"); *CW* 6. Cf. Ae 150 (Lion and Mouse). See also 407.

401) *CW* 6. A revision of 4. Cf. Ae 155 (The Wolf and the Lamb).

402) *OT* (12 July 1890) (untitled); *FF* (as "The Mountain and the Mouse"); *CW* 6. Cf. Ae 520 (The Mountain in Labour). Recall Horace's celebrated tag *Parturient montes; nascetur ridiculus mus* [The mountains were in labor; a ridiculous mouse was born] (*Ars Poetica* 139).

403) *OT* (26 July 1890) (untitled); *FF; CW* 6. In *OT* "Socialists" reads "Nationalists." The reference is to Edward Bellamy (1850–98), whose utopian novel *Looking Backward, 2000–1887* (1888) proposed a radical redistribution of wealth for the benefit of all citizens. Cf. Ae 130 (The Stomach and the Feet). See also 409.

404) *OT* (9 August 1890) (untitled); *FF* (as "The Cat and the Youth"); *CW* 6. In *OT* there is a final sentence at the end: "So she lived and died a lonely island of old maid in a shoreless ocean of pet cats." Cf. Ae 50 (The Weasel and Aphrodite) (where a weasel, after being changed into a woman, chases a mouse). In other versions of the fable (e.g., La Fontaine, Book 2, fable 18) the bride had indeed once been a cat.

405) *OT* (26 July 1890) (untitled); *FF* (as "The Farmer and His Sons"); *CW* 6. In *OT* "while they gambled" reads "while they improved the shining hour by gambling." Cf. Ae 42 (The Farmer's Bequest to His Sons).

406) *SFE* (19 February 1891); *FF* (both as "The Wolf and the Crane"); *CW* 6. Cf. Ae 156 (The Wolf and the Heron).

407) *SFE* (19 February 1891); *FF* (both as "The Lion and the Mouse"); *CW* 6. Cf. Ae 150 (Lion and Mouse).

408) *SFE* (4 March 1891) (as "The Hares and the Frogs"); *FF* (as "The Hare and the Frogs"); *CW* 6. Cf. Ae 138 (The Hares and the Frogs).

409) *SFE* (4 March 1891); *FF* (both as "The Belly and the Members"); *CW* 6. Cf. Ae 130 (The Stomach and the Feet). See also 403.

410) *SFE* (19 February 1891); *FF; CW* 6. In *SFE* the first paragraph concludes: "'. . . claim them; if they are it is wisdom to have them.'" Cf. Ae 11 (The Fisherman Pipes to the Fish). See also 387.

411) *SFE* (19 February 1891); *FF* (both as "The Ants and the Grasshopper"); *CW* 6. Cf. Ae 373 (The Cicada and the Ant). See also 369.

412) *SFE* (19 February 1891) (as "The Dog and the Reflection"); *FF; CW* 6. Cf. Ae 133 (The Dog with the Meat and His Shadow). See also 394.

413) *SFE* (4 March 1891); *FF* (both as "The Lion, the Bear, and the Fox"); *CW* 6. Cf. Ae 147 (Lion and Bear).

414) *SFE* (4 March 1891); *FF* (both as "The Wolf and the Lion"); *CW* 6. In *SFE* "war-dance" reads "ghost dance." Cf. Ae 347 (Wolf and Lion).

415) *SFE* (4 March 1891); *FF* (both as "The Ass and the Lion's Skin"); *CW* 6. For Bierce's views of militias, see 158 and note. Cf. Ae 188 (Ass in Lion's Skin). See also 576.

416) *SFE* (19 February 1891); *FF* (both as "The Ass and the Grasshoppers"); *CW* 6. Cf. Ae 184 (The Ass and the Cicadas).

417) *SFE* (19 February 1891); *FF* (both as "The Hare and the Tortoise"); *CW* 6. Cf. Ae 226 (The Tortoise and the Hare). See also 389.

418) *SFE* (19 February 1891); *FF; CW* 6. In *SFE* "The People" reads "The People of California." Cf. Ae 44 (The Frogs Ask Zeus for a King).

419) *SFE* (4 March 1891) (as "The Milkmaid and Her Pail"); *FF* (as "The Milkmaid and Her Bucket"); *CW* 6. The original of this fable is found only in La Fontaine (Book 7, fable 10).

420) *SFE* (4 March 1891); *FF; CW* 6. Cf. Ae 344 (A Wolf among the Lions).

421) *SFE* (19 February 1891); *FF* (both as "The Monkey and the Nuts"); *CW* 6. In *SFE* "Deformatory" reads "building."

422) *SFE* (4 March 1891); *FF* (both as "The Boys and the Frogs"); *CW* 6. The original of this fable is found in various eighteenth- and nineteenth-century editions of Aesop, but it is not in Perry's Appendix.

423) *NYJ* (3 September 1901); *SFE* (6 September 1901); *CW* 6. In *NYJ* and *SFE* ll. 16–18 read: "Then, charging blindly, hit or miss, / Fell whirling o'er a precipice!" It appears that one line was dropped, as there is no matching rhyme for "breast" (l. 15).

424) *NYJ* (3 September 1901); *SFE* (6 September 1901) (as "In the Land of the Snapdog"); *CW* 6. In *NYJ* and *SFE* "Sweetpotatoville" (l. 37) reads "South Asphyxia"; l. 39 reads "Had 'majesty,' and that they saw" (proceeds to present l. 43); "Glorypool" (l. 48) reads "West Squedunk"; l. 49 reads "With weep and wail and gnash of teeth"; ll. 58–61 read: "(Observe, O children, their despair / And of improvidence beware!) / That's all my tale—'twas good to see / Those dog-adoring persons flee, / Fall over their own feet and cease to be!"

425) *NYJ* (17 September 1901); *SFE* (5 October 1901); *CW* 6. In *NYJ* and *SFE* the last three lines read as follows:

> While he, the target of the jest,
> Bewailed (in slang), his lot unblessed.

Moral:
> To please the wise this is the mode:
> Don't be a monkey—be a toad.

426) *NYJ* (3 September 1901); *SFE* (6 September 1901); *CW* 6.

427) *NYJ* (17 September 1901); *SFE* (5 October 1901) (as "The Vanity of Cats"); *CW* 6. In *NYJ* and *SFE* "The Cat said" (l. 5) reads "Said pussy"; "condor" (l. 9) reads "eagle"; l. 13 reads: "She added: 'Ah, 'twould charm Your Grace.'"

428) *NYA* (15 September 1902); *SFE* (25 September 1902) (as "An Anarchist"); *CW* 6.

429) *SFE* (12 September 1897) (in "Prattle" as "A Practical Fable"); *CW* 6.

430) *SFE* (7 November 1897) (as "He Came at Call"); *CW* 6.

Unreprinted Fables from *Fantastic Fables* (1899)

In preparing the 1911 edition of *Fantastic Fables,* Bierce omitted ten fables from the 1899 edition. Bibliographical and other information on them is given below.

431) *SFE* (15 April 1893) (untitled); *FF.* In *SFE* "patriotic" reads "prosperous"; the final paragraph reads: " 'Vagrancy,' replied the Statesman, pensively: 'I was once a tramp.' "

432) *SFE* (4 April 1889) (untitled); *FF.* In *SFE* "A Forestry Commissioner" reads "A Yosemite Valley Commissioner."

433) *SFE* (6 December 1890) (untitled); *FF.*

434) *SFE* (14 January 1893) (untitled); *FF.* In *SFE* there is the following at the end: " 'Search his premises, destroying all his papers and models. Then draw up an edict forbidding any of my subjects to make an improvement in weapons of war, under penalty of skinning alive.' " This fable may have been omitted from *CW* 6 because it is too similar to 139.

435) *SFE* (6 August 1893) (untitled); *FF.* In *SFE*, after the phrase "the Christian Press made a note of it," there is the following: "and one good pious newspaper, the name of which is unknown to this Fabulist, was greatly pained . . ."

436) *SFE* (22 March 1889) (untitled); *FF.* In *SFE* "humble birth and no breeding" reads "humble origin."

437) *SFE* (1 August 1891) (untitled); *FF.*

438) *OT* (26 July 1890) (untitled); *FF.* In the last paragraph *OT* reads "General" for "Divine." Cf. Ae 64 (The Wrong Remedy for Dog-Bite).

439) *OT* (26 July 1890) (untitled); *FF.* Cf. Ae 7 (Cat as Physician and the Hens).

440) *OT* (2 August 1890) (untitled); *FF.* Cf. Ae 338 (The Lion and the Boar).

Fables from *The Devil's Dictionary*

In 1881 *The Devil's Dictionary* began serialized publication in *W;* entries from the letter A through the letter L appeared between 1881 and 1886. Two brief columns appeared in *SFE* in 1887 and 1888. In 1904 Bierce recommenced the serialization in *SFE* and *NYA,* continuing to 1906; but he had reached only into the letter R by the time he resigned from the Hearst newspapers. In 1906 Doubleday, Page & Co. published the volume (under the title *The Cynic's Word Book*), although it contained only entries from A to L; a second volume had been contemplated to complete the alphabetical series, but evidently the first volume did not sell well enough to justify it. Bierce revised these entries and published the rest of the alphabetical sequence in *CW* 7 (1911).

Some of the fables that are appended as elaborations or instantiations of the definitions appeared only in *W* and were not reprinted in later editions; others appeared only in the 1911 edition (none, oddly, appeared in the edition of 1906). The definitions accompanying the fables are given below.

441) *W* (28 October 1881). The definition reads: "The faculty that distinguishes a weak animal or person from a strong one. It brings its possessor much mental satisfaction and great material adversity. An Italian proverb says: 'The furrier gets the skins of more foxes than asses.' A different view of the matter, however, is taken in the following fable of the Rev. Father Gassalasca Jape, of the Mission San Diablo:" The first three sentences of the definition appear in *The Cynic's Word Book* and *CW* 7; the last

sentence and the fable itself do not. Jape is the fictitious author of a number of poems in *The Devil's Dictionary.*

442) *W* (7 June 1884). The definition reads: "A brief lie intended to illustrate some important truth." After the fable there appears the following: "This fable teaches that Justice and Generosity do not go hand in hand, the hand of Generosity being commonly thrust into the pocket of Justice." The definition is clearly derived from the canonical definition of the fable as given by the rhetorician Theon in his *Progymnasmata: logos pseudes eikonizon aletheian* [a false (i.e., fictional) story picturing the truth]. See Introduction, note 1.

443) *W* (25 April 1885). The definition reads: "That portion of the human body which is supposed to be responsible for all the others. It is customary in some countries to remove it, and many have acquired great skill and proficiency in the art. In ancient Japan, especially, this art was carried to a high degree of perfection, as the following incident shows. The account is literally translated." With some revisions the fable was used under the entry "Scimitar" (*CW* 7), the definition reading: "A curved sword of exceeding keenness, in the conduct of which certain Orientals attain a surprising proficiency, as the incident here related will serve to show. The account is translated from the Japanese by Shusi Itama, a famous writer of the thirteenth century."

444) *SFE* (29 April 1888); *CW* 7. The definition reads: "A vitreous plane upon which to display a fleeting show for man's disillusion given." The fable seems a variant of the story of the emperor's new clothes.

445) *NYA* (17 October 1904); *SFE* (24 October 1904); *CW* 7. The definition reads: "In politics the party that prevents the Government from running amuck by hamstringing it." For the name Ghargaroo, see note on 252.

446) *SFE* (6 November 1887) (in "Prattle"); *CW* 7. The definition reads: "One of the Creator's lamentable mistakes, repented in sashcloth and axes." In *SFE* the fable is incorporated within a discussion of a trial. It begins: "When Satan was flung out of Heaven 'with hideous ruin and combustown down,' he paused half way in his descent, bowed his fine head for a moment in thought, and finally went back. . . ."

447) *CW* 7. The definition reads: "In diplomacy, a last demand before resorting to concessions."

Uncollected Fables

The great proportion of uncollected fables appeared in *W* (1883–84), *SFE* (1887–1904), and *Co* (1905–7). They are found juxtaposed with other fables that Bierce reprinted in either the 1899 or the 1911 edition of *Fantastic Fables.* Six fables exist in a typescript found in a scrapbook of Bierce's newspaper writings at the University of Virginia; one of these is apparently unpublished, while the other five present texts varying slightly from their published versions. As the date of writing of these fables is not certain, the unpublished fable has been placed at the end of this sequence.

448) *W* (29 December 1883).

449) *W* (29 December 1883).

450) *W* (29 December 1883). See 243.

451) *W* (29 December 1883).

452) *W* (29 December 1883).

453) *W* (29 December 1883).

454) *W* (29 December 1883).

455) *W* (29 December 1883).

456) *W* (6 September 1884). Obviously an instantiation of the axiom of the pot calling the kettle black (not in Aesop).

457) *W* (6 September 1884).

458) *W* (6 September 1884).

459) *W* (6 September 1884).

460) *W* (6 September 1884).

461) *W* (6 September 1884).

462) *W* (6 September 1884).

463) *W* (6 September 1884).

464) *W* (6 September 1884). "Get thee behind me, Satan!" is an utterance frequently attributed to Jesus (see Matthew 16:23, Mark 8:33, Luke 4:8).

465) *W* (6 September 1884). A variant of the "Tortoise and the Hare" fable (Ae 226). See also 389 and 417.

466) *W* (27 September 1884).

467) *W* (27 September 1884).

468) *W* (27 September 1884).

469) *W* (27 September 1884).

470) *W* (27 September 1884). The references in the third paragraph are to a series of celebrated orators in ancient and modern history: Demosthenes, Cicero, Patrick Henry, William Pitt, and Dan O'Connell, a California journalist and politician who was Bierce's colleague on the *Argonaut* (1877–79).

471) *W* (27 September 1884).

472) *W* (27 September 1884).

473) *W* (27 September 1884).

474) *W* (27 September 1884). The name of the first character is a parody of Young-Man-Afraid-of-His-Horses, a Sioux chief.

475) *W* (27 September 1884).

476) *W* (27 September 1884).

477) *W* (27 September 1884).

478) *W* (27 September 1884).

479) *W* (4 October 1884). Abdul Ghafur (1794–1877) was the Akhund (or Akhond) of Swat, a region in northwestern India; he was long a thorn in the side of the British. When his death was announced in London papers in early 1878, the American poet George Thomas Lanigan (1845–86) wrote a comic poem, "A Threnody" (1878), on the "Akhoond of Swat." Bierce later wrote a political fantasy, "For the Ahkoond," *SFE* (18 March 1888): 13; in *CW* 1.199–216.

480) *W* (4 October 1884). 4 November 1884 was election day.

481) *W* (4 October 1884). Grover Cleveland was governor of New York (1883–85) when he won election in 1884 for his first term as president (he lost the election of 1888 but won that of 1892). The fable was written about a month before the presidential election.

482) *W* (4 October 1884). A hod is an open receptable for carrying mortar, rocks, or stones.

483) *W* (4 October 1884).

484) *W* (4 October 1884). The concluding quotation is from Tennyson's "You ask me, why, tho' ill at ease" (1833), line 28.

485) *W* (4 October 1884).

486) *W* (4 October 1884).

487) *W* (4 October 1884).

488) *W* (4 October 1884).

489) *W* (11 October 1884).

490) *W* (11 October 1884).

491) *W* (11 October 1884).

492) *W* (11 October 1884).

493) *W* (11 October 1884).

494) *W* (11 October 1884).

495) *W* (11 October 1884). James G. Blaine (1830–93) was the Republican candidate for president in 1884. On Lulu Hurst, see George C. D. Odell, *Annals of the New York Stage* (New York: Columbia University Press, 1940), Vol. 4, p. 212: "On July 7th [1884], Wallack's opened its doors to an astonishing vagary—Miss Lulu Hurst, 'the Georgia Wonder,' who, according to the advertisements, had puzzled 'scientists, physicians and wise men,' everywhere. According to Allston Brown, she had the power 'to resist and baffle strength by merely placing the palms of her hands against an object, thereby preventing the strongest man from keeping it under his control. She neither held nor pushed the object but merely kept her open hand or hands against it.' A billiard cue was one of the objects so treated, and she could, by putting her hands on a chair, force it and a fat person sitting on it to perform gyrations about the stage. Sometimes she failed to defeat her opponents."

496) *W* (18 October 1884).

497) *W* (18 October 1884).

498) *W* (18 October 1884).

499) *W* (18 October 1884).

500) *SFE* (4 June 1887). The *Alta California* (published in daily and weekly editions) was one of the oldest newspapers in San Francisco, having been founded in 1849. Bierce wrote for it briefly in the fall and winter of 1872.

501) *SFE* (4 June 1887).

502) *SFE* (4 June 1887).

503) *SFE* (7 June 1887).

504) *SFE* (7 June 1887). The *San Francisco Chronicle,* founded in 1865 by the brothers Charles and M. H. De Young, was one of the *Examiner's* chief rivals.

505) *SFE* (7 June 1887).

506) *SFE* (7 June 1887).

507) *SFE* (7 June 1887).

508) *SFE* (7 June 1887). Rev. Horatio Stebbins, although the frequent target of Bierce's attacks, conducted his marriage ceremony to Mary Ellen ("Mollie") Day on 25 December 1871.

509) *SFE* (12 June 1887).

510) *SFE* (12 June 1887).

511) *SFE* (12 June 1887).

512) *SFE* (15 June 1887).

513) *SFE* (15 June 1887). Dr. Charles Josselyn was the fire commissioner in San Francisco. He was evidently indicted on a charge of conspiracy to murder. See "Prattle," *SFE* (22 August 1887): 4.

514) *SFE* (7 March 1889). For "Silurian," see note on 261.

515) *SFE* (7 March 1889). For the Spring Valley Water Company, see 219.

516) *SFE* (7 March 1889). Goucher and Meany were both state senators in California; the latter was frequently referred to as "Goucher's Man."

517) *SFE* (15 March 1889). Loring Pickering was co-owner of the *San Francisco Call* and a frequent butt of Bierce's attacks.

518) *SFE* (15 March 1889). The fable is about Marcus D. Boruck, the personal secretary of Senator Waterman (see note on 531). Bierce frequently criticized Boruck for high-handedness.

519) *SFE* (15 March 1889). Possibly about Henry Vrooman (see note on 521).

520) *SFE* (22 March 1889).

521) *SFE* (22 March 1889). Henry Vrooman was a state senator whom Bierce attacked in "Prattle," *SFE* (2 September 1888): 4.

522) *SFE* (22 March 1889). For Senator Goucher, see note on 516.

523) *SFE* (22 March 1889). For "Yosemite Valley Commissioner," see 432 and note.

524) *SFE* (22 March 1889). Another fable on Boruck (see 518).

525) *SFE* (29 March 1889). Another fable on Boruck (see 518).

526) *SFE* (29 March 1889).

527) *SFE* (4 April 1889). The fable was written shortly after the inauguration of President Benjamin Harrison. See 224.

528) *SFE* (4 April 1889). The fable is about Claus Spreckels, nicknamed "The Sugar King" and part of a powerful California family that virtually controlled the manufacture and sale of refined sugar on the Pacific Coast.

529) *SFE* (4 April 1889). The new secretary of state appointed by President Harrison in 1889 was Bierce's longtime whipping boy James G. Blaine, who did not serve in the Civil War.

530) *SFE* (3 January 1890).

531) *SFE* (3 January 1890). Robert Whitney Waterman (1826-91) was lieutenant governor of California when Governor Washington Bartlett died in 1887. Waterman became governor and remained in office until 1891.

532) *SFE* (3 January 1890).

533) *SFE* (13 January 1890).

534) *SFE* (13 January 1890).

535) *SFE* (13 January 1890). See 523.

536) *SFE* (15 January 1890). Bierce's erstwhile commander in the Civil War, General William B. Hazen (1830-87), had been appointed by Rutherford B. Hayes as chief signal officer in the War Department, an office that was also connected with the Weather Bureau.

537) *SFE* (18 January 1890).

538) *SFE* (18 January 1890).

539) *SFE* (18 January 1890).

540) *SFE* (18 January 1890).

541) *SFE* (22 January 1890).

542) *SFE* (22 January 1890). Bierce was a vehement opponent of temperance.

543) *SFE* (24 January 1890).

544) *SFE* (24 January 1890).

545) *SFE* (24 January 1890).

546) *SFE* (24 January 1890). Colonel John P. Jackson purchased the *Wasp* in 1885, and may have been instrumental in causing Bierce's departure from the magazine the next year.

547) *SFE* (3 June 1890).

548) *SFE* (3 June 1890).

549) *SFE* (17 June 1890).

550) *SFE* (17 June 1890).

551) *SFE* (17 June 1890). Bierce's story "One Summer Night" (1906; *CW* 3) is about medical students robbing a grave.

552) *SFE* (17 June 1890).

553) *OT* (12 July 1890). Cf. Ae 184 (The Ass and the Cicadas).

554) *OT* (12 July 1890). Cf. Ae 229 (The Swallow and the Crow).

555) *SFE* (13 July 1890) (in "Prattle").

556) *OT* (19 July 1890).

557) *OT* (19 July 1890). Cf. Ae 210 (The Shepherd Who Cried "Wolf!" in Jest).

558) *OT* (19 July 1890). Cf. Ae 142 (The Aged Lion and the Fox).

559) *OT* (19 July 1890). Cf. Ae 257 (Lioness and Fox).

560) *OT* (19 July 1890). Cf. Ae 16 (The Cat and the Cock).

561) *OT* (19 July 1890). Cf. Ae 230 (The Turtle Takes Lessons from the Eagle).

562) *OT* (19 July 1890). Cf. Ae 284 (The Man and the Lion Travelling Together).

563) *OT* (19 July 1890). Cf. Ae 65 (The Travellers and the Bear).

564) *OT* (19 July 1890). Cf. Ae 451 (The Wolf in Sheep's Clothing).

565) *OT* (19 July 1890). Cf. Ae 17 (The Fox without a Tail).

566) *OT* (19 July 1890). Cf. Ae 201 (The Pigeon and the Picture). The reference is to Samuel Marsden Brookes (1816–92), an English-born painter of portraits, landscapes, and still lifes who came to California in 1858 and became a leading artist in the region.

567) *OT* (19 July 1890). Cf. Ae 702 (The Dog in the Manger).

568) *OT* (19 July 1890). See 422.

569) *OT* (19 July 1890). Cf. Ae 290 (The Oxen and the Butchers).

570) *OT* (19 July 1890). Cf. Ae 40 (The Astrologer Falls into a Well While Walking About and Gazing at the Stars).

571) *OT* (19 July 1890). Cf. Ae (The Frogs Ask Zeus for a King).

572) *OT* (26 July 1890). Cf. Ae 572 (The Kid and the Wolf).

573) *OT* (26 July 1890). Cf. Ae 55 (The Woman and Her Overworked Maidservants).

574) *OT* (2 August 1890). Cf. Ae 160 (The Disabled Wolf and the Sheep).

575) *OT* (2 August 1890). Cf. Ae 4 (The Fisherman and the Fish).

576) *OT* (2 August 1890). Cf. Ae 188 (Ass in Lion's Skin). See also 415.

577) *OT* (2 August 1890). Cf. Ae 509 (The Peacock Complains to Juno about His Voice).

578) *OT* (9 August 1890). Cf. Ae 406 (Some Dogs were busy tearing a Lion's Skin apart).

579) *OT* (9 August 1890). Cf. Ae 516 (The Bearded She-Goats).

580) *SFE* (27 November 1890).

581) *SFE* (27 November 1890). Clara Morris (1846–1925) was a well-known American actress of the period. She performed in California in 1890 and 1892.

582) *SFE* (27 November 1890).

583) *SFE* (27 November 1890).

584) *SFE* (27 November 1890).

585) *SFE* (6 December 1890).

586) *SFE* (6 December 1890).

587) *SFE* (6 December 1890).

588) *SFE* (6 December 1890). The governor of California at this time was Robert W. Waterman (see note on 531). Bierce criticized the frequency with which he, as well as his predecessor, George Stoneman (governor from 1883 to 1887), granted pardons. Cf. "Prattle," *SFE* (4 January 1891): 6: "After all, it does not greatly matter how many convicts have been pardoned by Governor Waterman. In a few months they will all be back in the penitentiaries again."

589) *SFE* (12 December 1890).

590) *SFE* (12 December 1890). Bierce frequently complained of juries' disinclination to convict women of murder. See "The Jury in Ancient America" (cited in note on 119).

591) *SFE* (12 December 1890).

592) *SFE* (12 December 1890). The reference is to the furor created in Great Britain over the Irish politician Charles Stewart Parnell, who was named as a co-respondent in a divorce case between Captain and Mrs. Kitty O'Shea. In November 1890 the British staesman and several times prime minister W. E. Gladstone threatened to resign as head of the Liberal Party if the party refused to abandon Parnell.

593) *SFE* (30 January 1891).

594) *SFE* (30 January 1891).

595) *SFE* (30 January 1891).

596) *SFE* (30 January 1891).

597) *SFE* (30 January 1891). The pestiferousness of people (mostly women) selling raffles or tickets was one of Bierce's bêtes noires. He addresses the point in one of his earliest articles, "Concerning Tickets," *Californian* 7, No. 32 (28 December 1867): 8.

598) *SFE* (30 January 1891). Another fable on Boruck (see 518).

599) *SFE* (19 February 1891). Cf. Ae 53 (The Farmer's Sons).

600) *SFE* (19 February 1891). Cf. Ae 503 (The Cockerel and the Pearl).

601) *SFE* (19 February 1891). For Governor Waterman, see 531. Frank M. Pixley (see 236) was presumably a supporter of Waterman. Cf. Ae 176 (The Man Who Warmed a Snake) and 617 (The Serpent in a Man's Bosom).

602) *SFE* (19 February 1891). Cf. Ae 291 (The Ox-Driver and Heracles).

603) *SFE* (19 February 1891). The reference is to Prescott Belknap, who had written a letter to the *Argonaut* (published in the issue for 13 October 1890) attacking Bierce and accusing him of cowardice because he failed to follow up on a whimsical offer to fight a duel with anyone conscientiously opposed to dueling. Later Belknap (apparently a minor) threatened to horsewhip Bierce. See "Prattle," *SFE* (19 October, 2 November, and 23 November 1890). Cf. Ae 520 (The Mountain in Labour).

604) *SFE* (19 February 1891). The editor of the *Bulletin* at this time was George K. Fitch. Cf. Ae 451 (The Wolf in Sheep's Clothing).

605) *SFE* (19 February 1891). Cf. Ae 17 (The Fox without a Tail).

606) *SFE* (19 February 1891). Cf. Ae 210 (The Shepherd Who Cried "Wolf!"). See 280 for an adaptation of this fable.

607) *SFE* (4 March 1891). Cf. Ae 613 (The Mice Take Counsel about the Cat).

608) *SFE* (4 March 1891). Cf. Ae 24 (The Fox with the Swollen Belly).

609) *SFE* (4 March 1891). Cf. Ae 15 (The Fox and the Grapes out of Reach).

610) *SFE* (4 March 1891). Cf. Ae 507 (The Cicada and the Owl).

611) *SFE* (20 March 1891). The reference is to Morris Estee, a Republican politician who had lost to George Stoneman in the gubernatorial election of 1882. It is not clear what incident is being satirized. Estee ran again for governor in 1894. Although professing to be opposed to the railroads, he was in fact secretly supported by the Southern Pacific Railroad in an attempt to avert even more severe governmental action against the railroads proposed by the Democratic candidate, James Budd. Budd in fact won the election. See William Deverell, *Railroad Crossing: Californians and the Railroad, 1850–1910* (Berkeley: University of California Press, 1994), p. 90.

612) *SFE* (20 March 1891).

613) *SFE* (20 March 1891).

614) *SFE* (20 March 1891). Probably an allusion to protests by naturalized Chinese Americans at the treatment of Chinese immigrants (coolies).

615) *SFE* (3 April 1891).

616) *SFE* (3 April 1891).

617) *SFE* (3 April 1891). See also 208, 269, and 352.

618) *SFE* (3 April 1891).

619) *SFE* (3 April 1891).

620) *SFE* (3 April 1891).

621) *SFE* (3 April 1891).

622) *SFE* (11 April 1891).

623) *SFE* (11 April 1891).

624) *SFE* (2 May 1891).

625) *SFE* (2 May 1891). The fable was written when William McKinley was a repre-

sentative from Ohio. He was already an advocate of protectionist tariffs, a policy he would vigorously continue during his presidency (1897–1901).

626) *SFE* (2 May 1891). The First Lady at this time was Caroline Lavinia (Scott) Harrison, wife of President Benjamin Harrison.

627) *SFE* (2 May 1891).

628) *SFE* (2 May 1891).

629) *SFE* (2 May 1891).

630) *SFE* (2 May 1891).

631) *SFE* (2 May 1891). For Bruner, see note on 138.

632) *SFE* (2 May 1891).

633) *SFE* (2 May 1891). The subject of the fable is what Bierce felt was the syco-phancy Americans displayed during Benjamin Harrison's tour of the nation in the spring of 1891, shortly after his inauguration as president. See "Prattle," *SFE* (10 May 1891): 6; rpt. in "The American Sycophant" (*CW* 11.296–309).

634) *SFE* (2 May 1891). See 189 for an adaptation of this fable.

635) *SFE* (2 May 1891).

636) *SFE* (1 August 1891). See 52.

637) *SFE* (1 August 1891).

638) *SFE* (1 August 1891). Approximately similar to Ae 360 (The Ass Eating Thorns).

639) *SFE* (3 October 1891). The passage in Aquinas is found in *Summa Theologiae* 1a.53.

640) *SFE* (3 October 1891). Richard Chute was a lawyer and lobbyist for the South-ern Pacific Railroad who was brought before a grand jury for contempt of court; but on 30 September 1891 Judge Daniel Murphy dismissed the jury on the grounds that it was improperly constituted. The case had not been resolved by the time Bierce published this fable.

641) *SFE* (3 October 1891). See also 177.

642) *SFE* (13 October 1891). A "boodler" is a slang term meaning "one who accepts or acquires boodle; one who sells his vote or influence for a bribe, or acquires money fraudulently from the public" (*The Century Dictionary and Cyclopedia* [New York: Century Co., 1902], 1:624). For Judge Murphy, see notes on 223 and 640.

643) *SFE* (13 October 1891).

644) *SFE* (13 October 1891).

645) *SFE* (24 October 1891). See 674.

646) *SFE* (24 October 1891).

647) *SFE* (24 October 1891).

648) *SFE* (24 October 1891). Bierce was a vigorous defender of the Mormons, criti-cizing the violence and prejudice they had suffered for decades. On 6 October 1890

Wilford Woodruff, president of the Mormon Church, issued a manifesto declaring that the church had given up polygamy. The decision was the result of a Supreme Court decision upholding the legality of laws passed by the federal government outlawing polygamy.

Jay Gould (1836–1892) had become part owner of the Erie Railroad in 1867 and through a series of unscrupulous practices had become very wealthy. The incident to which Bierce apparently alludes was a scheme in 1868 in which Gould and a colleague succeeded in forcing out another co-owner of the railroad by issuing a large amount of watered stock and repurchasing it for $12 million.

649) *SFE* (24 October 1891).

650) *SFE* (30 October 1891). For Morris Estee, see 611.

651) *SFE* (30 October 1891). Cf. Ae 87 (The Goose That Laid the Golden Eggs). The reference in the third paragraph is to bimetallism, an economic theory that proposed the establishment of a fixed ratio between the value of gold and the value of silver. See also 157.

652) *SFE* (30 October 1891).

653) *SFE* (30 October 1891). The president and secretary of state at this time were, respectively, Benjamin Harrison and James G. Blaine.

654) *SFE* (30 October 1891). For Bruner, see note on 138.

655) *SFE* (30 October 1891).

656) *SFE* (14 November 1891). A reprise of the Eastern or "Zambri" type of fable.

657) *SFE* (14 November 1891). For Bruner, see note on 138.

658) *SFE* (14 November 1891).

659) *SFE* (14 November 1891).

660) *SFE* (28 November 1891). A send-up of the Yale-Harvard rivalry in football.

661) *SFE* (28 November 1891). President Benjamin Harrison in fact lost the election of 1892 to Grover Cleveland.

662) *SFE* (28 November 1891). Five years earlier Bierce had written a poem, "The Restaurants of Oakland: By Their Victim," *W* No. 505 (3 April 1886): 6; later titled "Famine's Realm" (*CW* 5.80–81).

663) *SFE* (28 November 1891). One of the greatest earthquakes in modern history occurred on 28 October 1891 near Nagoya, Japan, killing 7,500 people and destroying 200,000 homes.

664) *SFE* (28 November 1891). Stephen T. Gage was an official of the Southern Pacific Railroad. Cf. "Prattle," *SFE* (29 November 1891): 6: "Mr. Stephen Gage, when before the Grand Jury, and duly sworn to tell the whole truth, is said to have persisted in affecting forgetfulness of everything that a man in his right mind would naturally remember."

665) *SFE* (28 November 1891). General W. H. L. Barnes had proposed to the Re-

publican National Committee to hold its 1892 convention in San Francisco, but the committee chose Minneapolis instead. The newspaper men's convention is mythical.

666) *SFE* (28 November 1891).

667) *SFE* (2 December 1891).

668) *SFE* (2 December 1891).

669) *SFE* (2 December 1891).

670) *SFE* (2 December 1891).

671) *SFE* (2 December 1891).

672) *SFE* (2 December 1891).

673) *SFE* (2 December 1891).

674) *SFE* (2 December 1891). The task of selecting a site for a new post office in San Francisco was placed in the hands of three federal commissioners (Postmaster General John Wanamaker, Secretary of the Treasury Charles Foster, and Attorney General William Henry Harrison Miller), but Bierce is probably alluding to the local commissioners — N. K. Masten (Chairman), John P. Irish, and W. J. Bryan — who, in early October 1891, actually selected the site at 7th and Mission Streets. There was much local opposition to the site because it was above a marsh, but the site was not changed. Bierce discusses the appointment of the local commissioners in "Prattle," *SFE* (1 November 1891): 6. The building was not built until 1905; it was one of the few structures to survive the earthquake and fire of the next year.

675) *SFE* (2 January 1892). The fable is similar to three early pieces in *Fun,* "Brief Seasons of Intellectual Dissipation" (21 June, 28 June, and 5 July 1873), consisting respectively of dialogues between a fool and a philosopher, a fool and a doctor, and a fool and a soldier. These items were reprinted in *Cobwebs from an Empty Skull* (1874).

676) *SFE* (30 January 1892).

677) *SFE* (30 January 1892). In the fall of 1891, in the midst of a civil war in Chile, two U.S. seamen were killed and dozens wounded in Valparaiso on shore leave from the U.S.S. *Baltimore.* The U.S. press demanded retribution, and for a time it appeared as if war might break out. President Harrison threatened the Chilean government, a move that angered M. A. Matta, Chile's minister of foreign relations. After a tense several weeks Chile finally backed down in late January 1892 and issued an apology.

678) *SFE* (29 March 1892).

679) *SFE* (29 March 1892). A political allegory in which Pataskatka is the United States, Novagascar is Chile (see note on 677), and Kamazemblagonia is Great Britain.

680) *SFE* (29 March 1892). "Vail" was at this time an acceptable variant of "veil." Cf. "Bankruptcy as a Military Resource," *SFE* (5 October 1892): 6: "Those imaginative persons at the various European capitals whose duty and, we trust, pleasure, it is to hear 'in every breeze that blows' a significant prophecy of that 'general European war' always imminent and inevitable seem pretty nearly to have exhausted their inge-

nuity, and might advantageously be recalled by their several newspapers and put out to reporting."

681) *SFE* (29 March 1892). For Silurian, see note on 261.

682) *SFE* (29 March 1892).

683) *SFE* (29 March 1892). See 674.

684) *SFE* (14 January 1893).

685) *SFE* (14 January 1893); rpt. in "Unpublished Fables," *Biblio* 4, No. 11 (July 1925): 827 (see also 199 and 688). Evidently an allusion to Ward McAllister, Jr., a state senator. The fable may refer to McAllister's failure in 1892 to support W. W. Foote in his campaign against Stephen M. White to secure the Democratic nomination for the U.S. Senate.

686) *SFE* (14 January 1893).

687) *SFE* (14 January 1893). William C. Bartlett was a writer for the San Francisco *Bulletin* frequently attacked by Bierce.

688) *SFE* (14 January 1893); rpt. in "Unpublished Fables," *Biblio* 4, No. 11 (July 1925): 827 (see also 199 and 685).

689) *SFE* (11 February 1893).

690) *SFE* (11 February 1893). For Stephen Gage, see note on 664. Colonel Mazuma is unidentified.

691) *SFE* (11 February 1893). "Hay" was this time a spelling occasionally used for "hey."

692) *SFE* (11 February 1893).

693) *SFE* (11 February 1893).

694) *SFE* (11 February 1893). The reference is to Queen Liliuokalani of Hawaii, who was deposed on 17 January 1893 by a group of Americans led by Sanford B. Dole, who was thereafter installed as president of the Hawaiian republic. See also 229.

695) *SFE* (11 February 1893).

696) *SFE* (11 February 1893).

697) *SFE* (11 February 1893). A variant of 265 and 412.

698) *SFE* (11 February 1893). In 1877 Bierce pseudonymously cowrote a book, *The Dance of Death,* purporting to condemn the immorality of ballroom dancing but describing the actions of dancers in such a lascivious manner as to be itself considered obscene. The hoax aroused considerable attention, and Bierce chuckled over it in later years; but his own prudery probably led him to endorse many of the book's positions.

699) *SFE* (11 February 1893). David Lesser Lezinsky was a local poet frequently twitted by Bierce. He published an article, "Delsarteism," *Californian Illustrated Magazine* 3, No. 2 (January 1893): 279–85, containing extravagant praise of a painter, Edmund Russell. Bierce attacked both Lezinsky and Russell in "Prattle," *SFE* (8 January 1893): 6. Lezinsky committed suicide on 4 July 1895.

700) *SFE* (11 February 1893). Every summer the Bohemian Club of San Francisco would put on a "Jinks," or a play written by one of the members (called the Sire) and performed by them in an outdoor theatre. For the Women's Press Association, see 218.

701) *SFE* (11 February 1893). The fable imitates the form of a celebrated anecdote about Voltaire that Bierce repeated on many occasions, e.g., the entry "Robber" in *The Devil's Dictionary:* "It is related of Voltaire that one night he and some traveling companions lodged at a wayside inn. The surroundings were suggestive, and after supper they agreed to tell robber stories in turn. When Voltaire's turn came he said: 'Once there was a Farmer-General of the Revenues.' Saying nothing more, he was encouraged to continue. 'That,' he said, 'is the story' " (*CW* 7.298). Cf. "Prattle," *SFE* (30 April 1893): 6: "Is not this the Moore who was a member of the late lamented Forestry Commission, and whom Mr. Allen Kelly pretty plainly and very publicly called a thief?" The precise nature of Moore's dereliction is not known.

702) *SFE* (15 April 1893).

703) *SFE* (15 April 1893).

704) *SFE* (15 April 1893).

705) *SFE* (15 April 1893). "Vaporing" means "Acting or talking in a pretentious or high-flown manner" (*Oxford English Dictionary*). For the subject matter, see note on 748.

706) *SFE* (15 April 1893).

707) *SFE* (6 May 1893). A reference to the Chicago World's Fair of 1893, designed to commemorate the 400th anniversary of Columbus's discovery of America.

708) *SFE* (6 May 1893). Probably a reference to Leland Stanford, the railroad tycoon who founded Stanford University.

709) *SFE* (6 May 1893). See 232.

710) *SFE* (6 May 1893). Another allusion to the World's Fair in Chicago, referred to as the Columbian Exposition.

711) *SFE* (6 May 1893). John P. Irish (1843–1923) was editor of the *Oakland Times* and *Alta California.*

712) *SFE* (7 May 1893).

713) *SFE* (7 May 1893). Another reference to the World's Fair (see 707).

714) *SFE* (7 May 1893).

715) *SFE* (20 May 1893).

716) *SFE* (20 May 1893). Bierce was a longtime foe of the "railroad barons." His greatest journalistic triumph occurred in 1896, when he helped to defeat the attempt by Collis P. Huntington, owner of the Southern Pacific Railroad, to pass a funding bill in Congress granting him a long extension to repay government debts.

717) *SFE* (20 May 1893).

718) *SFE* (20 May 1893).

719) *SFE* (20 May 1893).

720) *SFE* (20 May 1893). See note on 748.

721) *SFE* (10 June 1893).

722) *SFE* (10 June 1893).

723) *SFE* (10 June 1893). For Huntington, see note on 716. W. H. Mills was an official of the Southern Pacific Railroad. The fable may relate to the railroad's so-called pink contract, whereby the railroad, having choked off competition by water, raised their rates for carrying freight by as much as 50 per cent. See Bierce, "Fragments of Truth at Last," *SFE* (8 March 1896): 3–4. The fable is also somewhat similar in theme to the humorous sketch "A Cargo of Cat" (1885; *CW* 8.258–64).

724) *SFE* (10 June 1893). For the World's Fair at "Porkago" (Chicago), see 707.

725) *SFE* (10 June 1893).

726) *SFE* (10 June 1893). The allusion at the end of the third paragraph is to the assassination of Presidents Lincoln (1865) and Garfield (1881).

727) *SFE* (10 June 1893). J. J. Owen was the author of a column for a religious magazine in San Jose, *Better Times*.

728) *SFE* (10 June 1893).

729) *SFE* (10 June 1893). Joaquin Miller (1837–1913) was deemed the "Poet of the Sierras" following the publication of his first book, *Songs of the Sierras* (1871). He resided in a cabin on the hills above Oakland and called it "The Hights." Miller was a longtime friend of Bierce, but the latter was not above poking genial fun at him on occasion.

730) *SFE* (16 July 1893).

731) *SFE* (16 July 1893).

732) *SFE* (16 July 1893).

733) *SFE* (16 July 1893).

734) *SFE* (16 July 1893).

735) *SFE* (16 July 1893).

736) *SFE* (16 July 1893).

737) *SFE* (16 July 1893). The reference is to George Davidson (1825–1911), professor of geology at the University of California and author of many papers on the history and geology of California and on astronomy.

738) *SFE* (6 August 1893). The architect of the City Hall tower was Frank Shea.

739) *SFE* (6 August 1893). For the Mint, see note on 215.

740) *SFE* (6 August 1893). Mackinder was the editor of the St. Helena (Calif.) *Star*.

741) *SFE* (6 August 1893); rpt. *Figaro* (Chicago) No. 181 (17 August 1893): 421 (in "Fables without Morals"). Davis H. Waite (1825–1901) was was elected governor of Colorado in 1892, serving from January 1893 to January 1895.

742) *SFE* (20 August 1893). Bierce comments at length on the Midwinter Fair in San Francisco in "Prattle," *SFE* (25 February 1894): 6.

743) *SFE* (20 August 1893).

744) *SFE* (20 August 1893).

745) *SFE* (20 August 1893).

746) *SFE* (20 August 1893). The fable alludes to President Grover Cleveland, who had a summer home named "Gray Gables" on the shore of Buzzard's Bay in Massachusetts.

747) *SFE* (24 September 1893).

748) *SFE* (24 September 1893). The fable alludes to the Geary Act of 1892, sponsored by Thomas J. Geary (1854-1929), a representative from California (1890-95). The act stipulated, among other things, that all Chinese immigrants possess certificates of registration or face deportation. But by the fall of 1893, when it was learned that the cost of deporting the 85,000 Chinese who had failed to register would be in excess of $10 million, the government repealed the requirement for deportation.

749) *SFE* (24 September 1893). Grover Cleveland's second daughter, Esther, was born on 9 September 1893. She was not the first child to be born in the White House; that had occurred in the presidency of John Tyler.

750) *SFE* (24 September 1893). The reference in the final paragraphs is to Richard Olney (1835-1917), attorney general (1893-95) and secretary of state (1895-97) under Grover Cleveland.

751) *SFE* (24 September 1893). For Pixley, see 236.

752) *SFE* (24 September 1893). C. R. Bennett was secretary of the local branch of the Society for the Suppression of Vice who was later convicted of assault with a deadly weapon.

753) *SFE* (24 September 1893).

754) *SFE* (24 September 1893). Sausalito is a small town in Marin County, north of San Francisco and across the bay from Oakland.

755) *SFE* (24 September 1893).

756) *SFE* (24 September 1893). Noah's ark was supposed to have come to rest after the Flood on the "mountains of Ararat" (Genesis 8:4), which was assumed to correspond to Mt. Ararat in eastern Turkey. Several claims were made regarding the discovery of fragments of the ark on the site.

757) *SFE* (14 January 1894) (in "Prattle").

758) *SFE* (8 November 1896).

759) *SFE* (8 November 1896). A reference to Charles Shortridge, a writer for the *San Jose Mercury* who became editor of the *San Francisco Call* around 1889.

760) *SFE* (8 November 1896).

761) *SFE* (8 November 1896). Bierce was a longtime foe of woman suffrage.

762) *SFE* (8 November 1896). The reference is to Grove Johnson (1841-1926), a representative from California (1895-97) who had supported C. P. Huntington's funding bill (see note on 716). He lost his bid for reelection in 1896.

763) *SFE* (20 December 1896).

764) *SFE* (20 December 1896). Andrew Carnegie (see note on 193) was criticized by a Congressional investigating committee for providing faulty armor plates and steel plates for use in ships being built at the Navy shipyards at Newport News, Virginia. See "Defective Armor Plates," *New York Times* (5 December 1896): 1.

765) *SFE* (20 December 1896). The fable was written as President Grover Cleveland, who had served two separate terms of office (1885-89, 1893-97), was about to step down.

766) *SFE* (20 December 1896). A reference to Grover Cleveland's stance in regard to the Cuban insurrection against Spain. On 30 July 1896 Cleveland delivered a proclamation announcing strict U.S. neutrality in the conflict. In his annual address on 7 December 1896, as he was yielding power to President-Elect William McKinley, Cleveland continued to urge neutrality but stated that there may come a time when the United States would have to intervene.

767) *SFE* (20 December 1896).

768) *SFE* (20 December 1896).

769) *SFE* (20 December 1896).

770) *SFE* (20 December 1896).

771) *SFE* (20 December 1896). The fable is probably directed against C. P. Huntington (see note on 716), who had hired up to fifty lobbyists to win support for his funding bill.

772) *SFE* (24 October 1897).

773) *SFE* (24 October 1897).

774) *SFE* (24 October 1897); *Judge* No. 1587 (16 March 1912): [10]. In *SFE* there is an additional sentence at the end: "We'll detail some friends of the Prime Minister."

775) *SFE* (24 October 1897).

776) *SFE* (24 October 1897).

777) *SFE* (24 October 1897).

778) TMS, UVa; *SFE* (24 October 1897) (as "The Vigilant Policeman"). In *SFE* "owner" is printed as "Occupant."

779) *SFE* (24 October 1897).

780) *SFE* (24 October 1897).

781) *SFE* (7 November 1897).

782) TMS, UVa; *SFE* (7 November 1897). The title is an allusion to Frank R. Stockton's celebrated story "The Lady, or the Tiger?" (*Century Magazine,* November 1882; in Stockton's *The Lady, or the Tiger? and Other Stories* [1884]).

783) *SFE* (7 November 1897).

784) *SFE* (7 November 1897). Grover Cleveland's son, Richard Folsom, was born on 28 October 1897, almost eight months after Cleveland had left office.

785) *SFE* (7 November 1897).

786) *Life* (8 September 1898).

787) *Life* (8 September 1898).

788) *Life* (8 September 1898). An obvious allegory of Cuba (Oppressed People), Spain (tyrant), and the United States (Land of the Free).

789) *SFE* (30 April 1899).

790) *SFE* (30 April 1899); *Judge* No. 1587 (16 March 1912): [10]. In *SFE* the second paragraph reads:

> "My pendulous friend," said the Political Boss, sympatheti-
> cally,
>
>> Gives sorrow words: the grief that does not speak
>> Whispers the o'erfraught heart and bids it break.
>
> What's the matter with you, and where does it appear to hurt?"

The fourth paragraph reads:

> "This infernal dog, dissatisfied with my wag, has
>
>> cut me off
>> And left me naked to mine enemies —
>
> That's where it hurts," replied the Tail, its grief no moan abat-
> ing.

The final paragraph reads: "And ever thereafter when the Political Boss, a sadder and a wiser man, listened with a tender hope to the trumpet of Fame that candid instrument reminded him that he was stuck on."

791) *SFE* (30 April 1899).

792) *SFE* (30 April 1899). A variant of 586.

793) *SFE* (30 April 1899); *Judge* No. 1587 (16 March 1912): [10]. In *SFE* the fable reads:

> An Illustrious Orator was making a fervid speech in advocacy
> of Territorial Contraction as a party "cry" for the year 1900, when

some angels looked down from Heaven and wept upon him. The Illustrious Orator paused and looked skyward for a moment, then, observing the husband of his washerwoman occupying a seat on the platform, said to him in an earnest whisper:

"Go home and tell your wife to take in her washing off the line—I am about to urge the free coinage of silver in a ratio of sixteen to one."

794) *SFE* (30 April 1899).

795) *SFE* (13 August 1899). The allusion is probably to Commodore George Dewey's campaign in the Philippines. Bierce criticized the Philippine war as naked imperialism:

This is not a purely military war: like most wars it is partly political and sentimental. It is not conducted as it would be by one whose trade is war alone, and to whom defeat of the enemy in the shortest time and at the least expense of blood and treasure is the sole purpose of action. . . .

In such a war Dewey, having destroyed the fleet at Manila, would have left the city unmolested and returned to Hongkong, whence he would have pointed his prows to the Strait of Magellan or to that of Gibraltar. . . . That is to say, he would have joined the hunt for the rest of the Spanish Navy, knowing that with its effacement the Philippines, like Cuba, Porto Rico and whatever else we might need in our business, would come to us as naturally as ripe fruit falls from a shaken tree.

Why is it that instead of this simple and soldierly programme we have a complicated and enormously costly regime of invasion, requiring more than two hundred thousand volunteer troops?

"War Topics," *SFE* (29 May 1898): 18.

796) *SFE* (13 August 1899).

797) TMS, UVa; *SFE* (13 August 1899) (untitled).

798) *SFE* (12 May 1901).

799) *SFE* (12 May 1901).

800) *SFE* (12 May 1901). A reference to the blockading of Cuba during the Spanish-American War, specifically the siege of Santiago Harbor (1 June to 3 July 1898). The Spanish governor-general of the island at the time was General Ramón Blanco y Erenas.

801) *SFE* (12 May 1901).

802) *NYJ* (20 October 1901); *Cleveland World* (20 October 1901); *SFE* (25 October 1901). An allusion to Admiral Winfield Scott Schley (1839–1911), who engaged in a

controversial maneuver at the Battle of Santiago (3 July 1898) in which it appeared that he was leaving the blockading line when in fact he seems to have been swinging around his flagship, the *Brooklyn,* for a fight on a parallel line. The furor over the incident lasted for years; the public largely took Schley's side, but the navy generally regarded Admiral William Thomas Sampson (1840–1902) as the true victor of the battle. Bierce, with his many friends at the Army and Navy Club in Washington, clearly approved of Sampson and wrote many articles condemning Schley. See also 804 and 805.

803) *NYJ* (20 October 1901); *Cleveland World* (20 October 1901); *SFE* (25 October 1901).

804) *NYJ* (20 October 1901); *Cleveland World* (20 October 1901); *SFE* (25 October 1901). Because of the widespread dissemination of a hostile account of Admiral Schley's conduct at the Battle of Santiago (see 802), Schley himself requested a court of inquiry to investigate the matter. It sat between 12 September and 12 December 1901 and produced a verdict generally unfavorable to Schley.

805) *NYJ* (20 October 1901); *Cleveland World* (20 October 1901); *SFE* (25 October 1901). Another attack on Schley (see 802).

806) TMS, UVa; *NYJ* (2 November 1901); *SFE* (8 November 1901).

807) *NYJ* (2 November 1901); *SFE* (8 November 1901).

808) *NYJ* (2 November 1901); *SFE* (8 November 1901). For the name Ghargaroo, see note on 252. The whole fable seems a variant of 308.

809) *NYJ* (2 November 1901); *SFE* (24 November 1901). Obviously an attack on Andrew Carnegie (see notes on 193 and 764).

810) *NYA* (15 September 1902); *SFE* (25 September 1902).

811) *NYA* (15 September 1902); *SFE* (25 September 1902). An allegory on U.S. involvement in the Cuban insurrection.

812) *NYA* (15 September 1902); *SFE* (25 September 1902). On Bierce's view of trusts, see note on 203.

813) *NYA* (15 September 1902); *SFE* (25 September 1902).

814) *NYA* (15 September 1902); *SFE* (25 September 1902).

815) *NYA* (15 September 1902); *SFE* (25 September 1902) (as "Two of a Kind"); rpt. *Judge* No. 1587 (16 March 1912): [10]. In *NYA* and *SFE* "pig" and "hog" read "jackass"; in the last paragraph, "politician" reads "statesman" and "ass" reads "idiot."

816) *NYA* (26 September 1902); *SFE* (28 September 1902). A frequent complaint of Bierce's; cf. "Prattle," *SFE* (12 September 1897): 6: "A member of the eminent publishing house of Macmillan & Co. has had the thoughtfulness to point out to authors who would eat the necessity of having some trade besides that of authorship. I believe, however, that the publishers do not find it necessary to have any trade besides publishing. In a competitive examination in 'gall' this distinguished gentleman would take all the prizes — at least all the unguarded ones." Cf. also "Prattle," *SFE* (8 May 1892): 6: "What is a publisher? One of the most famous definitions affirms him to

be a person who drinks champagne out of the skulls of authors. Naturally that is an author's definition."

817) *NYA* (26 September 1902); *SFE* (28 September 1902).

818) *NYA* (26 September 1902); *SFE* (28 September 1902).

819) *NYA* (26 September 1902); *SFE* (28 September 1902).

820) *NYA* (26 September 1902); *SFE* (28 September 1902).

821) *SFE* (28 September 1902).

822) *NYA* (26 September 1902); *SFE* (28 September 1902).

823) *SFE* (17 October 1902); *NYA* (19 October 1902) (as "The Man with a Method"); rpt. *Judge* No. 1587 (16 March 1912): [10].

824) *SFE* (17 October 1902); *NYA* (19 October 1902).

825) TMS, UVa; *SFE* (17 October 1902); *NYA* (19 October 1902) (both as "The King and the Parrot").

826) *SFE* (17 October 1902); *NYA* (19 October 1902).

827) *SFE* (17 October 1902); *NYA* (19 October 1902).

828) *NYA* (17 April 1904); *SFE* (1 May 1904). A reference to Judge Alton B. Parker (1852–1926), nominated as the Democratic candidate for president against Theodore Roosevelt. He received the sobriquet "the silent candidate" because of his refusal to make any statements on public questions before the Democratic convention. He lost in a landslide to Roosevelt.

829) *NYA* (17 April 1904); *SFE* (1 May 1904).

830) *NYA* (17 April 1904); *SFE* (1 May 1904).

831) *NYA* (17 April 1904); *SFE* (1 May 1904).

832) *NYA* (17 April 1904); *SFE* (1 May 1904).

833) *NYA* (10 May 1904); *SFE* (22 May 1904).

834) *NYA* (10 May 1904); *SFE* (22 May 1904).

835) *NYA* (10 May 1904).

836) *NYA* (10 May 1904); *SFE* (22 May 1904). Theodore Roosevelt created a furor by inviting the African American leader Booker T. Washington to dinner at the White House on 16 October 1901. Roosevelt attempted to downplay the incident and rarely spoke of it in subsequent years, but it was repeatedly used by Southern Democrats to attack him.

837) *NYA* (10 May 1904); *SFE* (22 May 1904).

838) *Co* (September 1905).

839) *Co* (September 1905). See also 233 and note.

840) *Co* (September 1905).

841) *Co* (September 1905). An allusion to the battle against C. P. Huntington's fund-

ing bill in 1896 (see note on 716). In an attempt to portray Huntington as a thief, San Francisco mayor Adolph Sutro sent letters to congressmen in early 1896 with the words "Huntington wouldn't steal a red-hot stove!" written in red on the envelopes.

842) *Co* (September 1905).

843) *Co* (July 1907).

844) *Co* (July 1907).

845) *Co* (July 1907). A variant of 179. "Kairnagy" is another reference to Andrew Carnegie (see note on 193).

846) TMS, UVa.

꙳

A CHRONOLOGY OF

BIERCE'S FABLES

"The Fables of Zambri, the Parsee" (as by "Dod Grile").
Fun (13 July 1872): 23.
[2, 3, 4, 5, 6]

Fun (20 July 1872): 27.
[8, 9, 11, 10, 12, 13]

Fun (27 July 1872): 37.
[7, 1]

Fun (3 August 1872): 47.
[56, 16, 14]

Fun (10 August 1872): 57.
[46, 36]

Fun (17 August 1872): 71.
[28, 19, 15, 17, 20]

Fun (24 August 1872): 81.
[66, 18, 21, 22]

Fun (31 August 1872): 88.
[26, 24, 23, 25, 27, 29, 30]

Fun (7 September 1872): 103.
[31, 32, 33, 34, 35, 37, 38]

Fun (14 September 1872): 115.
[98, 39, 41, 43, 44, 40, 45]

Fun (21 September 1872): 125.
[42, 50, 48, 47, 49]

Fun (28 September 1872): 135.
[51, 52, 54, 55, 58]

Fun (23 November 1872): 217.
[86, 53, 57, 59]

Fun (30 November 1872): 227.
[61, 60, 62, 63, 64]

Fun (7 December 1872): 239.
[120, 65, 67, 68, 69]

Fun (14 December 1872): 243.
[70, 71, 73, 72, 74]

Fun (21 December 1872): 259.
[76, 75, 77, 78, 80, 79]

Fun (28 December 1872): 269.
[85, 89, 90, 91]

Fun (4 January 1873): 7.
[130, 81, 82, 83, 84, 87, 88, 92]

Fun (11 January 1873): 17.
[93, 94, 97, 96, 95]

Fun (18 January 1873): 27.
[108, 99, 105, 100, 101, 102]

Fun (25 January 1873): 38.
[104, 103, 106, 107, 109]

Fun (1 February 1873): 53.
[110, 112, 113, 111, 114]

Fun (8 February 1873): 57.
[115, 116, 117, 119, 118]

Fun (15 February 1873): 77.
[121, 122, 123]

Fun (22 February 1873): 85.
[124, 126, 127, 125]

Fun (1 March 1873): 97.
[128, 131, 132]

Fun (8 March 1873): 101.
[129, 133, 134, 135]

"The Devil's Dictionary."
Wasp No. 274 (28 October 1881): 285.
[441]

"Anecdotes of Animals."
Wasp No. 387 (29 December 1883): 6 (unsigned).
[448, 449, 450, 451, 452, 453, 454, 455]

"The Devil's Dictionary."
Wasp No. 410 (7 June 1884): 3.
[442]

"Fables without Political Morals."
Wasp No. 423 (6 September 1884): 6 (unsigned).
[456, 457, 458, 459, 460, 461, 462, 463, 464, 465]

"Fables without Political Meaning."
Wasp No. 426 (27 September 1884): 3 (unsigned).
[466, 467, 468, 469, 470, 471, 472, 473, 474, 475, 476, 477, 478]

"Fables without Political Meaning."
Wasp No. 427 (4 October 1884): 3 (unsigned).
[479, 480, 481, 482, 483, 484, 485, 486, 487, 488]

"Fables without Political Meaning."
Wasp No. 428 (11 October 1884): 3 (unsigned).
[489, 490, 491, 492, 493, 494, 495]

"Fables without Political Meaning."
Wasp No. 429 (18 October 1884): 6 (unsigned).
[496, 497, 498, 499]

"The Devil's Dictionary."
Wasp No. 456 (25 April 1885): 3.
[443]

"Fables without Morals."
San Francisco Examiner (4 June 1887): 44.
[500, 501, 502, 251, 187, 146]

"Fables and Tales."
San Francisco Examiner (7 June 1887): 44 (unsigned).
[503, 504, 505, 506, 236, 293, 507, 508]

"Fables without Morals."
San Francisco Examiner (12 June 1887): 44 (unsigned).
[509, 510, 511, 263]

"Fables without Morals."
   San Francisco Examiner (15 June 1887): 44 (unsigned).
   [140, 512, 513]

"Prattle."
   San Francisco Examiner (6 November 1887): 4.
   [446]

"The Devil's Dictionary."
   San Francisco Examiner (29 April 1888): 4.
   [444]

"Fables without Morals."
   San Francisco Examiner (7 March 1889): 4 (as by "A. G. B.").
   [514, 227, 148, 225, 515, 516, 147]

"Fables without Morals."
   San Francisco Examiner (15 March 1889): 4 (unsigned).
   [517, 302, 224, 518, 287, 519]

"Fables without Morals."
   San Francisco Examiner (22 March 1889): 4 (as by "A. G. B.").
   [520, 521, 285, 298, 294, 522, 523, 524, 436, 309]

"Fables without Morals."
   San Francisco Examiner (29 March 1889): 4 (as by "A. G. B.").
   [290, 299, 525, 526, 188, 296]

"Fables without Morals."
   San Francisco Examiner (4 April 1889): 4 (as by "A. G. B.").
   [527, 528, 259, 243, 529, 305, 432]

"Fables without Morals."
   San Francisco Examiner (3 January 1890): 6.
   [203, 530, 531, 532, 204]

"Fables without Morals."
   San Francisco Examiner (13 January 1890): 4.
   [533, 534, 295, 535, 143, 247, 145]

"Fables without Morals."
   San Francisco Examiner (15 January 1890): 6.
   [292, 536, 261, 279, 291, 253, 254]

"Fables without Morals."
   San Francisco Examiner (18 January 1890): 6.
   [226, 537, 538, 539, 540]

"Fables without Morals."
   San Francisco Examiner (22 January 1890): 6 (unsigned).
   [228, 541, 542, 167, 219]

"Fables without Morals."
    San Francisco Examiner (24 January 1890): 6.
    [183, 543, 544, 545, 546, 202]

"Fables of the Day."
    San Francisco Examiner (13 June 1890): 6 (unsigned).
    [547, 548]

"Fables of the Period."
    San Francisco Examiner (17 June 1890): 6 (unsigned).
    [549, 550, 551, 552]

"The Fables of Æsop."
    Oakland Daily Evening Tribune (12 July 1890): 1.
    [400, 391, 553, 369, 384, 388, 394, 554, 389, 396, 385, 381, 402, 387]

"Prattle."
    San Francisco Examiner (13 July 1890): 6.
    [555]

"Fables of Æsop."
    Oakland Daily Evening Tribune (19 July 1890): 1.
    [556, 557, 558, 559, 560, 561, 562, 563, 564, 565, 566, 567, 568, 569, 570, 571]

"Fables of Æsop."
    Oakland Daily Evening Tribune (26 July 1890): 1.
    [399, 439, 572, 405, 438, 398, 372, 377, 573, 382, 361, 363, 403, 376, 386]

"Fables of Æsop."
    Oakland Daily Evening Tribune (2 August 1890): 1.
    [370, 365, 371, 366, 574, 440, 375, 575, 364, 374, 373, 393, 576, 577]

"Fables of Æsop."
    Oakland Daily Evening Tribune (9 August 1890): 1.
    [367, 578, 379, 392, 390, 378, 380, 404, 579, 395, 368, 362, 397, 383]

"Words and Things."
    Oakland Daily Evening Tribune (4 October 1890): 1.
    [241]

"Fables without Morals."
    San Francisco Examiner (27 November 1890): 6 (unsigned).
    [580, 581, 582, 583, 584]

"Fables without Morals."
    San Francisco Examiner (6 December 1890): 6 (unsigned).
    [433, 229, 585, 586, 587, 588]

"Fables without Morals."
    San Francisco Examiner (12 December 1890): 6 (unsigned).
    [193, 589, 590, 144, 591, 206, 182, 592, 160]

"Fables without Morals."
San Francisco Examiner (30 January 1891): 6 (unsigned).
[231, 593, 297, 594, 595, 307, 596, 286, 234, 597, 598, 265]

"Æsop's Fables, Applied."
San Francisco Examiner (19 February 1891): 6 (unsigned).
[407, 599, 416, 406, 411, 600, 410, 601, 602, 412, 603, 418, 604, 605, 421, 606, 417]

"Æsop's Fables, Applied."
San Francisco Examiner (4 March 1891): 6 (unsigned).
[422, 607, 413, 419, 414, 608, 408, 415, 409, 420, 609, 610]

"Fables and Allegories."
San Francisco Examiner (20 March 1891): 6 (unsigned).
[172, 611, 612, 258, 252, 613, 248, 264, 138, 614]

"Fables and Allegories."
San Francisco Examiner (3 April 1891): 6 (as by "B.").
[615, 222, 616, 170, 617, 618, 619, 620, 621, 271]

"Fables and Allegories."
San Francisco Examiner (11 April 1891): 6 (as by "B.").
[622, 194, 198, 178, 195, 184, 150, 623, 164]

"Fables without Morals."
San Francisco Examiner (2 May 1891): 6 (unsigned).
[624, 625, 626, 627, 628, 629, 630, 631, 632, 633, 634, 635]

"Fables and Anecdotes."
San Francisco Examiner (1 August 1891): 6.
[220, 304, 289, 437, 636, 637, 288, 237, 638, 233]

"Fables and Anecdotes."
San Francisco Examiner (22 August 1891): 6.
[267, 282, 136, 162, 239, 221, 250, 235]

"Fables and Anecdotes."
San Francisco Examiner (3 October 1891): 6 (as by "A. B.").
[155, 152, 639, 196, 262, 255, 640, 210, 641]

"Fables and Anecdotes."
San Francisco Examiner (13 October 1891): 6 (as by "A. B.").
[270, 642, 300, 643, 274, 177, 644, 269, 174]

"Fables and Anecdotes."
San Francisco Examiner (24 October 1891): 6.
[260, 645, 646, 647, 137, 266, 648, 649, 276, 268]

"Fables and Anecdotes."
San Francisco Examiner (30 October 1891): 6.
[650, 139, 651, 652, 171, 205, 653, 654, 655, 301]

"Fables and Anecdotes."
San Francisco Examiner (14 November 1891): 6.
[238, 656, 278, 657, 658, 273, 242, 659, 306, 218, 249]

"Fables and Anecdotes."
San Francisco Examiner (28 November 1891): 6.
[660, 661, 662, 200, 663, 176, 664, 665, 142, 666]

"Fables and Anecdotes."
San Francisco Examiner (2 December 1891): 6.
[667, 668, 669, 670, 671, 672, 673, 674]

"Fables and Anecdotes."
San Francisco Examiner (2 January 1892): 6.
[283, 173, 303, 151, 257, 675, 246, 284]

"Fables and Anecdotes."
San Francisco Examiner (30 January 1892): 6.
[141, 676, 244, 232, 275, 313, 272, 223, 677]

"Fables and Anecdotes."
San Francisco Examiner (29 March 1892): 6.
[256, 678, 230, 679, 185, 680, 681, 682, 683, 180]

"Fables and Anecdotes."
San Francisco Examiner (14 January 1893): 6.
[199, 181, 684, 685, 686, 192, 434, 687, 688, 153, 208]

"Fables and Anecdotes."
San Francisco Examiner (11 February 1893): 6.
[689, 690, 691, 692, 693, 694, 695, 696, 697, 698, 699, 700, 701]

"Fables of the Day."
San Francisco Examiner (15 April 1893): 6.
[702, 175, 703, 149, 166, 431, 212, 704, 705, 706]

"Fables without Morals."
San Francisco Examiner (6 May 1893): 6.
[161, 707, 708, 709, 209, 710, 179, 277, 711, 154]

"Fables without Morals."
San Francisco Examiner (7 May 1893): 6.
[190, 217, 712, 713, 714]

"Fables without Morals."
San Francisco Examiner (20 May 1893): 6.
[715, 716, 163, 165, 717, 216, 718, 719, 201, 720]

"Topical Fables."
> *San Francisco Examiner* (10 June 1893): 6.
> [721, 722, 723, 724, 725, 726, 727, 728, 215, 729]

"Fables without Morals."
> *San Francisco Examiner* (16 July 1893): 13.
> [730, 157, 731, 732, 733, 734, 735, 736, 158, 281, 737]

"Fables without Morals."
> *San Francisco Examiner* (6 August 1893): 12.
> [738, 245, 211, 435, 739, 740, 741]

"Fables without Morals."
> *San Francisco Examiner* (20 August 1893): 13.
> [159, 197, 742, 191, 186, 169, 743, 744, 745, 746, 207]

"Fables without Morals."
> *San Francisco Examiner* (24 September 1893): 6.
> [747, 748, 749, 750, 751, 752, 213, 753, 754, 755, 756]

"Prattle."
> *San Francisco Examiner* (14 January 1894): 6.
> [757]

"Some Fables without Morals."
> *San Francisco Examiner* (8 November 1896): 6 (unsigned).
> [758, 759, 760, 761, 762]

"Some Fables without Morals."
> *San Francisco Examiner* (20 December 1896): 24 (unsigned).
> [763, 764, 765, 766, 767, 768, 769, 770, 771]

"Prattle."
> *San Francisco Examiner* (12 September 1897): 18.
> [429]

"Nine Fantastic Fables."
> *San Francisco Examiner* (24 October 1897): 18.
> [772, 773, 774, 775, 776, 777, 778, 779, 780]

"Fantastic Fables."
> *San Francisco Examiner* (7 November 1897): 18.
> [781, 320, 782, 327, 322, 783, 323, 430, 784, 785, 329]

"War Fables."
> *Life* No. 822 (8 September 1898): 188.
> [786, 787, 788]

Fantastic Fables.
> New York: G. P. Putnam's Sons, 1899.
> [156, 168, 189, 214, 240, 280, 338]

"Fables and Anecdotes."
San Francisco Examiner (30 April 1899): 12.
[339, 789, 347, 790, 791, 355, 792, 318, 793, 794]

"Fables and Anecdotes."
San Francisco Examiner (13 August 1899): 12.
[795, 358, 796, 353, 343, 797, 341, 333]

"Some Military Fables."
San Francisco Examiner (12 May 1901): 23.
[798, 324, 340, 346, 330, 799, 800, 801, 331]

"Fables in Rhyme."
New York Journal (3 September 1901): 16.
San Francisco Examiner (6 September 1901): 14.
[424, 426, 423]

"Fables without Slang."
New York Journal (17 September 1901): 16.
San Francisco Examiner (5 October 1901): 14 (as "Modern Fables without Slang").
[427, 425]

"Fables of the Deep Blue Sea."
New York Journal (20 October 1901): 16.
Cleveland World (20 October 1901): Magazine Section, p. 1.
San Francisco Examiner (25 October 1901): 14.
[319, 802, 803, 321, 804, 805]

"Fables and Anecdotes."
New York Journal (2 November 1901): 25.
San Francisco Examiner (8 November 1901): 14.
[344, 310, 806, 807, 808]

"Fables and Anecdotes."
New York Journal (17 November 1901): 25.
San Francisco Examiner (24 November 1901): Editorial Section, p. 2.
[809, 348, 350]

"Fables without Slang."
New York American (15 September 1902): 8.
San Francisco Examiner (25 September 1902): 16.
[810, 428, 811, 812, 813, 814, 815]

"Fables without Slang."
New York American (26 September 1902): 8.
San Francisco Examiner (28 September 1902): 50.
[816, 817, 818, 819, 820, 821 (*San Francisco Examiner* only), 822]

"Fables without Slang."
 San Francisco Examiner (17 October 1902): 16.
 New York American (19 October 1902): 23.
 [823, 824, 825, 826, 827]

"A Spread of Quick-Lunch Wisdom for Busy Readers."
 New York American (2 October 1902): 14.
 San Francisco Examiner (17 October 1902): 16.
 [338]

"Fables and Anecdotes."
 New York American (17 April 1904): 25.
 San Francisco Examiner (1 May 1904): 45.
 [828, 829, 356, 830, 831, 312, 314, 832, 345]

"Fables and Anecdotes."
 New York American (10 May 1904): 16.
 San Francisco Examiner (22 May 1904): 16.
 [833, 342, 335, 334, 834, 835 (*New York American* only), 836, 837, 315 (*New York American* only)]

"The Devil's Dictionary."
 New York American (17 October 1904): 16.
 San Francisco Examiner (24 October 1904): 16.
 [445]

"Fables and Anecdotes."
 Cosmopolitan Magazine 39, No. 5 (September 1905): 563–64.
 [325, 326, 838, 839, 840, 336, 841, 316, 317, 842, 357, 311]

"Negligible Epigrams."
 Cosmopolitan Magazine 42, No. 5 (March 1907): 585.
 [328]

"A Few Fables."
 Cosmopolitan Magazine 42, No. 6 (April 1907): 694–95.
 [308, 351, 349, 360, 354, 337]

"In Fable Form."
 Cosmopolitan Magazine 43, No. 3 (July 1907): 336–37.
 [843, 352, 844, 845, 359, 332]

"Fables from *Fun*."
 The Monk and the Hangman's Daughter and Fantastic Fables. (*The Collected Works of Ambrose Bierce*, Volume 6.) Washington, DC: Neale Publishing Co., 1911.
 [11A, 15A, 19A, 21A, 30A, 34A, 43A, 68A, 77A, 93A, 109A, 110A, 120A, 129A, 134A]

The Devil's Dictionary.
   The Collected Works of Ambrose Bierce, Volume 7. Washington, DC: Neale
   Publishing Co., 1911.
   [447]

[Unpublished fable]
   [846]

A Note on Attribution

It can be seen from the above that a fair number of Bierce's fables appeared anonymously, raising the question whether they are in fact Bierce's. If, of course, some of the fables in an anonymously published column were subsequently reprinted in one of Bierce's books of fables, then the attribution of the unreprinted fables is unquestioned; but for those columns in which no fables were reprinted, internal evidence — along with a knowledge of the customary editorial practices of the magazine or newspaper in question — must be our guide.

There is no doubt about the authorship of the "Fables of Zambri," as these all appeared under Bierce's acknowledged pseudonym, Dod Grile. I have already remarked in my introduction on the uncertainty of the fables in the *Wasp* (1883-84), none of which were subsequently reprinted, but I am confident that they are Bierce's. Of the fables in the *Examiner,* the majority were signed either in full or by initials ("A. G. B.," "A. B.," or simply "B." — the last being used for other works that are unquestionably Bierce's). The following columns of unsigned fables feature at least one fable that was subsequently reprinted, so that the authenticity of the others is guaranteed: 7 June 1887, 12 June 1887, 15 June 1887, 15 March 1889, 22 January 1890, 6 December 1890, 12 December 1890, 30 January 1891, 19 February 1891, 4 March 1891, and 20 March 1891. This leaves only the fable columns of 13 June 1890, 17 June 1890, 27 November 1890, 2 May 1891, 8 November 1896, and 20 December 1896 whose authorship is in doubt. I confess to having qualms about the Biercian authorship of the fables of 13 June and 17 June 1890, but not of the others.

There is always the possibility that other fables by Bierce remain undiscovered and uncollected. Although during the later years of his tenure with the *Examiner* Bierce maintained that he, being on a salary paid by Hearst, felt obligated not to write for any other periodicals, in his earlier years (1887 to at least 1892) he appeared to be under no such restriction, as his work appeared in the *Oakland Tribune, Town Topics,* the *Wave,* and perhaps other magazines and periodicals. Nevertheless, I am confident that this volume contains the overwhelming bulk of fables written by Ambrose Bierce.

❧

INDEX OF TITLES

✤

INDEX OF CHARACTERS

632, 666, 667, 691, 696, 743, 772;
Bright Young, 711; Country, 573;
Good, 670; Married, 154; Rich, 190;
(Women's Press Association), 218;
Young, 590
Women, Two, 326
Woodchopper, 362
Woodman, 29
Woodpecker, 102
Wool-Scourer, 494
Workingmen, 409
Workman, 626
World, 603
Worldling: Frivolous, 695; Muscular,
736

Worm, 75
Wren (King), 61
Writer, 748; Ambitious, 293; of Fables,
251
Writers: Convention of Female, 274;
Two, 417

Young-Man-Afraid-of-His-Record, 474
Youth, Fair, 637

Zebra, 65, 198
Zephyr, 14
Zodroulra, 257

www.ingramcontent.com/pod-product-compliance
Lightning Source LLC
Chambersburg PA
CBHW020651110726
47901CB00001B/144